I ___ YOU

All That Comes Between Us

MOLLIE MARDEL

Copyright © 2023 Mollie Mardel

All rights reserved.

ISBN: 9798873237500

DEDICATION

This is for everyone who adores the world as deeply as Sierra, or makes the same sacrifices as Sebastian with the same passion for rationale or love. This is for everyone who shares Alessandro's penchant for protection, regardless of the success of love's expression. This is for everyone who watches and learns like Betsy, and cares as Nicholas does. This dedication is limitless. This book is for everyone with character, a dream and a story to tell.

CHAPTERS

PROLOGUE 3
CHAPTER I: DESIRE 7
CHAPTER II: MOURN 15
CHAPTER III: DISOBEY 26
CHAPTER IV: FOUND 36
CHAPTER V: IMMERSE 48
CHAPTER VI: QUESTION 57
CHAPTER VII: HEAR 68
CHAPTER VIII: FORGIVE 79
CHAPTER IX: MEET 90
CHAPTER X: FOLLOW 101
CHAPTER XI: FORGET 111
CHAPTER XII: COMFORT 123
CHAPTER XIII: WANT 134
CHAPTER XIV: WRONG 147
CHAPTER XV: MISS 157
CHAPTER XVI: CHERISH 170
CHAPTER XVII: PROTECT 180
CHAPTER XVII: SAVE 190
CHAPTER XIX: TRUST 202
CHAPTER XX: ADORE 212
CHAPTER XXI: LOVE 222
CHAPTER XXII: KNEW 231

CHAPTER XXIII: IGNORE..242

CHAPTER XXIV: HELP 251

CHAPTER XXV: MISTAKE 265

CHAPTER XXVI: HOLD 277

CHAPTER XXVII: REMEMBER...289

CHAPTER XXVIII: GRIEVE 301

CHAPTER XXIX: NEED..311

CHAPTER XXX: SACRIFICE 323

CHAPTER XXXI: AWAKEN...336

CHAPTER XXXII: INFLUENCE...342

CHAPTER XXXIII: BETRAY..351

CHAPTER XXXVI: HUNT 354

CHAPTER XXXV: FEAR...361

CHAPTER XXXVI: WATCHED..365

CHAPTER XXXVII: OUTLIVED 377

EPILOGUE 381

DEDICATION

This is for everyone who adores the world as deeply as Sierra, or makes the same sacrifices as Sebastian with the same passion for rationale or love. This is for everyone who shares Alessandro's penchant for protection, regardless of the success of love's expression. This is for everyone who watches and learns like Betsy, and cares as Nicholas does. This dedication is limitless. This book is for everyone with character, a dream and a story to tell.

CHAPTERS

PROLOGUE 3

CHAPTER I: DESIRE 7

CHAPTER II: MOURN..15

CHAPTER III: DISOBEY 26

CHAPTER IV: FOUND 36

CHAPTER V: IMMERSE 48

CHAPTER VI: QUESTION 57

CHAPTER VII: HEAR..68

CHAPTER VIII: FORGIVE 79

CHAPTER IX: MEET 90

CHAPTER X: FOLLOW 101

CHAPTER XI: FORGET..111

CHAPTER XII: COMFORT......................................123

CHAPTER XIII: WANT..134

CHAPTER XIV: WRONG 147

CHAPTER XV: MISS 157

CHAPTER XVI: CHERISH 170

CHAPTER XVII: PROTECT 180

CHAPTER XVII: SAVE...190

CHAPTER XIX: TRUST..202

CHAPTER XX: ADORE..212

CHAPTER XXI: LOVE..222

CHAPTER XXII: KNEW 231

CHAPTER XXIII: IGNORE	242
CHAPTER XXIV: HELP	251
CHAPTER XXV: MISTAKE	265
CHAPTER XXVI: HOLD	277
CHAPTER XXVII: REMEMBER	289
CHAPTER XXVIII: GRIEVE	301
CHAPTER XXIX: NEED	311
CHAPTER XXX: SACRIFICE	323
CHAPTER XXXI: AWAKEN	336
CHAPTER XXXII: INFLUENCE	342
CHAPTER XXXIII: BETRAY	351
CHAPTER XXXVI: HUNT	354
CHAPTER XXXV: FEAR	361
CHAPTER XXXVI: WATCHED	365
CHAPTER XXXVII: OUTLIVED	377
EPILOGUE	381

ACKNOWLEDGMENTS

To the start of a journey, which wouldn't exist without this book. This is the first novel I've written, finished, dedicated hours upon hours of solace to, and felt prepared to share with the world.

To imperfections, and the knowledge that learning what to love, and what not to love, is part of the path.

To courage, to bravery and to lifetimes that are too short to let procrastination silence a story, or to allow doubt to shut away a world.

PROLOGUE

Secrets of London's Unspoken Outskirts
Chapter One

Though the emigration from England's capital city had been planned for quite some time beforehand, the attempt by a known antisocial group to blow up London Bridge on the 20th of December in the year 1884, provided an entire community the perfect cover, under which they could slip away from London. The records account as much as possible for the missing, though the case was promptly abandoned due to the move being presumed intentional by those involved. It did not arouse any suspicion of criminal activity other than those who had stolen away and left some debt behind in their name. Londoners admitted it was odd, that's all, that amidst the chaos, 32 men, 37 women and 4 children managed to flee unnoticed.

I have encountered people, of good nature, who believe that the move was simply opportunistic. These individuals are the sort to refrain from meddling in others affairs, however, and their opinion didn't much allow for contradictions to be represented within this book. As an author who strives for maximum credibility, across all works, I aim to portray balance when discussing such delicate mysteries. Consequently, in good faith, I presented a tape recorder to those who had decidedly more complex thoughts on the matter. You will find upon further reading, speculative voices, that tell of supposed associations between the two groups of note on that day. It is vastly peculiar, I was told, that pronounced London architecture was struck with explosives, and that workers in the gunpowder mills were among the vanished.

There was nobody interested in investigating the matter. The households that had disappeared were tight-knit, small, families therefore nobody remained who had high stakes in finding the missing Londoners. It was almost as though they had catered for everything before they left, except the debts, to ensure they wouldn't be followed. I have met individuals who believe they ran because these debts got overwhelming, but there was no common thread between the families that left. Many were consistent taxpayers, with ample funds to their names. Financial affairs were thought unlikely to be the cause of their departure. Although there was a distinct lack of interest, it wasn't long before curiosity manifested in people, including members of the police force. In June, in the following year, they established a search party and drew out a map. The congregation was split in four, each group covering 2 miles from central London to the North, East, South and West, respectively.

The North, South and West groups returned within the three-day window, with nothing. The East group, having ventured a mile beyond instruction, returned a week later, with stories of a settlement, called Colmoor. A town had been created, and the first census they had made accounted for all the missing Londoners. It functioned a little differently, in regard to society and economy.

In approximately six months, they had built a civilization from the ground. The report described the houses as similar to 19th century London, except made from wood and natural materials that were found in the surrounding area. They'd cut into a lot of the forest for resources. Unless these buildings have since been refurbished, historians suggest that the infrastructure of the houses will be bent and crooked in the modern day. Reflective of London's own social discrepancies, some people of Colmoor were literate and some were not. Those who were brought with them books from their shelves in the city, works by Shakespeare and The Brothers Grimm were seen by the East group. Thus, it can be assumed that a fair cultural and literary intelligence within their community has been sustained.

As there was no established bank in Colmoor, circulation dwindled, removing the need for currency altogether. The system became an interwoven reliance on favours and proportions. A process by which anyone was entitled to use any resource for the benefit of the community. Those proficient in farming, for example, would make use of the surrounding land, and harvest crops. They would then distribute resources using a formula that included household size, and took into account medical instances or young children within families. Each household that benefited would then owe a favour to the farmer from their own skill. A farmer could return to a shoemaker household and ask for the repair that was owed to him. The East group were impressed by the effectiveness of the system, but left doubtful. Colmoor was in many ways, regressive. The question remained, what would prompt a group to leave London, to start again? Though the East group returned, the reason for Colmoor's departure from the real world was still unclear to Londoners.

The location of Colmoor was calculated. It lies in the middle of fertile land, and expansive hilly grassland. Bordered by a forest on one side, and a beach on the other, it was elucidated as being well-obscured and private. Rumours resurfaced about the true intentions of a rural community erected so suddenly, when an anonymous article, later linked to a Colmoorian fugitive, made its way into London newspapers. It made hazardous and insane claims of a genetic phenomenon, in which female genes carried talents. Each daughter of her mother was bound by biology to adopt whatever talent ran in the maternal background of the family. These genes were also catalogued as recessive. If the mother was a magnificent painter, the daughter would be a skilful artist also. This was proposedly the same across any ability. This article was dismissed as hoax, and although scientists dissected the phenomenon briefly, they determined no probable cause.

However, neither Colmoor nor London had the expertise and technology of the 21st century, so it is feasible that the research done was not thorough. As a result, I have now committed myself to the study of genetic phenomena, beginning with Colmoor. The East group had made a sworn pact with locals in Colmoor, that their coordinates would remain a secret. I myself have ventured 3 miles to the East, in search of an off-grid ocean and forest, and have found nothing. Though, I have on multiple occasions, when I deliver my talks and lectures, said that this will not deter me from further treks.

As far as Londoners at the time, and heading into the 20th century, were concerned, all travellers in Colmoor had died. Nobody had heard from them, or interrogated anything from the East group. Word of Colmoor died, supposedly like its people. There is a chance that the naysayers are correct, and the unsustainable economy was destined to fall to pieces, but I continue to believe in something.

I have great anticipation that this book may encourage you, reader, to have a little belief in the impossible.

CHAPTER I: DESIRE

Sierra.

I have held every memory of tonight in reverse.
All Isaak said was "Hm, early today."
I am not looking, but I feel the assassin's eyes on me. For a brief moment we waited, until the hands that wrestled intention into the trigger stalked away into the night, leaving the fallen dying, bleeding out. Isaak had been counting down. The last thing I'd heard had been, "Two-" and then the gun clicked, the bullet fired, then embedded itself in my conscience.

Before that was "Three."
Then, "Four." Instinctual fear was already clouding my judgement. There would have been time to look away.

It all started with "Five." Isaak's dulcet murmur before I knew I would never be at peace again.

The twisted iron that confined us to our balcony was cold. A platform of stone, jutting out over the street. Aligned with bars frosted from spring rain in dropping midnight temperatures. Bars insinuated our safety was jeopardised, and Isaak predicted danger, but to try to understand his twisted way of telling me things was to touch upon sealed gates, or turn book pages without floods of words. Regardless, I was blinded by a desire, perhaps a compulsion or an ambition. A mission to explore the mechanisms that made up his mind. He stayed silent, either absorbing or searching, and the silence loudly called my name.

I assertively mutter. "You have no right to play with my attraction, and not let me into your heart." When I slice the quiet, he doesn't flinch.

Conducting his body in a way that is irresistibly on the brink of intentional, he manoeuvres to face me. Blasé always, and a frown, deceptive by a fraction I'll never decipher. He's feeding off the knowledge that he's denying me of my desire to be more to him.

Alarms howl somewhere unseen, piercing this scene, but in his darkened eyes it continues to play out. The atmosphere enhances and ignites all five of my senses to an overwhelming degree. We haven't been here long but it feels as though we've spent a lifetime in the city, and I'm still unsure if these sensations I feel for him are pain or passion but with each advance he makes toward me, he roots them somewhere ambiguous in between. A place I feel nothing but something. Something that is everything. And I know everything and nothing about him.

"Come here." His voice is steely, grounding, calm. There's affection, but incomplete, as if he had been born with a heart that had yet to be awarded a pumping presence to accompany stagnant blood. His veins are warm, but lack richness, powerful but with an absence of emotional connection. His empathy is incalculable, volatile, simply a tool for transaction. He hides a damaged wound, familiar to my subconscious. It's the only explanation for such an inhibited, hidden lover. My lover.

A grey turtleneck. A jawline etched with a permanence that relaxation can't attack. Unlimited. Unable to be suppressed. Eyes that seek danger with raw hunger. That look I desire, from my lover.

He embraces me in a way that if I didn't know any better, I'd mistake for love. He's an expert, aware how to elicit security in his hold. Against my recognised will, my fingers gravitate to the small of his back as if it is a necessity. He pulls my head, with tenderness, against him, so close to his heart I can hear it. Immersed in this moment, we are magical, magnetised. I am his, he feels like mine. But it is a place that is nothing, with an illusion. A gutting, artificial illusion of something more.

"I have no time for love when there's other things that need doing, things of importance. Life and death."

There's a precarious balance. His tendency to act on impulses acting as one weight, and his somewhat-innocent, arrogant as fuck predictability on the other. He regards me as his confidante, but in saying that, he never reveals too much. When he sleeps, I wonder if, and where, the raging thoughts vacate, or perhaps he dreams like he lives. Intensely. Fearlessly. Impossible. I'm sure that the thought of him dreaming sustains me.

I made an offering, into the contours of his chest. "Wouldn't life and death be easier if you had someone beside you?" His steady stance is unfaltering. But his tone softens, enough to add sincerity that I would even go as far as to identify as kindness.

"You know the way I work." Reminding me, of something I don't want to be reminded of. Reminding me that there is a lot I'm yet to understand. He releases me and takes a seat again with a ready breath, and is reabsorbed into the night. There, is love. Him and the city, the way he admires it. I am but a bystander. I am but a witness. To that type, his type of love.

I step back into our apartment, navigating around the curtain, delicate lace. It's flailing out of the doors and into the wind as if it wants to take flight. I understand the yearning so much it hurts, the yearning to fly, regardless of the fall. The flame that precedes the fire, the surge of current before the electric lightning. I felt it all that day. The day we ran away from a place I can't remember. My life now feels like flying. I am yet to fall.

If I have learnt anything from my lover, the first thing is how to ask no questions, expect to leave with no answers, and to prepare myself for the eventuality of him not returning. Our irreversibility will overcome us all one day. He cites that like it's written in a scripture of his fierce dynamic religion. I know he's fuelling my resilience, creating a refuge if ever he is faded, but it is unnecessary, unneeded. I am impossible to restrain.

The second thing I have learnt from my lover is how he likes his coffee. One. A fraction hotter than dusk in summer. Two. Darker than a soldier's nightmare of the cruellest kind. Three. More bitter than spite that spills from a broken heart.

At least that's how I illustrate my predictions of the activity alive in his mind. I picture an incomparable imagination, no boundaries, no limit. A free spirit, burdened by rationale. What would happen if someone were to set him free.

He likes his coffee - hot, dark, bitter. Like him. Nothing about a summer dusk or a broken heart. But it's a blend that always works.

"Come inside." I speak, clarity adorning my voice.

He grunts, facing me. "You need to be clearer if this is a choice or an instruction." He doesn't ask questions, so I have to play along, my half of the negotiation weighing heavily against his. I hope tonight he'll accept coffee because I'm not yet prepared to sell him my affection in blood, when the dosage of his affection comes down to merely a few glances and disciplined, tame touches.

I want to shut him out but I need to try to play my role. "I've made you coffee."

To try to persuade him is futile, fruitless. Other nights, coffee may provide the perfect lure, the strong smell calling him in from the cold. At times like tonight, not even the snare of liquid comfort or a woman wrapped in a dress robe, and only a dress robe, will entice him. The fixation is unbreakable. Handing him the coffee, my heart catches fire. It's all in his failure to mask gratitude. I couldn't replicate the way he looked up at me in a forbidden 'thank you' even if I had all the powers of creation in the world. His way of loving was loving the city.

He regarded the horizon's motor hum like an earthbound siren, in such a way that nothing could ever draw him away from listening, nothing could wrench him closer to wanting. I could never have what the city has. A million different lives, a million different lies, several thousand mystery crimes. My life only contains my song and I will never be a match for the city. The ever-changing lights of these million lives were his homeward bound beacons, he wasn't settled unless the air smelt like danger, he'd play his cards praying he'd be dealt a chase to keep him dashing around our city. Any new chance at a thrill-seeking, hypothetical death escape. He never stops his mind racing. My lover. My daredevil lover. He tempts the devil inside me, and dares me to dream.

"Go to bed soon, the cold is only ever a step behind the darkness. You told me that when we were out here yesterday." I try to override his ignorance.

"I don't have time for the cold." A retort that is clearly an excuse he tries to feed to me on a silver spoon. An excuse to stay outside and watch the entire city thrive. Cursing myself, I drink it up willingly. It keeps him around. My hand slips into his, he curls his fingers back, but there's no passion. He'll never tell you that he's my lover. Our relationship is more fantastical than it is established, more fictional than official, more burning lust and something to do to keep busy. To chain us back from entering the realms of insane.

"What a bloody surprise." I fire a sarcastic shot. The silence bled into my awkward agony. I'd give up my voice, for his smile, but nothing.

I ___ YOU

I asked him once to sleep beside me. The first and last time. It was eight months and three days ago in July, and I was horribly ill. My swelling throat gave way to a pumping headache. I was choking on my own saliva, swallowing felt abrasive, like clawing rips into my skin every time I'd breathe or speak. I hadn't cried for years, but that day tears glistened, like hot lava against my cheeks. My head was thunder, predators, conflict and percussion.

Before that day, and from that night onwards, his place is the sofa. Mine is the bed. It's better this way, he said, and resembling a drunk fool, I agreed. Every night since has passed, and I'm retreating to empty sheets that numb my love. He was long gone by morning, nearly every morning, but as a guilty pleasure I curl into the shadow of where he'd been, an imprint of the body I crave on the sofa cushions.

This is the way we work. In deficit and difficult. The only justification is that it nurtures our pathetic desire. I don't want it to be that he can't love me. But it is. I cut sharply away from my memories by blinking at him under the moonlight. Unusually, he glides his hand up to my forearm, touching my bare shoulder with his warm lips in the dim glow, something a little less than a kiss. Goosebumps bristle. Do you love me or not? Is what I want to ask.

I don't. Instead, I fell silent to his hold, until I melted completely into his embrace. I am a prisoner of criminal love. This night is timeless. Reality is a phobia and these moments are my sanctuary.

Whether he loves me or not, in this universe, at this juncture, I believe in what's between us. I am surrendered, by implicit force, by his casual devotion, by his sweet ambiguity, to my conviction that he reciprocates my care. I am coveting his attention to a point of no remorse.

He knows, as I fall to his grace. I know, as I transcend self-sacrifice. I am impossible, and with the spring's cold night wind curling my skin I ask him outright, "Will you ever stop staring?"

"Not staring. Waiting." He corrects me, and renders me silent before I can force any context, enfolding a guarding arm around my waist and drawing me in close. I'm asphyxiated instantly by his effortless charm and his scent strikes me like an arrow. It's distinctly summertime sunsets, from years of buried reminiscence. The beach, the spice of the sea air, the indulgence of time spent with each other that we knew we should resist. Somewhere far away from where the land and ocean rendezvous.

I don't remember much about our years before London, they were unsatisfactory for him. He always needed more, and tranquillity simply wouldn't deliver. Previously having encountered a malaise with the complexities of the world and its inhabitants, he was a man of fractured purpose until he became immersed in this urban purgatory. The single thing I know for certain, is that he'll never stray far from this city now. I believe it to be the pulsing core of his identity discovery. He protested little to the prospect of abandoning his childhood at the beach, eroded by the waves, lapped weakly at by the rocks, disintegrated by the sand. He was ready, and he knew the time was then, so he flew away from that life.

"Watch..." is his abrupt mandate.

There's an emergence of two silhouettes from the shadows beneath us, supernatural sorcerers of the night. Inferred caution glazes his eyes as he looks up at me. I understand the command. Keep quiet. There's a threat emanating from the way they move toward each other and the unnerving hesitation before either speaks. A strained conversation develops.

"Are we agreed then? You'll transgress. Our side." A voice like Isaak's, determined and sure. Exactly 6 heartbeats fill the space between the ask and the answer. "They'd kill me." Another man's brave tone cowers.

"Or I will." This alone could have told me death would soon be standing amongst us, and made me look away, but alas I was swept up in investment. I feel as though my eyes are a child's lens, I want to peep between my fingers and then hide away from the tension as if it'll make a difference, but I am an adult. I have to lean against my lover, who may or may not love me, and take pleasure in living like horror is amusement.

There's no pause for consideration this time. No time for me to count heartbeats. The first man seems confident, the latter weak. I debate with whom my sympathies lie, whilst sheltering under Isaak's muscle. Isaak. I repeat my lover's name in my head.

"Five." Isaak's voice now. I cannot comprehend how in the face of conflict he continuously remains so at ease.

"Four." I should have asked why he was counting so I could have known to look away.

"Three." His vocal cords don't produce anything that parallels the trepidation throbbing in my stomach. Alternately, his nonchalance is the first to challenge the adrenaline.

"Two-" The bullet clicked, then fired, then embedded itself in my conscience. The bullet barely stayed in flight. The shooter was centimetres from him. For the victim, the tsunami of pain vanished as quickly as it arrived and stole his life in its aftermath. For me, I was robbed of relief and the scorching lingers, stripping away at my mind's serenity.

I ___ YOU

The crimson dribbled over the concrete as the earth caressed another soul extinct into its gentle orbit, the consolation of perpetual rest awaiting him.
And all Isaak says-
　"Hm, early today."

CHAPTER II: MOURN

Alessandro.

We sat with our father for the last time in the decrepit hollow we called a kitchen. We were sixteen. We know nothing of the life of my mother, we know nothing of the duet she founded, we know nothing of how she was an inspiration, a renegade clothed in white. "I imagine she was beautiful."

"Stunning." My father replied, without snatching a second to think. "Her beauty as it was would have been enough to seal her fate. She had that going for her."

Our father is weary, losing our mother was his death sentence, he's never been quite the same. He tells us how lucky we are that we are boys, how lucky we are that we fall under the radar. Purely because of our sex, something so extensively out of our control, we evade surveillance. I feel survivor's guilt from that alone. A gift that our ancestors gave our mother ended up being the signature on her death warrant, and I could do nothing, absolutely nothing, to help her. It's the most powerless I've felt, and am determined to ever feel in my life. Never again.

He hates telling the story. It hurts him. We plead with him to stop but he says it's imperative that we know. You mustn't be the same, he implores us. He doesn't tell us the same as what or who.

"Sit," he implores, "or stand perhaps, need to be on your guard. Always boys, eyes low, awareness high. They'll be on your case if you don't. The only chance you get at standing out is fitting in. Your mother was a smart woman, but that's the one lesson she never learnt, the one that cost her her life."

Our father is a dominant presence, a repetitive thought whenever we leave the house - it is mindless to disobey him. He is a serious man, with a hint of rudimentary laughter that's been maliciously scrubbed away over time. The only time it reappears is when he mentions our mother, as if his words bring her alive again. He catches a glimpse of her before the reality of her death comes caving in and she is gone again.

"Your mother, could…" he says the next element like it's prohibited, a looked-down upon expletive, because in our world, the only world we've ever known, it is.

"She could sing. Lucia had a voice like an angel. Not the type that could just break the rules, but break your heart all in one note."

My mother. Singing her closing song in her last moments, and knowing it too. Singing for all the times she felt repressed, and as the grains of sand fell through the hourglass, she sang as a signal to heaven that her time was nearly up, a warning to prepare for her strength when she arrived in the clouds.

Her final breath was a melody dedicated to her sons; I know it. I know as she kissed us goodbye, she was crying a lullaby. I look over at my brother listening to my father now, and even though he was wordless, I could read it in his expression that he was thinking the exact same thing.

Identical twins with identical ghosts, churning haunted memories in symmetry. "She was killed for her voice…"

"No…she was killed because they heard. I told her so many times that she needed to cloak her talent, just until we could get away. She was so stubborn toward that, which surprised me, given how compromising she often was. No matter my protests, the secret meetings went ahead. The urges increased, overcame her, controlled her more whilst she was pregnant. It was as if having you inside her gave her something to fight for."

Through our father, we learnt that our mother had a close friend, an exclusive relationship that she had formed through an accidental discovery of exchanged talent. The woman was named Savannah. They fell pregnant at the same time and their friendship formed a support network for the two families, a chance to unite and perform their secret songs.

Father was at work the day the men raided our house - he had never forgiven himself for leaving. As we understood it, a traitor, a bastard of a weak man or a jealous woman, was to have betrayed us and leaked our address after hearing mother sing. The exact bedroom where Savannah and Lucia sang secret songs.

The shelter in which they let their fluent harmonies meld in sync and their melodies intertwine, was tarnished by their blood in the early hours of morning. Their screaming was heard beyond the four walls and into the murky autumn streets.

Sebastian came first. I came second, holding his foot as we left the womb. It was an innate technique of communicating that we needed to stick together.

Our birth, and the closeness of our mother's journeys meant that Savannah's labour started in immediate succession to Lucia's. Only, her twins were a surprise.

"I was only expecting one…" she breathed, exhausted but immeasurably fond, her maternalistic nature cleansing any doubts.

She called the first daughter Sierra, a name she had always loved. It meant mountain range. It was where one day; she had said she was going to escape to. A place she could sing into the abyss and be free. The second daughter, in the celerity of the circumstance, was called Betsy. A name for oaths and pledges. It was Savannah's instruction to her newborn to always stay loyal. She believed her twins were a message, and she accepted it adoringly.

Lucia, our mother, didn't have to promise us we'd be safe. We were boys. Society would take care of us, in a harrowing delegation of fate.

They were killed hours later. We were found, all four newborns, stashed under the bed like prized goods. Little did it matter, as the men with the bayonets were never after us. It mattered for Sierra and Betsy, which is why they were pushed behind Sebastian and I.

Father said that the town report that documented their deaths was just as chilling the hundred and twenty-fifth time he'd read it as the first. To begin with, he resisted telling us the details, but after Sebastian and I had found the scrap of paper inside his bedroom cabinet, he couldn't avoid speaking about it. The article read,

'L. Gray and S. Geneiva were exterminated this morning within the confines of their home, due to reports of prohibited expression of song. Three members of our armed forces carried out the instruction. Let nowhere be a sanctuary and have this be a warning to you all.'

Father told us that they had abstained from recording the brutality. He acknowledged that there was no need for it, for everyone already knew the horrors of the action taken by the society against women with talent, but I understood with intrinsic comprehension what he meant. My mother was recognised for her fate, not for the talent she had suppressed for so long. It amounted to nothing.

Reminders of our mother's death hung around us all the time, like stalagmites, imperfect and permanent, as we watched the world cave in on my father. We don't celebrate our birthday; it is only a gloomy anniversary for my father on the day he lost his lover. We accept this the way it is; we know we have no choice. Our birthday is a day for mourning, and that our birthplace is forever adulterated with the poison of blood and our mother's screams.

They didn't have long before the boots barged through the door, uncaring, unfeeling, irrational in their desire to pursue what they were about to do. The women were intuitive. Father said that Lucia must have run to the dresser where she kept her embroidery, he found it weeks after, smeared with blood, unfinished, and with the needle missing. The inkwell on her desk was tilted on its side, with the last bit of navy liquid held coagulating in a thin layer on the bottom of the glass jar. The rest of the ink was absorbed into the floorboards, painting them a dark shade of literary blue.

Post-investigation, my father had concluded that my mother and Savannah had marked us, each with identical tattoos, the inscription RWYA just above our hip bones, distinctly with our mother's faultless left-hand coordination. Sebastian thinks it represents a message for the four of us to stay united and solid in the face of adversity. I draw a far less profound conclusion. In my private thoughts, I imagine it as a cryptic final goodbye from my mother.

Our mother. She then watched, helpless, as the men plunged the knife deep into Savannah's stomach. Her face contorted as she attempted not to scream, but instead shrieked. Another ram of the blade into her temples and Savannah was dead. My mother wept for everything she had lost, she wept for a friend. A friend whose last words were Sierra and Betsy.

Our mother. With blood still dripping from beneath her dress, edged towards the door, where two men stood emotionless. She pleaded with them. All she had left where courage once reigned was pretence, fuzzy determination that may or may not have been an evolution of fear.

Our mother. Realised that escape was ineffective, accepted her fate and drew back. Desperate for one last glimpse of us, her babies, as the men discussed the best way to kill her in front of her eyes. In fractured sobs, she whispered to us, "Shh, my darlings. Be good. Be brave. Be-"

Our mother. The blade sliced through the mottled skin. The knife cut into her throat. The butt of the bayonet slammed into her cheek to knock her to the ground. Our mother, dead.

Our society originated from a group of women with incredible talents bred over generations of female reign. It was a soft world back then, one where compassion was handed around with generosity, instead of envy being thrown around viciously, as it is now. Colmoor's 'proficient' scientists had been studying for years to understand why the talent was hereditary, to no avail. It was guaranteed that the daughter of a woman would inherit her talent. And, what's more, the daughter of a mother's only son would be as talented as her grandmother. These same scientists turned sour when they could not find answers and merged with the oppressors.

Of course, over time, great problems arose for the men who were regarded with a lot more inferiority, the women didn't mean for things to evolve that way, but it happened naturally. At first, the men didn't speak up as they relied on women for their domestic abilities, it was rare to come across a man that had the patience to cook, write or sew. But there was a brewing fury that women landed the attention through their creative talents. Painting, singing, dancing, performing, being able to play a musical instrument, and an extensive list of others registered under Rule 2 Section 1A, were all gradually prohibited until the women lived in fear.

Some men obeyed the tradition they'd always known, they admired it and were enterprising in the face of these draconian changes. They engaged in romantic relationships to protect their women from discovery.

Others who felt victimised fell at the mercy of this growing patriarchal culture and hence banded with the authority who sought revenge. They ruled by a mantra, 'Bury the past, and with it the talented women too stupid to stay silent.' We were trapped in a graveyard, a spirit memorial, for all things joyful and passionate. Dissuasion and censoring of all things expressive were ripe in every family. You were kept tabs on, always.

And that is how our father died and joined our mother, in a place where he too, could be free.

I go back to my last memory of him, seated in the kitchen, talking to us yet again about our mother - it could never exhaust him. But this time is different because I brought up Betsy and Sierra. "Where are they now?"

"Still alive I believe. Savannah had no living relatives that I knew of, she never spoke of family, so when I found you four under the bed together, I set them up for adoption…" he trails off, breathing, filling his lungs with regret. "…took a long time to convince people to take them on, had to assure them they were from outside our community, no talent whatsoever, needed a safe place to grow up. I'm ashamed to say I played around with sympathy; it was the only way."

Sebastian rarely contributed to these conversations; he'd stand with his back pressed to the wall in the corner of the room. The darkest corner - he had an affinity for shadows. He thought of mystery as a virtue. He appeared idle but this was typically representative of a look that meant he was absorbed in the information, his dark eyebrows, like mine, furrowed in scrutiny. But this time, he spoke, taking us by surprise. "Who had them, in the end?"

A little taken aback, but masked well, Father replies. In his explanation he reveals that elderly women took them in.

The first, a woman who had never expressed her talent, and therefore was attributed to having a great deal of wisdom. She'd stayed quiet at the beginning when the adoption went underway, but then approached our father to one side. Didn't say much, except that she'd take one. She didn't want any payment or support of any kind so Father simply gave her Betsy.

Another elderly woman offered to take Sierra. My father forfeited the girls and all of the resources he had for them. He never saw them again.

I intercept this time, suddenly overcome with an insatiable curiosity. "Do you know where they live?"

Exchanging eye contact with Sebastian, the razor-sharp glance between us assured us both that we were on the same page. "I haven't got a clue, I never got involved."

"Could you not have taken them in?" Sebastian queries and I shoot him another warning glance that it was perhaps a conversation overstepping the boundaries into interrogation. He takes the hint and retracts. "Were you not able…"

Father is too quick for Sebastian to retrieve his words. "Grievance…is a mind-numbing concept. Unless you've experienced it, you will never know the feeling. It pained me so much to know that her last moments were spent fearing the world and vulnerable, permeated with uncertainty. I was too occupied with mourning her and raising my own children to care for two more."

I diverted my father's downward spiral; my default thought is back to the girls. There was still an intrigue ebbing inside, a want, no, a need to know more. We had spent the first moments of my life with these girls who are now strangers to us.

"Presumably they had talent too?"
"Of course. Savannah, besides your mother, had a voice like you've never heard."

Unexpectedly, it struck a chord, a sombre note inside me inscribed as a reminder that I would never have the opportunity to hear either of them sing. Part of me starts wishing that I could go back to the night she died, just before the men came in, and warn her, and we could have held each other like a mother and two sons should. We could have loved Sierra and Betsy like sisters before we were torn apart. I cut myself off as I realise, I am being insane and illogical. I am a Gray, I don't do illogical, I do practical. That is who I am. That is the way I work.

But then another heavy weight drags my heart to my stomach as I realise something serious. It hasn't yet dawned on Sebastian. I am never choked when I speak, but this shaky timbre to my voice is new to me.

"Father, you…"
"Lied, forged the birth certificates. They couldn't be the female kin of traitors." He finished my sentence.

Usually, I hate it when he does that, but now I'm thankful. I don't think I would have been able to reach the end of my train of thought if he hadn't. Sebastian reaches his delayed conclusion. He starts, taking over from me.
"You're…"
"Forbidden from doing that by Section 4.3. I am a criminal, in society's eyes. I understand what I did, my son."

"They must know by now…"

The word 'they' festers in the silence, the ambivalence of all our jumbled emotions uncomfortably ruminating. I feel uncommonly nauseous. Father inhales, calibrating and prolonging the breath.

"It won't be long. Sierra and Betsy would have grown up and started developing their talents now, they'll trace it back to me, I know they will."

The distressing truth manifests. Father's waiting on his death, on high alert for so long that it's breaking him. He's fatigued all the time, but it's because even into the nighttime he's wary of his surroundings, constantly on his guard. Every day and night for 16 years.

That was the last night we saw him alive. Sitting wistful, engaging us, protecting us, holding everything together for us. The first time we understood the magnitude of the laws he'd broken to ensure our safety, was 16 years too late. He'd told us, "Off to sleep." as the conversation drew to a close. We'd adamantly refused.

He said it again, stern now, "off-to-sleep", as if he'd known, at that point, they were already on their way, bullets ready to meet the roof of his mouth, ready for the abolition of his traitor status. For good.

He sounded weak, and so we agreed and retreated with reluctance to our room. I forever wish we hadn't.

My father. A Samaritan with your doom sealed. I hope that you found my mother again somewhere up higher - when you think of her you smile. You weren't smiling the night you were murdered. We found you with dirt smeared on your stubble from where they'd forced open your jaw to push the barrel of the gun inside your mouth. We found you bleeding from the head where the bullet exited. We found the bullet lodged in the bedpost covered in your mind and memories, that's how Sebastian told me to look at it so it wasn't your blood and pieces of your brain.

My father's death will plague me longer than my mother's. My mother's screams have only existed in my

imagination, my father's rings out as clear as anything when I close my eyes. It's why I hate sleeping. It's like watching the worst movie of your life. On repeat. Over and over again.
On repeat.
Over and over and over again.

CHAPTER III: DISOBEY

Sierra.

My lie. My one lie is that I break some promises. Isaak assigns me senseless tasks; I have a weak-willed determination to fulfil them.

Every night I recite a monotonous parody, he stays until commitment slips my lips. One of his deals is that he'll stay by my side until I fall into the slumber of circadian cycles and then he'll withdraw to the sofa where he sleeps. I'm addicted to the way he can see my mind's design, the stories I erect, as if they were the architecture building my dream empire up from its foundations, limitless.

There's no reason I shouldn't obey my side of the bargain as he does his. There's no reason I should be the way I am. There's no real explanation for being alive, able to interact with the world and be the ringmaster of my circus-like life. Assembling everything into perspective makes the truth look shallow. Everything in my unrequited love for Isaak is that one accidental, heart-stopping moment where your footstep encounters the deep end.

I want to be kind to him and fall asleep like he wants me to, I really do, but keeping my conscience awake behind my closed eyelids is rewarding. I sense the way he looks at me, drowning in his thoughts, I can picture his eyes looking at me in the way I want him to. Tonight, I feel him cup my wrist between his thumb and forefinger, a marriage of our skin in the moonlight. It's a new move, a contemporary attraction. Strange, for Isaak. Isaak who doesn't love me. But Isaak who might.

This is yet another night where my promise shatters like splinters of fragile china. I circumvent the fragments as I navigate the floor barefoot. If the floorboards wake him on my behalf I'd be condemned. I'd have chanced breaking his second deal, to enter the living room where he sleeps after dark. For this one, he doesn't offer a return deal, he proclaims it's undisputedly essential. I'm enslaved by his instinct.

A wooden plank screeches. Bated breath plugging my lungs, I expect Isaak to come charging. Unusually, the adrenaline simmers and the peace descends once more. He does not come running, nor walking, not even padding up the hall in the slippers he always protests don't age him. He never arrives. In a fleeting moment, I realise that I'm not afraid of him, I'm afraid of being without him.

I need water, so I mechanically destined myself for the sink. I find myself fortunate that the corridor is lined with a carpet, which delivers me safely to the kitchen tiles. Isaak is retired behind a door further ahead which prevents me from stealing a glance at my lover. My ears prick to a low susurration. The city can be infectious with its relentless and consistent echoes, Isaak and I are similar in that we concede to its magnitude and complexity without dissent, but tonight it felt different, edging on unwelcome. I shut it out, stopping its cries crawling in through the window and inhabiting our warmth. The subdued vibrations don't cease, I hear them again as I sip from my glass. Then, a strangled cry. Isaak. My lover. I'm coming.

The glass clinks as it hits the countertop. I'm coming, my love.

I compress myself by the door to the living room. Isaak has forbidden me to enter. However, the oak door dividing him and I obstructs nothing, he's hyperventilating, faster than I'd ever heard him breathe. He's smothered by the very oxygen that he's scrounging for. Intermittently, muted thuds occur, and my own experience informs me that it's the sound of a weighted head colliding with a pillow. A restless mind. He dreams like he lives. Intensely. Fearlessly. Or so I thought.

Momentarily consumed in abstraction, I don't register that he appears to have awoken. "Sierra, go." Isaak instructs. Shit.

I freeze, rigid, paralysed, trying to immobilise time along with me. His voice replays in my thoughts, so vulnerable in the dubiety of his waking seconds. Involuntarily I take my lip between my teeth, but all is enshrouded by lazy tresses of my abundant mahogany hair. Isaak's figure remains impoverished by my drowsy vision, although I can make out his splayed body on the sofa as I merge into the room, accompanied by the illumination of the stars, and into his eyeline. I cast my head down in admission, accepting that I, Sierra Genieva, am now a rule-breaker unearthed and penitent - overcome by misled passion. "Isaak…" I painstakingly search for the words, "Can I help you?"

"Nobody can help me." He decides.

I have a quick response. "Nobody *can*? Or you won't *let* anybody?"

I make him speechless under my instantaneous control, a rare occurrence. He has no comeback because my ability to psychoanalyse his behaviours and arrogance surpasses his means of defending himself and his pride.

His energy reserved to spark an argument is depleting rapidly. That's abnormal for my lover. He's always ready to challenge me. Now he's sinking down into the cushions, he'd already spurned the duvet for the sake of preparedness if anything were to happen, so where he should be covered, the t-shirt he sleeps in is riding up his waist, tangled to match the agony he was enduring minutes prior. Ordinarily, he has a flair for over exaggeration, hence the simplicity of him alone and existing as his nightmare's victim is foreign territory for us both.

I don't know where to tread for fear of being trapped, where to look for fear of being captured, I don't know the location of the mythical tomb containing his sacred secrets.

I've searched every manual, every map, yet his whole world is so far disillusioned, with none of his locked-up lies in sight. Living in a fantasy arena, the only key to success, or a magic cavern of secrets, is resistance, resilience and revolution. One day soon, I'll be staging an invasion of his memories, so that once and for all, the mutiny of past and present can be diffused and leave his future free from the shackles of time.

There is nothing left for him to say except a firm, yet clearly indisposed, "Goodnight Sierra. Try to keep your promises."

"But-"

"It's important to me."

There's an unheard beat in the stillness.

I'm not sure if it's right to say what I'm about to but before apprehension can hinder my impulse, I say it.

"You're important to me." It travels like a whisper, and concludes with his tolerant sigh.

Isaak and I are scarcely blunt with each other. Often, I offer provocative questions, tailored to embroider his subconscious with depictions of the relationship there could be between us. He is my opposite. He is a shield to emotional attachment and will cut strings before they've even been tied to our hearts. He will dust the remains off him loosely whilst mine stay clinging, like an ancient, unobliterable, cobweb riddled with sorrow. There are cavities of my heart chartered in his name, but not an inch of his body bears Sierra.

His laboured hand extends to me, beckoning me nearer. I know no matter how irritated he might be, he'll be benign.
Reassured by his mannerisms I approach him, soon becoming adjacent and able to meet his eyes properly. Taking great satisfaction in my hierarchical studying of his features, I observe how layers of sweat glaze his quivering lips where his fears have transpired to heat in the night. Now that I'm beside him I discern how he radiates warmth like a tropical flame. The phenomenon of him and himself being out of his own control should be alarming, but is instead remarkably inviting.

"I'll make you another coffee." I told him.
He clears his throat from trapped distress, the echo of the cough giving him time to collect his thoughts. A grunt, and then a bid at mild pacification. "Then you're going to sleep."

If it gives me permission to care for him, the deal is sealed. Oh, my dark, dangerous, difficult lover. Even in your pain you'll never stop pursuing any morsel of strength. One day, you'll find strength in allowing yourself to feel.

"Then I'll go to sleep."

Isaak indicates his approval with a light nod, it is my cue to absent myself to the kitchen. I can't straight away. Gingerly, I raise my fingers to his cheek, and he doesn't retract so following a second's pause, I touch him. His beard is shaved back, sculpted to reflect the partnership of his youth and maturity. His jawbone is sheathed by tanned skin, so honey in colour, like butterscotch and a rival to the bitterness of the coffee I'm now leaving to make. My fingertips travelled from his ear to his chin, balancing on the cliff of his facial features' curve. He didn't move a muscle, reactionless, staring into nothing as sparks of something were being uncovered between us. But it was enough. It was us. It was a reminder to me of everything impossible. It was bittersweet, like butterscotch coffee.

I'm glad when I tread back inside to greet him asleep, it means I can slip a cup of hot, dark and bitter on the floor beside him without conversation. The stars decorate his vacant frown, I want to stay to save him but it's a battle that he has to face alone, for now. He's overloaded with intramural torment. I envision the crescendo as a serenade of spontaneity, but it might be an emotion explosion. Either way, I will stand ready.

I retire to bed, thoughts compounding, wild and asinine. That encounter with Isaak sees my salvation, in the form of his imperishable strength, dissolve around me. I can't seek refuge in a broken haven, so sleep delays pulling me under for a while. I'm painfully and messily buoyant on an ocean of contemplation, periodically gulping the salt and sadness to be able to breathe again.

The coffee hadn't been finished by sunrise. The mug had instead migrated to the fireplace from the floor, alluding that he'd treated it to consumption - but it has scarcely been drunk. Collecting it marks the addition of more ceramic to the washing up assembly. Between plates, the liquid that remained is wolfed down by the sink, and as it is draining Isaak surfaces from the hall. My hand tightens against a tea towel, drying and deliberating, and I track his movements stiffly. Exasperation and analysis presently seem the same.

"You didn't touch the coffee." My statement is all of a question, a command for an answer and a desperation to understand why I can't figure him out. I beg for all of this whilst barricading him from my sporadic conclusions, by shielding behind my eyes, preserving him in a cold and calculated stare.

"I didn't have time." Isaak confesses, attacking his breakfast. Anyone would think he was suffering from starvation. They'd never have seen toast devoured with bites as flurried, frantic and ravenous as his currently are. The flustered nature of his eating circuits my gaze back to the cheek that I'd caressed only hours ago. He'd never let me as close now, as he's under improved consciousness. A slash embellishes the skin there. Blood in the butterscotch. I am certain that even in the dark I'd recognize any recent impurity in Isaak's wearied complexion. That can only mean one thing - it was opened this morning, it's a fresh wound.

"Did you go out again last night…uh, this morning…after I left you, made you coffee?"

"No." His neoteric obstinance is grating on me. I endeavour to sound more assertive.

"Isaak." He tilts his chin away as I speak, pretending not to hear me.

Leisurely, I release my apron and discard it atop the counter, followed by tying up my hair to charge my confidence and exude purpose. Orange juice rocks back and forth in a glass whilst I pour. It's without bits. I can't stand them. Isaak disagrees but he'd never waste his ardour over matters as trivial as breakfast, so I get smooth juice. The zest against my lips incites my articulation and I feel braver. I decide that he will give me an explanation. I'm accustomed to his contumacy and I am relentless in comfortably exercising my coercive devices.

"Isaak." I state a second time, firm and expectant, and curtly overemphasising the consonants.

He looks up this time, and I fight not to fall captive to his solemn, deprecatory expression. Isaak is never affected by natural stuttering as he speaks, prone to planning out his words before he presents them, or alternatively fostering a large proportion of invincible conviction with what he says. "I went out briefly."

My breath seizes reflexively and my fingernails still fervently patter on the countertop with impatience. He knows I'm losing tolerance for his midnight escapades. This venture totals the fifth time this month.

"I had business to attend to." Isaak justifies.
"At 4 in the morning?" I strike back, bitterly.

It's a counteraction that relinquishes us nowhere, we're at a stalemate. His eyes dart erratically, scanning his logic for how I would know the details of his departure as precisely as the time. I know the time was 4 o'clock because I broke my promise again.

There's a grandfather clock in the hall. Isaak insisted on having one in order to satirise horror films. He affirms that if you acquaint yourself with fear and become deliberately subservient to an uneasy atmosphere, you must, evidently, be making a mockery of all that fear intends to do and therefore cannot be disturbed. Fear is disabled without weapons; unfasten your apprehension and you are an unreachable target. I asked him why he was afraid of grandfather clocks. In return, I obtained a mumble about the grandeur and the jurisdiction of the chime. Coming from Isaak, all just romanticised crap that means he's hiding the truth from me.

The ivory hands protrude sharply from the middle like needles, it doesn't tick but standing close enough allows you to make out the ache of the gears churning within the ornate body of the clock. Sculpted into the wood are figures and scenes. I took the time to sit by them one day and trace the polished waves, occasionally encountering roughness where the paint has worn away. It depicts a tableau of torture, a man severed on a bed of nails, a coffin left to rot in the bowels of the earth, fire and hellish symbols of gruesome fate. On the opposing side of the base, portrayals of forests, wholesome demonstrations of sweetened and organic affairs. Predominantly female, harmonious, illustrations of fruit and flowers.

This clock is open to interpretation. This clock is heaven and hell. This clock is the wisdom of a grandfather, advisory and immortalised. This clock is in our hall, and as I sit curled beside it, obsessively fed by its philosophy, it strikes 4am in the morning with a strained knell.

It catches the light of the night's last ray of the moon on its glass face, and it dapples across the carpet, refracting towards Isaak's room with an air of counsel. I am compelled, his open door inviting. I wonder if fate, the forecast of heaven and hell combined are drawing me to him, if he'll hold me, in this world and into whatever comes next.

The reflection was one of accusation, I realise, as soon my eyes ascertain Isaak's deserted bedspread. Out of principle I close his door, and my hopes descend, the fourth chime sounds with earth-shattering closure. Isaak is gone, and with him, my energy. I recoup three more treasured hours of sleep, finding assurance under the watchful eye of the grandfather clock in the hall.

The grandfather clock, who at the very least, unlike Isaak, stays put.

It's tolling now to signal 8 o'clock, as I sit in the kitchen astounded by my stubborn lover's confidential cloak. All eight chimes sound before either of us verbalise a single utterance. There's nothing to say, everything that I don't know circulating inside his mind.

I need to leave for practice, my bag is packed, my brain is too, compressed full of Isaak's indignance and the day has only just started. Chancing an embrace before I leave proves to be the breaking point to his reticence. My lover doesn't retaliate, nor does he reciprocate as my affection graces his body, heightening my frustration.

"Isaak. I need to ask you a question."
"Your incessant fixation with questions will be your downfall, Sierra."
"This one is objective."
"You know my rules about questions. Ask none. Things will be easier that way." The want inside me activates with a wish to ask why. I'm about to refrain before my appetite says fuck it. "Tell me why that's a rule."
"I said no qu…"
"That wasn't a question, I said tell me." I quickly realise I've discovered a loophole in this order. He can't evade it.

"My mother died from questioning rules."
I am smacked down from my high. This is the first time he's spoken about his family. I want to be intrigued but I'm angry, my compassion is suffocated. I land straight in the point I'm trying to debate. "I saw someone get killed last night. A man was shot."
"Correct."
"Then that's all I need to know." I retort heatedly, and the front door slams in my wake, leaving Isaak and the grandfather clock in the hall, alone to dissimulate destiny. Destiny that Isaak debates and I create.

CHAPTER IV: FOUND

Alessandro.

Sebastian and I are brothers, twin brothers, who hate procrastination. If there is something that needs doing, we make sure it gets done. Our father's murder subverted the urgency of all we stood for. Before, we had just idly watched and worked out how the society around us operated, but now we are involved. I picture a red blotch marking our names as citizens of concern in thousands of books scattered across people we pass every day, friends merged into foes. We exist to entertain a world of inflammatory faith. If we want to be under inspection until we die, we stay. If we want to make a difference, we fly. Now.

Eighteen is the recruitment age, meaning we have just over a year to lay low, but there's little point. Not when we can act on our father's defence and our mother's daring whilst we have a head start in the race for our freedom. The girls are a priority, they will never be recruited but if they've developed their talents by now, they will be at risk by now, awake or asleep, in hiding or in the open. They will never survive without greater protection. Without us.

I searched the books. Father kept millions of paper copies of everything he could lay his hands on, from charity or purchase. He couldn't read, none of the books had been absorbed for their fictional brilliance and worlds away from here. The pages of distant lands stocked littered scraps of notes that evidenced and documented events that happened in our family. No information was safe to discuss openly.

Disorderly handwriting was here and there, exceptionally far from systematic. I had always loved the unpredictability, the way that a new story with moving explanations were uncovered in whichever book you opened. I can't begin to count the nights Father would reveal one memory after another. It was often every scribble we asked for, but he sometimes censored them for our youth. However, in a period of crisis, the irregularity was proving a hindrance.

Sebastian studied an illegal directory in the corner of the room under candlelight, nearing the window for illumination was too dangerous. A moment of exposure and we're done for. Firstly, he reads carelessly to omit the names, primarily reading for ages and sexes, eliminating his focus to any information except names and addresses of women over sixty years of age. With any hope, two would provide access to Sierra and Betsy. Our girls.

How we came to be in possession of thousands of identities was my fault. I'd found the brown leather book buried in the snow outside the forest boundaries and brought it home to show Father without realising it was the belonging of an officer. If we returned it, we'd be killed for knowing too much. Father had no choice but to keep it. "That directory should be able to locate them." I break the silence, but Sebastian just grunts dispassionately in response.

"Keep looking. I feel that I'm close." I offer a few words of encouragement to keep my brother searching.

Close to the evidence was one thing, but close to dysfunction as a result of my fierce predilection for adventure and high stakes roaming untamed was another. I think I'd heard someone somewhere refer to it as butterflies, which is an understatement in its masses. It's not butterflies, its vipers, writhing and injecting their venom, a poison that keeps my lungs burning from crusader's ambition.

Bridgette. Circled in fading charcoal inside a book of baby names. The cover looks old, presumably the property of my mother, confirmed as a purple scrap of writing paper flutters out. I see 'Sebastian?' written in my mother's handwriting as it turned in on itself in the delicate breeze. It melts into the damp of the windowsill before I can catch it, and I watch my mother's ink solvate to a blended indigo smudge. I can't help hurting.

My mother's signature ink was always shades of blue, and her works were always in pristine condition. The rushed charcoal impression wasn't her hand.

"Bridgette. 83." I whip around to see Sebastian gesturing to the page he's on. "68th Block. AXJ. 47588749," he continues.

"Give me just the essentials." I direct. I don't need the rest, he should know to only tell me what I need to know, and leave out the superfluous.

"7th Sector. Kildrift."

I debate the information, outlining the journey in my head. I've seen trickier things, done more difficult things than walking. Taking steps with a mission engages and reinvents me. "Outskirts of Colmoor, not far, but it'll take us to midnight."

Sebastian's mouth twitches up into a faint smile, catching my drift. "Ready?"

I returned it. "You bet."

Sebastian and I share a grin for the first time since Father died. It's nice, and a sudden reversion back to childhood when nothing mattered. I was oblivious to the fact we had everything then. Everything, a mother and a father.

We travelled the whole night as I'd predicted. Not much thought was given to what we left or took from our place. It was always a house above being a home. Four walls that had seen horror beyond comparison, there was nothing left to supply us happiness there.

I refused to knock; I didn't want to frighten an elderly lady to death if she thought I was there under orders for Sierra. That was if Bridgette had been the one to take her from my father those sixteen years ago. Standing on the doorstep for any longer than this we'd look like wanderers, intoxicated beggars. Sebastian, sensing my reluctance, heads off into the alleys to search for remnants of paper that we could fashion into a letter and ease the burden of a tricky conversation.

"Can you explain why you seem to be infatuated with my doorstep?" A sweet voice trickles from above me, as my brother strides out of view behind a brick wall.

I'm slightly perturbed by her brashness, and I accidentally reprogram my approach out loud, "Asking questions takes courage. Courage takes knowing you have nothing to lose. You're…"

"Sierra. Sierra Genieva. Nice to meet you, mystery dweller at my doorstep."

"You're not afraid of me." I'm startled. Women in Colmoor don't dare to speak to men with this level of flippancy. Only for the fact it is so easy to mistake the wrong person for the right person.

"Should I be?" She queries innocently, and I believe this is my chance to choose right or wrong.

If did know the fundamental workings of our society she would never dare to speak to a man so freely, especially one who was hovering by her front door in the midnight hours. I may have come to arrest her, but she doesn't seem at all phased. She is either stupid or uninformed, and neither predicament is all that appealing but there's an underlying assuredness.

"If I come down now, will you be there when I open the door?" Sierra solicits.

"Well, it's foolish of you to think I'm going anywhere when I've walked 4 hours to meet you."

For the first time, I look up to the window and Sierra defies any thought I'd ever had over what she would look like. Picturing a smaller woman, as my father described Savannah, the fact that she is slender, tall, and a light brunette is easily startling. I know instinctively that she is a woman governed by her heart, except with the additional mastery of an intuitive and witty mind. Her complexion, her gaze and her posture reveal in so many ways, the development of her maturity in the sixteen years I've missed.

As Sierra descends the staircase to meet me, tiptoeing the final stretch of our obscurity, a branch snaps from behind the garden gate, the cause of a hard footstep. Steps I've heard before. I spiral around, my hair prickles in preparation, but Sebastian stands ahead of me.

"SG." My brother promulgates, alerting me to lower my guard. This is Sebastian's code. Initials because they're fast to communicate and act as anonymous at the speaker's bidding. My shoulders slacken in recovery from my fight reflex, tension in my muscles melting away. A shrug masks the apprehension and instructs my body to reset the alarm, stand down, no threat. For now.

"The right house?" Sebastian wants to know.

"Yes. In about three seconds we'll have Sierra safe."

"I've got a few leads on Betsy," My brother almost looks excited. "Sierra's yours."

With 'Sierra's mine' coursing around my head, I cast my twin a concordant nod. A set of hinges squeal and I am level with Sierra's eyes, she uses the door to shield half of herself as if she doesn't trust me. Then again, she has no reason to. Yet. Glancing behind me, I learn that

Sebastian has fled, owing to the crucial importance of him finding Betsy now that I'm with Sierra.

"Do you have a name? I refuse to call you doorstep dweller for the rest of our time together." Her voice flows directly to my heart.

I suck thinly on my upper lip whilst I think, playing down my ascendancy so as not to intimidate her. I didn't plan ahead enough to charge into our first encounter with a goal or a demeanour, so there's an element of awkwardness whilst I discover who I want to be to her. I don't want to be Alessandro. Alessandro with the twisted past, chained by memories. I can't be Alessandro.

I give her a subtle smile, head tilted, chin marginally higher than what's ordinarily my greeting. I don't feel like myself, I feel melded forward from my background, I feel like more than I ever thought I could feel.

"My name is Isaak. Isaak Macaluso." It is a golden lie. An alias that brings me to life. A new identity, vitality by another name.

"Sierra." she breaks into a smile, "Sierra Genieva. Unused to strange men on my doorstep, and dying to know more."

I am seeing her properly for the first time, I see in her smoky eyes, the reflection of a man I want to be and never have been all at once. It feels like the beginning of a journey. The world's first sunrise. I can see beyond tomorrow. I can see Sierra, my escape.

I resent the urge to blink when I'm with her, I just want to keep watching her, observing how she walks and works, and refrain from explaining all about this world she's grown up in. Through abstruse hints after that doorstep meeting, I confirm that Bridgette, to whom Sierra has given 'Gettie' as an affectionate sobriquet, has told her adopted daughter nothing of the societal scandals that act like carcinogens to us all. My girl is blissfully oblivious. Initially, I was prepared to disclose each concept one by one, each regulation set in stone, but the more time Sierra and I spend together, the more it seems unnecessary. Until the day she expressed to me her love for singing.

We'd gone out a few times. Often at night when Gettie was sleeping. I preferred it this way, the atmosphere was a slave to Sierra's beauty, whereas the light that the day brought around, just amalgamated the surroundings and the sublime dark green jumpsuit she always wore. Tonight, we sat on the beach together, drawing stars and infinity signs in the sand because we both agreed that hearts are too cliché.

Poking the blaze was my task because the fire we contrived spat embers at us savagely and I didn't mind the burns. Sierra's hands were covered in bark and dirt anyway from helping to carry the logs we needed for the base all the way to the coastline. The ocean is hypnotic, an enviable gradient with the sky, Prussian blues meeting with the depths of the cobalt waters beneath, claiming you as a part of the deathless skyline. Stars interspersed with the air felt so close you could breathe them, or you could exhale and they'd be scattered like glitter, tossed to the waves, lost to time, like the sparks between Sierra and I. We existed solitary together, in a sentient watercolour of authentic soul delight.

We pretend to see a shooting star. There's nothing in life that's worth waiting for before you start believing in your wishes. Sierra quizzes me on what I'd wish for, and I didn't expect how difficult the answer would be. I could wish that my parents hadn't died, but I can't delineate that to Sierra simplistically. It would trigger too many questions. I despise questions. I could tap into her psyche. I could alleviate her doubts, help her to trust me.

"I'd wish for this night to last longer than any night in history ever has. Space is an expanse of night, perhaps I'd wish I could take you there. There's something about small lights in darkness."

Whatever impact I was expecting that to have on her, was not how she responded. That's what I love about her. My pupils dilate for her and her excitement, her passion and beauty, her eyes widen for life and the fortune of being able to live it. I see her mind ticking, I'm awaiting her wish. No matter what it is, I'll pledge it as a sub-assignment beside protecting her. Shit. I think this means I'm falling.

"I'd wish to sing. Gettie stops me at home. I just need to sing; I feel like I can't be me without…I don't know. I want to be a singer, Isaak. I guess it's mindless…"

The pressure of this moment is riveting. I should be trying to dissuade her, but I'm enthralled. I can't be too interested, but I want to hear her sing so badly. I've spent too long conjuring what singing might sound like if ever I'd heard it. My father is in my head telling me not to encourage this, but I shut him out. You sacrificed your better judgement for love Father, and this moment is mine. "It's not mindless. I want you to sing for me."

"Now, I-" Her cheeks heat into a rose-coloured blush. I'm almost disappointed. "You don't want to."

"No! I do. I just haven't sung…in front of anyone before. I never sing in the house, I usually sing by myself, I go out places, I sing here."

I sidle closer, picking up her consent from the way she moves away from the fire so I don't get burnt trying to approach her. Noticing her fingers twitch slightly as I get closer, I stop and look for more signals that she's okay, but when she touches my hand, sinking us into the sand I know this is what she wants.

"Nothing's different then, gorgeous." I reassure her gently, the adjective slipped out and now I'm forced to play it cool.

Sierra judges me. "Gorgeous?"

"Just, don't question facts. You're beautiful and I'm convinced your voice is the same. Close your eyes." I instruct her and she obeys calmly.

I ease nearer, navigating her face by the warmth alone. I close my eyes too; it feels genuine this way. I don't want to deceive her more than I already have. I'm drawn, helplessly and legitimately, to the individuality of her temperament and talent, but I know better than to ruin my chances. I try to accommodate myself in the memory of my mother and hers sitting and singing together before they knew they were in danger. Beside each other, bellies touching, Sierra and I even closer than we are now.

Her voice takes me to another place. The tones are sensational, interdimensional, countering reality in a 180-degree pirouette. I'm not asleep but I'm dreaming - of a new place where Sierra is all I can think, all I can live, where I can love every inch of her with no guilt or remorse. Where I can adore her without my father in my shadow and infesting each compass direction of my conscience. Where I don't need to protect her from anything but falling too hard in love. Where I can be by her side for normal things like marriage and a family, rather than bayonets and brutality.

In disbelief, I can't speak for the whole time we extinguish the fire, I'm speechless whilst walking her home. I can't stop smiling and she delights in it.

"Will I see you tomorrow?" is the only question that she wants to know the answer to.

"If you'd like that."

"I need you. You make me feel complete, in the strangest of ways. I barely know you yet that makes me want you more. I think when I'm with you I feel like myself."

Goodnights are always too short, the time away from each other is too long. I think over everything as I lie in the dilapidated bridge arch where I've found a crevice big enough to sleep, just. This is where I stay until she needs me again. Not much confuses me, but how I feel about her does. I need to keep her close enough that I'm able to protect her, but at enough distance that she doesn't risk getting hurt by our emotions.

Sierra rushes in my direction, tears streaming from her eyelashes when I turn up at her door the next morning. She's sobbing that she doesn't know who to go to, that Gettie isn't waking up, she doesn't know what to do. I follow her into the house and into a room where Bridgette lies motionless in bed, in this instance, she looks entirely how I'd expected, frail and with stern eyebrows, but with an otherwise kind appearance. Sierra looks on with desolation as I proceed with the routine of checking a pulse and listening for breathing.

"Is she...?" She can't bear to say the word 'dead'.
"I'm sorry, Sierra."

My arms act as provisional therapy, she thumps her fist against my solid chest in anger and in grief, but it doesn't hurt. I stay until she's stopped crying, holding her tightly. I'm wary about intimacy, but my vow was to protect her, and that includes her mental state. The day that Gettie died was the day I decided exactly what I needed to do. I needed to do it there and then.

"Tell me what you think we are." I whisper into her hair.
"Special. Elusive, a little like some of the dreams I've had." She lists. I commit her answers to memory, it's a

requirement for me to know exactly what I'm working with.

"Tell me how you see yourself."

"An artist in a colourblind world. My voice, my medium, and I've got a past to abandon."

I breathe in deeply, earnestness is not my strong suit, and give one last order. "Tell me how I make you feel."

"Easy. Alive."

She can't see me grinning powerlessly in response, and I have to shake this feeling. Calmer now, she leads me to the kitchen where she prescribes coffee as short-term medication for us both. Guiding me through the simple steps sidetracks her from her heartache swelling. She says what the coffee is in, is not important. What is in the coffee is important. It has to be poured immediately after being heated, it can't be allowed to cool, and you can't drain it too meticulously or you'll evict the flavours and the intensity. There is so much criteria, so I am enthused when it all goes to shit. She spills the granules all into my cup and across the counter, cursing. The obscenities might melt into tears if I let them.

"I'll drink it. There's no harm done." I follow through. I take it, steaming. I drink it, though it's deathly black. Strangely, I'm addicted. The bitterness, the darkness, the heat, matches my own darkness. It complements my stamina, teaches me resistance to pain. It's not perfect in theory, but in practice it overachieves, hitting every part of me it needs to be able to energise me. Coffee made like this, represents everything about the new man I am, and somehow reprimands me like drops of Sebastian in my veins.

"You don't seem all that poisoned, Isaak. Success."

I ignore her, still not entirely used to my new name, and straying into different, impromptu thoughts whilst she stares at what I'm putting in my mouth in disgust. I clear my throat. "Sierra. I want to take you away."

Rapidly, as if she had rehearsed the answer, she nods. "On one condition."

Sierra Genieva is intriguing. "Name it."

"I live with you."

So here it is - how Isaak met Sierra. I took her to the beach, away for a while, I pretended we had something so I could protect her from everything. It amounted to nothing. They are still after her, we are still running. My sweetheart. My gorgeous girl. A predator's prey and a figurine to an undisclosed game. Heroine to my origin story. For this to work, she has to believe she is no-one to this society. These are things of importance. Life and death.

If I let her know how much I fall for her, it is submission, so for now we are unsteady on the fine line of victims or lovers. It's all for the best that she doesn't ever know that she is my sweetheart. My impossible girl.

Signing out as Alessandro Gray, and in, Isaak Macaluso.

CHAPTER V: IMMERSE

Sierra.

Fuming over the morning's events does me no favours, so I regurgitate all the hostility onto the back of my receipt for my lunch, pulverise it in my fist, and watch it drown in the Thames. My schedule warns that I mustn't traipse by the riverside too long. There's a dress shop three squares up where Gala's fretting and pacing behind the counter. I'd forgotten what life was before my estimated time of arrival was being scrutinised to the second by a woman almost fifty years my senior. Gala sometimes reminds me of a sterner, more inquisitive Gettie. Perhaps that's why I've never sought after a new seamstress, it seems distant comforts enhance customer service. I should tell that to Gala on the rare chance that she'll ever ask me for advice on a managerial front - which is in the best-case scenario, never.

I'm dragging my heels to dislodge the cigarette butts that I've been trailing down the dirty streets. The door is whipped open as I'm reaching for the handle. I can't immediately tell if the greeting is one of impatience or relief that I've arrived. I twist my wrist to see the watch face, simultaneously being tugged from the elbow by Gala. "I'm not late!" I laugh, as the momentous amount of energy in her frail bones inspires me.

"What is the saying?" She drawls. "The early bird catches mice?"

"It's worms. The early bird catches the worm." I outline.

"Well, I always knew it as mice. Is your Isaak with you?" She clocks my expression, and offers poor consolation. "Your dress is waiting, perhaps that'll take your mind off the man."

I ___ YOU

My manager tried countless times to introduce me to designers, men in suits and far too many accessories who always claimed that my style was practically the only reason they were in business. They pretend to be in awe of me - but I recognise what awe looks like from my lover. The only thing their eyes scrounge for is the wealth, which they expect they can elicit from my body. Amateurs feigning experts. I abandoned their wishes for me with the contempt I learned from Gala.

This lady shuffled up to my dressing room in the interval of a performance last winter. I braced myself for praise, possibly mistakenly full of myself. The rush I get whilst singing is unequivocally amazing that in the moment I didn't question how she managed to bypass security. She scans me up and down and it's only when she speaks, I realise that she was studying my body language.

"And why is it that you settle for wearing something that makes you so uncomfortable?" She examines, her voice foreign and somehow able to make the start of a sentence sound like the middle of one.

Her question referenced the blue halter neck dress that I wore. I'd be lying if I said she wasn't right, and that I wasn't impressed by her deduction. Prior to the first half I'd refused to go on stage without a cloak, shawl or jacket to cover me - I hated how my back was exposed. I'd told my team the cold was bothersome, when really, I was screaming my insecurities towards deaf ears. The bust on the dress was too low, not that I couldn't fill it out, but I resent that the boundary between seductive and sensual is so blurred that I can't let my voice alone be my heart's advocate.

I told her that I'd exhausted my options and was tired of evading the standards set in stone very clearly for me. Someone somewhere is waiting to put my breasts on a billboard to advertise my singing, I joked, not prepared for the sharp look I got in response.

"Leave people like that far behind. Your body is not a trophy, you shouldn't believe that's how to feel pretty. I'll dress you, starting immediately." She snapped.

It took this prompt for me to realise how properly she was dressed. The hues blended perfectly and there was an aesthetic balance of jewellery, makeup and accessories on top of the dark purple coat she wore. It wasn't overpowering and allowed her personality to be the statement finishing touch. I imagined her styles on me and how it would feel to be dressed in a way that made me Sierra. A look that would finally hush the sexualised critique which had for so long suppressed the impact of my song.

I finished the show in a lilac jumpsuit with subtle gemstones. My manager marched up to me the moment the curtains united and declared me a disgrace. In a matter of furious seconds, I called out the industry, the people responsible for my degradation and the hunger of society for their nasty, annulled gratification for things material like a body over phenomenally intangible like a song. Heeding and needing visual clarity is but confirmation that the world's imagination isn't operating as it should. My song is my song regardless of how I dress, not enhanced by how naked I am. Close your eyes when you listen. And if you lose interest in the music because of your blindness to brash and dramatic spectacles, keep them fucking shut.

Gala hovered behind me, her narrow pupils pinpointed in the direction of the imbeciles receiving my wrath, evidencing her approval of my outburst. I walked and she walked beside me, leaving my manager open mouthed and sour.

Isaak's abrupt, unexpected arrival into the present startles my flashback and the memories start to fade, replaced with a flurry of images of my lover. I momentarily neglect a splenetic continuation of our morning because I'm too immersed in the way I feel around him. The windows in the door clatter, metal hinges on glass and wood, and I realise my ears are never safe from the sound of his voice.

He doesn't want me to say anything, the way he's standing gives it away. One utterance and I'll bolt, his stance speaks. I purse my lips as an answer to the question he'll never ask, and await the reason he's come. In place of rightful vexation, all I can think about is how he hasn't brushed his hair, and it suits him.

"Come to dinner with me tonight after your show, normal place, normal table. If life wasn't as short, I'd give you longer to mull it over, but I'm racing time so I'm going to need your answer now." Isaak pushes.

I nod numbly, falling dazed into agreement. Surrendering again. Every time. And then he grins, locking me in the thrill and leaving.

"He leaves that way each time!" Gala splutters, exasperated, crying my thoughts before I think them. My head is a labyrinth of messy, antithetical emotion and I shut it forcefully away, pounding from the inside out. I don't understand why I'm still in love, and yet being so desperately in love kills me like sweet murder.

Gala flourishes my dress with a proud presentation, the significance of the situation shining. Tonight's occasion marks the first dress I've worn onstage since I disbanded from my management. Precision and expression are crucial, and I had confidence that my new seamstress would bestow perfection. I take the navy fabric bag from her, cradling it gingerly whilst I latch the changing room door. I unzip it and remove it from its carrier to appraise Gala's creation.

I started off with weekly meetings with her, reviewing my schedules and designing outfits to suit my curves and comfort. Then it became almost daily, and now she's succumbed to my wardrobe as a full-time project, loving it, illustrating fashion and my style together with just her hands and an adept mind.

The dress she's made for this evening exceeds my expectations, arresting my diffidence. For the first time today, the muscles in my stomach and chest catch with traces of excitement. A bold black bodice encounters a baby pink skirt formed from chiffon and silver thread fastens diamante crystals around a high waistband. It's an illusion neckline, which is conservative enough to allow me to perform the way I want, but signals my readiness to leap from my comfort zone.

I barely have the words to express to Gala my immense gratitude for the outfit, and barely the time to engross myself in my reflection. I need to source some matching accessories in the adjacent shops to Gala's and get to the concert hall in time for hair and makeup. She accepts my money alongside a tight hug, then proceeds to fret about keeping the dress in pristine condition. I preserve it neatly in its case before leaving the shop with a much more contented heart.

"Good luck!" She calls in my wake.

I've mastered the urban jungle. I know where all of my accessory hotspots are. I know the duration of time I can run my hand along the banister leading down to the tube station before I encounter the chewing gum, my shopping bag handles dangling, conspiring with gravity to slice into my wrists. I know where the strangers are and how they stare, I know how to downplay the attention but sometimes it feels like eyes burn into the back of my head as soon as I cast my gaze back to the pavement. I shake it off, and shield my new dress from the pushy public on the train as the underground moves me into my evening.

It's a difficult task, for me or for most people, to sit in front of a mirror and not challenge what they see in it. My hairdresser frets and fumbles with my hair, continually deciding that she likes a style and then reversing the look entirely - but I'm coming to accept that unsurety is the dulled spirit of tonight.

I'm staring at myself, staring at me, and realising that I don't know much about the woman I'm looking at. I rely on Isaak as an anchor of my past, but beyond his face and the memory of Gettie I'm lost and my history is vague and blurry. Any opportunity I get to access Isaak, he tells me fragmented pieces of our memories, they often involve nature. He speaks of long walks and beaches, but keeps everything in the dark, literally. None of his memories feature an inch of sunlight, meaning that my past, what made me Sierra without Isaak, is eclipsed by the shade of his murky enigmas, obscured by the darkness of secrecy. I think, in this moment of introspection, the reason I'm so tolerant of Isaak is that I feel he's my only hope of setting in motion my life's light. He'll provide the answer eventually - in his long-winded Isaak way.

"20 minutes until curtain." A stagehand's echoed call travels up the corridor, and inexplicably, I'm arrested by my anxiety.

With the last of my lipstick extracted from its bottle, albeit a little slovenly, I have to dash outside to feel the cold on my face. The polluted London air doesn't hit quite as I wanted it to, but it reminds me of a larger world. To my left, late audience members are still arriving, scurrying across the roads, head deep in their purses and bags looking for tickets. All of those tickets have my name printed on.

I pull my hand back and forth against the ribbed wall of the theatre, needing the gritty rouge bricks to help me feel something to detract from my nerves. I'm humming, in reassurance that my voice is still operating the way it should - the song tangled in my throat, in my head, is Isaak's favourite song. To my detriment I keep making eye contact with passers-by in the street so I raise my focus to the sky. The stars are barely visible, but exist regardless. I feel the same. They'll burn out one day, and so will I, but not today. Whilst I exist, I'll shine.

I'm in a turbulent state to sing, unable to pilot my emotions with as much control as usual. Stepping on the stage, feeling so detached from the people surrounding me and tending to the last of my contemporary appearance, I snap a mental image of the ruby-red curtain so I can sing to my photographic memory and not the hundreds of people solely focusing on me. Gala made the dress with material that absorbs the shimmer from my sweaty palms, a blessing I've discovered only now. There's enough mental labour going into my forced breaths that the countdown is distorted in my ears. The curtain rises, a blazing spotlight incinerates my pupils and narrows my vision.

The audience is a cocktail of shadows and expectations, and my voice, a musical mixer. There's an intrusive taste of blood in my mouth and the best way to dilute the whole unpalatable beverage, is to down my constraint - and sing. I'll show them, like alcohol, maturity over time - they've waited to see the richness and I'm paying out in vibrato. I worry my arpeggios plague the smooth system of my song more like counterfeit notes, because I'm translating my brokenness to broken chords, but the rapturous applause heals all wounds of apprehension. But then it all starts to sound different.

My eyes shut, illustrating a performer's technique but also to maintain composure. I'm struck by a constructed visual of Isaak shifting slowly closer to me, I feel like I'm sinking, the sky is dark and shades of blue surround us. I know this is a memory, the first time I sang freely. The tension in my vocal cords weakens as I relax and I snap open my eyes at the apex of the song as imagination Isaak touches my cheek. Real life sees my head tilt upwards in response and the notes' departure from my lips happens easily. I can't hear how it sounds through my earpiece and the microphone, but I felt power.

Belting the highest pitches in this piece, I'm remembering the conflict with Isaak this morning. How I wanted to shout, but how his lack of reception makes anger pointless, I let the sun flare with my fury instead. It was shining on his flawless features - his deep cut, the last thing I saw before I left, somehow contributing to the perfect sublimity. Then I remember the source of the argument, the gunshot last night, and that's when the hundreds of clapping hands start to sound nasty and hideous. Fatal shots. They're killing out of oblivion, killing my confidence out of oblivion. But they're just people, not knowing how they sound, not knowing what kind gestures can mean, here to see my song, not knowing my past. And maybe not knowing my past, like me - that's for the best.

I'm relaying this piece with a rawness that I've never heard in myself before. Just remembering everything I saw last night is making my veins overheat, and terrified of them rupturing, I choke at the climax of the note I'm on - cutting it off short. In the silence, I find my breath, recovering sufficiently enough to come in on time in the next verse. My voice is still shaky but I'm pouring out an emotion inundation - enough for the whole audience to survive on, and with excess left over for the stagehands and surplus for my accompanist.

The spectators consume my energy throughout every song, feeding off it, some clamouring over it with their tiny notebooks. Critics are easy to spot, they're the ones with their heads peering down for the majority of the show they've come to watch. I'm waiting on the interval like it's Christmas, the people disperse, the curtains conjugate, and that broken chair hiding in the wings that nobody has used for decades suddenly looks all the more inviting.

I have everything I've ever wanted at my fingertips but I can't feel it. I have all the sounds I longed for, immersing me, but they merge into clusters of noise and I can't hear the beauty in it like I used to. I have the recognition I sought for, I'm making the impressions necessary for the vocal revolution, the media are my army, I'm the secret weapon - but the white flag is in my hand, and any second ready to be thrust to the skies. I'm done. I'm crazy for love that doesn't love right, I'm desperate for a fight I can't survive. By retreating from a hopeless battle, will I give up on my dreams or capitulate to reality?

My schema has me caged in a wicked circus. Towering over me the ringleader, theatre culture with a dictator's face and an eagle's scrupulous glare. With each whip crack, a spine snaps, another backbone shattered so that you can't defy tradition or procedure. Vertebrae and virtues all under possession of the people above. It's a cyclic carnival, and if I'm going to be exhibited, I'll tame the tigers and do it my way. Heads up high so they can't look down their noses. I wipe my forehead with my white flag, and leave it to rot next to my self-pity on the sidelines, a place I don't plan on returning.

"Ladies and gentlemen, please welcome back to the stage, Sierra Genieva."

I'm ready to flood Gala's dress in fame and eternal cherished flames. I'm charged, ready to electrify my song with so much worth that lightning won't phase me, ready to make my lying demons ashamed to uncover their two-faced heads.

I close my eyes a final time, fill my lungs, and walk into the light to finish what I started and take a longer journey than has ever been travelled. Because, ladies and gentlemen, people of the audience, my city, the world and its seven wonders, make it known, that Sierra Genieva, is impossible, and she adores it.

CHAPTER VI: QUESTION

Sebastian.

Alessandro stalks towards me in the cemetery, succession and success. Success and succession. It's dark but I know his footsteps, and I know the direction he's coming from as well as where he's headed. He can make his way to my location blindfolded. There's order, strife and pride in the way he walks like a matador in a detective's clothing.

I'm waiting by our father's grave, our mothers to my left. Our meeting place, and as close as family gets. It helps that my brother respects the dead more than the living, with the exception of Sierra and I. Why wouldn't he, when he has more relatives underground? Death seems like a heavenly society, meeting without him on an everlasting basis, but there's something about the danger of being alive that he relishes in and that stops him dying too soon - a bit of entertainment before the final chapter. After all, death has a bigger impact on a fruitfully spent life, and he's obsessed with the control he has.

As always, a silent regard for mother and father. We clench the silence too long, wringing it dry to release a sign from our parents, but nothing ever comes. It's nothing to dwell on. The moonlight absorbs our pain and we continue. Our interaction is as follows.

"You shot early." My brother starts with a breezily casual tone to his voice, and now I know why he called us here.

"That," I pause, "is an incredible observation AG. I applaud you." I'm surprised he doesn't pick on the sarcasm as much as the initialism.

"I'm not AG anymore. It's IM." He persists, besotted with his new identity. It is not freedom, but an excuse to forget how scared he once was of living.

"Yes…" I nurture, as a brother should. A brother should also keep him in check, "…to Sierra only, to me you're still Alessandro."

"I can live with that. All other questions about my name aside, I actually asked you a question."

He has a sustained, slightly annoying, dislike of believing people will reply to statements. "You didn't, you ought to work on that." I remind him.

"Just answer." Alessandro begins to get frustrated; I can feel it within myself when he's getting agitated. One question isn't worth an argument.

"I will respond to your statement." I jibe. I'm met with an expression devoid of badinage. When Alessandro is thinking in retrospect, it pulls open healed wounds and the only way he knows to counteract the pain is with ample nothingness. He calls me here to exchange his hurt, and to bury the past that's continually crawling back to life. To locate nothingness and burials, a graveyard is suitably perfect.

We fight in the present, individually but for the same cause. For the cause of our girls and for our justice, retribution for the deaths of our two mothers. It's just us alone, no colony like the bats that roam in the nighttime, working effortlessly to cruise the darkness. I remember once at age nine when I couldn't fall asleep, I left Alessandro, and sought out my father. I found him awake by the fire. He hid the photo of our mother that he was gazing at under the blanket covering his lap but I saw it. I saw his tears too. "Sebastian, come." he remarked hoarsely after noticing me.

I made my way across the sitting room that I never remembered looking so ransacked as it was then. It was likely I'd never noticed, but equally likely in hindsight that my father had been searching for something. Directing me to bring his alcohol bought him time to slide the photo under the cushion so I could sit on his legs without damaging it. Allowing me here was about as affectionate as he ever got, but I could feel his care in the way he stopped me shivering and how his arms kept me protected from the cold. Our mother's death had stolen a part of his heart that hadn't been returned. She'd be distraught to know that with her, his smile left too.

I learnt a lot from my father, things that didn't occur to me that I wanted to know, but always appreciated once I knew them. When I asked about the squeaking I could hear in that moment, sitting in his chair, that was when he first told me about bats, that they sheltered in our attic. I discovered how they're the only mammal with the ability to fly. It makes me smile to know that if the conversation were repeated now, I would tell my father how Alessandro tries to fly and defy what's possible, to be the elite and turn his back on expectation. If he's normal in a crowd, he's not gratified. I hope my father can hear the mortal sounds of Alessandro putting his life on the line for love. He'd be proud.

Alessandro knows I'm piecing together memories, so he doesn't press me for a response. Our pact is to never take pauses for granted, as new clues could emerge from all we remember. Shaking my head to break back into the conversation, I disappoint Alessandro with no memory significantly valuable to our history. I won't reveal to him the value it holds to me.

Alessandro's angst swarms the peace with immediacy, as he hears the distant sound of metal in the town. I'm suddenly intensely aware of Alessandro, and I find myself apportioning nostalgic sympathy. I need to ground him. Calm him. Calm him. Calm him.

"Stop." Audibly this time. I pull him in close, clutching his shoulders. I'm the only one that he allowed close, before Sierra.

"You're hugging me."

"I'm centring you, there's a difference." I reason, trying not to allow myself to be plagued with memories of my brother acquiring his phobia for the very first time. I watched it all happen, understanding but powerless. My grip on my brother intensifies in an attempt to extort his fear from under his skin, failing before I'd even begun, knowing that at the end of every day, fraternity is all we have to heal us. Time and time again, our unity pulls us back from the edge, long after the distress subsides and the bells have stopped moaning.

As animals forage for food around us, I'm disturbed too much by the sounds of the night to decrypt answers, which is rare. I embrace the nothingness. Alessandro, my twin and my opposition who has since overcome his inertia, does not.

"You killed him before the last second. You know we don't do that." He interrogates.

I cling on to the nothingness, but as my consciousness builds to bind it to my current state of being, the chaos of my whirring mind returns. The nothingness is thrown back into orbit, it is gone from its temporary lodging in my body to celebrate with the sun on the other side of earth. Chasing it is inane, trying to preserve it is fatuous, but finding Betsy might mean sharing my forever quest for solace with a companion.

"One more time…you killed him. Before his last second." Alessandro repeats.

"He saw Sierra. Beautiful by the way, that's the first I've seen her in person."

I see my words physically colliding with his comprehension and the instant gratitude. That's right, Alessandro, stay silent. Silent when you know you're vulnerable and your sweetheart may not still be standing if it weren't for your right-hand man. Let your eyes flicker until they find new context for diversion. It pleases me that I know his mannerisms so proficiently. As his twin, I'm the nearest to his thoughts there is, without the unappeasable appetite for defiance and enterprise.

"No shit." Alessandro responds after a beat. "Does this mean you're no longer going to confront me about the fact I killed him?"

"I mean, no shit she's gorgeous."

I perform a spectacular eye roll, and decide to tailor the man's mind back onto the valid reasons for taking a life. I'm not afraid to shoot and Alessandro knows this, but I will never do so hastily. I have to confirm they're a threat, before bullets are fired.

"Those ones are difficult. So difficult. They're a special faction of the force, they dodge before one. If you spent more time fighting and less time flirting perhaps you would have identified that on the night. The two? Essentially becomes the one." I explain.

"I know the feeling."

"Ah?" I say, not being able to help my eyebrows angling themselves downwards in confusion and distrust.

"At ease, brother. I just mean you're not around as much as usual." He teases, elbowing me to evoke humour but he sees it evaporate.

"I take it you haven't found Betsy." He tries a different approach.

"Working on it. She's been tricky to locate, I just pray it'll be worth it."

"She's Sierra's twin, if that inspires you enough."

"I forget. You make a good point."

"I'm not in the habit of making bad points."
"Now that's debatable."

Alessandro used to smell like ash and embers, always dusty and never caring. As long as his ambitions were presentable, it didn't matter if his clothes were. I only notice how his scent has changed because elements of spring are now apparent and fresh in our surroundings, with hints of freesia and hyacinth diffused in the breeze, and he doesn't contrast them anymore. Instead, he's matured, Sierra's influence has made him melt like scented wax, candles lighting up his pursuit of her. He smells like our father used to, before he let himself go fully and the scent became exclusively for socialising if he ever had to drag himself out of the house.

After we're disbanded, he'll be headed straight back to her, without doubt. She must be in good company otherwise he'd never have returned to the boundary of the settlement he left behind in the first place.

"You trust she's safe now?" I ask.
"There's no reason for her not to be. She's performing. No one would be stupid enough to touch her on stage, in front of thousands. I'm on limited time though." Alessandro evaluates.

"As always." I smile knowingly.
"It's the way I work. The only good way."

"Speak for yourself."
"Your methods aren't finding Betsy."

"She's not yet in the picture. There were..." he takes a thoughtful breath, "...complications."
"I see."

There's no need to spark hope in a conversation that doesn't require it. It's an ambition with two outcomes, either I'll find Betsy or I won't - the only variable is when I'll stop trying. I'm headed back into the town as soon as my brother leaves. It's risky territory, but where there is risk, there's reward. Perhaps my reward will be a heart at rest knowing that Sierra's sister is safe. Whilst I'm mapping my routes in my head, Alessandro sneaks a hand into his own pocket, withdrawing a thin metal chain that loops around his unwashed fingers. At the end, is a tiny capsule. When he holds it closer, I realise that it's a telescope. "I need your opinion," he explains.

"I'm flattered, but not really my style."

"It's not for you. It's for Sierra."

"Then there's undoubtedly a catch. You don't buy anyone gifts."

He smiles. A naive part of me believes he's about to prove me wrong, but I know him all too well. It's a tracking device, my experience points out each mechanism. A locator, concealed within a gold cylinder. I know why. It's so he can find her, and get to her quicker than ever before now that he doesn't have to rely on faultless logic, but the way Alessandro and I work is ethical. This would break thousands of conventional codes. I don't agree with it, or what he will do with it but then I know how many perpetrators are in the city at present.

Sierra made a name for herself. She represents London city culture, with help from my brother. Foolish but good-natured help. She is fulfilling her dreams with no notion of how many liberties she is relying on Alessandro to do so. Gettie raised her with no information about the threats surrounding her, Sierra was not allowed to sing, and that was the first rule in their family of two. To this day, Sierra doesn't know that she is being stalked. She doesn't know that at least ten in her audience as she sings, wish they had guns aimed at her forehead. She doesn't know that each time she walks, every street she navigates, Alessandro is two steps behind, dealing with men in fatal ways. We don't kill unless we have to, I don't join him unless we're predicting an ambush or a solo threat like last night. Some attackers get so thirsty to credit Sierra's name to their gun that they peel away from their patrol and seek her out on their own. Alessandro and I have murdered seventeen men this month. Sierra slowly falling for my brother is the last thing on our minds.

Having this necklace on Sierra would mean that we could make predictions even easier. It could mean less lives lost, not that they deserve saving, but we don't want to kill. Although immoral, it could increase her protection. It would make Alessandro's paths more accurate; it could leave me more time for Betsy. It could secure the safety of two Genieva sisters. Making a decision was that quick. With my eyes still rocking with the swinging amulet in my brother's hand, I endorse putting a tracking device around Sierra's neck. "Do what you have to do."

We're both trying not to think about what Father would think, but wait for a sign of dissuasion either way. A change in the wind speed, a screech from something in the night, a disturbance in the town. Nothing. It only happened once, when Alessandro and I met here. We were exhausted, our hands decorated with the blood of six men and with that many deaths on your name it's a visual setback. All these lives for two girls. We'd lost the balance. We were close to losing our morals, risking ourselves. I asked the question, because Alessandro still hated them.

"Is giving up on the girls the only way forward?"

All the spirits of our father, mother and Savannah came alive together, forcing themselves back into our dimension. Suffocating oxygen swarmed our mouths, an intense heat in the cold air, and we couldn't stand. Our bodies were weak, and all our strengths were being played with by things we couldn't see. My fingers bore into the dirt, ignoring stones, pushing further and further downwards, leaving me fearing I was about to come into contact with the bones of my father in the shallow grave we had dug. Leaves and nettles flew toward us, malice in the way they struck our skin and left red inflammations throbbing above our muscles.

The moonlight became more apparent, for the first time that night, highlighting the spectre of how many graves surrounded us. Then the whole world fell silent, and we had no pain. We had air to breathe. We had strength to lift our arms and lay punches. We had life, we were above ground, and our bodies could feel pain and power. We were alive. The dead are debilitated, which is why it's our responsibility to account for the living. They didn't die so we could give up, and just like that we had our answer.

Nothing happens in the air this time. We feel our strength without help. There's no resistance from the other side. Father agrees with our actions. The trees sway though, branches creaking, perhaps that's Savannah saddened by the measures that she had to accept to protect her babies. Alessandro pushes the necklace back into the depth of his pocket, and crouches to the ground. He doesn't speak, just acknowledges our father, touching his hand to the engraved name - *Jack Gray*. We're proud to be a family.

Father was buried beside our mother which is why every time we visit we bring a small memento of the world - because we know how much she would have loved discovering all that was on offer. The flower from two weeks ago is dead now, so we take it, sprinkle the seeds and replace it with the new gift. A shell. It's colourful next to the concrete headstone. Blue and purple, like her writing. I saw it on a walk and washed it in the saltwater, before slipping it up my sleeve. It looks perfect sitting on the grass here, but we have to cover it with an entourage of thick leaves so that it doesn't stand out that anyone has visited the grave.

"Until next time." Alessandro announces, straightening up and removing all the traces of his whereabouts from his knees.

I don't bother with a verbal goodbye; we don't like what it suggests. Instead, we share a glance and then he ascends over the hill. As he climbs, I realise how he's falling. He's the soldier he's always been, but he's looking past tomorrow in a manner he's never done before. It could hurt him, but I can't stop him. Life must be lived with intention, and his willpower alone determines his fate. I watch his confident march until the scenery is all that's left and he's a mark, accidentally the most admirable impression, in the distance.

I turn to my father's grave, kneeling and placing my temple to the headstone. I feel myself losing direction in what I seek to do. I need to refocus. Promise him. Promise him. Promise him.

"Father, when I next return to see you, Betsy will have been found and she will be safe. I promise you."

As I turn my back to the graveyard, upping my collar to remain on the down low, the gate opens with the wind. I don't need to be on my guard for anyone because I know it's Father's way of saying he has faith in me. I step through it, and head back to the town that made me an orphan.

CHAPTER VII: HEAR

Isaak.

"I should be inflating my rates, shouldn't I? This is every other night as of recently." The bartender scorns with a friendly smirk, remarking at my deposit.

"There's no amount I wouldn't hand over for her safety, Nicholas." I push the notes into his hand, holding his stare, "So up your rates, I encourage you. Dare you, even. I only have two rules, I expect them to be followed, no matter the price I have to pay."

He hands me half the notes back, nodding understandingly, and begins to pump more beer to expectant patrons hunched over their third drinks of the night already. I cross my arms, deadpan with dissatisfaction, leaning on the edge of the bar. Nicholas jams a pint in my face, which I swiftly set aside and survey him dismissively. I don't want alcohol. I challenge him again with another callous look.

"She mustn't leave under any circumstance. Anything she wants is paid for." he speaks slowly, handing me the information I wanted.

"Right. And don't forget it." I turn to leave.

"Can't the girl catch a break from you?" he retorts. His concerns are reasonable, but they're about to be invalidated.

"I'll be dead before that money is in the hands of an undertaker instead of yourself. Don't question my reasons. She's a strong girl, but evil is relentless." My glare pierces and burns all traces of his doubts. "Nicholas, you have beers to make."

He lowers his eyes to the counter, adjusting his eyebrows down, as I walk away. A warm wind snakes in through the door, slithering into booths and twisting up the legs of bar stools, coating everything in an energised city sweat. The malice of those that hide in the streets hisses in my ears, and I clutch my hand into a fist to avoid swinging at the whispers that manifest in the night. I remind myself who I am.

I see Sierra's face, illuminated on a billboard that lines the hall she's performing inside. I remember when that photo was taken, the day she brought home the previews and wouldn't settle until I had given my opinion on the one that I thought was most beautiful. They were all beautiful. I chose the one where her chin was angled slightly, making her look analytical and strong. I chose the one that made her fairy eyelashes look piercing and confident, the way they probe souls when she's angry. I didn't choose the girl-next-door Sierra because she was more than that. If a portrait had to be broadcast on every other building in London, I made sure it made the message clear to those that want to kill her. Good luck, because she's invincible, and she'll burn you to touch.

There's a ladder on the back of the building that nobody touches except for me. I know that because once I reach the roof there's litter which any caretaker who made the effort to ascend the height, would make the effort to descend back down with. Also telling is the fact that the metal has rusted, but if it can withstand rain, it can manage my weight. It hasn't rained for a while though, and my palms shine auburn with the tired iron that I've imprinted myself with from climbing. I suddenly smell salt, even though there's none around, and I realise it's seeping from a strong memory. Sierra's voice in the present air takes me back to the first time I heard her, intimate and close in the moonlight. If only she could see the moon now.

It shines in all its phases, phases I read about with Father at one point in the comfort of the past. I don't miss childhood, I carry the knowledge I earnt with me now, and despite time's joy in ageing and exercising me, it has also brought me Sierra. I spare a thought for Sebastian; time hasn't quite granted him a connection like mine yet. The celestial body appears in a waning quarter. One half of a whole. Sierra and I. Sebastian and I. The four of us, pure against corruption. Every beautiful light has its darker side, and on earth the darkness is all around the venue exuding Sierra's angelic song, ready to pounce. I shrink myself down behind a wall, as I hear voices from the ground.

"What time will Sierra be out tonight?"

A male voice. Not one I recognise. The answer is usually about five to seven minutes past eleven o'clock, factoring in how long she takes to change into something more casual to make it home without drawing attention. If this person intends to hurt Sierra the answer will remain the same, except the question ought to be when they can expect to come into contact with my fists. A sound like paper falling to the floor and fanning out echoes in the alley.

The voice jumps two octaves and no longer sounds like much of a threat as an attempt is made to gather the items that fell. I peer over the wall, still hidden from sight, and as suspected, Sierra's face on a t-shirt, on a programme, on a bag all dressing this one very bewildered looking and bespectacled individual is enough to make me nauseous. Nauseous, and resourceful. With a fan placed in her path, it'll stall Sierra enough for me to deal with her obstacles and be sat in the pub by the time she arrives. I'm growing to like the fumbling obsession of the man beneath me.

I have time to take a few paces back and recline on the roof. The auditorium is directly below this part of the ceiling and for a moment there's nothing I need to lend my ears to other than her voice. She's singing a few ballads from the 1970's today, working with some of the greatest artists of that decade, awakening the nostalgia in her audience. I sometimes take the time to observe those leaving the theatre and nothing could smile wider than their eyes. Every time, Sierra succeeds in painting smiles, wide with teeth and passionate uncaring joy. She's healing this colourblind world.

"You'll have to leave please." The sounds of the security guard reasoning with Sierra's fan are subpar to the sound of her singing. If her visitor stopped arguing to listen then he may catch the power in her songs. I'm immersed in the embrace of Sierra's voice, overcompensating for my pledge of never letting her understand how I've fallen for her. I want to stay and sleep in the hotel of what I'm hearing, until heat creeps in from the conversation on ground level.

"Let me pass."

It doesn't sound like a fan to be making deals that are decorated like threats. Whilst I skim myself soundlessly across the roof, I glance across to the windows of the building opposite. In them, I can see a man with his back turned, and a glinting badge meaning the guard is facing forward. The backs of my arms prickle, the first sign that danger is close. I start to assess the quickest ways off the roof. There's the ladder I used to get up here, but I know that if I used that as an exit route I'd be seen and shot, and no use to anyone. There's another ladder on the other side of the building, but that would impact the speed as well as the proximity. There are the indoor stairs, but that risks being seen by Sierra. There's a balcony above the window on the building opposite. There's a balcony.

It's within jumping distance. Just. It's wide enough for a few mistakes either side of the predicted trajectory. The conflict below is escalating which means my options are dramatically reducing. I shut my eyes and conduct my own countdown, then on one, my eyes are fixed open and I feel the air whip my face. The instant I land I collide hard with the concrete and produce an echo much louder than I'd wished. I push my back up firmly against the wall, befriending the shadows. The conversation pauses. I don't take a chance on a breath. I stay still, waiting for a conclusion, and then the voices resume.

"Don't think I won't hurt you, because trust me, I want to. Your badge, your keys. Your silence." The instructions were given without a hint of sympathy.

"Anyone asks, you misplaced them. Indefinitely."
"The security in the security guard means I keep things safe." I can practically see the cockiness gliding across his face, even though I'm still metres away. Still, I appreciate a man dedicated to his job.

"Well then, how much do you value your duty? More than your life?"

"Does that sound like a fair choice to you? Show me a little more of a threat and perhaps I'll feel like answering that hell of a question."

"How about this?"

It's not a gun. A proper handler would know to cock it in preparation, unless the intention was to taunt the victim first but there's never been a member of the force that bothered with that petty nonsense. If they were ready to kill, there'd be no waiting around for it. Killers like them don't need to await spontaneous bursts of motivation. Other murder weapons churn around in my head as I work myself down from the balcony, anchoring my arms around window sills, pipes and bars on the exterior of the building. Knives, quick but inaccurate. Could be a bayonet, like the one father said killed mother. A force speciality. I've heard they have exclusive training for murdering with them. Unlikely, but also possible, is a weapon of convenience - a nearby brick, scraps of metal, any dangerous material in the vicinity. Sebastian has taken the bullet from the wound of the last man shot, to see if he can figure out what weapons are circulating.

I approach them silently from behind, again blending into the darkness.

"Alessandro Gray." The man with the black coat rotates with a glib greeting. His shaven head hasn't been tended to in a while ago by the looks of it, the job clearly unprofessional, as the hair is starting to grow back longer in some places than others. He snarls at me. "Karian Hall. Pleasure to meet you. I was wondering when you'd turn up."

"Forgive me if I don't share your pleasure." I take a step closer, but out of his arms reach, he's hiding the weapon casually behind a fold in his coat. It has to be thin then, concealable. It narrows it down to something that could pierce skin, create a stab wound. Smaller than a bayonet, but perhaps even more deadly. Tread lightly, my brother warns as a voice in my head.

"You two know each other?" The security guard asks, reminding us of his presence. Before I can answer, Karian decides to smugly inform everyone that, "Oh, everybody knows Alessandro."

The questions press on, "For what? Is he famous or something?"

"You could say that. He's our path to Sierra. Of course, once we reach her, we'll have to…" he throws me a disgusting dirty look with an ill-fitting smile, "…cover our tracks."

He lunges at me, which I was expecting. He reveals the murder weapon, and I fixate on it, trying to figure out what exactly to prepare for. A green shard pokes out of his hand, coated in dirt, but still holds the glare enough to tell me that it's broken glass. Which means, as he clutches it, there's a sharp edge pushing into his palm too. The erupting physicality encourages the guard to step back, realising this was a fight above what he knew and likely above his pay grade. I've improved my dodging ability, so I weave the punches and hits, hoping this soldier will tire a little before I strike back. I meet his blazing eyes once or twice, and realise that the fury he has for me is drenched in desperation.

He doesn't want to kill me. The need that I sense is the same I sense from all of them. I'm top of the list in an itinerary that they all have. Everyone wants their chance to be the one to bring down Alessandro, and in doing so, the traitorous Sierra who defied a fake life so she could chase real dreams. Fucking pathetic. I'm not a man, I'm a red name on a checklist, underneath my father's name scratched out, and Sierra is a bounty. We're barely hovering above Sebastian's name. Which is why this maniacal protégé is not about to take my life tonight. Not him, nor any of his friends lined up in London's backstreets, waiting for their own try at my murder.

I perform a headlock so impressive that I almost hope that more of their men are watching, but as I'm forcing my elbow around Karian's neck my mind inexplicably drifts to connect with Sierra's faint voice from within the concert hall. It should be motivating, and it is, but for the first instant it's numbing, leaving my opponent free to weasel his way back to standing. His nostrils quiver, cheeks reddening with a fierce offence that he had been apprehended. As if he thought it'd be as easy as taking me down without resistance. I can't let Sierra get inside my head anymore. At least not for the moment.

Within minutes, there's no sign of anyone else around. The security guard has fled, no other support has stepped in to outnumber me. I credit Karian for a fair fight. They don't happen often. He launches himself at me and grabs my shirt, I feel his grubby knuckles so close to my chest and it makes my blood boil. He's ripping off buttons in a complete blind rage, as if it's really my morals, my chance at freedom that he doesn't have, that he really wants to dismantle. A smarting arises on my forearm, he's torn the sleeve and my skin. Beads of blood mingle with dirt and the hair on my arm. Another souvenir of a struggle, but for the fact I'm now going to have to deal with more of Sierra's suspicion, I punch him at a right angle, forcefully into his cheek, somehow releasing several colourful words. No blame aimed in that respect. If he hadn't said them, then I sure would have.

"You said I was your path to Sierra. Funny." I contemplate.

"Care to tell me what's amusing about it?"

Smiling, I reply, "That's a question. I don't answer many questions."

Apparently, that wasn't the response he wanted, and it only seems to aggravate him more. He tosses the glass towards me, but it only flies towards the floor as he realises, I'm quicker than the speed of his throw.

"I'll tell you why it's funny." I taunt, circling him. "It's funny because the path to Sierra you're looking for might just be a dead end."

Disagreeing, he lets out a sound that's hardly human, and I'm ashamed to say it actually made me laugh out loud. It conjures up images of what they actually teach these soldiers to do in their training sessions. I've witnessed more monumental grunting in this altercation than fighting itself that I'm starting to think I'm wasting my time. Usually, the people they send to combat me are more of a challenge. Unless, Karian came of his own accord, which isn't unheard of. Everyone wants a shot at Alessandro so they can prove they're the worthiest soldier. However, most come more prepared than a slice of broken glass.

I grab his wrist when he's distracted by a distant street lamp flickering alight. An advantage of knowing the area is having figured out that they do that automatically at this time of night and not because they've sensed movement. Still, it holds his attention long enough for him to be forced underneath me, with my leg across his neck. I spy the discarded shard of glass a few paving slabs away, and Karian scrounges below me to reclaim his belligerent angle. Purposely, I let up my knee slightly and feign a stumble so that he crawls away in the direction of the weapon. I never lost balance, so immediately reoccupied my position, now with the glass within reaching distance.

"Oh, you thought I meant dead end metaphorically. I assure you I meant it in a completely literal sense." I converse breezily.

Once the glass is in my possession, it tumbles and tosses between my hands carelessly. I know with both his arms held down by my weight he has no way of laying claim to it. His eyes jump with the juggling glint of green, already terrified that a slip will send it plummeting towards his face. I'm perhaps a little too jubilant. The fight's not yet done and the floor is shaking, with the audience's demands of an encore. It's a faint vibration, but I'm familiar. I wait until I hear a deep and full breath from Karian, the man I now hold captive, then I plunge the corner of the glass into his neck. And twist.

"I wouldn't bother screaming. It's not dignified." That, and it bothers me to know what I'm capable of.

"Wait…Alessandro…we-you know me. We were neighbours." He struggles.

I don't hesitate, I don't invest my energy in the lies. I force the glass in further, hearing more blood vessels pop.

Dark red liquid bubbles from the gash. I'm marginally surprised to see human blood.

"You don't believe me?" he chokes.

"My neighbours were dead by the time I was four. Nice try, Karian."

"You're..." He wheezes. I bank on sick, twisted, ruthless. All the usual names. Painful, because that's not the man I want to be, but it paints a picture of the man they've made of me. I've got to frighten half the world to be protective of one girl. "...more of a rebel than they said." Hm. New. Endearing, even. I'll remember that one.

I close my eyes as I administer the final injection of strength into his wound, feeling the life drain, flow up my arm. It transfers to guilt once it reaches my brain, so I break the link between my hand, the glass, and Karian's dead body. I don't enjoy it, I do it because there's a worse alternative which I will never allow to happen. Picturing the alternative that is Sierra lying dead beneath me, blood on her brunette baby curls, is all I need to make up my mind. I kill because I can handle it. It's just as easy as falling asleep even when you know that all awaits is nightmares - except a murderous mind has more control than a sleeping one.

I think about how lucky he is to be falling asleep for the final time to the sound of Sierra's finale, not many of my defeated men get that luxury. I leave his body where it is. The force will pick it up once they realise he hasn't been accounted for back at home. They're reckless, but not risky - they won't leave our society exposed to the nosy justice system out here. At least I know he's being posthumously returned to a place he deserves to be. Sierra's finale means that it's time to think about dealing with what lies in her way to Nicholas.

I ___ YOU

I smear the blood leaking from my forearm onto the hem of my shirt. It's black so the crimson obscures well. One down, however many to go. With the applause shattering the night, I head into the streets as Sierra curtseys. In all its danger, it's somehow what we've both always wanted.

CHAPTER VIII: FORGIVE

Sierra.

Every complexity of the day was forgotten in the midst of the applause, the exhilaration somehow igniting me. My heart is thudding against my ribcage in relief, as if it wants to adopt the stalls and seats in all its love. I can't help wishing Isaak was here to see me living this way, due to his faith in me. I hope I treated every ounce of faith with each piece I sang. Believing that reality is a phobia has delivered me up to this point but as I stand here and let my surroundings condition me and my bearings, I realise that the phobia is not of reality itself, but of not making something of yourself in the incredible world we've been gifted. When opportunity is everywhere, it is our fear of being blind to reality that holds us back. I would have stayed blind if it wasn't for Isaak.

I can't escape quickly enough, picturing Isaak and his hand around a drink. His gaze as I walk in the door. How it feels like no other woman, albeit, person exists when mine and his hearts beat in the same space. No matter how much I dislike Isaak at points, I will never be able to not love him. He is more than an answer to the emptiness that lurks within me - he is the reason I found it, and the reason I seek to fill it. He is the reason that keeps me waiting for love.

Covering up with a jacket, I head out the back route, keeping my bag tightly fixed to my side, because there's no trust in city streets. There's litter and all sorts that pack the alleyway I exit through. In a stacked array of flattened cardboard boxes there's a pool of liquid and broken glass. There are drunkards everywhere, a lesson in just how careful I have to be. Part of me thinks I smell Isaak's scent, but then I realise that's just because that's exactly what I want.

Darkness forms an aura around me, but strangely returns comforting memories of sneaking around with Isaak after Gettie was fast asleep. He'd wait for me under the flowers in the arch on our porch. They were nothing special. A few dying dandelions that the old lady had picked up when she could walk enough to make it to the border of our town where things grew. Flowers weren't often seen, unless you knew where to look. Isaak took me on a tour of these places that night. Forbidden places, he said. I wasn't quite sure what he meant, but it would have been a shame for anyone else to discover them and ruin the beauty that lay there. He let me pick a flower each time, from each location, as long as I kept it to myself when I got home.

The first time, I chose a daisy. I relished its simplicity. I admired the edges of baby pink near the middle, showing vulnerability emerging well before the white innocence of the petals. It stood for everything I felt I was at the time; naive, patient, a small part of something much bigger than me.

"There's an otherworldly prophecy attached to those things." Isaak mutters.
"Please elaborate." I laughed, offering up my pick.
Twirling it between his thumb and forefinger he recites a rhyme. About love. He alternates between being in love, and not, in love, and not, then stops. "You're supposed to pluck each petal, with each fate, until you're left with one. I've never done it. Things as big as love should be left alone to grow naturally. Like flowers."
"Isaak...do you think there's love between us?" I chance, and he instantly recedes back into his cold heart.

"I can't answer that." He spells out, simply and painfully.

"Because you don't know?"

"Because I don't have the time. And I don't like questions." I knew that was as far as he would go with the conversation, so I let him push the flower into my plait. The slight intimacy made my skin tingle and my heart ache. I wanted so badly to know how he felt about me. More than I wanted any flower on earth.

"I'm taking us home," he said.

Then there was no more said about love until very recently, now that my confidence is peaking and my curiosity is becoming more insufferable. I took that daisy out of my hair when I got home that night, and I pressed it between two pages of a book that I'd read a million times over so I'd never forget the words that the flower's imprint hid. That book was actually one of the only possessions I'd taken when Isaak and I had run away. Except by the time we set off, every word was illegible, filled with memories of our time together, with flowers of every colour.

The pandemonium of London traffic doesn't affect me as much as it did in the beginning. I got used to the constant commotion, and I loved that the engines were less uproarious than the drivers themselves. People have so much hate inside for others, clouding their every other judgement, which I will never understand. I am a girl that sees life romantically, noticing every detail. The way the rain makes the road look shiny, and how oil turns to rainbows when it's split which goes to show how some mistakes can be the start to wonders. I hear ambulance sirens, blue and red lashing around in circles, people coming to the aid of people. Accidents that bring humanity closer, despite the pain and heartbreak. The human instinct to care without selfish regard for our own harm or losses. It's why I give the change in my pockets to a man wrapped in a blanket on the side of the road. It's why I smile at the grandmother and her grandchild. I stop romanticising when I see my initials, SG, swiped into the back door of a dirty van, alongside other phallic images and insults aimed at 'Brendan' and 'Micky'. It's enough to make me stop, but not to stop my eventual continuing. There are plenty of people with my initials, of course. My face is on a billboard. I can't take a fancy to anonymity now, when all is said and done.

I slip in through the doors of the pub on the corner. It's more of a cafe throughout the day, until customers turn to alcohol in the late evening, by which time, families with children are gone. The selection of cocktails is what draws me to this particular place - for me to handle alcohol I also need to taste fruit. My favourite is a passionfruit and mango fusion because it's served like a sunset. I order it as soon as the server comes over. I haven't seen Isaak yet so I assume he's running late. Naturally, my eyes explore the decor. I'm perched on the edge of a leather seat, tucked into an alcove. The seat is more than spacious enough but I'm not ready to relax, anticipating Isaak still gives me butterflies, and my eyes are helplessly excited, flickering to everything and anything around.

Lamps on brass handles award the interior a darkened feel with spells of glowing light. There's a burnished look about the whole place, the pumps on the bar seem newly refurbished and there's a collection of paintings hung in varied metal frames - copper and golden. Some perfect squares, others rectangular and large, as if to boast their picture the loudest. All the images exhibit powerful moments in time, whether that be through action in battle as the men on horses portray, or tranquillity, as a naked woman sits beside a candle and an open book showcases the power of solitude and vulnerability. There's a stark contradiction in the layout of the features here too, and one I can't help but notice during my scrutiny. The first, the floor. It's configured in two sections - tiled and carpeted - with a sharply straight and angled strip of metal dividing either material from each other. The floor lies beneath the bar, made up of a contoured wooden surface which travels smoothly around a bend manufactured to fit the shape of the room invitingly. Such artisanal attention has been paid to the room's wooden attributes, that the ornamentation, in the forms of leaves and twisting waves, etched into the panelling on the walls are noteworthy.

"Paradise Cocktail?" a server arrives beside the table, tray in arms.

"Yes, mine, thank you."

The waitress sets down my drink, without a coaster, but hovers eagerly. I'm drawn to her name badge, with a merchandise pin of one of my programmes attached to the outside of the lanyard. There's no disputing that she knows who I am, so it's only kind to offer her a photo even though my mascara is blurry and my gaze is wide in the pre-stages of weariness. Happy and grateful, she leaves me to my drink, the first sip tasting nicer knowing I've made another set of lips smile.

Forged from thick wood, the table is slightly less adhesive than I would imagine is normal for a surface so frequently prone to spills. It does mean that I'm less conscious about resting the sleeves of my jacket down onto it, elegance forgotten in my lust for Isaak. Speaking of whom, is nowhere to be seen yet, and the clock is ticking into twenty-three minutes past the time we were due to meet. I'd message him, but he's always insisted on neither of us having phones, he says we'll lose our born connection. I can't argue with that, or with him. Although in moments like these it makes clarity harder to reach, and all I can do is reassure myself he'll be here soon.

My inspection recommences to let my surroundings seize my head with interpretations rather than letting the queueing invisible thoughts top me up with sadness. A low ceiling gives the property perspective, and means that the booths and zones require separating by stained glass with rich colours and deep character. There are hand painted signs on a few spaces on walls between other decorations, with slogans and expressions encouraging people to drink, releasing them from potential restraint or guilt around their drinking habits. Really, it's the copious bottles of carcinogens behind the bar, luring people into drinking enough that they can no longer consider the risk to their health that keeps the money spilling into Nicholas' pockets, as the bartender and owner. Nicholas heads over now, another Paradise Cocktail dribbling over the side of the glass and down his carrying hand.

He crouches over the edge of my table, ready for conversation. It's somehow not invasive though, he's oddly gentle when he addresses me. Most people stress the start of my name, but he elongates the end, and with it comes a different regard. Like he's really bothered to take the time to listen to me, and get to know me on an emotional level, that regrettably said, Isaak hasn't reached yet. Nicholas must be at least twenty years older than me, attractive features but the sort that draws a person in to listen to his stories of childhood, not the sort, like Isaak's, you can get lost in. I thank him for the drink, and welcome him to sit. If Isaak is running late, it's only fair that I take the time to catch up with a friend.

The time I spend talking to Nicholas runs away from me. I keep drinking as he brings me my favourite concoction, and more new things, to try. In flooding my system with alcohol, the memories inside my cage of denial begin to burst out. I feel them simmering but not yet clawing at the top of the precipice.

"Are you trying to get me drunk?" I hear myself slurring, but can do nothing to control it. I'm not sure I care what the answer is. I trust him wholeheartedly, so I know if he's anaesthetising me then he may be recognising my downfalls before I'm willing to admit them to anyone.

"Sierra, I believe you need this to get off this optimistic carousel you always hold yourself accountable to. It'll help you really understand what you're feeling. Isaak's already paid for all that you have."

I gasp with a forced smile, "Is he actually planning on turning up sometime?" I pause. "You know, it doesn't matter, it's nice to talk to someone who actually answers my questions."

Nicholas smiles knowingly. He lets me talk, which is a mistake, because doubts and danger are starting to spill from my mouth. I saw a man get shot last night, Isaak confirmed it, and the reality of that is dawning on me. I've never seen death in its full wicked form before. If death was a person, he'd be sketchy and sly, always knowing the things you don't, but death is more than a person, it's an entity that steals from the living. He steals values and virtues, he steals strength and stamina, he steals experience and innocence. I'm struggling to understand what inside the man yesterday that death wanted and took.

"Nicholas, do you think there's any justification for taking a life?" I stop mid-ramble to ask.

He pauses. "The world gives tools to us. What if I said the tools were the qualities of life, empathy, forgiveness, acceptance, discovery? Do we have any right to each other's property?"

"I suppose that's a good enough justification for some." On that wavelength, something else comes to mind.

"Isaak was okay with it though..." I recall, "he was counting down, he must have known it was going to happen…" it puts a weight in my stomach realising how calm Isaak had actually been.

"If you think he did have something to do with it - does that scare you?" Nicholas meets my eyes. For the first time since I boarded this train of thought, the carriage shudders to a halt, the steam clears and I feel a glimmer of my conscious return.

"No." My heart answers for me. "I feel completely safe with him."

"Even when he doesn't turn up for drinks with you?" he tries.

"Even then. Still." I let Nicholas take my hands, in a gesture of compassion, he holds them between his. I didn't see that I'd been trembling. Death has an apocalyptic impact on the mind. I feel out of control of myself and can't configure myself back to mettle. I think I'm sweating, but pins and needles make my arms and legs feel cold. The alcohol in my bloodstream must be on its way up to my head because my ears are humming and distorting the sounds I hear; a crushing pain is starting somewhere in my skull and the dizziness is overwhelming.

"Perhaps more caution with the alcohol in future Sierra. I apologise, I wasn't quite sure how much you could handle." I sense sincerity in his voice despite my drunkenness. "Isaak will be here soon, I'm sure."

"Yeah, how much shall we bet on that?" I grunt, rather unbecomingly.

"He will. Listen to me for now, until he comes. Sierra, your understanding of the world is what makes you special. If anyone knows how to use the tools to live life to the fullest, it's you. I see your face on the sides of buildings every day when I walk around London, I see your m…" he breathes heavily, "I see your magic everywhere I go. You've made a difference to the beating heart of this city, because you have just that. Heart. Not a greed for money, or a scrambled attempt at fame. I know I'm just a bartender…"

"A friend." I reinstate, barely gripping onto consciousness. "You're a friend."

"If that's how you see me, then allow me to say I'm proud of you. I'm so proud of you, Sierra."

I look up, my vision scattered and erratic, seeing the naked woman in the painting with her expression fearful of the candle's flame, the glare of the surfaces like twinkling stars and then what looks like tears held back in Nicholas' eyes just before my head sinks onto the wooden table. I fall fast asleep with my hands still tucked inside his.

"You're welcome." Is the first thing that Isaak says when I wake up. I'm back in my bed, fully clothed but under the duvet. The room is barely lit but I can make out Isaak's figure leaning forward in the armchair, that's usually in the corner but is now directly adjacent to my pillows. "I carried you home asleep, you looked dead."

I'm too angry to see the humour. "I thought you were when you didn't turn up last night." I try to sound scathing but I know I still sound drunk. It's as frustrating as someone flicking through a dictionary, picking random words, and calling it conversation. I don't even try to continue, which apparently gives Isaak permission to come closer to me. His warm breath on my cheek makes me fathom how cold the rest of my body is. I shiver. After resting his arms on his knees from crouching, he uses the side of the bed to support him. Our hands are so close. Alarmingly close. This may be an apology tactic but I can't buy it. Not when he's just let me down.

"Firstly, as soon as you're sober you can be as angry at me as you want, and I'll take it. We can make a day of it. Secondly, I know you don't want excuses so I have an apology gift for you instead." He sneaks his hand into his back pocket, but then the edges of his mouth fall, ever so slightly. He keeps his hand in his pocket voguishly. "It'll be in your hands tomorrow, with me right in front of you, on our second date." Date...

I must be dreaming. I am again soon, falling away into nothing.

Isaak's impatience doesn't let me sleep long. A tugging at the corner of my pillow. A scaled down earthquake jerks me out of the forgotten dream I was entering.

"Sierra..." he waits for movement. I twitch slightly, my eyes slanting open thinly.

"Forgive me. For not turning up to you tonight." That's it. No reasons. No persuasion. It's not a question, and I'm still hungover, so as it stands, Isaak Macaluso - always a man of mystery, on my doorstep, in my life - has his furtiveness forgiven once again. His Sierra Genieva, secondary to his stealthy ways, sleeps until morning.

CHAPTER IX: MEET

Sebastian.

It hasn't always been this way but it's all I've ever known. Grey paths to grey houses. Everything beautiful is dead, or dying. People walk around at any hour of the day - there's not a single thing much more frightening or threatening in the dark than the horrors our society has brought to light. I'm advancing through the sage cover of the forest, an impatience now in my step as I see the road that'll take me to the centre of the town. Beige grass crunches underneath my heavy tread. Even the grass is no longer green. I can't fault the town's neglectful regime for that, it's the rain that won't divide the thick canopies to find the ground from the skies. For this reason, I've been using the forest to rest since Alessandro and I set out to find the girls.

A couple of days ago, I made the mistake of passing the ruins where we used to live. In our hearts, the idea of home was already a broken one, but arriving to find it torched to the ground in restless pursuit of the missing Gray twins was too much for even the shoulders of courage itself to bear. The floor map is easily distinguishable. I can make out the room Alessandro and I shared, the bows of the bottom of Father's rocking chair now charred in the desolation. Rubble to anyone else. Reminders to this grieving soul of mine, of what the defiance of two men left behind. The first hint of doubt slips into my mind, and I have to slip away from the scene before I convince myself into believing my faith was uninformed and unjustifiable. Alessandro hasn't been back here yet, he hasn't seen the emptiness, and I pray he never will. The memories of our house remain better in his mind, and tucked safely into a pocket of the past, where it wasn't a home by any means, but it was the four walls that concealed a family holding on to each other.

For a dictator so dismissive of women, it was one woman from whom this all started. At first it was a deep maternal love that he shared with his mother when he was young, but then she left him alone as a child to follow her passion for music, and a hatred that nobody predicted began mutating. His name was Jasper, and he rose to power in our small town, gaining control, and what rose alongside him was the dawn on the first day of the Era of the Conventional. Jasper was a political figure at the age of thirty-five.

In the words of my father, it was the morning that never came. He was right. There's never been a morning as fair since. My father - Jack Gray - was a boy at the time. About fourteen. It was his father, my grandfather, who'd been the first to enter his bedroom that day.

"There's been some changes in this town overnight, Jack. I know it doesn't gratify your curiosity to abide by what I must ask, but please remain in bed for the time being. I must check in with the townsfolk, but I don't know what this may mean for us. Your mother is here. She'll bring you food."

"How long must I stay, Father?"

The food never came. Jack spoke these words to his father, not knowing they were to be his last. It's why he loved his own boys beyond measure, before his own untimely death. The second to enter his bedroom was a guard dressed in uniform at around four in the afternoon, when Jack was hungry and his curiosity, now with an unhealthy spice of unease, wasn't enough to feed him. Jack was taken in by the system, something he refused to go into too much detail about to Alessandro and I. At fourteen he was under the age to enter into service and patrol with other cowardly men who either agreed with Jasper's foul ways, or were too weak to protest. From then, when I heard about it, until now, I've held such an enmity against those who didn't overturn the regime that very same day and prevent history from happening as it has.

Jack didn't see his father again until after he'd been nudged and kicked by the system into eating when they wanted, sleeping when they barked the order to, and carrying out jobs at their command. This went on for four years and had him convinced his father and mother were dead. He had a faint memory of his father saying he'd come back, but on reflection those words were never spoken to Jack by anyone, and it holds him from his bitterness towards them. It was in the first few months of his stay in the system that his lasts became so much more meaningful. The last time he ate food from his mother's kitchen, the last time he snuck in with his parents when the night got too starless.

I'm striding between the streets with my head cast down and with my collar flared and upright. The cobbles I'm treading over have been worn down, and walked before.

Jack was eighteen, and free. That is, as free as he could be, being enlisted and abandoned. His mind was almost free too, from the trial that sentenced him to years without parents, until a man crouched down, with hands more cement than skin, and helped to build a road. It was his father, but only on the outside. Startled doesn't begin to describe the first look at a shell of a man that left you alone. The man that Jack's thoughts raged between missing, and wanting to rot, bruised and suffering the way he did. Somehow, seeing him bruised now, crippled and quiet, older and broken, doesn't have the same remedial effect it had in Jack's imagination and two tentative steps was all it took between panic and answers.

The old man looked up, mouth peeling open as he recognised his son for what he was now. A broad-shouldered adult, painted with pain. A child of a system, not of parents, not of love. Jack knelt, for his father couldn't stand. Deplorable irony. Only a collection of dry lips and brittle bones laboured at ground level. Faraway pupils stared up at him in vague recollection and then away again. Jack didn't need answers anymore, the construction played on as it had for 4 years. Cement. Brick. Ease into the gap. Push. Slap into place. In front of him wasn't his father, it was a man who lost his way too long ago to warrant rescuing. It was the end of a road travelled, and the start of a new one to follow.

Jack's mind was made up. The jigsaw fitted, his childhood completed, boxed, framed, forgotten. His father forgot him, grafted into a routine that makes a man forget what love is. What love ever was. In his head, the balance was neat this way. In what had begun with his father taking final steps away from him, he would take the final steps away from his father. Questions were blacklisted. One he had been asking himself so long produced an answer that was an expensive waste of heart and time. He'd been following orders for too long to find meaning, so from now, he'd work to fit in, and take the orders from himself to move on, and right now, his head was telling him to walk. Walk. Walk. Walk away.

Walk. Walk. I tell myself I have to keep walking. I'll never find her if I don't look and I will never stop looking until I find her. I have to swallow down the toxins, fears enough to make me stop walking and cynicism that has me talking to myself. The stones that my grandfather laid could be any of these I tread, I could be rooting my step in the fruits of his labour. I could learn from the consistency and effort, but I could never learn from a man who gave in so easily and chose monsters over men. Lost a son to complacency. Lost his revolt so easily. If only I'd had the chance to turn to you - I'd tell you that you'd have to lay a thousand more bricks before I become the sort of man you were, grandfather.

It couldn't have such an elementary and facile ending. Plus, there was one last question.
"Where is my mother?" My, because that woman could no longer be one they shared. The father he knew wouldn't have left her side, even through the worst of the weather. Edge the brick in. Push. Slap. Pound again. Stop. His father raises his greying head slowly, idly, focusing somewhere past Jack's left shoulder. Hot breath trickles onto Jack's arm, and drips down over the prickles that start to form. He turns to escape the heat of the unknown, meeting the sharp-edged chin and cheek of his father's officer, his superior by several tiers. The scent of his mother's perfume and struggle reeks from this uniformed ignoramus. Must have slipped the simpleton's conscience to button up his trousers, fix his belt, rub away the strained and fresh scratches from his neck, drain his ego. Must have slipped the simpleton's conscience to not fuck his mother. *Jack's fist twists into itself, hardening in fury. He envisions his knuckles flying into this man's smug smile, grounding him, irreversibly. In reality, he stood stock still. He met the bastard's eyes, exchanging a darkness there isn't a word for, and walked on. An encounter with Jasper that wouldn't be Jack's last.*

The history of these bricks is the foundation of my present. This road circles the town, if I followed it until the sun goes down, I'd be where I'm standing now. These people live in a place in which society doesn't know they exist. People of this generation don't know there's a world out there. Potential has been spurned for the perceived greater good of the community - there's only one man allowed to prevail. His name is Jasper. That's why men don't do what I do - what Alessandro does - and break the rules. That's why the women don't dare to do what they do best. This civilisation is breathing through punctured lungs and broken ribs for a reason. That reason has a name, and that name is Jasper.

Angry at Jasper, keeping my hood up, is when I see her.
Loathing Jasper, keeping his dignity in check, is when he sees her.

She is beautiful.
She is beautiful.

Sierra's duplicate, yet the similarities fail me and I'm drawn to her every uniqueness. Every quirk. She is her sister's twin in body, but it is clear her mind doesn't need saving. It didn't occur to me that upon meeting Betsy I'd become a deer in headlights. This is a woman that isn't, and never was, in need of saving. This woman is saving me, the longer I watch her move, the longer I sync the blinking of my eyes with her smile. My heart softens for the dimples in her cheeks. I sigh, for she is so unaware of the sweet rose thorns that she's sent knotting tightly around the lines in my life I would cross for her, the walls I'd let my heart destroy for her, and the risks that the fire in me would run toward for her. For Betsy, forever. I almost fall short of the sight of her and the orders in me return telling me to move, for as of now we are still strangers. Move. Move.

Her brown eyes don't hide her sadness, beauty or talent. His eyes don't hide how he feels for her. Their eyes connect, and explode, the stare held between them killing traces of Jasper's stringent control over the town in meteoric burns. A supernova shining, the start of something new. A man who grew up on nothing hadn't got a thing to lose but this moment, so it takes seconds before this woman steps, following his lead around a corner, and one more, and they stand across from each other in the brick corridor, waiting for the other to be the first to define the feeling frothing in the middle of two strangers turned soulmates.

I move towards her, and synchronously everything else moves towards me. I keep an archer's gaze to her, steady, calibrating. If she's heading right, I plough left, ready to meet her somewhere in the centre. Betsy's chestnut hair is distinctive but a camouflage all the same, which, equitability, may be a benefit later on. Impulses to talk to her are overcome by relief of having found her, but I need to remember that I don't have her, yet. My entire being is an arrow poised in her direction, and I have this single shot.

"I don't know who you are." She breathes first, but she's not running. She wants to know.
"I'm Jack."
"That doesn't mean I know you, Jack."
"There may be a day we miss knowing this little about each other." Jack urges her to consider, he wants this and nothing else. This spark is a star he can't let die.

She entertains it. "I'm Lucia."
"Please." Which means nothing. It fell out of his mind. He's out of his mind, out of his depth. So lost in her.
"Can this be the least we ever know?"

"How much more is it you want to learn?"
"All of it." He pulls a stranger in and leans in with every good intention there ever was, to kiss a friend. A woman. A lover. "All of you."

"Is that Alessandro?" someone shouts. "A Gray brother!" bursts out another, and all at once I am smothered. My road to Betsy, literally, temporarily abandoned in search of desperate shelter. This isn't the first time I've been noticed but it's the first time it's mattered as much as this. It's another loss I don't need in my life. I dash between a gap in buildings that I don't think anybody knows isn't a dead end. Instead it comes out into the forest, a space for me to catch my breath. Pummeling my anger against an oak trunk, I curse out the village that turned the final triumph of seeing Betsy into a tragedy. This tree is getting so abused by my thumping fists, I almost feel bad. My hands are stinging with premature bruising, and the smarting distracts from the floored beige leaves that crunch behind me. I glance over mid-defeat to see her grinding the heels of her pretty black shoes into the ground.

"You've been watching me." Betsy accuses, and I can't tell her she's wrong.

"You've noticed. Says a lot."

"What exactly does it say? I believe it says more about you, Sebastian. Or, Seb, do people call you Seb?" A brave response. Her facial expression emphasises her weathered wit, a buffet of acumen with none to feed off her challenge, and she almost looks dismayed when I throw the dynamic off balance. I'm too stunned by her, and too occupied rearranging the way I'd portrayed her before I'd known her.

"Nobody calls me Seb."

"Well, now it's nobody plus one more. Come on, Seb." Her eyes shine, and I watch the leather wrapped around her chest crinkle as she twists away from me. Her skirt bounces too, exposing her ankles and white socks, and I can't help thinking she's far from innocent. She knows who I am. Innocent people don't do their research. Innocent people don't know the Gray twins. Innocent people don't lead dangerous men into the forest. I'm so enamoured, intrigued. Ever since I can remember, it's been me and my orders wherever I go, the two components of my mind acting interchangeably. Betsy's presence stops the orders, stops my conscience, and it's just the two of us, alone. I follow her, this time the order comes straight from the heart.

"What would you want to know?" She dictates as we walk. "I know who you are because I put two and two together when I hear people talking about the Gray twins. I know how every person in this town acts, and you aren't the same. I figured it must be one of you coming back."

"Who's to say I'm not a threat to you?" I have to stretch across a larger strewn log to catch up to her.

She grins. "You had control of your destiny and your first instinct was to get away from this damn place. No, I'm not worried you're a threat. Everyone who is a threat to me, lives here."

"In the forest?"
"Funny."

We keep walking until we reach a cottage in an area of the woods I'd never been before, like something from a fairytale. Betsy forces open the door, causing it to swing, and leaves the echo resounding off the trees. Birds take flight, wildlife scampers, and I follow her inside. The instant she closes the door, my eyes adjust to the minimal light and devise my surroundings. Getting to grips with my environment is a survival tactic I've come to adopt. The place is unfurnished, but somehow homely in its own regard. It isn't sizeable, the whole house is just a fraction larger than the bedroom Alessandro and I shared when we were younger. There's a single bed pushed up against the corner of the room furthest from the door, with an itchy looking duvet dumped across it, stuffed with material from the woodland.

It excites my curiosity to see the bed made so messily, but the few sculpted ornaments, clothes and food containers arranged so flawlessly. Perhaps she was expecting a guest. Perhaps there was no need to make the bed if she was expecting to make her guest her bedmate. There'd be no need to make a bed clean just for it to be trashed again. These are new thoughts for me, a presumptuous and irresponsible drifting of my mind. We have only just met, I don't know anything about her aside from her virtuosic and razor-sharp ingenuity. It's barely a large enough living environment for her, but my hope half rests on it being big enough for just us, so that I don't have to spend the rest of my life running.

"Where's your brother then?" Betsy asks, gliding down into a chair, gesturing for me to sit. I don't. I remain standing. She looks me up and down, impressed by my disobedience. From what I've gathered in our brief time together so far, she's not a woman used to being ignored.

"Who's to say I have a brother? The people that claim it are two faced, what's stopping them having double vision?"

Emphatically, she throws her hand up to her wall, silencing me again. I can't decide if I love or hate her. Posters and sketches of my face, and Alessandro's are scattered everywhere - and she doesn't seem embarrassed. The majority of them are peeling, showing me that these decorations aren't recent, they're an obsession.

"It's not an obsession, despite what you may think. She's just curious." A orotund, matter-of-fact voice hits me from behind.

I revolve around immediately, one hand unconsciously resting on the gun in the innermost pocket of my coat. A jacketed figure steps out of the darkness, and is completely nonchalant in the face of my defensive stance, leaning casually on the door frame. Already, his mannerisms don't correlate well with my senses. His height is the first feature to stand out to me, but I'm not intimidated. Clearly at home, he saunters towards me. He's not in a uniform that tells me he's poisonous, but I'm damn sure he'd suit one.

"Relax. This is Warner, he's a friend." Betsy says, drifting past me. By the way she lays a hand on his shoulder, I'd say he's a little more than that. I stand like an awkward fifth corner of the room as they make eye contact, Betsy smiles like a child of lust and Warner simpers like a relative of the devil. Protecting her could be a completely different logistical exercise than I was expecting when I threw myself into this. I didn't realise it'd be a tussle of emotion, and I'd be lingering on the outskirts of the comfort zone palpitating from Betsy and Warner.

The orders take full throttle again. Protect. Protect. Protect.

CHAPTER X: FOLLOW

Sierra.

I come here when I need to get away. Even dreaming can get tiring. Living inside a dream can exhaust you even more. The sounds of wind on the water, ripples from ducks and rented boats in the lake all meld together to ease the lonely memories of last night, and make wanting to see Isaak tonight easier. I come here in the mornings when people are less likely to know me.

There are flowers in this part of the park. I don't need any more but I still like to smell them all the same. You begin to miss floral perfumes when your life is spent orbiting the city, the businesses here capitalise on nature and turn fragrances artificial and commercial. It's hard to resist being drawn into it when the real way to tantalise the senses is outdoors, like this. I think the trees, like me, need to do everything in their power to hold onto their roots before they come crashing down, bleeding seeds on this cement playground that succeeded their growth. If trees could bleed the way I do, I can't imagine we'd be much different.

I have a mixed relationship with London. I love how open I can be, how London loves me back. Things I don't get with Isaak. Yet I curse the city for maybe being the reason, the wedge that drives me and Isaak apart because he's so non-negotiable and sensational about disappearing into its night's silver lights and its day's tumult.

The fourth hole in my watch strap is crumbling. It would be easier to tell the time if Isaak let me have a phone, but he keeps steadfast in his adamance. Most often I feel time is running away from me, my energy spent in bundles panting and pushing ahead, but this morning the race is over. Instead, time ambles beside me, almost holding back. These small rare moments of ghostly synchrony. I'm not scared that time will at any point escape me like a bad first date.

Time lends its services to me to reflect on my faith, which also lies in London. It's a connection more like a deposit I can retract once I can put my faith in Isaak. Isaak in all his inconsistency, is really the only consistency I have. The only link between my past and the present. I yearn to know what he does in secret, alone in the streets, alone on the sofa. Given the option, I'm not sure which of Pandora's boxes I'd unpack first and how much of the contents I'd hate, how much I'd love - how much about him, like now, I hate loving and love hating. The knowledge that there's more that I don't know makes him all the more attractive to me.

The unhealthy feeling of time beginning to quicken its pace beside me, suddenly evolves into a stark visualisation. Time possesses the leaves in my path and the patches of shimmering sun on the ground ahead of me. It mocks me with every next breath. I find myself running - racing nothing. The people I pass don't take a second look. Time doesn't taunt everyone the same. Why me? Does it feed off my ambition, or my fear that death will take me too soon like Gettie? My feet hurt. I'm not in shoes for running, but time never caught anyone prepared.

The clockwork uses the environment to leap further away into the distance, running a track to an immortal world that I simply cannot keep up with. I'm out of breath, my throat scorches from hastily breathing in and out time's casted oxygen lures too fast. The hands of time leave me in monotony, and two more powerful hands grab my waist, lifting me so my soles scratch against nothing. I go to scream and raise the alert level until I realise the hands are one part gentle to two parts devoid of affection. Why is he here?

"This is new. Bloody hell Sierra, I was not ready." Isaak pants, only a little out of breath. How long has he followed me?

"I run, sometimes." I say, only half-convincingly. "Right. I'm going to need some warning next time you decide to sprint a half marathon." He doesn't have to say he doesn't believe me. His face says it all.

"How about giving me a warning when you're going to make a spontaneous appearance in the morning? I didn't think the vampire inside you allowed for that." Snarkily, I begin to keep walking so he has to follow me if he wants me. There are occasions I can't tolerate Isaak's antics, and now is one of them. I'm still in indecision about where we stand with each other.

"You ought to be nice to me. I brought you your present." He comments.

"Tonight's present?" I'm instantly more interested.

"I thought you'd like it now." He reasons, whether it's sweet or suspicious is unclear.

I slow down, answering to the novelty. His arm is outstretched, making my heart beat faster until I realise his hand isn't meant for my touch. The bone in his wrist protruding and blue veins prominent, he turns his palm up to cradle a small golden chain. At the end is a telescope, and I ponder the significance. There must be some meaning, Isaak doesn't do things half-heartedly. He looks at me, hopeful, needing me to accept. I'm wary, because the other thing Isaak doesn't do is material things - he speaks, in his own convoluted ways, every love language except gifts.

He'll bring me to a city with the power to kindle my dream and birth my career and to some extent this is what I consider quality time, despite him being absent for half of it. He chooses accurate times to be away. I'm not sure if romance lies in being there when I need him, as he always is, but never there when I crave him. Physical touch is a dubious one, but again a love language he exercises just above a frequency of extinction. He healed my grief by letting me hold him. He was there in body, but that's perhaps all it is. Occasionally, he'll let me get close to him, commonly more so when he's distracted by the world as he was that night I'm trying consciously to forget.

Words of affirmation are scarce, but truthful when they appear. He doesn't say anything he doesn't mean, and he doesn't speak in the tongue of regret. Compliments are few and far between, but he has called me gorgeous, once, and meant it. He says my name, like it means something. I can't ask for much more, no matter what I would give to hear him whisper statements that are stronger and more saccharine than compliments.

Isaak's acts of service are invisible, he coordinates the special things in my life. My drinks are always paid for. It's like those days where you truly believe the universe has everything lined up for you, except I don't need constellations in a perfect pattern when I have him.

"Sierra, please take it." He pushes, some apparatus in his voice sounding smaller, subjecting me to weak knees. If Isaak can give a gift, and satisfy the fifth and final love language, then there remains a chance that he may satisfy the fifth sense and let me taste him.

I take the delicate chain between my fingers, trying to ignore how Isaak watches me. His eyes keep flickering back and forth between the park and the telescope swinging from my hand. In jewellery partisanship, I am proudly a golden girl. Gold fits every season. The glitter of summer and the drowsy ache of autumn, orange leaves sighing for a final time before the winter. Golden baubles and ribbons make Christmas timeless, and when the spring comes as it is now, it matches the golden-yellow of new flowers.

"Isaak, I love it. Thank you." My pitch develops highs and lows, my song shining in my happiness. How he reverses my stubborn mind is unforgivable. The things he does, and doesn't do, to me are unforgivable. I eat it up, I keep wanting the opportunity to refuse him and then be induced by him. It's a dizzying paradox.

His sigh of relief is almost audible, but my focus on his breathing dwindles as he runs his hand into my hair. I shake when I make coffee, let alone when I'm nervous, but his hand is entirely still. There are severed nerves in this man and everything leads me to believe he ran with the scissors that caused the tears. Isaak must have suffered a hurt so bad that he had to cut it out himself, be the surgeon operating on his own cancerous sadness before it could spread. If he is consumed by a virus he thinks he can control by keeping contained, that might be why he keeps himself from me.

I should have brushed my hair with more attention this morning, I realise, as Isaak can barely pull it up away from my neck without getting his fingers tangled. He likes a challenge. I have to remind myself to avoid being embarrassed.

"Hold it there," he instructs. I take over gripping my ponytail, brushing past his hand in the process. He doesn't react, but my love does. It feels right to be so close. So right that I don't know how he doesn't feel it too. The necklace is cold when he puts it on, and I breathe in sharply as the telescope drops down my chest before gently being inched up to fit the length of the clasp. The cold stays anchored to my heart long after Isaak steps away, back to the distance he's used to. It hurts me to see him instantly more comfortable.

I wait for the one-sided emotion, my love monopoly, to crash down, to die so that I can turn and face Isaak who stands in a different world of passion to the one I'm in. We're centimetres away from touching, but centimetres don't mean seconds. It could take centuries to meet in the middle of this seesaw. In my city of stars, he is my sun. The light in my days. If only his past didn't darken him so, he'd stop being a beautiful eclipse and burn on his own. He'd scorch these centimetres, and incinerate centuries. His past isn't simply a burden, it's a blackout.

"Stay a while." I tried.
"I'm afraid the vampire inside me won't allow for that." I almost admit defeat when I receive his reply. In fact, I'm sourcing the best place for me to lay to rest, I need somewhere to bury the blood that's rising into my cheeks. I can hide my blushes in the pink baby's breath that carpets the trees perhaps. I'm too preoccupied hunting for a hideaway, that when I look back at Isaak, he's not himself.

I say that because his eyebrows have narrowed again, only slightly, but of course I notice.

"I'm going to walk, and you're going to follow me," he wastes no time in saying. I'd love to disobey, just as I do with his orders some nights, just to see what would happen, but I forget that my curiosity exists. I cannot forget my love exists either. My emotions sneak back out of their place in the moss and hedgerows, back inside my body and propel my steps in Isaak's direction. His strides stretch further than mine, and I have a flashback to racing time. However, Isaak is tangible, somewhat at least, meaning I have no excuse for letting him get away. I take a chance on running the next few paces and swiping at his wrist.

He turns, touching me back. Before my mind and heart have been mutually inveigled, his arm is across my back, supporting me by my waist. I wonder if my bones are beginning to melt over his embrace. He is not just letting me touch him, not just a simple gesture. *He is holding me back.* I look around for the apocalypse, blinking uncontrollably as if reality will conduct a sudden reboot. Nothing. I try to remember the placement of his arm, carving the fingerprints into my waist. Please don't let me lose this feeling.

   He's not in a state for giving answers, that hasn't changed, but there is a spark of intention I've never been able to believe was there before. I'm so enraptured in this lottery moment that I don't register Isaak's ceaseless head turning. He's going to have to get used to the daytime eventually. Our pace begins to slow, and I keep tripping over my own feet because my blood is churning more quickly than the energy I can expel. Nobody said butterflies would feel so welcome. I picture swarming time with these butterflies next time it tries to isolate me, deactivating the flow of the world. With Isaak here, I have all the time I need. The time to hold him. The time to love him. The time to be two, in an afternoon, in a morning. Time to discover us.

   "Isaak Macaluso, this is highly unusual." I manage to regain part of my voice when we've been slowing for a while. He doesn't reply, just smiles with a fraction of his mouth, down at the floor. We've followed the winding path of one of the rivers that crawls away from the large lake in the park. The path has vanished, and most of the people too, save for a few park goers with what I assume are the same escapist and romantic views as us.

Even though we've slowed, Isaak is still cradling me to his side. The trunks of the trees look witchy and sinister under the shadows of their own canopies. There are capsules of darkness and solitude under each one, the reflection of the branches leaking into the water below like black liquor. Isaak guides me to a willow tree, parting the curtains with graceful regard for the leaves, to reveal a hollow pastoral cavern. The trunk of the tree itself is warped, suspended above the brook. We went from a park to a fairytale in a matter of Isaak's hand around my waist.

He releases me, his expressions less contorted, stress echoing less and less from his face as he moves me. Emotionally, miles. Physically, towards the base of the tree, edging my back down until it's arched over the bark. It's only a slight angle, but I have to hold him to stop myself falling. It strikes me that my dependence on him is something he wants. The beating of his heart is copied onto the knuckles of the hand I have pressed against his chest.

"I've never known your heart to beat so fast." I confessed. My other hand is trembling against his back with effort.

"I've got you." he points out my struggle, deflecting the attention away from his body. His beating heart. These premiere emotions.

Falteringly, I try to relax and realise he has me safe. The additional weight causes him to stand over me a little more, and shakily, I press my other hand to his chest too, my touch on him positioned like a defibrillator wanting to excite the walls of his chest. I'm trying to trace his ribs but the muscle prevents me.

"My heart always beats faster in the daytime. There are people around."

"People who won't hurt you."

"Historically, people don't take too kindly to vampires."

He's been amused by this vampire metaphor so long to the point I'd expect fangs to pierce my mouth should he try to kiss me. I still feel the potential of a kiss is as fictional as vampires, unless he were to prove me wrong - and this moment certainly invites it.

There's a threshold that he slips under, for a fraction too long that he loses control of my mass and we become unbalanced. All my weight backs onto the thinner branch behind me and I see the momentary acceptance in Isaak's eyes before I go plunging, taken by gravity, to the bank of the river. All concern forgotten, he is clearly entertained, immorally and immaturely, by his high ground as I lie on a decline surrounded by verdurous underwood. I'm watching Isaak closely. In those few moments we're apart, he takes an astute glance at my right hip where my tattoo is. I don't know the radix of the ink. It's just always been a part of me.

"I'm a nightmare, Isaak." I concede, and half-apologise. I'm sprawled on the floor, if my hair was knotted before there's no way it isn't now. I like my relationship with the earth, I'm an elemental person when I get the opportunity but this is perhaps a little too untimely considering I have to work again this evening. For some reason, I find humour in imagining what Gala will have to say when I arrive dressed by my encounter with the wilderness. Isaak extends an arm to me which unfortunately doesn't go to plan. The weight distribution sends us plummeting down into the river, and I scream. Isaak lets out a disgruntled sigh. His soaking hair now drooping over his eyes makes him look so sad. It brings out the child in him. Soaking in a stream, against his will, but not entirely against his joy. Did he intend for this to happen? I will never understand. All I understand, when I push my head against his drenched shoulder, is that this is the best and most unconventional source of happiness, and not how I expected today to go.

"Sierra, I've had worse nightmares than being in nature beside you. I'll see you later."

He gets up, helps me to my feet, takes a look around and stalks away - leaving me dripping with pond water and algae, incredulous. I sweep up a water lily that's been floating around my shins, to add to my collection of memories with Isaak, anticipating the effort of drying the flower and finding the perfect space for it. This is going to be the first update my flower collection has had for a long while.

I'm not dissatisfied, in the middle of a park in London that I love with a telescope around my neck. I understand his desire to leave so quickly. Living inside a dream can be exhausting.

CHAPTER XI: FORGET

Isaak.

I have had worse nightmares than resisting Sierra. I've had nightmares that tear me apart. I've had nightmares asleep and awake. It's hard to hold anyone accountable to a feeling, nobody wants to take responsibility if there's no evidence to crucify them for their mistakes. The place I was born in is so remote that nobody has evidence for anything, people can murder as they please, because the justice system wears the crown of the executive and nobody remembers the dead. I can't say the same for the disappeared, they remember us, and they haven't stopped searching. They won't stop searching, until Sebastian and I have bullets inside us, Sierra is choked by her voice and Betsy's bones are broken, irremediably. Our town is off the map, but the people have their wily ways into London. We're not safe here, but it's large enough to ensure Sierra will be safer for now than any other city. I dread the day, if it ever comes, that I'll have to tell Sierra about Colmoor.

Colmoor. The town where we were born, the town I met Sierra, the town Jack met with Lucia and Lucia sang with Savannah so many years ago, the town we escaped from, the town Sebastian's scrounging in this second as I walk the London streets, the town that killed my father and my mother and my freedom. The town that couldn't cope with success. The name sounds disgusting, stabbing in my mind, sticking to my teeth as I mime saying the letters. I'm disgraced by the word; my dreams are possessed by the word *Colmoor*. I shove the name to the back of my mind, to bubble and fester away, I don't need the memories. My only agenda is to get back to the apartment, and get rid of this sodding pond water before I get any more blasted looks from any more strangers.

I can't pretend I'm not to blame. I overstepped the mark I drew between Sierra and I for the sake of safety. Protecting her is a moral mind game. I didn't want to end up in a river, but I didn't want her at risk. I didn't want to entangle her in love, but I didn't want it to be the end of us. I left her soaking, but I left her safe.

As my first priority, when I'm inside the flat, I head into the living room and ease a grey tablet out from the stack of old newspapers that Sierra won't touch. It took me the whole of this morning to figure out how to get it to work. It has one function alone, and that is, like a moth to a flame, to guide a city explorer to a telescope.

It performs as an electronic map, the technology is advanced here, unlike home, and before I had a reason to, it was too confusing to be worth bothering with. Paper maps would do their duty, except paper maps can only do so much to give me live updates of Sierra's location. Digitising a hunt is as much of a help as it is a hindrance, as soon as information is in an invisible network then dangerous people could have access, and I wouldn't know. Although there's hope that if it's taken me a morning to make sense of this system, it would hopefully take longer for those who have since now, only known a society in a primitive technological age. I'm taking no more risks than are necessary. Hence why Sierra has no phone. I'm taking my chances on a telescope around her neck.

The tablet reports back, through a pulsing red orb on the screen, that Sierra is with Gala. From what I understand, dress altering is an arduous process which allows me time to shower and prepare for meeting Sierra after her show tonight. I don't know what to say to her to follow letting her fall into a river. I don't want to think about it or the stale water scent that hangs over my clothes. I'm frustrated and rethinking the day to this extent makes me feel ill. I'm not one for introspection, I prefer a practical approach, so I pull off my jumper and start to unbutton my shirt. A better use of the recent surge of mental activity in my brain is wondering what the hell they put in the water to make it smell so bloody awful, like rotting plants and seaweed. It's like what I'd imagine Colmoor would do to the beach Sierra and I frequented if they found it.

Showering in the dark is unironically not the brightest idea. I was wrong to think it would switch off the thoughts I'm starting to have about Sierra. I reach to turn off the water, but stop. I let it pour. I am in darkness, except for the slivers of the afternoon sun through the slats of the bathroom blinds I closed before I let my lack of clothes undo my muscles. I have my shower so hot the air goes hazy, the sort that doesn't fill you up if you try to take a deep breath. I keep my breathing shallow for this very reason and sink to the floor, my back sliding down the tiled wall. Every bruise I've sustained for Sierra is drumming in the agony stages of healing, against the stifling mist.

It's gratifying feeling clean after a fight. Watching the blood drain away, letting the guilt flow with it. Letting the scars that remain on your body preach your sins so your conscience is dismissed from its post. I study my arms, my hands. Thick skin, unbreakable. All I remember seeing in my father's hands was overuse and misfortune that caused him to look so old. There was probably a time where he looked down at his own hands and they were like mine, and he thought they'd never change.

In today's case, it's gratifying to be able to wash away the dirt, but I'm struggling to filter the image of Sierra's face, just before she fell. The adolescent acceptance, her inability to prevent the fall, the way I fell onto her smile and we got separated by the ripples in the water as we crashed. How, in that moment, I'd realised my mistake. I saw the love in her eyes and knew it couldn't be requited. I can demand that she follows me more than I can demand she fall out of love with me. If I was Alessandro alone, maybe love would be welcome to fill the void of all I've lost, but for now my tenderness hibernates because Isaak Macaluso has a lifelong job to do. Emotion will only foster lethargy, and feelings too strong for a woman I will only lose should my affection overcome my protection.

I can still hear thunder after I turn the dial to stop the shower. It's not in my head, I know the noise of my cerebral storms. It must have picked up outside as a spring torrent, nothing peaceful lasts forever. All that's ever been reinforced is that rage and hunger live on, sprouting fresh from the cremation of love as if love never was - or was but fleeting theatrics. It's maddening how purpose is only assigned when it is no longer due. Abhorrent how rage gets to dictate, when nobody in a sensible state of mind elected for it to. Then again, it makes sense. Humanity walks in circles.

This man of dual identity walks forward, his programmed attitude broken for purpose, to let the hope of a better humanity wreak havoc with the pessimism of the majority, letting Sierra be the cause and the start and the answer of defiance. I start with a walk to the window, allowing in the thunder. To feel the pelt of the rain against my naked chest is resuscitative. To know that the freeze of the weather is biting yet I, the bait, won't take, won't surrender, and will never, let myself fall in love.

Love is espionage in a flawless enterprise and I'm too much of grief's veteran to be deterred by the small highs of affinity.

I'm pestered by my reflection. The bathroom mirror is cloudy, my figure a blur, but I lock eyes with myself in a place where the steam has evaporated. I see Sebastian. There's nothing that can tell us apart except from Sebastian's birthmark on his right shoulder. The only mark on my body is the tattoo our mothers gave us, which I hide from Sierra. She knows I've seen hers but she doesn't know about mine. The grandfather clock in the hall chimes four, I flinch, knowing I can't seize up whilst I stand so vulnerable to another's eyes.

I can hear screams that take over from the thrash and the majesty of the old grandfather's bell. Screams that won't stop. I see a road, a red soaked road. A woman lying lifeless. Sebastian is beside me again, and in him I see that we're both younger. I know this virtual feeling. I know it has captured me once again and there is nothing I can do. I'm standing in a place that I feel I am but know I'm not. I see my double in Sebastian but my brain is unused to being a clone of itself as reality courses around me in a forcefield. I become again, the vagabond child I grew out of, vandalised by the memories he didn't give licence to stay.

As the screams oscillate, acquiring a louder volume and a stronger pitch, my instinct tries to distinguish Sierra's tone in the suffering. It's not her. I hold my hand in front of me and it's swaying from side to side, like watercolour waiting to dry, and if I try to look straight ahead the action is clear but the distance is rocking too and not a single element of the landscape comes into focus. I know where I am, of course. I can't forget an inch of Colmoor, I had time to digest the captivity. A lion knows every corner of its cage, for the tedium of being trapped.

The screaming crosses a boundary into howling and with it I sense myself flinching, but I don't see it enact into my body. Blood surges into my fingertips but to look at, they remain apathetic, swinging in this dizziness, my nerves struck with some sort of dreamy narcotics. My conscience tussles with this robot. Conscience is a brain inside a skeleton inside skin and yet I'm somewhere beyond my conscience. I need to take the wheel. I need to find it first.

My father is beside me. I know he should be buried but he's walking around, and I'm terrified that my brain is zombifying the truths I've come to terms with already. I don't want to go back to confusion. I can't afford the damage that permeates my progress there. Nothing about this makes sense, except that I am back in Colmoor and I am half my age - and in a gut-wrenching loop which brings me straight back to the beginning of incertitude, nothing about Colmoor, or my dad being alive, or the incessant screaming makes sense.

One by one, the jigsaw pieces arrange themselves. This is a replay. It is not real in the time I'm in, but it was happening, in a time and place where I was. Now, it's happening again. If I look straight ahead, I'm staring into a clinical white tunnel with colours of beige and crimson, and still the noises, in my peripheral vision. Anywhere I focus is erased. To have any hope of resisting the pain of this flashback I have to gain control. Make the memory just that, a memory, and not a lesson in the futility of trying to reshape and forget the horror.

I can't be hurt by this simulation. I test that hypothesis, and confirm it, as the intense sun only fades away without blinding me. I edge my focus to the left of the events I want to see. Two men have their arms around a woman, holding her to the floor in a fashion that's surely breaking her bones. They aren't helping her, they're hurting her. All she's done is been a little less careful than she needs to be to live in this society. She will die. There is no doubt about it. I will watch. I have no choice. I know this woman from flashbacks before, and she is lifeless by the end. I watch them murder her again and again.

Sebastian is taking it in, seeing what I see. I don't need to meet his eyes to know. Even in an archetypal reality I can attest I know his every action. I didn't look at my father on the day this happened and this flashback won't let me contort what I saw that day. It also won't stop me trying. My weary head slumps to the side. My father is erased. Where he should be is a bright white expanse, which becomes greyish tiles as my own, actual, reality gives my eyes depth and shadows to learn. I'm awaking, but falling again, without energy to shake myself to the peak of revival, without life on the other side of sleep being accessible enough to break this psychosomatic problem.

After my cursory hiatus, I return to the absurd world that I'd never completely left. No matter how much I try I will not be able to see my father, so I give in and relive the torment. The woman is being pinned down by the neck to the ground now, any disease she might pick up from the dirt on the streets is less lethal than the weapon being poised at her head. The town still holds its breath even though it knows what is to happen. I hear Sebastian talking to my father, I know what he means but the words don't make sense. *She is done now. What has she feared, will not hurt her more, it has hurt her most already. Singing and done and dead. Anything and done and dead.* Sebastian never speaks in this code. He has his initialism, but often his sentences still are comprehensible.

I ___ YOU

A shot smites the nebulous memory I'm in, the population inside this matrix falling by one. It doesn't have the effect I thought it would, but then again, my heart doesn't fully exist in this place, it exists in a body outside of it. A crowd quickly appears. They watch the woman get dragged away by family after Jasper's men leave her to die. Try as I might, I cannot move to get closer, I cannot see. Mechanically, my feet turn for me towards my father, and if I stare past his shoulder making Sebastian the mass of white erasure, I can vaguely make out my father's height, and at a stretch, my father's face. As I am smaller, I can feel the trauma brimming inside him.

He told us he didn't see our mother die because he was at work. Perhaps he did see. Just moments too late, through a window, through a crack in the wall, and he didn't want to tell us so he didn't have to describe it. The damned story of when Jack lost Lucia, left dusty on a shelf in a mind I don't have inside access to, and now never will. I can only speak to my father in my dreams. The hardest part is what to say.

Turns out I never get the opportunity. Father speaks to me first, and it is a first, for this dream I keep having.

"Don't fail me." I see my father's mouth moving, and it is his voice, but it is my words. My father would never condescend.

"Do you hear me? Do not leave me to die, Isaak. Don't you let them do that to me." Now I know it's not me, for all the questions he poses. It's still not entirely him though. I'm missing something. Something about this whole fucking dream won't make sense. I don't have time to work it out because the proportions of the dream shift, I can see so clearly, I believe I've woken up. Except my father still stands here. He's taller, standing tall as he talks down to me.

"I know you'll let it happen. You're not wise enough yet, not smart enough yet. Not awake enough."

Sebastian isn't being targeted, I wonder what I've done so wrong. Somehow it seems my train of thought is written on my face. "Sebastian's gone, Isaak. Your mother is gone. Sierra is gone. I will be gone. You'll have nobody. The force will pick you up. If you don't keep running."

"No, Father, you're wrong."
"Do you see them?"
"This isn't real, Father."
"Do you see them? They're coming!" he agonises.
"Father, you aren't real. You're dead. Already. It's happened already."
"I don't want to die. They're coming, Isaak, for me. Sebastian! Isaak! My sons!"

This isn't patronage anymore. This is my father's fear. A scene I've been imagining since we woke up as orphans. His hand clutches my shoulder, it's greying, it's crumbling. He can't hold on. I know it's a dream but I try regardless. His wrist disintegrates, I'm left clutching dust. I can look at his face now, straight into eyes that are filled with fear.

"Lucia. Lucia!" The scream is bloodcurdling and lasts forever. But then it turns delirious. "Lucia, my love, I'm here, Isaak's here with me."

"No, Father, you can't take me yet. No." I struggle with him, "No."
"He said no to me, Lucia. Shall I take him anyway? Control away from a man who loves it."

"I don't know who the fuck you are-" I shout before lashing out, my first coherent deliverance in this whirlwind followed by a fist. I can't punch my father's image but I can push him aside. This imposter has nothing on my father, but knows how to tap into my guilt.

The more I listen, the more there's an edge to his voice. His face is morphing. Into Karian's. He grabs me with the hand that's still attached, and his grip burns as it sinks into my skin. "-but you are not my father. You are not Jack Gray."

"Sebastian!" I cry for help as the searing pain in my shoulder worsens. I regret looking up. The face is not my father's anymore, it's horrific and macabre. The skin is peeling, either black and rotting or red and flesh like. There are tiny holes, poked like stars, which at first let me see straight through to the world beyond, until jet streams of blood start spurting out, covering all of the facial features that remain in an iron-tasting death. Sebastian should have stepped in by now.

"Sebastian, dammit. I need help. Please. This fucker disgraces our father's name." I look around for my brother, and all of a sudden, he shatters into view. Like a stone dropped into a lake, the picture pulses and gets larger, but that's when I realise, he's not alone. He's with Betsy, who looks indistinguishably like Sierra, my head hasn't given her a separate identity yet. My brother is above my girl, or his that I can't tell apart, and is smiling. Loving on her. Touching her. Eating up his prerogatives and privileges. He's fucking her, as she sits on a chair, to call it what it is. Adding more screaming to mine.

"Sebastian, you absolutely useless prick. More time fighting less time flirting, my ass."

He turns to me, insulted. "Father's fine. See for yourself. You're disillusioned Alessandro. Take a break AM."

He's right. He's made me look like a fool. Somehow, I'm holding both of my father's hands, still pressing them against me. Father is smiling at me. He looks smaller, frailer and isn't scared anymore, I know that it's happened. He is past his death. There are scars in and around his mouth to prove it but they're old scars. He's not bothered by them. The air is quiet, I notice. As if we've all been swallowed by the deletion. By the erasure. My father opens his mouth to speak.

It all starts again. The heat, the noise. Sierra's screams, the power in my brother's concessions. My father's face and tone, though, remain his. I remain sceptical. He pleads, "They're coming. You've got to keep running. Keep running Isaak. Keep running." Sebastian's voice joins in. He hears the orders in his head louder than I do. "Keep running…" the voices crescendo. I try to run, but the sky has begun hailing dust and dirt. I have become smaller. I trip over my own feet. I can't stop myself from becoming horizontal. I start to realise what is happening.

Sebastian and I dug my father's grave, now this dream is digging mine. With a paranormal scream, I push back into reality, wherein my cry sounds significantly weaker, as my vocal cords grasp that they are awake.

I have moved nowhere, just as I couldn't in my dream. There's a flaming cramp in my shoulder from having bashed the sink cabinet. There's also a darkness outside of my mind, and a frost inside my body. One of those things is easily rectified, I pull a towel across me to warm myself, and to redeem myself. I cannot reverse the time.

Whilst I've been stalled by my nightmares, Sierra has been waiting, sat and stood up, and whilst I know there's ways she can forgive me, I've never felt more guilty. I pick myself up, walking off the nightmares, putting on clothes that make me a person not a puppet, and head out to bear Nicholas' disapproval and Sierra's disappointment.

CHAPTER XII: COMFORT

Sebastian.

I want to outline that I am doing this because I offered and not because I was told. I simply saw the fire had burnt cold and I protested I knew this forest like the back of my hand. In truth, I offered because I needed the time out to walk and pace and consider my place now that Warner is in the picture. Trust is a funny concept. You can give it, you can lose it, form it and break it. Trust is therefore the most malleable source of friendship. I trust Alessandro but we are not friends, we are brothers. Does that make trust an expectation? You don't choose your family, but you can choose to trust them. Even then, some don't deserve it.

I should trust Warner, for all that I know of him is that he protects her, but sometimes that's not enough to know her heart is safe too. This must be how Alessandro feels, he has a messy imbalance between love and duty. The only difference is he intends to hide his love from Sierra, whereas I intend to shower Betsy in mine once I'm sure it's her. It has to be her that gives the go ahead.

With the first chunk of wood I collect, I try to reckon where trust begins. I start with no trust at all, and let the other person contribute to my attraction to them. It's hard not to run the race this way when fear lies in everything around here. I know some people who run the race backwards. They trust wholeheartedly until they get hurt, they call it the benefit of the doubt but it's a poor way to live. These people trust once, love once, and never take a chance again. There is only one person I have met thus far that lives in the middle. One person who mastered trust in a way I didn't think was possible. Betsy made a judgement how she'd trust me before she knew me, going off the strength of her objection and the sources of subjection from the town. She made a gamble on me, so the stakes are higher to not let her down. It's the nervousness to prove her right that's making me so unlike myself.

By the seventh piece of wood, I've debated trust in every possible direction, wrangling the idea backwards and forwards through every dimension. It doesn't answer why I'm so beset by my lack of understanding. I don't believe it's an encyclopaedia of trust I need, it's an action plan. It's, and I hate to say this, someone to tell me what I need to do. It used to be my father. Now I obey a ghost. It's the confidence Betsy has that I'm drawn to, and I know my homage to her is far from over as she still manages to become relevant to every conversation, I have with myself.

It's time to head back to the cottage when the twilight makes it impossible to tell branches apart from roots. I can hear hedgehogs, somehow safe in the nighttime. I envy them, until I remember once my father said envy breeds procrastination. I don't envy them. I listen to them instead. I'll take any chance I come across to practise my aural skills. There's a rare good memory from my youth where my father sat Alessandro and I down by the window and made us listen.

I started, as children do, by asking what I was listening for, but he only told us to write down what we heard. I tried. Isolating my ears from every other sense. The squeaking, my father reminded me from before, was the bats.

Until now, I'd never seen one properly, funny little creatures with zigzag wings, flapping in suspended halos in the night, habitually astray.

I ___ YOU

Alessandro got bored of the task quickly, as he does, however I'll give him credit in that his patience has improved, but only when he knows there's something to expect. There wasn't a better incentive than nature that our father could give him.

I wrote and wrote that night. The whistling was the coexistence of forest and trees. The shouting, if not accompanied by words, was foxes, howling to each other in the darkness. We didn't have wolves here, aside from their appearance in rumours and legends, but they died out long ago when mothers realised, they didn't need stories to make their children afraid. Colmoor did that for them.

We didn't live close to the forest, so some noises I hear now are the ones I've learnt since my father died. I've had to spend hours on my own which has helped me know that finding sounds that mean you're less alone is comforting, unless the sounds are human. Hedgehogs, for example, as one shuffles by now, were a phenomenon I discovered not too recently. I like that they're led by their nose, I like that bats are led by listening, I like that foxes are led by their fear. Spiders are among the most fascinating of them. In the darkness they are led by the bounce of their web when something catches. They feel strong vibrations and are drawn to the danger, all eight legs scrambling with urgency. These adaptations of creatures smaller than myself are novel and nocturnal. If I wasn't tied up with the fast dynamic of the human race and trying to make each day of a short life count, I might have done more research into the lives of little things.

I'd stayed next to my father, who was reading a book too advanced for me, about an hour longer than Alessandro. When I got up, finally feeling like sleep was on the cards, I glanced over at my brother's paper and leaky pen. All that he'd written was: Monsters. I took it quietly into my hand with a rustle the man thought was just leaves, so Father wouldn't blame himself for how scared Alessandro truly was inside.

I covered for him that day and I still do. He knows it but it goes unspoken that he doesn't thank me for it. There are things going on that are larger than us, are larger than gratitude, and those are the things we choose to talk about when we meet. If one of us had to be ultimately responsible, it would be me. Alessandro is the reckless one, but I allow it because it brings him passion, and if it came down to it, it would be my life before his. I would die for anyone I loved. If I could I'd die in the place of Father, or Mother. I'd die for Alessandro because it's right. The parliament of owls in the trees all around me seem to ask who I'd die for because I can't live without them. They ask whose ghost I would readily take orders from if I were to die second. Who might I love? Betsy. It can't see it being anyone else.

It's hard to make out in the dark, so much so I almost missed it, but there's a figure pressed up against the back of the cottage when I return. I'm too close to hide, so I stand tall, making my silhouette as broad as possible but when the figure sees me, I'd know the sparkle in those eyes from any distance. Betsy points at me and cocks her head, directing me to join her. When I start to walk forward, she puts her hand out as if to slow me. I follow her lead, something I'm rather not used to doing for anyone, but I keep compliant even when I reach her side. I'd explain my surroundings but what is there to describe when I'm in the dark.

She's acting strangely. I'm not one to talk about hiding in shadows so I can't complain about that, but the way she rubs her thumb across my cheek before she pushes a finger to my lips to keep me quiet is new and captivating. Stunned by her touch, I almost forget to question why we're braced like we're under attack. Then a door slams, and I can't feel for my gun because of the wood in my arms.

"I should have known you'd run off to the fugitive to protect you!" shouts Warner, storming from the entrance of the cottage and presumably referencing me, unless there's someone else I have to be wary of. For the moment I know we're alone, I've been checking for any other movement in the forest. We're on the opposite wall of the house but it's only a matter of time. My reflexes tense, and I talk myself through all the ways I could shield Betsy. Behind that tree stump a few feet away, back inside the house in a barricade. Worst comes to worse, and there's always a possibility, behind my body and letting my back bear the weight of what is to happen.

The load in my arms lightens as a log is taken off the top. I can't lay the rest down without risking them toppling and revealing our location. If I choose to act, it has to be as and when the danger strikes, and within a split second. I'm more apprehensive as I don't know the sort of fighter that Warner is. I usually have time to track people before I engage in physical contact with them, but Warner could have any strength, any weakness, that I'm not aware of. In this situation, Betsy might have more of a mind for the fight than me. She knows him.

For two seconds, and only two seconds, Betsy and I take a shared breath, and then I start preparing but Betsy is already there. The fiend is smacked to the ground before I've even registered what has happened.

Her sweet voice says words that suit her so very much. "I don't need protecting," she spits, her saliva mixing with the bark imprinted on his forehead, "and he's not a fugitive. Look at yourself first, asshole, then perhaps we'll talk. You're looking a little worse for wear, and so far removed from anything you could ever call home."

Mesmerised by her, so badly, I only have the beggarly strength to say, "You're never talking to him again are you?"

"Absolutely not." she smiles.

"We have to move. We can't stay here." The next thing I introduce to the conversation is a schedule for movement, we need to deliberate over what will stay and what will move with us, and we need the whole process to start and end before Warner's concussion wears away. It is needless to say that the information on Alessandro and I can't stay. I wish Betsy could have knocked everything Warner saw from his head too, suddenly the reason he stayed so long without killing her makes so much sense. Not only does he know as much as Betsy, he knows I'm still alive. He will give back all that he knows to Jasper, and with it, warp me into someone treacherous. My only pride is that he will have to deliver all this information with a tree trunk stamped into his reptilian face.

I think it dawns on Betsy as we're packing away the minimal number of belongings she has, how much information she has given away, in trying to make sense of me. She is subduedly filling a basket full of the photos from her wall, when I choose to deal with Warner. I have to be the one. Even with Betsy's strength, Warner's ego weighs him down and she simply can't move him. I don't want her close to him either. I drag him to a clearing where the trees in every direction look identical. It will have to do to lose him, until we can lose ourselves.

Betsy is still filing when return. I understand her needing to slow down, but this isn't the best time to stall. She's stopped on a photo of me, and her eyes are inspecting it closely. The magnifying glass is unpacked again, dragged from its place as a paperweight in the basket. I know we're undoing our progress but I want to know what she's thinking. Initially, it enlarges my chest but she descends the area to my waist, then my hip. My tattoo. I don't know how they have a photo, but I'm hardly surprised. Colmoor has everything. It just means I need to be so much more careful.

"You can look in person if you want, to save time. You do have to pack it if you want to take it. I'd rather not walk the forest like an inspector's apprentice." I speak softly but it startles her all the same, so engrossed in her task that she didn't hear me come in. For a woman often so alert, it's a signal to me that she's processing. I turn up the bottom of my shirt, for her eyes only and in this small embroidered image of intimacy, I feel like my tattoo is suddenly the only thing I feel like she can see, the object of her every desire. I've never seen a longing manipulate somebody's face quite so much. The photos in her hand are placed down, the magnifying glass goes back in the basket, and I feel like she'll walk over, until she takes a step back from me and touches her hand to her own waist, shielding me from her tattoo.

A twig snaps outside, and I turn sharply, shirt dropping, bond destroyed, assessing the limited earth I can see. A badger, just a badger, but a badger that galvanises us to leave. Final goodbyes to places that were once sanctuaries come naturally to me now, less naturally to Betsy. She tells me she isn't interested in watching herself walk away, so I must watch her, to confirm she has done it when she is eventually ready to accept why we had to go.

I hold a bag containing books and ornaments, another with the bedding. Betsy carries her precious research with two hands and I admire her so much for that she values knowledge the most over any of her possessions. When we entered the cottage knowing we were relocating, Betsy gravitated straight to the wall of her souvenirs and connections.

I don't record how long we walk for but judging from how far the stars have moved since we started, it's been hours. At least an hour since either one of us has spoken. Nothing feels strained. There's been time to think over everything. Betsy has tripped a couple of times, either her mind is somewhere else, or her energy is - but I now need to implore her to rest. Her presence is no longer enough to make the orders cease. Find a safe place. Find a safe place. Find a safe place.

I strike up a conversation, to keep her awake, whilst I keep an eye out for places to settle.

"Have you been alone all this time?"

"Arlen died when I was nine."

Arlen. A male name in Colmoor.

"I'm sorry." My apology is sincere, given that there was no guardian around her I had already invented the conclusion.

She sighs. "I'd be sorry too if I'd liked him. I left when I was eight, he was too weak to stop me. I only found out he'd died through the town. I doubt you would have liked him either, I have reason to think he was the one who alerted the authorities to your father..." her voice trails off.

I stop. There's nothing I can do about it but it hurts to know. I changed the subject before I could get too inside my own head or heart. I'd make a note to talk it through with Alessandro later. "I was under the impression you were taken in by a woman."

I find out through Betsy that the woman, Arlen's wife Cecile, was lovely, she was the one who wanted Betsy. She was the one who my father handed Betsy over to, but she died when Betsy was four and Arlen was left with a child he never asked for. About seventy years her senior, he wanted nothing to do with her. Betsy said that Cecile was the only reason that she could put up with her degenerate husband; the lady insisted that one day she'd know the answers. When she left, knowing that there were answers to find, it became her obsession, and with the Gray brothers being the only long-term unrest, she started her research there.

"You found the cottage after you'd left?" I ask.
"I found Warner first. He knew that there was a murder that left a place available." she explains.

It doesn't sit right with me. "Did he…"
She knows where my sentence is headed. "I don't know. I'm still trying to convince myself he didn't." I believe that's her way of saying she's aware, and embarrassed, that he did.

"I wouldn't put it past the bastard."
"You'd laugh at my reasoning. When I met him, he was a saint compared to Arlen."

"What did Arlen do that was so bad, Betsy?"
"I know you've seen the scars. Who did you think they were from?" It's not an accusation, it's a passive and mournful sadness. I know firsthand what it's like to mourn childhood. Who, not what. Her word choice is clear.

I have seen the scars. On her shoulders. On her neck. Behind her hair when she moves. Signals after signals of abuse, that explain the resoluteness. I want to wrap my arms around her. I want her to stop, properly stop.

"Will you sit?" I guide her to a mossy patch on the floor, "I need to make somewhere for you to stay. It might take me a while. I don't work in halves."

I'm expecting a clever response, but none comes. She sits down on the ground, following my gesture. I watch as she lays on the floor, not caring about the soil in her hair, my beautiful brunette, hair darker than her sister. I pull the bedding from the bag, and rest it over her, making sure the frigid spring winds of night don't freeze her.

Mother Nature hates Colmoor, although how anybody could hate this girl enough to chill her, I don't know. How Arlen could touch her with anything less than love, baffles me. I won't forget his violation against her. I've saved a unique emotion for him in a holding cell in my head.

I labour the whole night through, checking on her all I can. I've never felt as much peace as I do when watching her sleep, and it sounds so wrong to say I fall for her more every time I see her dreaming. I keep having these thoughts until I hate myself, for not averting my eyes like a proper gentleman, enough to redefine this dynamic. I have good intentions. She must know this if she's allowed her guard to be replaced. I've become her conscience, her eyes and ears. This is trust. The trust I was trying to define from the start. For all she knows I am a fugitive. For all she feels, I must be something more to her. The trust keeps me building and climbing long after my fatigue sets in.

The sun wakes her up. I'm still high up in branches when I see her shift.

"What in the name..." she mumbles, rubbing her eyes.
"It's a treehouse." Worry envelopes me, "You don't like it?"

"I know what it is, Seb, and of course I like it. It's just how, why even..."
"You. You are why. Surely you know that much." I executed a controlled drop from the tree, coming to her side, looking up at my creation for the first time. We're both observing with fresh eyes. I've never made a shelter so ambitious, but all things considered, I've never made a shelter with so much meaning. I want nothing to harm her.

"It's safe I assure you. Get some more sleep, make yourself at home. I'll be back tonight." I attempt a rigid pat of her arm, but she steps towards her new home so my hand drops straight into the space she leaves behind.

"Seb." she calls and I stop, thinking I've forgotten a joint, or a ladder or a patch in the roof to keep her dry. I scrutinise the mental list of things I've done. There's not a single thing I can think of that I've missed.

"Please stay." she entreats. My heart skips a beat. I think staying is perilous, I've fallen too hard as it is, who knows what would happen if I were to stay longer.

I make up a phatic excuse, I'm hoping my newfound friend, truth, doesn't display in my cheeks. "I'll only bother you. I don't sleep well."

She steps a little closer. "You are an awful liar."
"I'm not lying." I lied. She can be infuriating when her mind has battery and somehow, I still like her charged wit. Plus, I can sometimes convince myself of different feelings to avoid sharing the ones I actually have. I did it with my father about my mother, I can do it to Betsy about what she does to me. I reverse her recital of power. "You slept there, and you were perfectly serene. Why was that, hm, if not for being completely solo and self-sufficient?"

"You are why. How's that for persuasion, Seb?" This woman can spin a reversal on its head, she makes me feel drunk and delirious. Champagne, whiskey, any alcohol that can simultaneously sober you up, back to life, and give you a kick up the ass. This woman is it, and I've had my fair share of alcohol tasters whilst defending myself in the city and keeping a third eye on Sierra.

"Drop the Seb and maybe I'll oblige." I juggle speaking with the lump that's risen in my throat, but she already knows I'm addicted, and the worst thing is I think she's more in love with taunting me than in love with all that I do for her. I'm hooked.

CHAPTER XIII: WANT

Sierra.

I am still happy. I have fallen in a river, lost a race against time and had a lacklustre night today - not necessarily in that order - and still I am happy. Happiness is certainly a jump. It's standing on the mountain you've climbed and looking down. Except in London, mountains are glittering skyscrapers and in the centre of the city, it stays warm because as sundown hits, the kitchens start cooking and people start getting ready to go out. I know when I look out at the members of the audience who have come to see me, that it is only the start of their night.

What I love about people is a fascinating concept called sonder. It's the realisation that everyone you pass is writing their own story. One person in my audience may be sitting on their own, listening because a friend recommended that they go out to take their mind off their own sombre thoughts and they've grudgingly accepted, clueless to the fact that the couple sat beside them plan to go out to dinner afterwards for their third anniversary. They may be sitting in front of an elderly couple, years ahead of their young love, who don't care for my voice but care for the venue - it brings them life, makes them feel young and in love again. How many shapes and sizes a night out can present itself in. I love life's variety. I love that special word *sonder*.

This particular venue is a favourite of mine. I've performed here since last winter, for a series of evening shows that they use as fillers when no other entertainment is booked. I cannot care less. I am not at the top but I sit somewhere in the world of music that I'm happy to be. If I were at the top there'd be nothing to learn, my song would lose its personality. I am more than comfortable with letting the venue speak volumes of the history of music, the journey of song. I am merely there to supplement the surreal experience of sitting in the Royal Albert.

Not being a master of your craft is humbling. Most artists, of any occupation, are so set on a destination that the path is forgotten. It's only afterwards, like a too-little-too-late eulogy, that they talk about giving anything to return to the game and persuade themselves that it's worth the effort and worth the fight. I think it's rather more touching to feel the effort and feel the fight and know that whichever destination you end up at is a certificate of your trying.

I like to get on a bus to nowhere, and I liken that to having no direction in my working life. I enjoy what I do and I'll trust that to carry me. It's about what you visit on the way. The people I meet, how the atmosphere is tactile, forcing me to be tactical. I've learnt to read a room, know an audience, unearth every little detail to play with subtexts of the songs I sing. I don't only sing. I talk to my audience between songs. It's a new thing I never used to do, but when you have five thousand friends for a night, it's fun to open up. I don't have much of a history that I can remember, so I talk about the future, I talk about what the songs make me yearn for. I explore what the lyrics suggest that is out there for me. Love. Pace in life. A debt to the world I'm in and the people in it.

I often orate an anecdote about the bus each night. There is so much to say.

It sighs heavily, the same way every time, sinking as it welcomes me. Everyone is interested as I walk into the stretch of their space, some recognise me, but they stay quiet. I am a stranger here. I am not Sierra on stage, I'm Sierra getting public transport for pure joy and I look like

I'm more in my zone than when I'm performing, I think this elicits an element of confusion. I try to smile at everyone, I want them to know I'm a servant to sonder. I have a small part to play in the movies they're making, some starring without realising it. I treat them each as their own protagonist. Isaak hates that I do this. He says be careful. Nobody has given me a reason to need to be careful yet so I just think he takes the world too seriously.

I don't tell the audience that last part. They don't need to know that there's parts of all that's out there for me that I haven't quite grappled with. They don't need to know the crazy way I care for him, care less for his opinion, and care quite so little for the way he sees the world. They don't need to know I'm committed to altering his perspective. Isaak is, with all his twists and turns and changing minds, so much like a wild dream that when I speak of him, people respond as though I'm talking about one. They simply don't understand, so I stopped trying long ago. This includes Gala. Nicholas seems to recognise my feelings to a large extent, bless his heart, but I somehow still feel alone in love.

The bus rides with the weather. I've been in London for a while so I've seen rain, thunder, sweet sunsets, everlasting daylights and occasional endeavours of the sky to snow. Through that strained sleet, even when the clouds are white, like cotton suffocating a lively city, I know the smell of every food and the placement of every lamppost. I know how London changes with the seasons, both with nature and with commerce. I've seen London for the first time myself, but then so many first times through tourists, their eyes becoming wider windows when they step into the postcard that is the Westminster streets outside Parliament and when they queue cameras in hand for the world's most famous ferris wheel. All things that until you're here are just pictures or otherwise, imagination. I see this all from the window of the bus. Sometimes they even board and I can hear them chatting, excitement is unitary in every language.

The next song is one about travelling. I lighten the load of the emotion, but still regard the world dutifully for its brilliance. It wasn't the performance that was lacklustre, it was what followed. A laptop gets thrust forward to me by a supervisor backstage. I have to strain my eyes because I'm not used to the electric light it produces. I negotiated with him to make it less bright. After he does so, I receive the good news. My ratings have gone up since the shows here, even though I'm just a filler, they want to start booking me for main shows. My eyes glaze over the computer, and I see a white strip at the top of the screen with the words 'search for anything'.

"Would you mind if I borrowed this, please?" I effuse.

"Yeah, I guess, for a second, but I can't stay, I've got to speak to another member of the team, can you put it in my office when you're done? It's just on the left here." He replies, and I nod, half listening, as he scuttles away down the corridor, lanyard clicking as it bounces.

I've never had the thoughts of the world so available, accessible. I'm not quite sure what to do. I want to know what is thought of me, so I start to type in my name. It takes me ages. The letters it gives me aren't alphabetical so I have to find each one separately. I've seen people tap away but I've never had a way to learn. I communicate with work in person and by writing notes. It's not practical in a modern world but I prefer living a basic life with a pen and paper, more similar to how it was once lived by everyone. I feel it's an example of staying true to mine and London's roots.

I ___ YOU

As each letter is added, suggestions swap around below the word. It's guessed what I'm trying to type by the time I've written the 'Geni' of my surname. My name no longer stands out to me. It's that, below my name, there are two suggestions that catch my attention. The first:
sierra genieva where was she born
The internet has no answer. I don't know any better. I can tell the people what my house looked like when I lived with Gettie. What the beach looked like, and my side of the town - but the name of the town escapes me. My childhood before Isaak found me is gone. Memories that aren't exercised become consigned to oblivion. I have no more answers than the biggest source of information in the world. The biggest *modern* source, granted, but that's not all that's out there. My weekly attempt to fly to nowhere on the chassis of the bus, suddenly becomes a mission to find a library. Next, the question underneath it, poised by someone somewhere I hope I will never meet.
sierra genieva where does she live
The answers are only London, no more specific, which helps me to breathe better. The prickles on the back of my neck relax, remembering I live with Isaak, remembering I'll see him later today. I am safe. I am slightly perturbed by the images that spring up. Professional photos of me, ones I knew were being taken, ones I knew that existed. Then there's others. Me on the streets, sitting in the park, buying food, and I realise the eyes I see every day are not all friendly. Some are sick, taking surveillance; agents for the internet. Isaak might actually have a point, and that makes me more irritated and infatuated all at once.

I pack up quickly, leave the laptop where designated, and head to the pub for the second night running. I don't take the bus, I walk, not wanting to raise my head for people I don't know. I only want the home around me, the nest my lover creates with his stupid smile and brown eyes. I've got the world all wrong, but maybe that means I'm more right about him than I first thought.

A hand reaches out to me. An accident, but everything scares me. I can't help but look up and the hand is still near me.

"My apologies" he starts, before stopping, "I thought I recognised you from somewhere."

I coyly pointed to my face on the billboard behind him, wrapping my coat tighter around me, surprised that for the first time, I wished it was Isaak who touched me, but it wasn't. This man is gentle though, although he is tall and obscures the streetlight so I can't see his eyes, it helps me to believe he didn't intend to bother me. There's also no camera in sight. When he turns back around, he holds his sleeve to his mouth, like he's investigating me for features that scream I am the woman on the sign and that I am not an impersonator.

"Are you aware of a man named Alessandro, by any chance?" He queries.

"I'm afraid not." I begin to rush, exiting modestly. "I have to go. I'm sorry."

"It was lovely to meet you but I have places to be, please have a good evening."

I always hate when people have the audacity to dictate how my evening will go, but I am either too tired to take offence, or I found this one amusing. "And you."

I begin to walk away. The man turns, adding, "I've been looking for a show to watch, I'll come tomorrow. If you'll see me again, I'll be here at this same time. Goodnight." I don't ever see his face in the light, I'm too far absorbed in the thought of Isaak waiting.

The thought is all it is. The booth is empty when I get there, but my excitement searches for the benefit of the doubt, forcing me to wait the minutes until Isaak arrives.

It picks up outside. Thunder, the perfect pathetic fallacy of how I'm beginning to feel, and then the rain, lots of it. The weather ushers' people in from the streets, and the bar begins to get congested. If Nicholas wanted to come over to talk to me, he couldn't with the extent of customers now needing service, but he gives me the occasional glance, and then the empty seat opposite me a follow-up glare. Tears prick in my eyes, but Nicholas doesn't see them.

I take my chance whilst I can see it being successful. I've been staring at the bookshelf in the pub without touching the secrets it contains for far too many nights, and if one more thing than my heart will be broken tonight, let it be the streak of not knowing what knowledge lies in plain sight. All the books call for me. Tourists' eyes blaze into my back, into my seat. One by one they file into my booth, careless and disorganised with their wet anoraks, maps and the least fruity of drinks. I'm not standing up for myself when they're already sitting down, if they want to be there, so be it. It's now obvious to me that Isaak won't take their place.

I imagine him striding in here, clearing the table with one compelling instruction, he can make anyone anonymous do anything with the way he talks. It's hard to answer comments that aren't questions but I've learnt to get used to it. Feeling isolated and crushed two nights consecutively, not so much. Isaak and I haven't had time to converse properly since the shot I witnessed, all of our interactions have just been arguments or drastically mythical in the way he comes and goes, leaving me to wonder if his legend is worth more than his love in the grand scheme of things.

The bar is an ancient place, the unofficial looking plaque outside tells its history as a bank, and as an inn long ago. People will ignore the history to get straight to the hysterical hallucinations of the alcohol, to which they forget their own history, either waking up at home with no recollection and a hangover, or in a stranger's bed. I think I've realised why, since I've accessed the world's largest portfolio of connections, I've felt so disconnected. I am doing everything I can to remember my history, whilst people everywhere have such an incontrovertible urge to forget the traces of their own ancestries that lie at their fingertips.

The phantoms of my own ancestors are wandering streets somewhere, waiting to be found. I cannot bring them home when home is what is lost.

Home is not exclusively the feeling of safety, or company. I feel safe when I sleep in a room three doors down from Isaak, I had company with dear Gettie. There is company in everything if you look hard enough, sometimes I have to be my own company and I have to say I am rather skilled at it, but it does not feel like home. Another reason I struggle with direction may be that I am midway up a flight of stairs that I don't recall starting to walk up.

I don't know what came before I had the instinct to fly. I don't remember what my feet felt like on the ground. I'm beginning to realise that Isaak and introspection won't last as a handrail forever. I'm less scared about the hall that means death at the top of this flight of stairs, than I am of falling, and ending up wherever is below me in a basement of my lost childhood. Down never had the answers, which is why I've always looked up, but I think it's time to give in to the pull of the past.

The book I've taken from the pub's bookshelf is exactly that, a leather bound, dust bound cover, each page setting the hourglass backwards, sand spilling upwards. In particular it reminds me of the books at the apartment, a place I don't currently want to go if I know that Isaak will be there. My library is special to me. They are the books Gettie used to read to me. We used to read the days away from when I was old enough. Her voice could become an entire cast, flitting around from one character to another as if they sat in a circle around us to declare their own tales. One story is flooding back into my memory now, about a tragedy, in which a girl lost a man she was yearning for because he confessed his love too late. It stuck for a reason, and now I feel I'm living it. Isaak is that outlandish spirit Romeo, and I am Juliet, isolated in thoughts I experienced from a balcony. Except they were in love, and we are in limbo. They are dead and gone, and we live on. There's still a chance for us.

I hover awkwardly, wanting to turn the first page, but not wanting to start the process of my mind's divulgence and submission publicly. Opening a book that I've never come across before is always a luxury. I appreciate Gettie for teaching me all she did, about the way that words dance.

A suited combination of letters clutches a dressed-up meaning as a partner and swirls, as they deliver a raging tango or a paced waltz, their positioning in relation to each other quickening or softening the action. Adjectives, verbs, adverbs, nouns and more in a masqueraded ballroom of linguistic possibility, where every pairing begins footwork in a synchronic tango titled: Imagination. New words on words. New ideas on new concepts. New ways to imagine and new ways to think.

I open the book and my eyes are reading, but my mind is still piecing together a faint recollection of Gettie. A time where the first word of a book was replaced with a knock at the door. Somewhere a little out of my mind, I find the door down to the pub kitchens and I sit on a flight of stairs that I've never seen anybody use along the corridor. Balancing with my head against the wall and my tiptoes pushing me up into a comfortable position, I pretend to get lost in the book, when really, I roam the past. I ought to do it whilst these memories resurface, something may hold the key.

There's a man in our sitting room, gruff and with squared shoulders. A little like a grumpy mediaeval king with a grey beard and no crown. In my memory he sits too close to Gettie, I would never have allowed that now, given how frail she appears in my memory. At the time that was just how she looked, at a time before I comprehended ageing. but she was always so calm and collected so I never had to assemble my guard around her.

Visitors were fascinating to a younger me too, purely because they were so rare. Gettie and I lived alone with each other, we could go months without seeing another face if we didn't have to, except from the keeper of the grocery shop.

They are in the middle of a conversation with each other.

"I tell stories." This is her answer to his question after question on his occupation, he is ticking boxes more than he is interested.

"Stories..." the elderly man repeats, attempting to process Gettie's words, seeking to find a reason to reject the acceptability of such a creative pastime. He can think of nothing.

"Any kind you like, Sir." Gettie continues, entreating him to listen even if it went against his will. Her words, even now, are like words curling out of a book.

"Even if they weren't the truth?" He navigates around the notion. The love for fantasy in my mind almost

*lurches out of my mouth before Gettie's look silences me.
I think to myself, this man has never read fiction.*

I had goosebumps. The door was still slightly ajar and it was winter, so the snow outside became the snow inside the door, and the cold in my lungs. Gettie was wrapped up in a blanket, so the freeze didn't snap at her the same way, but when she lifted her hands from the arms of her chair, they left shiny damp marks. At the time I didn't know she was sweating, I thought it was just how snow worked, that the furniture leaked like the icicles on our porch and melted like the snowflakes on the windowsill. I'd never seen Gettie sweat, perhaps she'd never been scared.
Why did this man scare her so?

Gettie goads the man. "Most of the best stories are fictional dear. That is what makes them stories."

He takes a sly look at me and backtracks. "You can't sew?"

"I cannot."

Gettie's answer only seems to make him want to expand his list, so he adds. "And you cannot cook, or grow food…" he scratches his neck with agitation and not an ounce of hygiene, "but you can tell stories?"

The enthusiasm returns with the old woman, meeting his condescending stare, you'd never tell how her heart flinched with dread, because her eyes kept so confident. "I can write them too. Give me a pen and I'll write whatever you like and it'll be downright convincing. Won't it lovie?"

It takes a second to compute that she is addressing me. I nod, not knowing how much is too much to give to the conversation. It is an adult conversation, and I am not one yet, so I say nothing more.

"There, Sierra knows." Gettie saves me from having to speak.

"Sierra..." the old man tastes my name, the whiskers on his moustache and chin edging up when he talks, and I don't like the way he stares as he does it.

"That's quite enough for today. I ought to get started praising the way you've treated my small family. Jasper ought to loosen up and start arranging promotions, he's too old now to be stingy like he was."

The man, not realising, turns without much fluency to the door, hearing the name Jasper seems to upset him. Gettie preys on this, her words pushing this man away from our house. He tries to recover.

"I'll be indebted to you if that were ever the case, lady. A pen can only do so much." he grunts.

"If you believe that then, by default, you are right. Still, I shall take it upon myself to prove you wrong."

Only now can I read his lips as he leans close to Gettie. I should kill you, he mouths. I didn't hear this at the time. I didn't know the context or concept of death. He must intend it humorously, for Gettie only welcomes him back, leaving the door open metaphorically and literally. My shivers return.

"I might just." he accepts her invitation, "Goodnight Bridgette."

She hates hearing her full name from this man, but smiles like a child. You wouldn't know how she seethes as her way with words saves her. Then they both turn to smile at me, cross legged on the carpet, like nothing was the matter. I wish I'd had the strength to disagree.

The strength to disagree is all I need. Positivity is a curse when all I need is something to malfunction to bring to light life's impurities, something to focus on that's not Isaak, or lusting after impossibilities and let downs. The pages of the book I hold will suffice. My eyes droop as I read. I get to the first four words, "The universe was disquieted." before my shoulders drop and I sink into sleep with no care for who wakes me. For after all that has happened today, I have to pretend, I am still happy.

CHAPTER XIV: WRONG

Isaak.

Nicholas twists the knife. Instead of being disappointed, he unwraps the look on my face, all by saying nothing. It is clear he has had enough of me. Several mirrors caught my reflection on the way over here and each time it was Sebastian frowning back. There's a correlation with my nightmare in how I see him. He is worthy of Betsy, whereas I feel I've stolen Sierra - to a place she thrives, but does not belong. A place I'm no longer managing to keep safe for her, because I'm deteriorating. The city brings back a longing for unity. Don't get me wrong. I never want to return to Colmoor, but that isn't to say that there's not aspects of Colmoor I wouldn't want to bring to London. My brother, for instance. I want him and Sierra to meet. I hadn't begun to think about Betsy and Sierra meeting, but I like the idea the more I envision Sierra's excitement.

Life is lived in theories and three ways. I am obsessed with things in three steps. Firstly, synaesthesia makes the world joyful under false and illogical pretence, pretence because there is so much out there with the potential to hurt. Kinaesthesia to feel every last drop of synthetic slime, people's lack of mercy and morals. Finally, anaesthesia to feel nothing at all and wear away how much ethics are the governing state of the good. All the good desire is to feel numb, the evil are all numb already. I don't want to feel numb. All I need is a cup of Sierra's coffee, which in my mouth becomes all three methods of living.

The grumble of the pub, a collation of individual conversations, scorns me as I trespass. Society gives me a face I don't want, but actually for now it helps to cache my vulnerabilities away from Sierra. To file the flashbacks beside the nightmares and have done with them. There'll be trouble if they stay. Sierra is asleep on page one, her thumbprint dreaming on page two, her hatred for me flying free as my steps on the floor wake her. I brace myself to be dismissed, and get ready to convince her I have to be the one to take her home, no matter how much tension it brings to us both.

In an unvarying pitch she clarifies, "I forgive you." Her hair is in front of her face so I can't see either a smile or sadness. I don't know whether to believe her. "I just want to go home. Take me home, Isaak."

Dumbfounded, I took her hand, sheltering her under my arm. I'm not relieved. I can't describe it. It's like I've hurt her beyond a fathomable point and she has lost the spark I know. Hating on each other, deliberating on what we are has become a routine, I've always thought I knew who I am to her - her saviour, her volatile solar flare - but my actions have meant that I'm not that person anymore. On top of that, I still don't know who I am to myself.

Nicholas has called a taxi even before I've led Sierra past the bar. It's waiting outside with its engine running, and I'm angry that I won't get the walk. This is the price I have to pay for being inadequate at the only job I claim to have. Protecting her. Her pull on my arm is strong, and I need to let it happen. She's fallen too much at my hands this evening already, I can't believe there isn't an ulterior motive behind her forgiveness but I know she wouldn't do that to me. The truths we manifest about each other to keep us interested are slowly fading away. I realise that our dynamic runs on mystery but when she is no longer invested in the answers, the spirit is extinguished. Sierra has decided she doesn't want to fight me. I don't know how to deal with people who don't want to fight me. Compassion is a foreign concept to perceive long-term.

In the taxi, the driver seems nervous. It's my fault. I'm not used to this way of getting around so my eyes are locked onto the pedals and the steering wheel. A metal case, constantly changing direction and swinging around corners. A stranger, responsible for my life, and Sierra's. It makes me horrifically unsettled, and I am so relieved when the ordeal is over. I don't listen to the price. I just pay it. It is worth every last penny I have that I'm back in control of my own two feet. This is why I will walk anywhere, the distance to Colmoor and back, just to avoid little tin boxes controlled by people I don't know.

She can't stop yawning. Through the door and up the narrow stairway to our apartment she flashes her white teeth, her open lips a brilliant red beside the beige wallpaper that lines the lobby and the landing, and the black matte door handles that I ease open quietly to give her access straight from our hall to her bedroom. Flustered, she frets in circles, unknotting her hair with her fingers when we get in. I kneel at her feet. I cup one ankle and bring her foot onto my leg. I don't care that her heel is almost injecting my thigh, at least I feel a connection from her, an outreach and another show of acceptance, even if it is pain. Pain I couldn't care less for if it comes from her.

I coast my hand down her calf to her ankle, the temperature of her skin after she's come in from the outside cold is indelible. I undo the straps of her shoes one after the other and leave them by the door, causing her to return to her usual, shorter stature. Her coat goes on the hooks, my job, and she alternates arching her feet and curling her toes as she stands to try to work out the muscles, and perhaps delay working me out. It doesn't get far. I'm glad for it. I don't want her to work anything out before I've had a go at it. All I get is a frown - a hybrid of despair, sleep and disdain - and the last look at her for the night as she stumbles to her bedroom to sleep.

Sierra's room is the only bedroom in our apartment. The bed is big enough for us both, but I like her to have the space. I also wouldn't be able to cope with being so close to her at my most vulnerable, and not knowing what her presence would do to the nightmares. Not to mention the effect that me in that state may have on her. I'm not fully convinced that on the times she's walked in on me asleep, beyond my control, she's seen the worst of it. I'm not fully convinced that I have. Which is why when I leave her to fall asleep, I stare at the ceiling until my eyes start stinging with a tiredness that doesn't make me drowsy.

There's one thing on my mind. It is that there are two different paths available to me, I need to choose which to follow, and I need to choose tonight. The signpost, of right and wrong, is illegible to a conflicted mind. One eye reads as Isaak, who is confident, a protector and knows that the way to be close enough to her is to make her want me. The other eye reads as Alessandro, who is tired of messing about and wants to reciprocate, the only love in his life that he can interact with before the inevitable happens and they are taken away the same way as everything else I've ever known.

I need a coffee. First, I can't find the granules, then when I finally pour them into the cup, too many fall out. I clean the mess on the counter, and go to shake out the excess, when the pot drops and there's beads of coffee scattered dustily across the kitchen floor. Shoes coming off so I don't carry the sediment to the carpet, I leave the kitchen for later, and make haste to check I haven't woken Sierra with the noise of the container falling. Being barefooted in the apartment feels odd. I feel unprepared. I feel so tired. Like I just want caffeine. She's fast asleep, and I feel like a foreigner in her room, alien and awkward, so I leave as quickly as I arrived, knowing her eyes are closed and breathing is as it should be.

The kettle is clicked, and growls as it heats, beginning to vibrate as it lets off steam. I use the time to sweep the floor back to its usual marble look, almost. I'm lucky Sierra likes to keep herself too busy in the mornings to walk with her head down otherwise I'd need to mop it clean tonight too. I take a breath of relief as the light on the kettle flashes from red to off, and I don't care for the heat of the handle as I carelessly tip it into the mug. I've had enough mistakes ruining every moment of today, and a scalded hand to add to the exasperation can't hurt - my mentality as I scoop up the cup in my open palm. I am disciplined by the coffee. Hot, dark, bitter and fucking painful. I feel it burn before I register the reflex. My blood bubbles to the surface of the skin. I shake it as though that's going to help, and bite down hard on my lip so that Sierra doesn't hear my suffering. It's just a minor flame, often something handleable, literally and figuratively - so what about today has made me so subject to misconception about what it is that Isaak can cope with. I blame it on the bloody flashbacks.

The coffee doesn't hit the spot. It's not made by Sierra and that's perhaps the only difference, but it doesn't infuse my blood how I want it too. My thoughts are still clouded.

My collar starts to get tight. I hate it. I need to breathe. Frantically, I tear each button from the top down, I get to three before my hands shake so much, I have to stop. I push both palms against the window to stop myself lashing out at an inanimate object that doesn't deserve it. The glass sends a coolness through me, and with it, I roll my neck trying to snap out of this weird and inopportune funk. I don't want to lie alone on the sofa, I need company. London calls me.

In the distance, the lights stop somewhere and stars begin, and I'm so intrigued. Stars are lights that shouldn't exist. If there's something bigger above us, Sierra shouldn't matter so much to me. What is bigger than us should triumph, we should all be fragile and robotic rather than able to lead our separate lives. Along the way we've been given a choice and I've been given two. I've been given a new identity. I am one of the lucky ones. Or, Isaak is one of the lucky ones. Alessandro is wandering aimlessly in a maze.

The stars might be the exact carbon copies as those Sierra and I saw from the beach that night. The moon is one and the same, it sees everything. Each bold decision I chance, each mistake I make - and each journey, on foot, back and forth to Colmoor to meet Sebastian when Sierra is sleeping, singing or being stood up. By me. It feels so barbaric to make her an animal in London's cage. I won't allow her anywhere outside the city, because I'm scared that I can't carry the world's geography on my shoulders and its corners in my conscience. Killers could be anywhere. All I can do is learn the city and narrow the scope.

I work by predicting her every movement, now with the help of her reconnaissance jewellery. Her routine is not at my command but at my hands. If I tell her to wait, she will wait. If I tell her to walk, she will follow my heels. She doesn't know another way - I led her to happiness, now I'm just leading her blindly. I know if I ask questions, I'll be encouraging her to ask them. I don't want to answer and unveil the types of hell that lie above ground. Hell better left unmentioned. Hell in the hands that killed her mother seconds after she brought Sierra and Betsy to life. Her smile is too much of my everything to damage it.

My conflict is too much to manage now. On my own. I'm done with doing this to another person, another life, when she doesn't know the reason for my manipulation and my facetious love. It's not human. It's cruel. It is not who Alessandro was, or Isaak set out to be. I need to rewrite the rules.

There's a rainbow around the moon. More colours than the black and white world that I've seen so far. I should take the opportunity with Sierra whilst it's here. I don't know what will happen tomorrow, and if something happens to us, this can't be my last memory of her. I can't stay out on the balcony too long, Sebastian isn't below me anymore, so I don't know who could be looking up as I look down. I could have a target on my head and not know it, even though my mind is bleeding as it is. The coffee bleeds into the sink too. It's too strong to drink, and that says a lot about my state of mind.

I'm noticing little details around the apartment that agitate me and I don't want to fall asleep. Those two features of my fear combined mean that I spend time scrubbing at the rings that the cups have left on the table and the counter. The dustpan and brush help me collect the flakes of whatever I had for breakfast off the carpet. I can't stop cleaning, because I know when I do, it'll be time to step straight back into the flashbacks. The floor is being attacked by the brush so much that the fibres are being unknotted, it's a compulsive behaviour to avoid my obsession and I need to stop. I need to face the truth that what Sierra and I have isn't sustainable. I can't live this way, for her.

Alessandro sees a light in the hedges, a way out of the maze, at the same time Isaak realises what he has to do. I have to learn from Sebastian. I've not been running behind Sierra to cover her tracks. I've been looking for an excuse to leave the past behind and using her as a reason to keep sprinting. I need to accept that I can't run forever, that life doesn't go on forever, that I need to attract love whilst it lasts.

The grandfather clock hits midnight. I'm frozen in place as I try to see through each sound. Each of the twelve reminders of practicality. It drags me back out of my head, it draws the cleaning equipment out of my hands, it marches me out the window, making me face the balcony and whatever spies on me in the dark. It is recovered, and continued by London. Engendering the appetite for power and discordant play that has been lost on me since I woke up on the bathroom tiles with my body's frame aching. It must have led to some disfigurement of my ambition also. London, dependable in its stirring, maelstrom and incidents, returns to me my motivation.

The sirens, the shouts. The twenty-four-hour plight for justice. I realise this whole night I've been delusional. The city cries for someone to take a hold of it. It is brimming with revulsion, it's pathogenic, full of abusers, killers, sadistic ways and lonely lives. It's disgraceful I ever considered stepping away from this. I have no right to indulge in a life nobody else can touch. Chasing a love of my own when others are loveless. I must live like the dogs of society. Feel what they feel. Eat the same shit, walk in the very same gutters. My mother suffered, not for me to walk free, I didn't stop my father's death, only to walk free. I don't protect Sierra, for a chance to walk free. Sebastian is not free from Colmoor yet, and I refuse to walk alone. I'll not start my life until I pay back the debts, I owe to those I've lost, in pain and in suffering, and in entering every fight for Colmoor's innocent dead, and for its innocent living.

If failure is currency, then I declare this bankruptcy. I will not fail by easily falling in love, I will use the love I have and fight with it instead. This is the one and only way I work.

And more so, I will make Sierra know this. In obligatory deceit or spontaneous closeness, she will know the man my love for her makes me. I will do what I have to do. For Sierra and the spirits I loved until and beyond death.

I start to put the kitchen back together, making sure Sierra knows nothing of the way I was tonight, and that I wasted coffee beans on my inexperience. My head wants everything in order, so I can hit the ground running when I wake up, so I straighten the cushions, wash the dishes, and with regret, close the curtains to shut the city outside. I know there's no way I will be able to sleep if the lights want to kidnap me back into the streets. I have a purpose here, to keep her safe, and to stop the thoughts of Colmoor escaping out of these four walls.

Snapping off the lights, I think I see, only briefly, something moving in the dark. I can't walk away from an illusion, no matter the extent I can talk myself out of it, so I fumble for the switch again. In the light, there is nothing there. My eyes and my mind need to start cooperating. These false perceptions aren't working for me at all.

If I make a peaceful sleep a mission perhaps I'll be more likely to succeed. Climbing onto the sofa, I repeat this mantra so no other thoughts can invade. I've checked, and the door is thoroughly closed this evening, because the thought of Sierra stepping into my nightmares a few nights ago makes me realise I have a responsibility to never let her suffer like I do. Not for me. Not because of me. Not at all. Her eyes when she sees me like that cause me to feel like I'm sinking. In my own embarrassment, in my own feeling of stupidity and weakness that I can't sleep over a mother I never knew and a father whose actions I wasn't responsible for. It is just the way it goes that the living are billed by the dead. I refuse to die and put that burden on another. I will never do that to Sierra.

The only alternative to this is sleep, so I last until morning without another issue.

CHAPTER XV: MISS

Sebastian.

I know I'm far from Betsy because I can't think outside of the orders. I can't just think it once, it has to be three times so that it's stuck and solid and sustained, this time they're telling me to reach Alessandro. We meet when we can, and often we don't decide a time. I walk when I need to, and so does he, and our telepathy brings us together on the nights we need it most. Tonight is rare in that he already stands there in the same place we always come to. Perhaps there's news, but I need to get in there first. I know something. Something that could change this deadly game we have a hand in. Something fatal. The orders morph to warnings. Danger. Danger. Danger.

"Don't speak brother." I extract the bullet from my pocket. I've cleaned it since dried blood covered it, and it catches the moonlight. Its shine reminds me of Betsy alone. I have to make this quick. "See, here." I gesture and he cocks his head in acknowledgment, following the pattern of my pointed finger. Alessandro knows what the ribbed edges mean. There's a machine, albeit not a very good one, but the heat of a gun has seared the edges of the metal as it's been ejected from the canister. They've had machines here in Colmoor for a while. The one that killed my father was entirely low range, it fell from behind him when he was shot, the strength of the gun was not powerful enough to keep the bullet accelerating and get it lodged in the wall. Then there were the ones they began to take to London when they lost us. At first we were wary. Until we realised that the issue of range had not been conquered. If they wanted to shoot someone, you'd have to see down the barrel. You'd have to look them in the eyes if you were within the medium range needed to kill you, or avert their gaze if you were afraid of death. If you were going to die, you'd know.

These are the guns Alessandro and I keep. Effective above all else. They will give an accurate death, proven only a few days ago, with my fingers at the trigger. They share the same bullets as every other in Colmoor, and are not like the unfamiliar bullet I'm squeezing. I did all my research. I found a use for Betsy's magnifying glass, that was far from close moments pertaining to illustrations on my skin. Without using the glass, there was no way of warning Alessandro of the metal. There are new guns. Guns that could kill from a distance. The threats have become more than we can see.

Lack of long-range guns has been the reason Alessandro's concern for Sierra has remained pragmatic. My revelation makes a wreckage of pragmatism. The gravity shows on my twin's face. He can't protect Sierra from these new types of guns, no more than he can survive one himself.

He'll hate to hear it but it has to be said, "SG might have to stop singing for the time being. To be safe, AG."

"Sierra will be safe. She won't have to stop singing. It's immoral."

"It's all immoral." It's pointless to paraphrase what is crystal clear. Sanitised language is wasted on the Gray twins. We have seen and heard everything there is to consume.

I remind him. "AG, you're not a foreman to fate."
He knows. "I'm a slave to surrender if I don't try." His stubbornness shimmers brighter than the bullet, he wears his confidence like a badge.

"Do as you will. My words won't make a bloody difference. I know that much of you."

My brother lowers his head, he won't meet my eyes. I don't care. I'm too focused on ending this conversation and returning two brothers to two sisters. Then I remember he had something to say. His expression is vacant, and it's beginning to unnerve me that I see Alessandro again rather than this front of 'Isaak' he's constructed. If his face is vacant then where is his mind engaged? He needs to talk. Make him talk. Make him talk. Make him talk.

Then it occurs to me, his thoughts have retreated to a time when his passion was underdeveloped and a changed identity was unnecessary. I speak sternly, trying to gauge him.

"You went home."

"No, I took a book when we left for the girls. I found this inside." He pulls out a photo. One I've never seen before. Of all the reactions, I'm surprised that it's heat for Alessandro that seethes inside my chest.

"How long have you had *a photo*, as far as I know the only photo, of *our* mother and not told me?" Speaking slowly allows me to organise my anger from my thoughts. The worst thing is, Alessandro doesn't show a hint of deterrence. I should think he can tell by my tone I'm unhappy with him. I often stand beside all his decisions, even if I don't agree, but I will not stand for this one. Alessandro has seen our mother's face longer than I have.

She's smiling in the photo, making me nauseated to know that she is dead and I decided it was best to become angry with my twin instead of sharing his love for her. Through gritted teeth, I render my temper unworthy of this little time we have to meet. I snatch the portrait from him, and he doesn't fight back, or flinch. He lets me have it. I study it.

Alessandro's warmer skin colour comes from our mother, now it's obvious. It's difficult to look people in a photo in the eyes and not be able to alert them that their lives are compromised. It's this very notion that makes the paper less ergonomic in my hand, I don't want it there, there's nothing I can do about it. I don't know what Alessandro expects me to do with the memories. It's a campaign flyer trying to get me to enrol in pain when my subscription has already expired. It's not hard to see that the situation that decelerates us, is that one of us is looking to the future with a woman he's just met after searching for so long. The other is regressing to the past and dragging an ambitious woman with him as a companion and an excuse to not face the world.

Facing the world starts with taking a good look at yourself in the mirror, and Alessandro does not know who he is. I am his mirror, for we look the same, and I think because of that, he thinks we act the same. Assuredly, we don't. I have never felt more different from him - perhaps it is because I have found someone else to love whilst he's denying himself Sierra. The photo will cause a rift between us eventually if it is not put away. I hand it back to my brother and tell him I don't wish to see it again.

What preoccupies me more? The fear of the mess Alessandro will plunge himself into whilst trying to defend Sierra from new artillery, the audacity of him to keep family history from me - or the urgency with which I need to return to Betsy. I picture Warner crawling out from the dirt, getting to her before I do, and finishing what he started - with a vengeance that smiles at her downfall through his disfigured features.

"AG, I need to leave." I'm done with this situation and tell him straight.

"You're so in love and it's written all over your face."

I ___ YOU

He makes it sound like a bad thing. I'm not even sure that love is what it is for now, love is a timeline, lust is the moments, and attraction is dangerous because it could lead to nothing or be everything. I'm not in love yet, I'm risking it all with love as the target.

"You're so in love and standing here lazily like you aren't." I retorted. We often toss around sardonic comments, but this one felt personal. It takes a second for my words to disperse in the cemetery. I know Mother and Father feel the rift between Alessandro and I, and I feel like it is worse than the distance between us both and them.

"I find it insulting that you think I'm not in control. To think I'd react in any other way but devastation should anything happen to Sierra." Isaak speaks slowly, not meeting my eyes, blazing vision centred on the words of Father's grave.

I don't feel like my initial statement was loaded with the expectation that he doesn't care for Sierra - I think he's unloading his guilt without even realising. I unintentionally may have found the crux of conversation hidden in Isaak's silence and stifling of the bewitching photo of our mother.

He leaves me with the words "I'll never drop the strings I hold. You'd have to cut them from my composting hands, Sebastian." He leaves just as I work out that there's so much more we need to discuss. What point we're at with how much the girls know, about us, each other, Colmoor and their survival. Our states of being. Killing, injuring and fighting with no down time is bad for me, but worse for Alessandro. For every fight I have, he's having five.

As much as I want to return straight to the treehouse, I have to retrace my steps for peace of mind.
Unfortunately, the route bypasses peace of mind, and

instead sets it pacing frantically when I realise that where I left Warner, the dust is disturbed and the leaves aren't where I'd left them. More so, I can't see the vile creature in any direction, or hiding behind anything. I move at whatever pace is sensible, usually, but I've never run this fast. When I finally get to the treehouse, I am completely breathless, not a vulnerability I need when I may have to get aggressive.

Betsy stops me in my tracks. I'm breathing so heavy that I can't see her properly. She's a lot more alert than she was when I left her, and I'm significantly less energised. I can't help but relax as she touches my shoulder, asking me if I'm okay, why I'm running, where I went, what happened. Too many questions, when there's only one answer. Her safety. My attraction.

"He's not here?" I pant, looking for signals all over her face, that Warner perhaps might be forbidding her to speak, but she seems calm. There's no ulterior recreation here.

"Who? Warner? I haven't seen him. I'm okay, Seb." This is the first time she calls me Seb naturally, without a spark of playfulness. In a strange way, I'm comforted but my head is programmed to jump to the next stress, riding the adrenaline. Alessandro, heading back to London, heading straight to the fire of a gun. I sink down into the meagre patch of grass, cradling my head in my hands. I thank everything and anything that she's here and perfect, with not a scratch on her skin or tears in her eyes. I want to keep her spirit glowing this way forever.

"Betsy, will you sit with me?" I piece together the words. She crouches to my level, knowing I can't feign the weakness in my voice, and waits for a stipulation, ready to be summoned by my needs and pleas. Her hands are on my knees, an eagerness to help leaps from her smile but caution holds her back. I spread my knees apart so she sinks down onto my chest, her hair spilling across my ribs. I'm too tired to imagine what would have happened if that was a move too fast. That it would have destroyed the moment, and I'd have overstepped my own authority, my role to her. But that's the thing about love, it will happen naturally or not at all. As if she can hear my anxiety and the orders struggling to be heard, she places her hand on my forehead.

I don't know what changed, but we feel connected. Puzzle pieces, ingredients to a familial recipe, the sun and moon on rotation to make the days. Betsy is my days, and I am here for her each night. Like a sundial, I seek her for direction, and like a sailor, she seeks the stars in my darkness for guidance. From this moment, will our cycle be endless, will it repeat on and on, and one day, from our planet, will love evolve?

"Did you go to Alessandro?" she asks, innocently enough but my skin prickles at the mention of my brother's name, patience simmering over as he's brought into the space between Betsy and I when I've just forgotten about him. I don't want him here. He's not invited to my heart's federation, where my secrets lie undone and open to this woman. I also don't want Warner here, and I keep looking around as if he'll appear. Betsy is keen with the questions, I'm not too sure she knows how to handle me right now. She's not used to emotion pouring fluidly into her hands, not used to being trusted, not used to being loved - the right way.

Keeping going, she is now meditative, and I am the mediator between her impulse, instinct and logic. Guilt consumes her. I know what that looks like, my old friend rearing its nasty aesthetic in the face of my companion. Karma is a killer, spite is a swindler, guilt resurfaces in her because I dismissed it so long ago. "I hit Warner. I hate him," she stops, pensive, "but I can't help feeling as though he didn't deserve it."

"Maybe that's not the question. The question is, did you deserve it, what he did to you, how he treated you?" It turned into a list, unintentionally, I could write Warner's sins on every square metre from here to London. It wasn't rhetorical, but perhaps the subtext passed her by. She doesn't answer.

My voice fills the gap she's left. "The answer is no, you didn't. These souls we claim, through violence, through heartbreak, through injury and death aren't ours Betsy. They're people, and you're right, the only soul we are responsible for is our own. But angel, if anyone tries to threaten that, never put yourself at risk. I will never let you put yourself at risk, understood." I reiterate, trying to attach the message to the moment. "These souls we claim aren't ours."

She takes a deep breath and sighs, "Sure feels like it." She's still not convinced, and begins to get up, deciding she needs more memories from her day than lying on my chest. I try hard to savour what we have had, more than I ever expected when I told Alessandro that Sierra was his. Betsy is not mine. I am not hers. We are each other and she is capable without me, which is what makes me surer that she is the one. She reduces the exigency.

Alessandro was never as present with our father as I was, so I had a lot of time to ask the questions that my brother refused to.

"Will I ever find love for myself?" I feel ashamed to say it, because my father was held back from his eternity with my mother, but he seems keen to answer. He made me walk with him, there was an errand he had to run in town, but I think looking back on it now, he just didn't want Alessandro to take the burden of knowing that love was

another service he had to take on before his time on earth was up. My brother already suffered with the weight of responsibility far too much.

My father didn't explicitly answer my question, but he answered every blank in my knowledge around it. That conversation I had with him as we walked together is the reason I'm not convinced I know what love is now, and why I'm okay with not being certain. I'm a man who likes to know things, but love is the one virtue I will let make me blind.

I hypothesise. Once you know love, you can't ever go back. Love is the reward of getting to know someone, too well, it is packaged with commitment and belonging. If it's true love, it's irreversible. My father never loved before my mother. He never loved that way after. Love is loyalty. Love is knowing there's nobody else there for you in quite the same perfect combination of everything you cherish. Love is missing company when it leaves a hole. Love burns when threatened, repairs when nurtured, dies for nothing, not even mortality. Love matters. Love lives forever.

My father was dead before he died. To be buried with my mother made him complete, I know it. They are together now, headstones inscribed with each other's names, laughing more in heaven than they were permitted to in Colmoor. My eyes prick with tears, as I look at Betsy.

I want her name right under mine on my stone, and my name on hers. I want her last name to be Gray, and her first name to be the only word I speak when we're alone and I can't breathe in her presence. I want righteousness for the first time, righteousness in my life that goes by the pseudonym *Betsy*.

"Betsy." I call after her. I know when she turns, I have her full attention, "These souls we claim through conflict aren't ours, but the souls we claim through love are shared. I'm prepared to give my soul up to you," I stumble on my words, caught up in the mess that is her magnetism, "for you. There is nobody better to share it with."

Everything relies on her being accepting. If there was distance between us, I don't know how I'd cope. I want her more than I've ever wanted anything.

I think her face complements all my fears and fortitude, and introduces anger among these concentrated emotions. I don't feel susceptible, responsible or dominated by the ferocity in her gaze. She's not hating me, she's hating every minute before this, of her entire life that she's been devoid of this feeling of care. I want to tell her, come here. I want to tell her I've got her. I want to lay claim to her as long as she'll have me, I want to hear her say I'm hers. I want to tell her that neglect is something she will never know again.

Now is the moment. Not to confess to her, not to lay myself down. To bear the naked truth, to let her see the battlefield and the bloodbath it will cause. I don't want to do this at all, if our page isn't the same.

"Do you know about Sierra?" I lacerate the moment's energy with the hope of taming it. This is it. There's no going back now. Oblivion has staged its final adieu.

"Sierra..." I see the cogs turning in her darling mind, trying to figure out what corner of the serpentine web she's missed. As if we were back in the cottage again, her eyes drift across her mental notes and pictures of the situation. Sierra is ringing no bells, it becomes increasingly clear. I brace myself, praying I'm doing the right thing.

"Sierra. Your sister."

A new expression that I'd never seen on her before, makes her mouth climb, and fills her eyes. "I have a sister?"

"A twin sister."

Through tears that she is trying so hard to keep custody of, she tries to use her humour to stay presentable. She doesn't have to be presentable. As long as she's present, I couldn't give less of a damn whether she was made up or not, as long as she feels safe to be herself. Comfortable, individual, home. "You failed to tell me that earlier, Seb. You could have spared me the embarrassment of these tears." With that, I'm right by her side. I'll let her feel anything she needs, but not cynical of herself on my watch.

I know what it takes to lighten her. "If it helps, I feel that way towards Alessandro sometimes. So frustrated with the knowledge he exists, that I could cry." An overstatement, a slight exaggeration, but given today's events I care little about accurate overextensions of what's gospel. I make a joke, waiting for her response to validate if I've chosen the time wisely. It takes her only one step to reach me. She pushes her forehead into my chest because standing up, that's all the height she can reach. "Oh Seb. I'm not sure I could ever see you cry. It'd hurt too much."

I'm trying to diffuse the weight of her processing, and somehow with a smile, as is my helpless way around her.

Her fingers gently lift my jumper, stroking my tattoo. There's nothing that could make me stop her. My heart is thudding faster than any chase I've ever endured. "I didn't tell you I have one too," she admits. Suffice to say this is not news.

"I'm aware." I chuckle.

She uses my simple two-word phrase for deduction. "Have we all got one?"

"All four of us. You, me, Alessandro and Sierra." I kneel down solemnly as I explain, taking polite advantage of her quiet. "Betsy, can I touch you?" Instantly she reverts back to herself. Top form. The Betsy I met the first time in the woods.

"Let's find out. You have my permission, the real question is whether you have desire."

This paradigm shift, a breakthrough in our relationship that I've been keeping myself so held back from, is proof that not all questions need answers. I peel down the band of her skirt, revealing her hemmed lace underwear. She stares straight on to the distance so she doesn't have to look down and imagine I see her the same way she sees herself. I can't touch her when she doesn't appreciate the joy that she, in her totality, brings to me. "Look at me. I can't have desire, if I don't have your faith in me."

She obliges, slowly meeting my eyes. I nudge her vest, and don't allow a hesitation to let overthinking and fear suffocate me. The ink sings to me. I push my lips tenderly against the tattoo. I am so lucky. I am blessed. This is the first time I've kissed life and love, the first time I haven't missed life and love. I can't take my lips away.

CHAPTER XVI: CHERISH

Sierra.

In sleep, I have a dream about Gettie, and what would have been if we'd had longer together. Awake, I have a dream to be with Isaak, I want him here. I know he's here because I can hear his footsteps somewhere in the apartment, but I want him closer than that, in these sheets, next to me. That's when I remember I'm supposed to be angry at him, but then I begin to mentally repair the chronology of last night. My forgiveness. The journey home. He doesn't love me the right way, but he loves me his way. He wouldn't be crashing around in the kitchen trying to make me breakfast if he didn't. I have to decide if his love is the love I want though. If he can't tick the boxes I want, and makes me keep waiting, potentially for nothing, then I can't hand over my heart on a silver platter. He has to earn it.

The sunlight tears through the curtain, London is waking up and so am I. Even angels have their dark side, I need to use my love to look beyond my lover. I have more to give, so if he won't receive, he's going to find himself left behind. I start to wonder what constitutes boundaries if they only mean something to you. What if boundaries are just criteria, a judgement of who I let close, a trial of affection? Maybe I've let criteria and boundaries become blurry. I let Isaak close, but whilst he's lacking what I need. I need closeness, I need love, I need sex, I need things that make me feel. I am human, after all, and passion without application is wasted.

Being in bed doesn't help. The warmth calls out for him, so I get up and crawl out of my want for him and into a dressing gown. It is useless. I am in sensory poverty, and a motivational slump. Food may help, so I don't reject his pancakes when he pushes the sickly maple syrup drenched plate toward me. It's a slow morning, but that's okay. I can recharge my energy to deal with the world tonight. Knife and fork in hand I'm missing something completely, and it can't be significant, because I'm within minutes of waking up. I blink and it comes to me. In the day's alternative to a nightmare - eye contact with Isaak. The easiest part of him to read is his eyes, even if his posture, actions and speech say otherwise. The first time we look at each other in the morning is our claxon to start the day, we race through our lives apart, until the evening when we say our last goodnights. A last goodnight can be at 8pm, it can be 10pm, it can be midnight, whenever Isaak shows up, or never. If it's never, the race begins again the day after.

It's fun toxicity - because what kills you might not necessarily make you stronger, it might make you weak all over, and you might love it.

I don't know where he's come back from, but I find I don't mind all that much. It's also probably easier not to know. I don't want to know where he gets the marks, the cuts and the scratches. He can handle himself, I've never doubted that, but I never see a need to get physical with troubles that simple words and empathy can rectify. Then again, Isaak seems to have been less fortunate in empathy, than in the way he looks. I'm struggling to take action, a shower that is supposed to energise me but instead makes me so sleepy, falling away with the furry diamonds that the hot water makes me see. I wash myself until I'm dizzy and submerged by the fog that I've stormed up in the bathroom.

My wet hair is dripping arrhythmically onto the floor, escaping through wormhole channels in the tied-up towel. I try to finish a cup of hot chocolate on the kitchen island.

It's not really a morning drink, and it's making me more tired. With my fatigue, comes a flurry of emotions I didn't know were stocked up. I start thinking I've woken up on the wrong side of the day, but Isaak's been the reason for my late nights, so I'll blame him. I'll blame it all on him, because he doesn't care, and because I don't want to believe I'm unlovable. It's easier to look out a window, than into a mirror, and cast away the insecurities to a place, in my case a person, that won't give them a second thought.

I'm doing all the wrong things. I'm reading again, and I know that getting myself engrossed in fantasy worlds to cope with the disjunction of my waking life isn't helping me rise from the insecurity, but I enjoy it. I am tired, no matter which lens you use to look at the word, but the subject shapeshifts. I'm not tired of myself. I'm tired of listening to society and its long list of expectations. I'm tired of attending lectures slurred by my own heart every moment I get alone, I'm tired of being Isaak's sheep, who every time I think we get close, he runs out the door. I don't need him to round me up in this big city, I don't need him to take shears to my overgrown imagination.

The book I've chosen has a distinct cover, one my young eyes remember. Something I probably used to love, probably used to obsess over, probably used to know every word to. My thoughts are so repetitive, not resembling the woman I usually am at all. It's simply not possible that I've changed this much, and it can't be regression because I don't think I ever was this woman whose shoes I walk in now. Sierra with a broken heart, and the constant overhanging knowledge that she has a fractured past, hasn't walked London's pavements yet.

Albeit when you start a book you have no knowledge, and the author feeds you little snippets of their own dreams. They craft miracles with words on paper and by the end you're in the world and don't want to leave. You cry for ink characters, and hurt the same for fictional love. Maybe my confusion is just a *tabula rasa* and the pain I feel right now, that exhausts me down to my bones, is just growth. I could look at this as a last page, or a first page. I could fall to pieces and sweep them under the mat, or gather the pieces and discover who I really am.

If Isaak knows, if Isaak has been stealing my past from me this whole time, he'll be committed for his double dealing before he has a chance to know what I know, and to know what I've done. I want to be in control of every aspect of my life, I want to learn the past and create the future with the same power I eject in my voice, and most of all, I don't want to continue living as a puppet, crushing on a man that is nothing more than a shadow.

I'll definitely start the independence process once I'm out of the house and on my way to a performance, but I need to let myself grieve the old me or I'll forever be bouncing back to this state of mind. How to give myself closure to a love that has lasted as long as I can coherently remember though, is slightly more challenging. Then the quote of the day reoccurs. *Even angels have their dark side, I need to use my love to look beyond my lover.* That is exactly what I do, and it starts by curling up on Isaak's sofa, like a sombre, celestial angel in the dark, laying divine on his bed, and wrapping myself around his upholstered cushion bed mates. This is using my love and my addiction to give me strength to evade loving him from now onwards.

I don't know how long that I've spent with my eyes closed, and inhaling the scent of his cologne that he's left pinned on the fabric. This room always stays darker longer than the others, so the rising sunlight doesn't give me much indication of how long I've been hypnotised. A silhouette that I'm not anticipating makes me jump as my eyes splinter open, directed out the door where Isaak's coat hangs in the hall. It is one of the two he owns. This one is clean, so the dirty one is somewhere skulking around with him on his shoulders.

I blister away from the sofa as soon as I feel that it's hurting, not helping, to remind myself of him. I hum the songs I'm ready to sing tonight, but these melodies, like a wild animal, aren't all that satisfied being contained. Babbling, turns to patchy vocalising, turns to whispering, turns to belting. My head voice wastes no time in hoisting my chest into its campaign to be heard. My lungs excrete my agony and leave me feeling healthier. I sing away the pancakes, the thought of Isaak, the darkness and the fear. Isaak's reasons for missing the opportunity of this relationship. The patience of my neighbours to deal with living beside me, I will never know.

This is one of the rare performance days where I feel as though Gala is unneeded, and I actually feel confident in my outfit today. It's minimal - grey with a bright white top. Like a lawyer with an added touch of rhythm. My wrist is singing too, in weird cadences, as the metal bangles smash together, like an on the move instrument that orchestras would hate for its lack of perceptible organised musicality. Contemporary.

London greets me as it usually does, with difference every day, and originality at every turn. New people, old people, all people that the city sensationalises. In the spring, most people are flocking to the parks, but there are still masses of people in the narrow avenues and walkways trying to get to work. One of life's most stressful jobs must be operating the vehicles that support people in the city on the regular, as there are often pedestrians where pedestrians shouldn't be, and red lights may as well be green given the number of times they are mistaken. I put extra effort into smiling at the bus driver this morning. I feel good, and others deserve to feel the same, even if they are clustered and crowded by those that don't care.

Often, I try to catch sight of Isaak, but I feel detached from the need to, the people on the bus are more interesting. A case study, maybe, an observation. That's how we'll pass the time, the miles and the monotony from here to work.

There's a man, with glasses, sitting to my left across the aisle, and writing in a small journal. Not inspired by his immediate surroundings because he doesn't look up, around and down again to write. He just keeps going, the pen whispering to the paper the whole time, every time I look over, he is scribbling something. Notes for a meeting maybe, but he's not dressed in a suit. He is wearing a scarf, in spring, which makes me think he is a writer, drinking up the harsh stereotype.

As much as I'm captivated by some books, I don't fully understand why people write them. If people could live their life like it's a book, creating their own dialogue in conversations, featuring the people they like in their story, and defeating those they don't in psychological terms, there would be no need to fictionalise anything at all.

The flip side is dark and daunting, full of desires nobody speaks of. There's horror, because people have crippling phobias they hide from behind a page. There's sci-fi because people are unsatisfied with the world as it is, or have innovation that needs to be heard. There's crime, because there is darkness in people, which contrary to my first view, means I'd much rather people write books, to stop them from acting upon their impulses in reality. Nightmares need to stop at their materialisation on paper, and not make it into the courts.

The man disembarks a stop before mine, leaving the mystery of his notepad forever unanswered, and on my mind as something to debate for the remainder of the day. There's another untravelled path, that my brain hasn't quite accustomed itself to yet, which is the silhouette I encountered in the street last night. In fact, I hadn't given it too much thought until this moment, now that I'm walking the same street again.

It's lighter this time. He said he'd be outside tonight, and made it sound like it would be affording him pleasure and honour to meet with me, and something about the favouritism, the prioritisation, sparks something. Flames that Isaak has never stimulated in me. The feeling of being truly needed. Not the feeling of being truly used, the entertainer of Isaak's inconclusive wants and the sole one he messes with when he's done with packing the rest of his time with getting into trouble with the wrong people.

I try to think how I'd tell a wrong person apart from the right one. There's a natural attraction, a chemistry between morals, so when your intellect and heart match with another, there is an instant click. Conversations with them become existential, but grounded. Your touch becomes physical and intense, but passionate. Arguments are meaningful, and a step backwards always ends up swinging you back around into love that's learned and experienced. Real love is an industry for the masters.

Nevertheless, real love for the right person takes time. You can like them first, you need to like them first, like training for the finals. A masterclass for the demands of marriage, which is a beautiful unity I discovered, was a thing in fairytales, where you pledge a place in your life to someone, one person, out of billions. Marry a person who you can stop from breathing momentarily, with laughter. If you can stop their heart from beating for a fraction of a second, they are in awe of you. They bring you happiness, happiness, and in equal parts humour and garbled hatred for the little trivial things, which at the end of the day you'd crave if they were to disappear. This is friendship in your shot at love, the unique code to the safe. The wonderful thing about life is that you can shoot your shot again and again if you miss. Of course, anyone can break into feelings even if they're reinforced and reluctant, but if it is controlled and consensual, it is clear you are in love.

Chemistry and connection. I have both in Isaak, plus a little calamity. *Had* both in Isaak. There's no love or friendship anymore.

That is until after the show, when everything changes, and like always, normal is destabilised. The man said he'd be waiting, and I want to know his name. It is all I could think about as I sang, the potential of another Isaak, another love. Another chance to fall for someone worth falling for. Someone who waits for me, and I'm never left waiting for. He said he'd be waiting for me on the same street I found him. Different scenarios play out in my head, wondering how our interaction will happen. If he'll remember me. Of course, he'll remember me. I'm feeling doubtful, but that's possibly a positive, it means there's a deeper feeling thrown into the mix.

The earth seems so much prettier when you're in love. Lights become mistletoe, to kiss beneath. There's a bucket list of locations I want to be kissed. Under the streetlights, under the sunlight, under the moonlight, under the stars. In addition to the where's, there's also a multitude of how's. At first something gentle. Then something experimental. Then a fix to something detrimental. Then an impulse, an instinct, a habit, a result of subconsciousness. Quickly when they're leaving and in compensation and slowly when they return. Bottom lip, top lip, it doesn't matter, I'm careless and desperate for either. My neck, my shoulders. Warm, cold, frozen. Any temperature adds feeling. If a kiss causes goosebumps, it's a good one. It matters little where or how. If it's perfect in the end, it also matters very little when. The one thing that needs to be unrivalled, is who.

I'm ready to walk away from the theatre, past London's restaurants and hotels, to meet a 5-star lover and leave a review on his lips.

I'm excited, so my anger when my past doesn't even let me make it out the door is augmented. He's standing there in the coat that wasn't hung up this morning, declaring himself a bouncer, not allowing my serotonin or dopamine to dance.

"Isaak, you need to leave. I'm meeting someone." I say breezily, walking straight past. He stumbles, that's how I know I've won. He wants to ask me who, but he's trapped by his own promise not to ask questions. His eyes scorch my back. I can't help adding to it.

"I'm meeting someone I may or may not be interested in. Someone who might love me without conditions, constraints or conflict, Isaak. Someone not like you." My words are so spiteful they hurt to say them, but they don't lack meaning. He begins to walk but stops right in front of me.

"Sierra. If this is what I think it is, you're the sweetest of irritations."

I swallow, wanting to prove him wrong but I can't think of a single thing. My brain is deactivated. It must be the way he's looking at me. "It depends what you think it is." I remark.

"You're riling me up for passion." I can't tell if he thinks it's admirable. But even then, it's still not the truth, not what I'm doing. He's depositing ideas directly into my head. I don't want passion from him. Nor do I want to give him any of my energy. That ship has sailed.

"I won't say either way." I purse up my mouth, trying to keep a stout attitude.

"Then, I'm right. It's not healthy, Sierra."

"Neither is your obsession with chasing the nighttime for nothing, even when it's hurting you." That came easier.

"The only thing that hurts me is not being able to do things to you that I obsess over." He rushes his words, forbidding me freedom of movement with his telepathy, he must be doing something as he locks eyes with me. I swear I can see the sparks.

Fear is the first instinct. I'm afraid of myself and what I will do. I've never been able to feel afraid of him, but I'm scared of how he makes me feel.

"What do you want to do to me?" Warily, I take a step back.

Isaak doesn't answer questions. He never answers questions. Instead, he lunges forward, hesitates for a moment to make sure I close my eyes, and kisses me. It's not 5 stars. It's a galaxy.

CHAPTER XVII: PROTECT

Isaak.

I want to cry. I've never wanted to cry before. I want to cry because I don't know what to do. So, I do what I should have done for a long time and take her out to dinner, at her favourite restaurant, and order as many of Nicholas' Paradise Cocktails as he has left. I hate this feeling. I hate what I've just done. I hate that I'm feeling so much confusion that I can't function when I should be elated. I hate that I'm sounding like the voices my brother hears in his head, all the hatred marching and spewing. I think I need to be sick.

A few beers clean up the nausea quite smartly, and I'm left to study the lips I just kissed as she does nothing but smile. I think of those familiar Colmoor predator eyes standing behind her, as I went for it, making no predictions on what it would be like. Alessandro wouldn't have been as drastic, and neither would I. Having kissed her, I still can't form a conclusion. I don't know what it meant, I don't know what I've made her feel and I don't know why my only instinct is to do it again. It can only mean I'm greedy and insensitive to how significant it was to have the one.

I'm not at ease here. There are too many faces, and too many people turned away from me so I couldn't see them scheming. I try to tune into every voice, but they're all talking about Sierra anyway. If her fame had any downside, it'd be the constant murmuring I'd abolish, I can't separate the lovers from the liars, even when I've got characteristics enough of both to be able to tell the difference. It's when two men dressed in black Colmoor coats enter, that we need to leave. For Sierra to move, it has to be the spontaneity that entices her. I sincerely hope the potential of the towering metropolis and the power of our first kiss will be enough to drive her out the door. Two of us, out of a single exit, at the same time, side by side. Lives change so fast.

A fraction of me is glad that there's evil around, it's not comfortable but it's my comfort zone. I'm happier in hypervigilance than I am simmering in the guilt of kissing Sierra without thinking it through first. I didn't think there could be anything worse than the flashbacks but this is a close second. I've never experienced so much love and anger in equal measure, the voice in my head that interrogates me for my sins is like a demented lullaby. It can't be a sin when we're both happy, yet I still feel imprisoned. Boundaries are a factor nobody seems to be able to respect tonight. I couldn't help myself as I crossed the line, and the force seems to be in the city more than usual. It might have something to do with the eagerness to use their new guns, or it might be worse. It might be time. Long enough that they've grown impatient. I need to get her away. Lock away the girl that seems to set me free. Only for protection. That was the goal all along, that I've lost sight of so many times. I'm getting grievously distracted in my only duty that I need to obtain my brother's diligence and constancy. I need focus. There's nothing I need to do now other than what I've done since the beginning. Protect my girl. Sierra Genieva.

She assumes we're not going home the instant we take a new turning. There's nobody around. People remind me of insects sometimes, the way they scatter and scurry back to safety when there's danger in the streets. Humans didn't evolve to run, they evolved to conquer.

In spring, like now, and summer the leaves hang from the trees and conceal my strategies, but it rains less. Logically they should be greener in autumn and winter when it rains the most, but I never listened to my father talk to us about nature. I found it pointless, it's indolent to thirst for peace when there's so much energy, action and intensity to drink up beyond grass and flowers. Come November onwards, I guess the darker and colder months need green. It'd be helpful to make the world realise it's not supposed to be hibernating. Darkness doesn't mean you don't get out. The cold doesn't mean you pull on another blanket. If the world challenges you, embrace it.

Visitors from Colmoor being here, is a challenge. Sierra not knowing the danger she's in as she jumps puddles, and spins in the streetlight, adds more to the undercover fun. I'll take her to the Southbank, where there'll be us alone, with people and places around. It's the safest, closest, and our destination. Sierra reaches the wall that borders the Thames before I do, itching to peer over the concrete, raising her feet off the floor to lean over. My thumb runs straight into the belt loop on her jeans to bring her back down to earth. She's content to rest her head on the ledge. Ignoring her disdain for hygiene, I turn to the view, my companion from the first day we stepped into the capital.

I attribute the sparkle in her eyes to anger nearly all of the time. Each time I'm not the man she expects of me, each time I prevent what she wants from us happening, I make her head declare battle. Her conscience grinds against her long-term love and short-term frustration, and brings stoppage to the affection she shows me. I have to keep it that way. Grenades explode in her mind, flashing, bright and nuclear, and her eyes are a direct window to the crusade I've caused. She doesn't know I see the hurt. She doesn't know I'd stop it if I could. She doesn't know that stopping it, loving her, kissing it all away, could be the death of us. Our mortality, and our life together, even if love is beyond what we can call it.

This might be the first glint I've seen that is a peace treaty. A negotiation between her, me and the city to freeze everything except the flowing river, and stop attacking the present with ignorance. I don't take enough time to stop usually because the flashbacks are the understudy of my rigour, and will step in, if I don't keep up to scratch.

London is strange because it has diversity that Colmoor never knew. The types of personalities, the food, the strength, industry, architecture and infrastructure. All the inferences and implications there just by walking. Sneaking around the backstreets, reveals a lot about the city's cryptic history. Skyscrapers live next to monuments that still stand after years. This is a city that was burnt to the ground, was born again from the ashes and rose. I discovered that in a book I read, and it was the last thing I told Sierra before I took my hands away from her eyes and let her absorb her new life. She imbibed the message well. I hear her whisper it to herself in front of the mirror in the mornings. On the day we broke from Colmoor, she became a phoenix taking flight, clutching the opportunity to sing freely as her own almost as immediately as we got here and in the days that have since ensued, she soars with elegance. I can't deny my love for the power of this city, it is the first love I have felt that has brought me no harm, and poses no ephemerality. I will love London forever for it has delivered two travellers from a lonely and lachrymose place.

Sierra looks out over the Thames, her head in a sad tilt. She feels me staring and says, "It's not quite the same as the sea."

There are parts of Colmoor she remembers. The pretty parts, not the painful ones. I helped her avoid as much of the morbidity as possible, and it worked, because out of everything, the coast is what sticks with her. "You sound disappointed." I feed back into the conversation she wants.

"Not disappointed as much as I'm mesmerised by it." She explains wistfully.

"It might do you well to notice that London has one thing the beach doesn't." I go to her, and pull her in tight from behind, pressing my palms to her heart. It's romantic to her, but the real reason is that we're not safe yet. They could be anywhere, there could be more of them and I need to be a shield. She's entirely encased by me should anything try to hurt her from afar. My muscles have always known to prepare to take bullets. I murmur a phonetical nothingness, a hint of fervour, into her hair to encourage her to speak. It's not a question, but I'm hoping the similarity will show her I'm breaking down some boundaries to be able to make this night what she needs. What I need to stay in her sights.

"A heartbeat…"
"A pulse," I correct her, "An adrenal pulse."

Her head tips back onto my shoulder. My heart and the moon are full. It's heavy but wonderful, like a satiated stomach. I know the liaisons of life with love though, and it's not too long before an empty ache will arise to eclipse what we have. I'll see the light again, when the sun comes up, and I'll know I can't be with her. I should stop now, for I'll keep letting her down in a domino effect if I don't stop falling for her when the night clouds my sensibilities. My tight hold on her loosens, by a fraction. My head is saying let go, but at the sound of a distant crash, my instinct holds her closer before my heart has had a chance to confer. I need to keep talking so the culpability doesn't creep in, "What I really mean, Sierra, is people. Lives everywhere you look."

"There's a word for that, Isaak. I read about it somewhere-"

"The waves, watch them. Imagine they're shuddered by the aftershocks of the fame in this city. You." I find myself meaning every word, no matter how much it severs my throat to know I won't mean them come sunrise.

Turning around, she holds my forearms rigidly so I can't leave her side, regardless of the fact I never planned to. It's beguiling, being face to face. When she had her back to me, I couldn't see what I was doing to the emotions inside of her, now I can read my prophecy starkly in those crystal eyes. I haven't chronicled yet how close our bodies are, and for how long. We've never been this close, this long, when time wasn't a third party before. I'm not missing its presence. There's an ambulance, and blue lights rebound off the rippling water further up the bank, but I don't feel an admonition that I should be following them. I don't want danger. I want to stand here next to her. I'm going to need to stop at a hospital on the way home, and request a godforsaken lobotomy - rip out this bloody love disease I'll tell them, I don't care how much it costs. If you can find the guilt whilst you're at it, rip that out too.

"Sonder." she indicates, unannounced. I couldn't even tell by her body or her breath that she was about to talk. Her words, or singular, make no sense, but then again, I was snapping in and out of my medical syllabus. I let her explain, I'm too busy thinking about scalpels and surgeries that could remove the desire in my veins.

"The sense that everyone has a life as deep and complex as your own. I'm going to make it into your life Isaak, I promise you, however fickle your masquerade, however scared the real you is of this happening to us. I know there's love in that capricious shell of yours."

If anyone else attributed me to the term 'capricious shell' then there'd be trouble, but when she says it, it just makes my mouth twitch up into a knowing smile. "You can just say you want another kiss. Trying to trick me into an argument isn't the only way." I say, catching her halfway into whatever she was trying to do. I'm not sure I'm ready to deal with the explosives that will come with another kiss, but I sure as hell don't want to ruin this moment with another petty debate, especially as I need to maintain this safety net.

"I want another kiss," she mumbles into my neck, and then has a change of heart and says it confidently, right to my face, "Isaak, I want another kiss."

Her eyelids flutter and chin tilts up, as I move my wrist to cup her ear, bringing her so close. I don't expect her breath to be so cold. The only breath I've ever felt is my own, warm when I run, and hot when I wake up in darkness, in the middle of the night, from the flashbacks. "And I want to take you home. Take my hand." Still with the tips of our noses touching, her hand slips into mine, and I'm surprised my body allows it. If exasperation could talk, it'd be screaming. From Sierra's open lips.

As we walk home, we're away from the main street, less cooking cuisine means the air gets colder. The hospital we pass is tempting, with the needs of earlier still drumming in my head, but with her hand in mine, I can't convince myself to tear away. It's embarrassing to think about offering her my coat, it's covered in all the muck from the drains I've crouched next to, all the dirt I've mutilated, and all the places I've hidden. Though tonight is about overcoming inhibitions apparently, and so I wrestle off the sleeves, keeping one arm in a subtle protective arch around Sierra. I'm left walking, voluntarily, in a single jumper as she wears two coats. I wish the equation stopped there, but I can hear three sets of footsteps.

I flick through every memory of today. I imagine our apartment, with its grandfather clock, abundance of books, the fortress that is Sierra's bed, and the kitchen counter that has seen so many breakfasts. The kitchen counter with its empty canister of coffee granules. Please say she noticed. "Sierra, it's the perfect night for a coffee." I insinuate.

She smiles, rubbing the back of my hand, and taking the bait as planned. "I can't agree more, but we don't have any left."

"Run into the shop. I'll wait." I encourage, pushing money into her pocket. The third footsteps get louder, but they won't hurt her if she's bathed in the glitching porch light of the newsagents. As she navigates the shop, she looks up and down the aisles and shelves with her face smothered in her scarf which she won't take off even though the nights are starting to get warmer. It's a wonder how she can see between that and her hair, but I'm not adverse to her taking her time. Whilst smiling at her, flourishing the delusion that everything remains typical of a late evening walk, I have to speak through gritted teeth.

"Get...lost..." I mutter to the shadow that has stopped and is waiting four paces away from me, out of view of Sierra. A sensible choice. What's not sensible is that they don't move when told to. I reiterate, whilst continuing to send Sierra a comforting expression, "I said...get away from here. Now. Don't make me list all the things I could do to you."

The figure steps forward once, unnervingly normal and unthreatening, revealing a skinny frame and deep voice. It isn't long before his words make up for it. "The list of what I could do to her," he says, nodding in Sierra's direction, "is, equally as long."

I feign a laugh. "You wouldn't even get to number one. If I were you, I'd leave before I make certain your legs are so broken, you'll have to crawl back to Colmoor. Don't give me a reason to hurt you."

"Tell me, Alessandro, have you ever failed before?" Sierra's paying at the desk. I need to end this transaction before she walks innocently into harm's way and I'm taking no chances because I know he has a gun on him, I can tell by the way he's stood, and the narrow way he has to walk. She's distracted talking, so I use the window to turn to the soldier. It becomes obvious why he travels between the shadows, he's got a horrific purple bruise spanning the width of his face. I wasn't the first rebel to meet him it seems. If I sported a bruise that ugly, I wouldn't want to show myself either. I'm desperate to joke, but it's dangerous territory. I would taunt him if Sierra wasn't in the premises. I made a disingenuous compromise. "You won't get the satisfaction from a fight now. It's too easy. How you kill us will be the story you take back to them. It'll be your legacy in Colmoor forever. If you're going to do one stupid thing, above all stupid things, try not to do a half-assed job of it."

"Fine." He agrees. "You'd better hope you mean that, otherwise it'll have bad consequences."

"I'm not scared."

"For her," he finishes.

"Isaak?" A gust of central heating from the shop hits me as she opens the door, and then she darts within proximity enough for me to resume caring for her. She raises the coffee like a trophy. I don't need to look behind me to know that the imposter is gone, I can't smell blood, sweat or weakness anymore. All I can smell is the perfume that films Sierra's wrists, and the proleptic sting of coffee. In a manner of ways, including the promise that I'll not leave the apartment again tonight, I convince Sierra to walk circles around the block to indulge in the last ever moment the Earth will ever experience this calendar date, and with that justification, I can wait several more moments for coffee.

She's so lost talking to me about how the world will never be the same today as it was yesterday, and as it will be tomorrow, that I can steer her into three right turns and register no footsteps without her noticing, or questioning. The state I like things in. Non-interrogative. Rolling on our own courses, that like tonight, might overlap when it suits.

Wanting to please me, she sets straight for the kitchen the instant we enter the apartment, not stopping to take off either of her two coats or shoes to hit the kettle. She only sheds her layers when she has prepared for the boiling water with a cup, a heap of coffee and a teaspoon, and there is nothing else for her to do until it's ready. Which means she ends up going to change, mixing coffee in her pyjamas, stirring up the drink as well as something inside me as her shoulders edge bare from her vest straps, and I see more of her than I think I can handle. I need to take my coffee and retreat to my room. To sign off as Alessandro as I did long ago, and just until morning, sign off as Isaak. To shut down and act only as a placeholder for my absent thoughts, for as long as it takes to forget everything that has happened since the last time I woke up. I pray that Sierra and her soul looking so tormentingly beautiful will succumb to dementia as I sleep. The only issue being, my dreams don't let me forget a thing. Tomorrow's aurora will come, and she will still be beautiful.

CHAPTER XVII: SAVE

Sebastian.

I don't want to talk about one half of today, so I'll begin with the other half. I'll explain as my head scrambles to recover. Recover. Recover. Here goes, the perfect half of a broken chain of events, starting and ending with Betsy, the perfect half of me. I've still only kissed her once, to savour the single special moment. I could have kissed her again, I could have kissed her all night, no questions asked, copying principle from Alessandro, but I don't want to overdose on her. I can't risk making the memory of that first kiss overwritten. If I could save only one memory from amnestic peril, that'd be the one, with all the heat of her skin and the fragility of the gaze we shared. The first time I've felt that Betsy has allowed herself to abdicate control. The fact she gave herself up to me in particular, is nothing short of a privilege.

Time for bed didn't arrive last night. I kissed her, and then the impact of what I'd done and what it meant kept me up. She lay awake with me, not tired enough to sleep either, with her skin still glistening where my lips left their signature. A part of us always has to touch each other if we're going to continue without words, at first it's just our index fingers interlocking, but then I cup her waist and pull her to me.

"Do you remember much about your father?" Betsy asks out of the blue, looking up at me through the silver moon's reflection in her eyes.

"More than Alessandro chooses to. His reality is more dark fantasy. That's the consequence of trying to forget, so I just let it happen."

At this, she nods with understanding, trying to fold into me more as if our hearts will fuse. Once the silence sets in, I tune into our hearts and they're beating out of sync. I've never tried willing my blood out of its natural rhythm, to meet the pattern of another's. My mind is proud and my heart is madly percussive to be alone, and infatuated, with Betsy.

There's a topic we haven't touched on yet. Her sister, Sierra, what she is like and what she can do. There is much to say. Betsy delights in the fact that like myself, she is a twin, and I decide not to tell her, right now at least, of the challenges a reflection with its own will and way can present. Although I don't see Betsy and Sierra having tension like Alessandro and I. They've got joy to cover their journey apart from each other.

She's done her research too, as much as she could, and I'm thankful for it. It means there's less to explain in the way of technicalities. She knows the basic principles. Every woman in Colmoor has a talent, it is genetic, and forbidden. By powers of deduction, she knows she must have her own.

I start objectively. "Sierra is a singer. Wanted to do nothing more with her life than sing and be heard, so my brother took her to the city."

"The city?" It's amazing how limited this small excuse of a town can make ambition and knowledge.

"London. It's a runaway's playground. Alessandro is devoted to it, and devoted to your sister, but he's yet to admit that to anyone. He can't help that it's written all over his face. Sierra sings there, in halls, to people. Everybody knows her voice."

Worry rushes over Betsy, I can feel concern and safety on her mind just by laying a hand to her rosy cheek. She doesn't want to learn her sister is dead, moments after she learns she has one. I dealt my best hand at reassuring her.

"I wouldn't be here if I didn't trust Alessandro to protect her."

Trusting me, that familiar spark bounces back. "Nonsense Seb, you're here because you can't stand to be away from me." I know where these boomerang emotions are coming from. How can you get attached to someone you've never known, just because they're family? She wouldn't have cried for Sierra, if she never knew she existed. I begin to doubt my actions, but then I look at the woman looking back at me. She is old enough to understand, maturity years beyond her youth, maturity beyond my own. It has to be now, because if not, it'll keep being tomorrow until tomorrow doesn't arrive. I only laugh off her comment, because I can't contest the truth.

She blinks whilst I'm chuckling, feelings flipping for a third time. I've never seen exploration and curiosity for what they truly are, such a comprehensive and convoluted process. I'm relishing how it colours her face. She's trying to navigate a lifetime with a map she's had for mere minutes. I'll be her compass, until she's satisfied. With me, she'll never find herself lost again, she's been in that darkened place before and I want to make sure any direction she walks is waiting for her with open arms. Anywhere she walks she will be welcome. Anywhere she walks she has my protection. Finally, she speaks. "I had heard talents were hereditary. That means I can sing too?"

"That's why I'm here, sweetheart." I whisper sincerely, but sneaking my hand down to her hip again, pushing gently until she's underneath me. Her waist is easy to manoeuvre, which makes me think she's allowing me to move her. "I'm here to stop you singing. It's proved incredibly taxing so far, with all the melodies you insist on belting out every moment of the day."

Off the back of the sarcasm, our mouths break into smiles, hers demanding another kiss, but I've at long last found the strength to resist the orders. She only has herself to blame for that. I know my resistance from brass temptations, her eyes, her golden hair, her sand-coloured skin, will be worth it, to treasure her ruby lips when the time comes. I'm an adventurer, a voyager, I don't take the facile road. "Seb, seriously, do you think I can?" she breathes.

"Mhm. You've got that sort of manner about your voice when you speak. That, and you'd defy the evolutionary science of our community if you couldn't." Only at the end of the sentence do I notice that she's been looking at my mouth as I spoke, with a blank, dreamy look. I move the conversation on. "Can you try?"

She fumbles over some notes. Then, it occurs to me. How do you sing when you've never heard a song? For most it's like breathing, albeit in tune, but Betsy has never had that instinct. I can't fault her oblivion, I fault Colmoor, as one more misdemeanour on this town's reputation is barely noticeable anymore. I try to encourage her. "It can be about anything you like."

She smiles, readying herself, working out which ligaments move at her bidding, and which of them have connections with the command she already has over her voice. Clearing her throat she asks, "Can it be about you?"

I give the honest answer, as is customary. "If I make your heart sing." At this, she looks me in the eyes, as I continue, "The only rule is passion."

"Then no more needs to be said." Her subtext tells me how much there is to let the song take over. Stringing together her thoughts, she tries to make the words make sense, getting more confident as she sings. I don't consider how it's not perfect, she's not trained, there's techniques she hasn't had the means to adapt to. I'd argue that rawness is the perfection learned people seek but never reach. The standalone impression I get, having heard Sierra sing on rare occasions when I'm circling London, is that there's something in Betsy's voice that her sister doesn't have. An edge, a soul, a natural ache. True pain. It translates inimitably, and this is the moment that I know I'm in love. I am in love with her, and try as I might now, it will never not be her. I am utterly in love and a fool in that it has taken me so long to name it. I've tossed around love, searching for a definition, but I have found it now. Because of her and her song, I will never be clueless again, her music is my meaning. I love Betsy Genieva.

It gets better. I think she might love me. I don't act without evidence, speak without substantiation, so allow me to present the lyrics in question that she sings for me, in a night nobody else can hear, an auditory euphoria:

There's a way you saved me, touched my soul. A gentleness, my body thought I'd never know. I'm indebted to you, my unexpected heartbeat. Thank you for being the reason I lose, and safely, sleep.

This concludes the beautiful half of the day, and that's when time twists into mayhem and I will never be able to retrace the steps that caused the loss of this reality forever. I suggested we go to the town. For adventure. For adrenaline. In hindsight, out of sheer stupidity, and naivety to the fact I'm still being hunted. Alessandro would wince at my momentary drop in conscience. There was a reason, we needed food, and we can't keep living from the nutrients that the forest provides because we'll eat all the good until all that's left is poison. I should have gone alone and left her here but I don't do things my brother's way. I can't deny her from darkness anymore, we are equals and our tortured past is something we have to embrace as one.

We walked to the epicentre of this cultural madness, all the way there I taught her how to walk tactfully, unnoticed, with silent steps. I think she's getting it. Betsy is a quick learner, which is essential when you treat every day spontaneously - she's absolutely the woman I want to take along for the ride of life with me, in fact, sometimes I think she leads the way. Until she stops dead still. We haven't entered the main square yet, it seems too early for her to get cold feet, but I silently pledge that if she's scared, I'll walk her straight back to the treehouse and return again to feed her. I never get to reach the end of that thought process, because whilst I've been thinking, I've been tracking her eyes, predicting and plotting our next move. We aren't going to move for a while, because something else slithers, with a skin-crawling tap, tap, tap. This time the repetitions aren't in my head, they're on the stones. I swore the repetitions couldn't jump outside of my mind but they manifest here, and Betsy swore that Arlen was dead.

How am I so sure of it, that I can match a name to a figure? I watch Betsy's face. I watch the scathing trauma relight in her eyes, a mixture of retrospect and redemption, with deep-seated lesions of distrust and innocent fear. Arlen is elderly now, as if he wasn't already in her memories. She's terrified of him. More than she ever made out to be. I'm not. I want to kill him. I'd kill him and it'd take one heartbeat. How dare he ruin her. How dare he rob my Betsy of a childhood. I want to strangle him threefold for every finger he ever laid on her neck. I've seen the scars, and now I want him to pay. I want him to burn.

"Don't." Betsy hisses, not easing my anger, but stopping the impulse in an instant. Damn the way she knows me. There's a limit to my control though. My love for her and the way my fists curl for justice are representing the divorcing of my sanity from my fury. Betsy does exactly as I teach her, and I do the opposite. She sneaks past Arlen, I'm in admiration for how she can stalk alongside the embodiment of her adolescent shackles. I watch him sniffing at his surroundings, an olfactory sixth sense for his prisoners. He attempts to hobble after her as she circuits the corner, darting out of view, her splaying skirt pleats the last of her I see. Arlen's head cocks, trying to figure out her face, rifling through the victim portfolio that's stashed in his withered brain.

My elbow catches his neck from behind. Spluttering, his cane clatters to the dirt, the tap, tap, tap ceasing. His thin arms flail like branches trying to grab at nothing, wondering how the world can change in the space of nine minutes, and not in his favour. I plead with the world to not let Betsy turn back around that corner, she doesn't need to see this because I almost think that having seen her, Arlen's gestures call for Betsy to save him. The subversion, the role reversal of predator to prey, is audacious of him, and unluckily for the old man, only enrages me more. I've never held someone so close to death before, with this much wrath coursing in my veins. "Don't you fucking dare. Do all but look at her, and I will make sure nobody will ever remember your name for anything else but what you are. A sadistic, inhuman pervert."

"And you are?" He croaks.

"The end of you. If I ever see your fucking face again." I don't feel my usual post-conflict mercy for this abuser, and I permit him all of ten seconds to get lost, not bothering awarding him the coldness of a stare. He deserves nothing. I step around the corner to reunite with my love, the one who deserves everything except the way Arlen defiled her.

I remember seeing the place we were going to search for food, but we never made it there, and that's what makes the end of the day so horrific - that we were so close to nothing happening at all. There is sometimes animation in Colmoor, of the children that run around in the streets, enjoying the limited freedom they have until they show intelligence enough to undertake Jasper's orders. Hence, all the littles I can see must be around six years old, and I suddenly become very aware of my height, my age, the way I've progressed from being so vulnerable into a protector, as is life's metamorphosis. I'm thankful I got rid of Arlen when I did, the threat of him around these children is unthinkable, but what's harder to process is that these children, a scrawny blue-eyed one in particular, would be the cause of destruction. They draw attention to themselves, acting erratically, playing with their imagination like they don't know they're in a place where you simply can't do that. Jasper's spies could be around you, at any point, and if that's the case, you don't want to be the one standing out. Being of a certain age doesn't make them any more lenient, if they want you, they will take you. Betsy seems to share my concern. She dashes me a look without a word - where are this child's parents? Everyone is well aware of what will happen to those who are different.

I see others looking around now. At the child. At me. I hear murmurs, delusional rumours. I need to leave, but Betsy is alert and steady, like a watchman on duty. Every time we have needed to move from danger today, Betsy has remained still, and I need to make her walk. I can't quite get to grips with this girl, perhaps trauma inhibits the instinct to run. I stand closer to her, under my breath breezily whispering, "I know you're used to this, but I'm with you now. I'm targeted. We need to move."

Numbly, she shakes her head, "You go ahead. I need to stay. I'll come and find you, Seb." I don't like this. I knew creating distance between us was a gullible idea, but I know Betsy enough to understand how her plans are fixated, and she will respond to nothing I say if she is certain of her actions. Lightly and affectionately nipping her hand with my thumb and forefinger, a silent goodbye, food becomes my new direction. Until I take the bread in my arms, the fruit hanging from my teeth to carry them, and head back to her. I am lucky that Colmoor shopkeepers are there to do a job only. Given how many imbeciles and criminals stalk the area, they never look up from their desks and never ask questions - which is handy for me, a wanted man.

I've worked out what happened from then onwards through spending hours deciphering Betsy's gestures. Whilst I had my head turned, the road became the runway for a horse-drawn cart. It was pulled by two large horses with a stocky build, taller than me, ferrying Jasper's men across the town to destroy livelihoods. Jasper doesn't patrol himself now that he's in his sixties, instead he gets easily influenced men to undertake his dirty work.

Transport isn't permitted for the rest of us, which is how I know the carriage carried someone vile. The speed of the animals barrelling down the narrow path, with houses on either side, is what she saw to begin with. What she was looking out for from the beginning. Arguably, although now I can only guess this, why she spent so much unnecessary time in a town of prosperity thieves, to protect the children whose parents weren't around to protect them themselves. Oftentimes, it ends safely. All the time, even. Nobody gets hurt. It's never ended in chaos before, and this time was the curse.

The carriage hurtled exponentially and Betsy knew there was no chance for the child without her interference, and her intrusion saved the blue-eyed boy from possessing a single scratch. She was the difference in the rest of his life, and the prevention of his early death. That transaction happened swiftly and harmlessly, it wasn't the first time she'd done it, but it was the first time her skirt had been caught. It was taken by the first wheel, and to protect herself and her dignity, Betsy threw herself towards the axis to unfasten herself, which she managed somewhat successfully. Somewhat, being that the force of the acceleration swung her body like a rag doll right back around until she can't motor her limbs to do anything against the wind that whips her. The ordeal lasts seconds, but for her racing heart it's more. I can't bear to think about the next details. I have to speak through them slowly.

As she was spun helplessly, away from the carriage, her skirt still remained entangled and her hand was urgently trying to prise the material away. They provided a pivot, and the momentum threw her straight to the wooden body of the carriage. A rusting nail protrudes at a crooked angle. She sees it and can do nothing. The whole time she screams, and this is what I hear, as I try to get to her. The food is lost, the horse's hooves' pound, and her blood is all I see as the nail sinks deep into her neck and severs the skin, clicking against bones and cartilage, and ripping the existing scar tissue open again from side to side. As the nail has nothing left to catch on, the horses turn a corner and she is dropped from the charging vehicle. I reached her instantly. The orders aren't there, replaced with exclamations and panic. Shit. Shit. *Fuck.* I refuse to lose her.

I pull her straight onto my lap, immediately grabbing my sleeve to pull apart at the seams and wrap around her.

Red leaks through it. It's not enough. Blood is sputtering from her neck, whilst I remind her to focus on survival. Try to breathe, and find something that is marvellously irrelevant to the pain, whilst I work. I'm not letting her die. What she decides to focus on is the parents of the child, who have just returned from the direction of the graveyard and now it all makes sense. Happily, they reunite, and Betsy knows she has done an angel's exertion. She wants to die knowing that, but I won't give her the freedom of death whilst I still have fight, and love for her, inside me. Incredulously, with a slashed neck, and what looks like a broken wrist clasping my shoulder, she is still trying to speak.

I try to stop her. "Betsy, I've never once ordered you to do anything, ever in my life, ever in the time I've spent knowing you, but please for the love of everything good darling, shut up. I will fix you. I swear to you." She doesn't listen. Of course, she doesn't bloody listen.

With every small movement of her trying to talk, more blood pulses from her, bubbling, spurting, spilling onto my chest. There is so much crimson I can't tell where the wounds begin and end. If she won't listen, I'll ask my father. If you have any power up there, stop her talking, please. Please. Please. Her speaking is whistling. Thankfully still through her mouth, but it sounds as though there are holes straight through her neck to her windpipe. Not to mention her breathing is all wrong, that's not how humans should work. That's not how she worked this morning. The world can change so much. Her eyes shift from scared to determined, I see the physical alteration. "Sebas." She croaks. "Sebastian." My full name.

Not Seb, not a diminutive. Her last word is my birth name. My eyes are starting to tear and I can't stop them. There's only one thing I know. I will not let her die on me. I understand what my name means now. It means, 'I'd love you in full if I could have done. Every word would have been spoken to you if it could have been. I love all of you and I hope that is enough.'

   She will always be enough, and yet she still tries again. Air wheezing from her bruised vocal cords. Her lips move together and apart but nothing. No name. Her last ever word was Sebastian.

CHAPTER XIX: TRUST

Isaak.

I have done the unthinkable. I have expanded outside of Colmoor's regressive constraints, and been a hypocrite to Sierra. I have bought a phone. One for Sebastian too. I need a lifeline as the stakes begin to inch beyond control, maybe the Gray brothers together can suppress it enough to escape with our girls. The strength of us both. The love for Betsy and Sierra. Our hate for Colmoor. Working together never seemed like an option, but now it's presenting itself as our only choice.

Sierra's telescope provides a clear red radar around the concert area. I walked her there. I'll walk her back. In the meantime, she'll be safe, I'm taking no chances. A principle my father always tried to encourage was a strong and sharp memory, you never know when you'll need information, but unfortunately alongside all the data I'll never need, is all the darkness I can't forget. And a single phone number. Sebastian will have the right words. The right advice. He makes things seem even, after we've overcome the odds. The dial tone vibrates in my hand.

When Sebastian, this time, doesn't start the conversation I know he's either not quite worked his way around the technology, or been affected by something grave between now and the last time we spoke. After hearing everything, probing it from him with my silence, not questions, never questions, I piece his fragility together. I can't fix him, but unlike anyone else, I can complete him. He is genetically my equal when I don't operate to standard, and for the first time ever, I am part-Sebastian when he can't function. He needs that time to process. Killing with morals, witnessing justified death - doesn't compare to seeing the blood of a lover.

It's a twin trait to be competitive. For everything I do, he is a step ahead, and now that I have news, he has more. I have no doubt now, my brother is stronger. I struggle with reigning in my emotions, he struggles to have them, the short straw is in his hand. How he can see anyone hurt like that, let alone the woman who has just lent him her voice, is beyond comprehension. How he can't express the pain, as much as he tries, is concerning. This call has taken up a higher priority, because if Sebastian isn't whole, it means Betsy isn't safe. "No." My brother sighs. "Explain."

"She can't talk." Applying the evidence to the conversation, on repeat, won't help. We can't heal the past or the injuries. I feel as though he's slightly gathering a point from the way he's breathing down the line. "Meaning, she can't sing. She's safe."

"You're not, they're still after you." I remind him. "That's easier to handle. You can pull your hand away from a match that burns you. You can't control somebody else's muscle memory."

His analogical train of thought is always on fire. It must hurt to be in his head, I've never acknowledged that being a half of one another might mean we share the pain of Father and Mother in different ways. I feel the guilt from not taking time to know Father whilst he was here in body, Sebastian feels the gap where Father used to be. We both mourn Mother the same, a name on paper, the impression Father conjured. We love her like folklore, detached, in denial, but like a legendary fable that meanders around us as time moves on. Teaching us through interpretation. The musing what she'd be thinking if she saw us.

I can hear his voice seize when I address him by name, and it's not clear what I've done or why it's hurting him. I don't pry. Even though my version of events seems far more inferior, in comparison to Sebastian's, we must tell each other everything. I can't wait much longer to tell him, or I'll know I'll back out and say nothing at all. Then he'll curse me for secrecy.

"I kissed her." I say breezily, trying to pass off something that made me feel so hot inside, as a cold nothing. There's no fooling my brother, and he stays quiet, waiting for the catch. This'll be the first time I disclose this information, the real reason I kissed her, the thing that made love stumble into danger's dominion. It wasn't entirely a stumble. I was on the way down as it was. The soldier from my run-in outside the shop earlier, was behind Sierra as I kissed her. Ready to take her. Salty at my ability to be where he doesn't want me and where she needs me, and Sierra never noticed. "It was either kiss her or let her wander straight to a soldier. There's one I can't shake at the moment, by the looks of it, he's been hard done by, by somebody else. Explains the sourness."

"I'm going to need to know what *hard done by* means in this context, AG. There could be someone after him, after you. Especially if he's followed you without permission." I hate the desperation my brother has for details, but it's all relevant. So, I tell him about the height, the snarky nature, and lastly the facial discolouration and shallowness. All things he'd want to know, in that order: what to look out for, a personality trait, and what makes one viper distinguishable from another. Important when there's so many of them out for us. In response, Sebastian's voice gets quick and breathy. "Warner."

A traitor we know by name is rare. Incredibly rare. This is the first time it has ever happened. Someone Sebastian calls by their full name is even rarer than that. We always know they're coming but are usually only introduced once we're face to face. Most often, we wish they'd spare us the foreword, so the anonymity can speed up the killing.

"AG, check your surroundings. Check SG. Make sure nobody is around, that one is…that one is something else." He continues to panic. It is difficult to believe he is my brother sometimes. Thinking over Sierra and her safety is all I've been doing this evening, looking at her empty bed through the window, through the slit in the curtain. I'm on the balcony, she's performing, but as soon as she returns there and sleeps peacefully, we will be safe. Sebastian worries more than he should, I have dealt with soldiers, I can deal with one more. Still, I take a courteous glance down into the street. Nothing, not even shadows masquerading as people. Nothing is awry tonight. Except my twin, but he's an exception.

The line goes dead when Sebastian is mid-debrief, the discernible fear of Warner in his voice saying more than his words actually do. Bloody battery. We only get one life each, yet phones and cats reap all the benefits of multiple. I don't think I'd like to live more than one, I want to give all that I've got to this life now. Living again would mean loving again, and it will have to be Sierra right now or not loving at all. My solitary mind used to drift to the city when alone, so it intrigues me that I'm missing her presence in her bed, and not caring for the lights that extend miles behind me. I'm concerned for my brother, still checking my tablet for Sierra. Then, it starts to rain. The sky understands, and cries so I don't have to. I have more important things to do. Matters of life or death.

If I sit, I'm only postponing the action. Bringing the soldiers to me, risking Sierra's safe place. My plan is to leave, catch them off guard. Find this Warner before he finds me, before he reaches her. Locking the balcony door once on my way out is not sufficient, I double lock to be certain, although I know if they're desperate they'll break glass. They've done it before. Smashed glass. Karian. Blood. My father. The funny feeling encases my head again, putting pressure on my eardrums from the inside out. Odd what can be a trigger, but flippancy will not recover me. I'm too far gone. It's happening quicker and quicker each time. The flashbacks melting my focus, I need to be the barbed wire around Sierra to keep out those that trespass against her and I can't fucking think.

My brain feels like it's vibrating, and instead of striding out of the door with confrontation my only aim, I stumble to the sofa and force my head into a cushion trying to transfer the hallucinations that are topping up my head, somewhere else. Just somewhere else, to tie them down to the sofa, so I can concentrate. Concentrate on protecting her, and pushing away the imposing and advancing battalion that is the thousand evils festering in Warner's fractured smile.

I'm still holding the tablet, but it's slipping from me, her light flashing red, red, red. The colour of love. The colour of danger. The colour that tells me, Alessandro, you can't stay here whilst she's still out there. The voice in my head is deeply resemblant of Sebastian's. I know he's right but I'm in another reality right now, one that has already passed me. My father, lifeless, up against the bed frame, whitening stripes in the flesh of his back from being pressed so hard up against the headboard to escape the fire of the gun. He must have tried to dodge the bullets, but he was the one that told us that the force doesn't wait until you're tired, or compliant. This must have been why they grabbed him, clamping their hands around his cheeks to force the gun between his teeth, cock it, and shoot, before we could reach him. I heard the screams. Sebastian told me to wait until morning. I wanted to leap out of bed and be by my father's side as he died, but I would have run straight to the soldiers, offering myself up as a sacrifice. Now I know it would have been an instant death, both my father's and mine.

The flashback this time is the horrible morning, like an antagonistic sunrise, walking into father's eyes wide open, covered in a cloudy film. An imprint of his alarm, captured like a photograph. The blood, pus, mucus where his body couldn't heal itself. The chunks of brain matter. The awful silence that let the moment be unorthodoxly unbearable, and then the ringing. The sounds. The chimes I've tied, in a neural way, to terror. The masses and floods of red. Everywhere. Still.

But the singular red pulse is moving. Sierra. The danger. The moment. There's opportunity now to leap, rehabilitation for a dead father, and nobody to tell me no this time, because of a blessed dead phone.

I'm barely two steps from the apart lobby when Warner unfolds from the shadows, back pressed up against a dark wall and his arms crossed. The rain that still descends from the heavens is dripping silkily down his wounded skin. He's too happy as he saunters over. The air hangs, holding its breath, the light around us dim. There's a chance he's returned for the fight I suggested he suspend. My fists curl. Completely ignorant, he walks past my side, uneasily close. "I've walked a full square." He raises an eyebrow at me, expecting me to be impressed, and when I'm not, he starts again, spouting his cryptolect. "I've been counting windows."

I've realised he's not blinking much. It's borderline psychotic. He wants my death more than I thought, he demands it, circling me standing like he wants my body on the ground. He won't stop talking to me, but he's not picking a fight. "Do you know what that means Alessandro?"

I stay silent. He snatches it up. "Ah," his face breaks into a smile, "Your brother said you weren't a fan of questions." At this, my eyes darted to him, studying a man that's met my brother, my sights a little blurred by the flurrying raindrops. A man who my brother appears to have trusted, it explains why he was so afraid. Thinking it through gives me no answers right now. Warner is still prowling. "It means that it's only a matter of time until I find the right one."

There's some concealment to his manner that makes me cold on the inside, the sort of freeze where the goosebumps operate your body so you're a robot of yourself. The chill where you have to walk, or else. It'll take him less than a week to search every apartment. A deadline. I haven't had a deadline for too long. I don't usually schedule the races I partake in, but Warner will be ruthless competition.

There are two types of force members. The first type, those who are reared for a riotous life. Violence, savagery and an innate austerity to end the life of anything that speaks a word against them or their leader. The system raises them like this. They are wasted men from the start.

The second are the helpless, those like my grandfather. Those who didn't join, or leave, by choice. They lack the drive to rebel, but don't inherently want harm. However, they are the more dangerous of the two, for the longer they carry out orders, the less agentic they become, it only needs a year of killing innocent people under false accusations for the technique to rewrite their psyche. They'll kill out of habit, independently, with initiative. They are more dangerous because compassion is something they have learnt to shun, and put away. They are hatred retentive as a cause of self-murdered empathy, they are the reason they are what they are, rather than never having learnt of love like the others, who at a push, or a shove, could be taught. I lie, there are three factions of the force - empty puppets, internalised prisoners and Jasper, the felonious orchestrator of Colmoor.

"I have places to be. Excuse me." I mutter, not caring in the slightest whether he excuses me at all. I'm committed to being anywhere away from him right now, my concern for him is less than my concern for Sierra.

"No matter," Warner says, "I'll walk with you." I've not done my research yet on how to detach bloodthirsty leeches from a practical man, myself in this instance, who has his mind set on other things. On one woman in particular. On the flip side, Warner could have chosen anything to do to me tonight, and he chose to walk - which I do routinely. If he wants to follow me, let him. I can walk into the night and out the other side if I had to. Sierra will just have to wait.

Unsurprisingly, Sierra doesn't have to wait at all, or at least not for very long. After leading Warner to the other side of London, I circled blocks of houses until he sulked away. I didn't see or hear him leave, but once alone, I raced back just in time to catch Sierra walking away from the venue, despondent. She lights up when she recognises my footsteps. A simple apology, and it's like I'd never left her. I've left Warner, though. Out of sight, and out of mind.

I look at her. Really look at her. With updated eyes, for remembering the outlook of Colmoor, has made me analyse and refigure my own attitudes. I have to find the root of my ambitions - and I have whittled it down to two things. Love to maintain. Schema to protect. One will serve me lifelong, if I get it right, the other downgrades as my body gets less able and weary.

I can't gloss over what I called it. Love. A foreign locution. Looking at her, the word love just melded artlessly into this reality. This is how I know I can't run from it like we ran from Colmoor.

I've always had a directional, chronological approach to living - that's how I've organised myself so that I don't miss or mistake anything in my environment. Yet, now I'm starting to realise the importance of evolving my perspective, and looking beyond what I know. It becomes the difference between mastering myself, and making myself. I can be content with the man I am to Sierra, or I can mould the lover I want to be out of protecting and providing for her, and be at my happiest. I am my only obstacle. Not the situation, but my mind's diegesis. That's what has made me subjugate to my brother, the fact his pride and past never stood between him and Betsy whereas I have let mine dictate me.

I want direction, and perspective now gives me a crossroads. I can run in a way I choose, without being mindless about it. I can follow what my caged heart has been saying right from the day I last spoke to my father to the day I searched directories with Sebastian, to the day I met her. Take her with me. I can be wild. I can chase stars. I can put out fires, and light them too, when my duty calls for it. I can't do all of this rotating around the bubble I've kept her in, she has to stand beside me throughout it, come with me, like I knew to be her role from day one. Otherwise, there's no meaning to my mischief, or drive behind my deeds.

Somewhere along the line, I have let the notion of protection blind me to all she has given me from the beginning. Purpose.

Presently, lots of lenses are binding together the events I have endured. In seconds, as I hold her hand, I feel we are facing the future on a shared platform. I walk her home. A home I've made possible for her, in the dream I've accelerated. When she's asleep in bed, bound and wrapped in the duvets and the promise that nothing will ever touch her, I stalk to the living room and push the door to a close. Retrieving my tablet from its privacy, the importance of lenses magnifies, gets larger and larger in my mind - for technology has treated me. I shouldn't have been so quick to judge it. Two lenses. Two red dots on parallel paths that will never meet as long as I'm alive.

CHAPTER XX: ADORE

Sierra.

I wonder how many accumulated hours I've spent holding Isaak accountable for my loneliness when he's nowhere to be seen. I wonder how many minutes I've wasted in Isaak's presence, not taking the opportunity to explore him, to unlock the manacles that tether him to his hollow outlook on love. I wonder if, given this past week's adventures and revelations, now might be my only chance to kickstart his heart. Sierra Genieva, again willingly and parlous, breaks her rules and goes in search of a restricted lover. Third person makes me seem like a protagonist, and not a lowlife making a peasantry crawl to bland and shallow intimacy. Sierra Genieva is unafraid. Except on the inside, where the fear invades, redefining the frontiers of what confidence I thought I possessed. Performing is a breeze, but trying to connect with a loveless statue on my own accord - when I usually follow his lead - is an untrodden step.

Am I wearing something that'll make his head spin with want? It can't matter. He shall have to take me as I am for I'm too far now to return. I worry all courage I summoned will be suppressed if I head too far back to the domestic comfort of my bedroom. I need to find my way to the minimalist, cold cavity that constitutes his bedroom, even though I want to scatter my senses underneath the mat, and drown back into the sleep that just took me hostage. Return to the kidnap, in safety, where intuition and instinct and love won't let me do anything drastic. Sleep stops the urges I feel for Isaak. Sunlight hours let me enjoy them one at a time, through daydreams.

Alas, it is too late. There's a rustling.

"Sierra." The same response every time. He hears my footsteps and my name has become the command to return to where he positioned me until morning, with the hope I'd stay.

I let nothing pass me by. I am not a girl that works on lost opportunities. "I don't care what you say. I'm not making you a coffee. My presence is unconditional, I'm not leaving with any bribe less than a-"
"Come in." He offers.

Impolitely, "Huh?" is what I end up grunting.
"I've denied you once too many times. If you want me, have me. Sit."

I don't know what is happening. I came into this without the weight of submission and I won in some faction of his affection. Weakly, I perch on the cushion beside him. It knocks the air out of me when he reaches around me and hauls me downward. Now I'm lying on Isaak's chest, and it's a mind game. When did our relationship turn horizontal? What did I miss? I'm trying to think what I did or didn't do to cause this. I've rolled the dice and cast a seven. A new turn, a double take.
"Sierra, say you won't leave me."

"It's not in my plans. I had an agenda this evening Isaak, and you've sent it into a whirlwind. You're an ass for it." I put the words out.

"I'm glad I make you dizzy, you wouldn't long for me as much if you were rightly sensible." I think he's joking, but there's a sadness.

I want to ask why I'm on his chest, but he won't answer, things aren't completely different to this morning, he is still resistant. I may have cracked the shell, but cracks won't shatter satisfactorily when inside of them is just empty air. He needs to feel. He might if I stay. So, I wait, and I breathe deeply, and I want him.

It isn't love yet, if it were then I'd know it, but I'm still uneasy. He's rigid with delicate touch; he can move me, manipulate me but when he starts to caress me it's not natural. That's not to say I want to leave, so I do the only thing I know to do to connect. I sing. It's a slow song. A private one. Lyrics written by another person stood invisible in this room, watching over our situation and narrating it, knowing who we are, what this is and where our relationship stands before I understand it myself. For once, Isaak listens without getting restless, relaxing me so the words flow clearer.

"You're sending me messages." He works out, over the sound of my voice. I don't stop singing, protracting the time before the confession. Nevertheless, he touches my arm in rhythm, beating my words, beating with my heart song. All songs have to come to an end, though, then I'm ordained to speak my own words, unable to ride on the coattails of someone else's any longer.

"I just want to know what we are." I whisper, avoiding looking at him. The pads of his fingers still pulse on my shoulder, but now with the tempo of his angst rather than with music.

"You're an artist in a world that's beginning to see colour, and I'm," he hesitates, atypically of him, "more of a rebel than they said." I didn't process this the first time because I was still searching.

"Give me more than that, Isaak, I need to know what we are together."

"We're bound. Neither one of us can live or love to our capacity, together. I restrict you from your full affections, and you restrict me from a simple life." There's a sudden change in tension, a product of his built-up quietude.

It hurts inside me, a nerve struck that I didn't know existed. I am a harp, a violin, an instrument of love that can no longer, and will no longer, be played. He is the cymbal, the snare, the crashing that stalks me from behind, snapping at my ankles and stopping my march forward. I don't want him. With force, I raise myself from his chest, and stumble away from him. The concern in his eyes tries to corner me, and keep me encased in this psychological cell. The door is right there, my day clothes are next door, and there's a world away from this outside, but Isaak's words create a forcefield. To break it, I need answers, which means asking questions.

"More of a rebel, Isaak. What does that mean? Who said that to you?" My anger is scathing, it's gutting me, and I don't care what it's doing to him. "An individual who knows more than I do about you, no doubt, despite my every attempt to be close to you!"

This sparks a new train of thought. Another woman in his life, to explain the nights away, the intense bruises, the constant second-thought format of his actions. I have been blind. He said, *I restrict him from a simple life.* A simple life with another. I won't hold him back from what he wants anymore.

I've been brandishing these thoughts out loud, because he stands up and protests there is nobody else. Liquid lies. They seep out of his mouth, through the floorboards and into the apartments below us. It makes the room damp, and I want to wade through the wasted moments and be on my own. Creatures of deception that I've always known but never accepted swim in the water that Isaak's pleading floods the floor with. If I stay here a moment more I'll go under.

"You underestimate me." That's his only comeback. I don't have to probe, as he keeps going, walking towards me like he's going to reabsorb me into the pain and the repetitive lack of loving. I retreat backwards. "I could leave and I would have done so, if I was involved with another woman."

I'm in a corner. He is close. I don't feel threatened, it's a different feeling. It's a pity for him and all he's lost is his pride. I'll hear him out, then I'm getting out, and putting my foot down for all the times he's let me down. "Then leave." I exhort.

"I'd rather die." His breath on my neck is warm. Then his forehead is on mine. My hand finds its way to the back of his neck, and pulls him forward, onto my lips. There's a second where everything is still, and then I'm kissing him, out of hatred and months of longing. After draining him of the love he hasn't given me, I finally blink open my eyes, and my cheek is wet from a single tear that streams from Isaak's eye.

"We're okay." He breathes through deep panting, with the emphasis on his words sounding so close to a question, but still without the strength to ask in the common way.

"No, Isaak. This is goodbye. Because killing me countlessly then kissing me back to life, is not the way I work." I adjudicate.

"Sierra Genieva..." he begs. I wasn't supposed to hear the, "you're impossible" that followed as I left the room. He's quiet as I get changed, I almost think he's left, but then he's standing in the doorway when I turn to go. Shirtless. Apparently trying every way. I have no interest, until I see his emblazoned skin. A tattoo almost identical to mine.

"Where-" I say, my voice convulsing, "-the fuck did you get that?" He can answer the bloody question before he takes another movement, takes another breath. "Answer me, now, before you have time to think of another lie to spin me."

"I saw yours." He explains, steadily. I'm looking for any trace of a lie, whilst an embarrassed hand pulls my jumper over my waist at the thought of him seeing me naked. "I got it done. I wanted to show you that you are my only temptation. My only love." He stares at the wall, past me.

I tread decisively towards him, my hand slides up his chest, over his abs. I have to crouch to see what he's done to his skin with the ink. It's not identical, on closer inspection, it is the same concept but the lines and dots are messed up. Done in a rush. Loyalty is apparently not worthy of time that is considered, thoughtful and proper to him. Still with my hand pressed against Isaak, I stand up straight, searching in his eyes, building a boundary in my mind.

"You're lying to me. Either that, or you're a poor excuse for a lover. Find someone else to worship from a distance, so they'll never know, like I never knew. Too little too late, Isaak Macaluso. I'm going out. When I get back, I don't want to see you." My blood boils, my heart breaks, and I can't look at him.

I used to see love in his eyes when we first met, even if he didn't say it. Now I see nothing except a man worn down by responsibility he hands unto himself. I grab my coat, but he follows me, sliding his coat over his bare chest so he can chase me into the night.

Each step I take down the staircase echoes. He's shouting my name, tripping over himself to reach me. I turn to him, in a last-ditch attempt to drive his behaviour back to the basics. What we were before London made us cheaters, and he lost his love for me to the city. "You don't like questions. You substitute feelings for facts. I need personal love, sentimental love, love like we used to have where my heart was more than just, like nowadays, a sidelined statistic." I list haphazard ways he's made me feel my worst since we've been here.

His face tells me he didn't know I felt that way, but it is implausible. We exist in each other's space. It is inconceivable that he doesn't know how his behaviour affects me. I hate this conversation. It's making doubts creep in, making me ask myself if I'm overreacting and if I've just taken out my loneliness on a man who despite his flaws, has always been there. Always, but incrementally, periodically. Always, but not all the time. I stop. If hands could extend from his stony eyes to restrain me and keep me close, they would.

"You just can't accept feelings without there being a reason. Love without condition. That's all I want." I accuse, and wish, through a murmur, unsure of anything. My fight or flight hormones are still churning, using up far more energy than I have to spare.

"If this has anything to do with that night on the beach, you're still gorgeous. I called it a fact because I was too afraid to admit that it was more than that. It was a feeling." Isaak resolves, and with his words, that night comes flooding back. A mixture of music and the moon, and nothing beyond our relationship mattered. Now, everything matters except it. Still, he remembers. Yet because I can't send us back to the past where he showed me another level of sensuality, I send him to the next place in the hierarchy that is appropriate.

"You'll keep making excuses until you're sick. I can't hear you love me when I've not reliably felt it, there's nothing hard to understand about that. Go to hell, Isaak." I strike, beginning to walk again, but he captures my hand.

I know this contact. This intensity and this vulnerability makes him squirm. I don't like making him into someone who doesn't conform to my ways. I don't want control over him, just my own life, just a little bit of power to stop myself from implosion.

"Listen, even if you don't like it. Please." He argues. I allow him a sentence, then I must leave him for his sake and my sanity. We can't continue in this heedless ricochet.

After I sigh half-heartedly, out of forbearance, he unravels. "Sierra, I've been to hell a thousand and one times to keep you safe, and trust me," he laments, "it's a lot more accommodating than the shit that goes on in this world, but I am by your side and following in your footsteps because you are my light in the darkness. Not this city. You." I can't tell if he's crying or if his tears from earlier still stain him. He's gripping both my hands now, tightly, curling them into a ball between his palms, with desperation, with helplessness, his hurt hurting me and mine hurting him. "I want to know you, Sierra. The things that make you, things that break you, things that make you want me and things that make you crave each tomorrow."

I pause, then ease my hands from his pressurised cocoon. "Tomorrow will always arrive. It's about making myself ready, and I need time. Give me time, and I will have patience for you." He nods, with a deadening expression. The bottom of the stairwell looms closer as I scurry down the rest of the steps, and take one last look at Isaak before I'm welcomed by another beating heart. The one I need right now, because it has never condemned me to an apartment. An open city, called London, that tells me the tales of an open world. I know exactly where I'm headed. To stories and secrets. I'm heading to a place that contains them all.

The libraries I usually frequent are closed, for it has gone midnight. I am used to returning home at the witching hour, but not leaving home to stimulate my mind and stay awake. It is not a problem. It is London, after all, and one place is always open.

It is silent aside from the squeak of cloth on glass as Nicholas washes cups, succeeding my entrance with a knowing bow of his head. He must be the only person that sympathises with my escapism, and I have never seen him with another, which means he must be content in being alone. But people who are content in loneliness, have at some point been hurt in company. I know this myself. One argument with Isaak has driven me out onto the streets on instinct. London is the place for life's soloists, if people want to watch you or if people don't. I can sing out sorrows in front of an audience or curl up in a dim corner at the back of an empty bar and read at my leisure, in my time.

Nicholas' bookshelves here are more bountiful than mine at home, and this is the first time I've noticed. The clutter in the bar every time I make my choice of a book, means I am swift and careless. I'll read anything with words and new ideas, when I turn a page, I want to step through a door, and that is my highest expectation. Now, I can take time to decide. Each spine looks eerily like the books I have at home though, the ones from Bridgette, the same auburn colour. The same binding. Perhaps that's what books of a generation once looked like.

The titles are vague, and perfect. A quintessential air of mystery that I need forever to breathe. I'll never get through them all unless it is at the sacrifice of the rest of the beautiful things in my life. There is a debacle, between real life and printed wonders, but in times like these, monochromatic pageants overcome my desires twofold. Arguments need augmented healing, that can only come from broadened knowledge and unveiling a timeless chimera. Both of which can be achieved through books. I scan the covers, listening out for their calls.

Life of an Illusionist. The Things People Work Towards. Secrets of London's Unspoken Outskirts. The Army That Gained an Angel. Lost.

The penultimate one speaks to me until the pathways in my brain connect and 'army' reads as 'violence'. I need no more anguish tonight, if I need activity, it'll be proactivity and not reactivity so I pull *The Things People Work Towards* into my arms, cradling it until I can melt into the crevice of the booth furthest from the door. I unfold the book in my lap, taking a brief look at the clock. 1 in the morning.

It's going to be hours and hours before the nation wakes up. Until then it is just me, an isolated individual lost in pages of ideas. I'm delighted.

CHAPTER XXI: LOVE

Sebastian.

Human beings are not programmed to be successfully and consciously constant. They thrive on change and momentum, and quells of ambition, troughs and peaks of motivation. Monotony is a secondary cancer.

I am thinking about the constancy of breathing. When we're told to breathe, it is seen as a solitary thing. To breathe is to focus on the oxygen you pull in from your environment, and busy your body with nothing else. Yet, breathing is constant. There is occasionally a requirement to take a constant and turn it into a focus, when a situation calls for it. Which is why although Betsy has breathed since day one of life, when we first met, to now, when we met again - I cradled her in my arms and begged her to breathe.

Breathe. Something that had remained so constant, in all her journeys, reliable and dependent, subconscious since birth. Betsy suddenly became incapable of all but a whistle. Trying with her mouth, and all that she couldn't take in, in the capacity she needed to live, being filtered through her damaged throat. She is a fighter, and always has been.

The circle of doctors in Colmoor offered to tend to her, but I don't like their methods and they want nothing more than money. Life - her life - is a fee to them, and I don't see living that way. I have limited medical knowledge, but love for this woman in excess, and have promised I will not let her die under my care. At the bare minimum, I am a man of my word.

A clearing in the forest, not far from our treehouse, has a stream that spouts clean water, that I'm not aware that anybody else knows of. It is pure, and the first thing I think of to ease her pain. If it cannot mend her, it will numb her, so that her grit is recycled until she's herself again, minus the beautiful tones she could once make. I know it is selfish to be sad, but I feel I have lost her voice along with her, just one night after I heard her soul. Cogs in my mind begin to reposition themselves, I have to lose the tenderness, or I might lose the state of level headedness and prudence.

She is asleep. Nearly dead, but for the telltale whistling she now produces. Her blood turns the water murky, which is a minor inconvenience. For the most part, it is resolute, as it means I am almost ready to diagnose the trauma to her neck more specifically than I would have been able to with her neck covered in blood. Common sense recommends cleaning the wound of rust, dirt or anything that could make Betsy susceptible to infection, but common sense can only manage to a degree. The specifics of her injuries need an expert assessment, not just a lover who has spent his conscious years as a protector. I'm not educated as a doctor, and therefore know nothing about physical healing. Although I may know more than most about emotions, and calming her is going to be paramount in her recovery.

It looks torturous from an outside perspective - the way that a headlock, with Betsy settled in my lap, is the most ergonomic way to stem the bleeding. I don't really care what it may look as though I'm doing to her, because we both know my place. It is next to her, a permanent position, until she is back to suitable health. If this is what a nail and a few seconds of distractions will do to her, I feel obliged to not let her in human company again, because there is no knowing how much they could hurt her.

In as long a time as it takes for the sun to go down, the bleeding around her neck has dried, crusted, and is adhesive to my sleeve. There is no way I can peel it away without waking her. I have to do it the second worst way, and gently kiss her awake to tell her.

"Blink hard when you're ready." I instruct. She tries to take a full breath, fails, then blinks purposefully. I wish she wouldn't stare at me, in the helpless way she does, when I ease each fibre from the blood. It is all for the best, but my second wish is that Alessandro was here, as the twin that is much better with blood.

In getting closer to her to tend to her, now that the twilight brings darkness, the purple throb of her neck becomes more apparent. She is not only bleeding from the surface injuries, but the force of being swung against the side of the carriage must have caused incredible swelling. A pressure on her vocal cords that I'm not sure will ever be relieved.

Her wrist is still tender too, she squeaks slightly when I adjust it but that is all. Otherwise, she stays quiet. I made an executive decision to lay her down in the grass, facing the stars but angled slightly so she won't choke on her blood or saliva. I need to find something. Unfortunately, the forest has a supply crisis when it comes to modern day treatment, and the town I was raised in is no better. And London, for all its medical progression, is too far to take her. Not to mention all the paperwork and questions, when Betsy's name isn't featured in any census of this world.

All I can gather is moss, which will have to be enough to cushion Betsy's wrist in position as it heals, but as I bring it back to her, I know that I can't leave her in the open all night. I'll have to set her up again in the treehouse.

The last of my energy is spent carrying her and the moss to the treehouse and repositioning her wrist, ever so slowly, to where I think it looks the most like it should. Everything takes twice as long, carrying her over my shoulders up the ladder, maybe even three times as long. I've sliced my palms with the stress of holding the wooden rungs so tightly. Realising that by four steps up, her life and mine, rely on my hands. At the same time feeling the trust of her heart and mine intertwining compels me against gravity, I feel like I can float, until responsibility reminds me, I'm still tied.

With Betsy, I completed one climb, then proceeded to do six more, with canisters in each hand to collect clean water for her. I travelled back and forth from the source until my legs would barely march forward, yet as I lie against a full tank of water and by her side, I know I still need to walk. Exercising my brain, figuring out what the hell to do. Distributing my own trauma into manageable bites. If I swallow it in intervals, it might not hurt as much.

"I'll be back, Betsy, love." I whisper into her dreams, leaning down for yet another kiss, wanting to extract her pain with everything in me. Her childhood had handed her enough, now this is a double dose, and has torn open old scars for me to see her bleed.

There is an abundance on my mind, and yet I still take the device Alessandro has given me out of the corner I conceal it in, and it must be a psychic power that it rings when I'm less than a mile away from home on my emotion-fuelled march. I'm busy protesting all the little ways that life has to be. When my brother calls, I channel my protest to him, across fields and expanses of land, through a small screen held to my ear, and tell him everything. His concern is evident, and I don't want to give him reason to come racing back to Colmoor, but I can't stop. I hate it. I hate the distant thrum in my ears of *march, march, march*. They can stay distant. In the hours since Betsy has lost her voice, the minions in my head are starting to realise the potential there is to return, to control me. I say no. I say no, amongst a lot of other things, to Alessandro.

I say no to believing that Betsy won't ever speak, or sing, again. I say no to the fact that I still have to run away, even though they hunt something that is lost to time that I no longer have to protect. I say no to Alessandro, implicitly, not wanting to think about stepping in again to stop him fighting alone. I just need to be alone, myself. Alone with myself. Simply alone. For the moment, until I can be alone with Betsy.

I say no when it comes to realising that Warner is on Alessandro's trails. My mind shudders to a halt, and my steps do too. So caught up in my head and the input/output learned way of processing information, it takes a while for the name to trigger thoughts. Warner is in London, and so is my brother, and Betsy's sister. I need to go to London, because Alessandro won't be okay forever. He's been breaking already, and Warner's cheap humour and pursuit of murder will be the straw that breaks the hero's back. Moreso, the bells do not help, and yet it is not the bells.

He does not realise but bells toll in the background in this phone call, he lives in London where the city clock is a staple. They don't affect him. He has told me of the grandfather clock Sierra has bought him for the hall, and I refuse to accept that it only chimes as a rarity. It sounds every hour, but he does not fall with it every time. Only I know the reason.

A grandfather clock stood in our Father's room, and rang ten o'clock as Alessandro processed what was left of Father's bloodied face. What Alessandro didn't know is that because I was the second to enter, I remained a few paces behind him, taking in my father but along with the sight of him, every other aspect of the moment. The lighting, the danger, the risks it posed and the future risks it caused, and most importantly the sounds. The ringing I know was funnelled into Alessandro's understanding of the situation, but amidst the bronze was silver, silver metal, light metal that collided and fed into my brother's psyche in a messy high clamour.

Our mother's necklace was suspended in the open window. Father had hung it there since her death as a sign to the town of what they'd taken from us. Savannah's was hung next to it, as he didn't have a soul to give it back to, and decided it was the best way of memorialising her, to let her jewellery sway next to Lucia's. The necklaces struck each other in the breeze as Alessandro saw our father's face, and translated it to death. It is not the bells, but the chimes he didn't know he heard. I have always known.

In the graveyard, when I held him, loose copper tributes on some gravestones broke into our silence long before the bells did, and he began falling away. It is a specific sound, not of coins jumbled in a pocket, not of glasses collected together, but of windchimes. The type of noise that starts loud and trickles into the air, into the ears. I guess it is bells, but not the heavy kind, small shavings of metals, like icicles, that send their earworm droplets into quiet rooms, and quiet minds.

It is silent again now, because the line goes dead. Resenting the reinforcement, I know I need to reach London. I need to leave a wounded Betsy behind. I'll leave tomorrow, and in the meantime, I'm relying on Warner to restrain himself until I know my girl won't die whilst I'm gone. I have hope, but I'm wise to what hope does to people. It is the same as love. A chance. A shot in the dark. A gamble.

The body has all but one substitute for morphine, and that is pleasure that'll cancel out the unsettling pain.

I say to her, "Can you write? I'll find ink. We brought plenty of paper with us." Bless her heart, she tries. Scrambling her working arm across paper that I hold above her whilst she's flat on the floor, and a barely legible Y, or perhaps an R, is all that she produces. It is a waste of our time, and limited time, now that I have decided I have to leave. Her left hand is a farce, and her right hand is broken. We need a supernatural medium, and something that is going to work.

Her left hand may be incapable of writing, but her touch acts the same as it always has. Able to raise my temperature. Betsy has evolved from my weather, my sun, to my climate. I changed with her she has changed me. For as she touches me, I don't fight back despite defence being what my instinct always has been. I sink down underneath her fingers. It is lazy to begin with. Slow, gentle, but my skin is yearning, and I am rarely an impatient person unless I want something to a ridiculous degree. This woman is barely a day recovered from her deathbed, and now she is the making of me. Teasing me, tempting me and the only one I want to see me at my most vulnerable.

"Betsy," I breathe, trying to pace the lurching in my veins that just wants to envelope her, and provide for her in ways only a lover can, "Can I, I mean, will you, I don't know…fuck. I'm making a mockery of you sweetheart, I'm sorry. I don't mean it. I'm scared. It takes everything to admit that to anyone, and you, you're so precious."

She can't move her head widely, but her eyes are solely concerned and besmeared with the urge for me to continue talking. I have to deny her, it feels unjust to express myself whilst she can't, in romance, in life, in love and in sex. "In the name of justice, nothing I say will be for my pleasure, only yours. Consider my lips sealed, unless I speak for you. I'll be looking at you until you're satisfied. You are more than your silence, and you deserve to be without pain darling." I pause, looking at the epitome of luck I have safe in my arms. "Let me take it away."

Then, her shoes and socks are beside us. Her underwear too. "Let me take these away. Let me free you of everything."

With sudden fear and strength, she latches her left hand onto my bicep. I understand her, for all her actions are. "Although it may infuriate you some day, you will never be free of me."

She tries a smile with the muscles that are left, but I'm looking at the way her eyes sparkle. The way she lets one of my hands guide her legs open whilst the other one supports her back, says more than words ever could.

It's a faint inhale that represents a gasp, when my hand returns to her tattoo, finishing what my lips started. There are two things on my mind: how her heart is speeding up, yet still not surpassing the mileage of mine, and how close I am to her. I can tell by her hold on me that she hasn't been touched before. She can likely tell by my trembling fingers that I've never touched before. We are both surrendering, and scared. That's what makes us need it so much, the call of losing our inhibitions to love.

She breathes a little too fast, a little over tempo and my concentration is entirely on her. "It stops here if you've had enough." I gently remind her.

Betsy rejects the concept of ending this, purely with a split second of expression and her eyebrows. Passion engulfs her in record time, and before even this, she tugs at my shirt. A shift in mood, her admission and subservience, has turned to instruction, begging for my weight, my warmth and my service. The silent pleading gets deafening, overwhelming, steady and my heart is just a passenger. It is now or never, all or nothing, now or nothing, all or never. This night may not repeat itself.

I am naked, but for my tattoo. She is naked but for hers. This is the first time I've wondered what it stands for, the RWYA. Betsy doesn't know either. But right now, we choose to be stressed in the best of ways, finding a natural rhythm. Emotionally, mentally, literally, metaphorically, physically, all that I have, inside all that she is. Connecting in a way that a foolish number seeks for sustenance, but I see as a statute.

Betsy's Law, I will call it. In a perfectly weak, desperate and passionate end to a defective day - love is the answer. Love is the purpose. And our love is forever. Embossed with Sebastian's seal of approval, entrenched, and codified in an eternal constitution.

CHAPTER XXII: KNEW

Isaak.

The fire consumes me. It burns. Sierra's anger, Sebastian's mind. The heat of my flashbacks when I don't need them. Fire must be furious because all mankind does is contain it: to fireplaces, to lanterns, to cook with and to a single day in November, months from now. We ridicule fire and insult it with our ways. We deserve to be burnt.

I deserved Sierra's outburst, and all the pain that came freely with it. I am less than myself, less than a protector and less than a man in whatever definition being a man adopts. I have let her down, and before I can lose her for good, I need to grasp this last opportunity to love her. I will sit on this balcony for as long as it takes to work out what my heart needs to say.

It is harder than anticipated, because between thoughts of Sierra that I love, there is the sight of her back to me, leaving down the stairwell for the streets. At midnight. My low tolerance for love has sent her out of the place I made safe for her, and following her seems like the worst thing to do. London is huge but only extends so far, it has boundaries, and is a giant hunting ground where Warner and Sierra might find each other at any given moment. I'm restless here. Knowing I have to sit and wait, whilst wanting to find her and keep Warner away. Fuck.

It is worthwhile to unlock my mind, lay down this exhausting identity and become Alessandro again. To remember Sierra as a sweetheart and not a project.

I used to take her anywhere away from home. Midnight used to be our time, and now somewhere along the way I've let it all fall apart. It was quite possibly knowing that every excursion had a time limit that kept us addicted to seeing each other. She adored Bridgette, but Bridgette never knew about me and we tried so hard to keep it that way. Secrecy made what is normal now seem exciting. She didn't know about the places I took Sierra after dark, the beautiful ones and the dangerous ones. Deep down, I know even if the lady was aware, I know she wouldn't have said a thing, because Sierra was happy and saw something more than just four walls, and that was something both of us wanted.

I remember the day I swore myself away to Sierra, so invested in who I wanted to be, I attempted to convince Sebastian that Isaak was here to stay. He never believed it, if the initialism was anything to go by. AG are my letters and IM is, when all is said and done, a forgery. Alessandro wanted a lot more from love before Isaak's fear interfered. Isaak was a way I could distance myself from her, to make her last forever, when Alessandro just wanted to savour the moments as they came. The balcony is giving me no answers and neither is the view. Instead, I feel like I'm on display, an exhibit. Colmoor, look at me, the one that ran away - with a pulley attached so you can find me and pull me back. I must not be in the right state of mind, wanting to go back to Colmoor. I know exactly why it appeals to me, and it is because everybody in London is on a different tier and I skulk around in the shadows out of mandatory principle. I love the city, but like an affair. I admire its beauty from a distance and use shadows to disguise what I am. A Colmoorian. I'm here because of love for Sierra, and it has saved me from a much worse fate, and I owe that to both of them, but I will never be a Londoner. Isaak is in a scandalous relationship with this place, using it as an exotic distraction from the weight of the danger a relationship would cause to my heart and to her. I've been acting up and wild, fighting appetisers for too long when there's a feast of violence to follow. Alessandro needs to be faithful to his roots. Which is one girl in this big city, who is alone right now, and vulnerable, and who believes I'm someone I'm not. A brave man called Isaak, whose darkness shrouds a mystery.

She doesn't know I am Alessandro, whose darkness shrouds his fear. The more nightmares I have, the more my childhood trauma puppeteers me.

And as for the mystery, it exists as long as Sierra doesn't know the truth, no matter what name I call myself. The truth of the tattoo, her birth, and her lover.

I can't be outside any longer. Frantically, back inside the apartment I search for things to retain these memories of my past in the limited items we brought with us. The books. I flick through them. Nothing helps, there is nothing here. I need to know the ways Alessandro once thought, and make me want to be him again.

The clock chimes. The grandfather clock. It's 1. The sound isn't hurting me. I'm too stressed about the length of time Sierra has been isolated to work out why I'm not cowering with the ringing, and the one strike is over before I can investigate my brain. I can't shake the eventuality that she's walked straight into Warner's invite to meet, but she's not that bloody stupid. On the other hand, I haven't told her anything, I haven't taught her what to avoid. The fault is all mine if she's out somewhere with a knife to her throat. I simplify my night into two steps.

Step One. Find myself.
Step Two. Find her.

I'm still peeling open these leatherbound covers, looking for handwriting from a distant memory. Mania is creeping in. Each book gets brought up close to my face so I can try to extract a smell that I remember - but it's just the scent of antiques and a universal comfort, which is exactly what Colmoor is not. It is all words and nothing substantive that makes me truly feel anything. Sebastian is distressed with his own problems. Sierra has reached a limit with me.

I am alone.

Completely alone in a country of killers, and with a woman I can't keep kidding myself I can protect.

Alone but for the flowers that fall out of the next book I open.

A daisy and another white one I don't know the name for. A faded purple one, crushed into pale yellow petals. A couple, in fact most, are dried until indistinguishable, but there's age in the stalks. I've never seen half of these flower species in London. The waterlily by my feet I recognise from being half-drowned in a park river with Sierra, only recently. This is a book under constant review, her memoir of the past transcribed in flowers. No wonder she only remembers what was positive, and no wonder I didn't select the book sooner. It was the only one without a dusted exterior.

Sierra's treating the past with the present, and she's on to something. After all, nobody can live without time's assistance, and I see a new opportunity to get ahead. Protecting Sierra became my task as soon as I decided I was Isaak to her, but finding Sierra in the first place was an accomplishment of a different man. It was Alessandro, because what Alessandro wanted was never one girl to protect, it was all of them. It wasn't his mission just to curse his hometown. It was a father, a mother and a system to avenge.

Too much blood has been lost in Colmoor, on time's watch. This is bigger than Sierra, her future is more than my capabilities. This will only end with a conversation. An old, frail Jasper and the Gray twins in a room where three enter, and two leave.

Right now, things just boil down to flowers. All over the floor. I don't do delicacy, and my scramble to recover them just ends up snapping and breaking each stem. The petals disintegrate in my hands, an ugly metaphor for the way I feel about the history of my relationship with Sierra. I leave them where they are, ready for her eyes when she sees her memories destroyed on the carpet and I won't have the words nor the courage to apologise for breaking her heart and mind in one day, under the same moon.

Alessandro and Isaak have one thing in common. They love Sierra too much to bottle up her voice or her ambitions. They will run with her, far away from where she and they belong. They will exist gormless and floating in empty space to make sure she can touch the stars. Right now, both identities are in one man, they will run to her to stop her from falling. None of Sierra's screams or blood will be drawn on Isaak's nor Alessandro's watch. I'm finally ready to hold her tight without an alibi, without an excuse. I need her to know I love her, so she'll never resent me for sneaking around anymore. I need her to know that everything that I've done has been for her.

With the tablet in my hand, her location locked on Nicholas' pub for now, I make my way out of the door. All I have on my mind is her bearings, her smile, my love for her, and a pledge to end Jasper. I need to find Sierra, then I need my brother's help to make sure that this is the final chapter.

This should have been the end of everything, of Colmoor as we know it and the end of the Era of the Conventional. This should have been where Isaak and Alessandro stopped being different people, but the world doesn't turn for happy endings.

Nicholas mutters as I come in the door, not quite low enough for me to ignore him, "Might as well be open bloody twenty-four seven. One exception for Sierra, then the boyfriend, then the whole of bloody London." His sigh overwhelms his anger.

Amazingly, he is sitting behind the bar without being active. Often, he's washing, or serving. I've not seen him completely inactive before. He looks tired, like he shouldn't be lending his energy to the bar at 1am. I want to shake him by the shoulders and tell him to go to bed, but I'm aware my words won't make a difference to a stubborn man. It infuriates me because I see Nicholas as an older, more sedentary version of myself. Too scared to skip the action in favour of sleep. Too enthused by people to live a quiet life. Nicholas must know everyone in London, visitor or local.

I know the places in here that Sierra prefers. In the booths, or in front of the doors that waitstaff try to carry food through, and somehow none ever request that she moves. Nicholas has had a word.

I've been led into a trap, and the shutters of my hope and horizons and expectations close, locking the light outside. I don't see her smile, or her head bent over pages and invested in characters I will never have the empathy or intelligence to associate with. The empty corner and closed book hit me like an avalanche, she hasn't even replaced it on the shelf. Sierra hasn't ever neglected a book, treated it any less than perfect. I know I've treated her less than perfect, I know it, and I feel guilty for it. It's not the fire I'm consumed by, it's the guilt. I want to put it right, but I can't if she's on the run. Storming back the way I came, I'm drunk on apprehension and fake excitatory scenarios that fill my head as a result of my panic. All of them have Warner lurking in the background.

I need her to be here. I don't understand what's gone wrong. My control was perfect. I had control. I've lost it now.

"I had her, Nicholas! The fucking dot is still on my screen. Fucking look at it!" I'm thrusting my tablet across the bar and into his face, fear dripping from my teeth and messily on my chin.

"I believe you son, but it won't change the fact she's not here." He accepts, batting away my advances, whilst trying to convince me he didn't see her leave.

"She was the only one besides you in this fucking pub, damn it!" I sink onto the bar, soaking up the leftover alcohol into my clothes. I'm seeing my delirium reflected in Nicholas' eyes and I know I need to get away from him before I shoot a sloppy gun of blame, and have this pub on its knees vying for mercy. Deep down it is clear to me it isn't the bartender's fault, but my hands are shaking and if I can't reach into my tablet and pluck Sierra's teasing red location from there and put her next to me, I will extract red another way. From anyone who stands in between me and Sierra.

The cubicle doors swing on their hinges from the moment I ignore the signs and enter the bathrooms, they are all open, empty, taunting Sierra's absence. Then they swing from my kicking them out of frustration, every limb in my body aching to collide with something. I wonder if the neighbours heard my scream. We'll see in the report of civil disturbance that comes in the post tomorrow. If tomorrow arrives. My anger sweeps back to Nicholas, who's now stood up and is pouring me a drink. I guarantee whatever he has I need something stronger, a drink that is the most dangerous for his reputation to sell. The ones they lock up in their bottles.

"I'm not going crazy, Nicholas," I down half the beer between one breath and another, "I'm not crazy. Her necklace is here. She's somewhere here." In a fleeting sober moment, I see myself. Brandishing evidence that I'm a stalker for my girlfriend in the face of a man I've met with less than a dozen times in three months, and never personally. All I do is demand he looks after Sierra when I can't, and demand he takes my cash. Branding Isaak as possessive, obsessive and a control freak, and downing alcohol like I haven't drunk in days, just to reinforce the madness.

I can explain to him later, smooth this shit out. It's low on the list of priorities right now. Sierra might be getting exploited somewhere unsafe whilst I'm self-reflecting on my resolutions to decide I'd be less of a fucking absolutist this year. As it turns out, Isaak has failed, and he doesn't like to fail.

"Let that go before you crush it." Nicholas refers to my reddening hand, squeezing around the now-empty pint glass, needing something to hurt. A punishment for losing her. This incident isn't private, I have to share my mistakes with Nicholas, and my faults are not isolated to tonight. It is an accumulation of the nights I've let her cry herself to sleep because I won't touch her. It's the nightly balcony rendezvous that have evaporated in the frost, and left us retiring to bed with frozen hearts. It's the times I've rejected her for every unnecessary means, that I ashamedly put above her. Sleeping has nothing on her. Neither does the city, neither does the night. This tablet has nothing on her either.

It's bleeping here, here, here, but she's not here, here, here. My brother's in my head. The alcohol's in my head. Nobody's here for me. The bar is empty. Nicholas is nowhere. Sierra's out there alone, and I'm just drinking it all away and then I realise. I've been deceived. I take the drink, and he takes his leave. Then, just as me and my sweating jacket turn back to the London streets, Nicholas takes me by surprise. He holds Sierra's telescope from his hand.

"Left it in the book. She's not here."

"Told you I'm not fucking crazy." I smile, with half a heart and half a hope she's still alive, for I've found a last resort.

Not the sort of last resort I ever wanted, or expected, to abide by. Mistakes give people second chances. Games give people second lives. I've never believed in second chances because it makes it easier to kill the guilty. That was until I acquired myself a second little red dot, that still moves breezily along a street, mere minutes from here, if I head there at running pace.

I hear footsteps charge behind me and before they can reach me, I twist and land a blind punch. My estimate was correct, my calculations executed perfectly, except my mathematics left a dent in Nicholas' cheek.

After regaining his balance, and seeing me trying to avoid staring at the damage I caused, he tries to accept it. "You're forgiven, let's not mention that again. Hell, there's force in those hands." He speaks whilst winded, leaning over to support himself, hands on his knees. Sucking air through his teeth.

I extend an arm to help him. "Nicholas, you're a bartender not a vigilante. Get back to the pub. You can't be with me."

He straightens himself up. "I'm a bartender, it's the London equivalent. I've seen more fights than I've made drinks. Let's go."

"Fine." I grumble, secretly admiring his volunteering. I've always found bartenders curiously philanthropic. "Don't hold it against me if you die. There's not a waiver, just my word against yours if something were to happen, and something will absolutely happen."

"You think there's a chance I'll die?" That's all he takes from my caution. At least I tried.

I give him the answer I give anyone and everyone. "I don't answer questions…"

We walk into the night, with Warner's red dot blazing from the plate in my hand. Occasionally, I glance at Nicholas whose gaze is fixed on directions.

"It's quite possible you'll die." I continue quietly, after I decide it's been long enough, and I feed off the little bit of pleasure I get from hearing Nicholas swallow the cold. He keeps walking though. I'll credit him for that. I've never gone into the lion's den with an apprentice.

"I hope you don't have a family expecting you. These aren't the sort of errands you run if you have family at home." I'm not sure if this counts as explaining or oversharing, or dissuading him from taking any more steps with me. I don't want his life in my hands.

"I have to disagree. They're the only errands that are necessary, if you have family." Nicholas replies affirmatively.

I'm beginning to like him. He's my type of vigilante, but I have to insist he leaves. It takes stopping in our tracks and an intense reinforcement of the potential fatality of whatever we're going to walk into. The sealing statement, "Nicholas, if anything were to happen to me, I need someone I trust to watch out for her. Please, go back to the pub." I've never begged like that before, and I know as he nods and walks back in the direction of the pub without looking back, I'll never earn his companionship again.

I walk. I want the skies to bring on the thunder and the clouds. Maintain the rain that's been hammering all night. I need the right weather for a good fight. I don't want whoever I kill, for touching Sierra, to see the sun when they die. That'd be too much of a liberty.

CHAPTER XXIII: IGNORE

Sierra.

It seems like midnight has lasted forever and fruit won't cut it. I'm coming down from Paradise, these cocktails don't match my mood in the slightest. I turn to bouncy flavours when I need energising, but I've never skimmed the other side of the drinks menu to find something to restart me. Nicholas watches me reading abnormal words, rude and vulgar names of drinks that astonishingly, or maybe not for London, are common orders. People must be in dark places to order these potions that sound like they could share their name with prisons, asylums or curses. It's like there's a certain threshold where people let go of everything. Their sadness, sensibilities and place in this society. I glance over at Nicholas, who instead of resuming his tasks, keeps staring at me. He must watch people lose themselves all the time, and keep serving them regardless. What is his role? To save people or to enable them to disappear? I take over the menu, ready to find out.

"I have books, Sierra. You don't need that." The bartender reminds me. I grit my teeth because he sounds like Isaak, telling me what I should and shouldn't request. I closed my eyes and set the menu in front of me with all of the poisons facing the bar's orange lights on the ceiling. My finger stroked every name that I could choose as a tribute to my pain, to introduce to my throat. It passes over Apocalypso, The Last Sunrise of Grapes and Graves, and Forest Nightmare because I know where they all are on the page. I want to select something completely new. From a new orientation, a blind one, and let my instinct guide me to my doom. I want to fall asleep and not wake up until the pain has passed, at least until the end of the week. I want to come back to a parallel universe where Isaak loves me, and I have to fight him off my body and battle his desires. To be trapped in bed with him all day, and out in the city all night. The perfect cycle.

"The Lunacy Cocktail." I ordered, reading from underneath my finger.

"There's books…" Nicholas tries one last time.

"I know what I want."

He sighs in defeat, but I know I'm not bound to his wishes for me. The shot glass itself looks mystical the more layers he adds to it, if this won't give me the release I need, nothing will. The music that Nicholas has playing in here, seems to swell between volumes just from me bringing the drink up to under my nose. I cough with it. There's no distinct smell, just acid, but there's a certain taste when it all goes down. Peppermint, kicking my stomach like rogue toothpaste, and a flavour that dries my tongue. I feel my brain dissolving already and the puzzled face of the man in front of me. This is, as advertised, a ludicrous way to break up with my feelings.

"I don't feel crazy." I recognise, as I'm still conscious.

"You're not. That was peppermint cordial, Sierra."

"You're not allowed to do that…" I say wryly, embarrassed that I can't distinguish between alcohol and flavoured water. I didn't want this. I wanted to be out of my mind, because it's a confusing place to be at the moment. I don't need any more riddles or tricks, especially from a bartender I trust.

"Then surely it shows how much I'll consider stepping around my rules for you. You don't need that sort of stuff. That's for people who've given up. I thought there was more fight in you."

"More than enough, Nicholas," I exhale heavily, heat rushing to my head, and into my fingers with bitterness. "More than bloody enough. I have so much energy that I don't know what to do with it all-" I realise I'm slowly shouting, "-excuse me."

I remove myself before I can cause any more damage to this caring man.

The bathrooms are the only place truly away, he won't try to counsel me here. I don't know where it comes from, but I hear it before I feel it. A blood curdling scream. My own. I've never heard myself sound like this clown. Who is this? I'm afraid to turn to the mirrors. I lock myself, after a few shaky attempts, in the furthest cubicle from the door, and sink down. Away from reality. I've never felt as low, or alone. My hands search for Isaak, who obviously is not here. My heart can't comprehend that I was the one that caused this. He broke me apart, smashed me up little by little, there was nothing else I could have done. I just want to live without loneliness. Live with Isaak ideally, but he casts a dark mask where the truth should be. The good moments are just a little too good, and the bad ones are abysmal. Surely, there should be a comfortable medium, not just space for a throne that seats the truth he's hiding. I know I need to care about myself the way I want Isaak to care about me; it's poor, and teenage, for me to want validation patchwork. It's immature to have this latent mantra that one hundred percent of me is only half of a bigger picture. It just goes to show, you can be living your dreams and still have a habit of dreaming beyond what you have. It will never be enough to achieve dreams just as they are, knowing there are always zones of success and capability yet to exist in.

I claw at the floor. There's nothing to it. I can't pull up the ground and make it take me. I want it to take me. Bloody hell, please. I've been on the up and up, and it's delivered me to hell. I want to go the other way. There must be something I'm missing. Something down there. Down, down and somewhere under the soil, the bones and the mud, to heaven. People don't bury people, who await heaven, in the skies. Ground, take me please. Unfortunately, I'm lucid enough to know that it is impossible, and I have to live in the real world.

I'm still on an enemy basis with the mirror. I don't want to see myself, and I don't need to look, and it would be doing the mirror an injustice to have to portray me. I count up to ten and down in my head. It is supposed to calm me, but whoever came up with that has never met Isaak before. Numbers and facts is all he is, and it just reminds me of the orderly way he does things.

I need something fantastical, borne of human imagination for human consumption, something that promises to exercise the mind. Words. I need to read. I think, inside, I knew that all along. The most fantastical literary item I can find beyond the bathroom is another menu, a food one, with the pub's logo detailed at the top, and the phrase *hoc est in domum suam* beneath it. Latin is a pretty language, but it teases. I can't read that any more than hieroglyphics.

Putting the menu down, I slip past the door frame without Nicholas noticing and collapse onto the stairs where my book still lies, fanned open. I glance at the parts of me I can see. My wrists, and my clothes, my shoes and my jewellery. I don't like to embellish myself with colour, my music does just that, but a bit of gold makes me feel put together. Which is when I remember what he's done to me. This stupid telescope hangs around my neck like a collar, a psychological persuasion to act at his beck and call, to degrade myself to an animal that stays loyal to a man. A fence, a cage or a necklace won't contain me, Isaak. This is the part when I say I'm free from you.

Yet, I can't. Not completely. I'll leave the necklace in the safest place I know, nestled in someone else's narrative. Tucked inside *The Things People Work Towards* on a page that begins with the line 'Try to stop me flying, when you don't have the wings to catch me. I'll watch you try and faint, from my seat on the moon, love. I work towards being free of what we're supposed to be'. For a time, when maybe, a necklace might just mean friendship, and I won't be moored to a love ship sailed. Still resignedly attached, but knowing I won't ever see him again the way he was.

I get an ugly feeling, like I'm not supposed to be here. I don't want to be here. Instead of a clammy London pub, I want to be outside in the rain. The discomfort seeps from knowing this is the first place Isaak will come for me if he's had enough of waiting, and there's only limited time. He's bedevilled with my whereabouts, who I speak to, and what I think. Never what I feel.

I resent his tattoo. I forage underneath my shirt to find mine, pulling my skin taught so that the ink and my stretch marks slide, to see if it's truly the same. RWYA. What does that mean? Nicholas ought to hope he isn't looking at this self-examination. I feel small, and an outsider to my own body. I should have some recollection of my skin being tainted, but I don't. I feel like I'm tiptoeing around a conspiracy, around a room that contains all the secrets about me that I don't know. What if it's not a room, what if it's a city? Keeping low, I edge towards the back door to the pub and tug the lock. The hinges swing open and I have to fall into the alleyway to stop it slamming with full force against the wall. I've committed now, one shoe is deep in a puddle and the draught will find its way to Nicholas if I deliberate too much longer. I left last night behind and entered the morning, closing the door behind me, with one last look at the book that treasures my necklace more than I do. I hear the latch lock itself upon closing.

I vaguely remember the last time I stepped away from grief, knowing I'd never return. It would have swallowed me whole if Isaak hadn't been there to shine a light. I would have been pulled back into my past unless I left Gettie's home, but the secrets are all still inside that house and whatever became of it. Isaak left her lying in her bed, with a last bouquet tucked under her hands. I wish I had done it but I couldn't see through my tears. We took her books with us when we left, for angels have no use for them, and now they're all stacked up in the apartment as artefacts of a life I once lived.

. *My mind is in bits and pieces, but I can only remember three things from who I was before London. I remember the ocean, I remember flowers, and I have flashbacks, without warning, of things that happened in those four walls. Nothing outside of those three things. I thought four walls was all there was, until I met Isaak. We always performed our excursions at night because he didn't want me to see what was in the distance. The house was in the middle of nowhere, and I couldn't explore because I was only allowed to the end of the fields and no further. A forest obscured everything else, and when we needed resources then I'd stay at home whilst Gettie left and returned hours later.*

I felt awful lying to her, when I left at night whilst she was asleep, but I figured that nothing bad could possibly happen to me when I was with Isaak. Everything I was afraid of, all of the not knowing, just melted away and left me open to be taken wherever.

I was too trusting. This flight that I've taken with Isaak has left me stranded, with a man I don't recognise anymore, and our love is expelling feathers like a cushion. What was once comfortable is becoming empty and I haven't got the motivation to fix it, because even at its best, it's worse. I have a man who shuts himself up like a fortress, and I'm starting to think that, irresponsibly, nobody ever made a key. Nobody knows how to unlock him. I used to see that as a challenge. It was exciting to think that one day I might decrypt him, and yet here I am, pissed off in the rain because I can't access something that's been keeping me out, tempting me, warning me not to get too close, from day one. Sierra Genieva, may be impossibly stupid, and that's a burden I have to carry on top of the weight of being the focus of the media, the focus of the public, and my own arch nemesis.

When did my thoughts get so dark and detrimental, like cognitive burial? I think the contamination happened when I realised the light was overwhelming. The spotlight and the sunlight are all too much and you're taught to avert your eyes, but we're all fireflies, thinking we're indestructible. Destroying ourselves with the pretty things, for superficial bliss.

But we're all so small, so incredibly small, and so alone. We can't battle the darkness this way much longer, so in the meantime, we flit around helplessly, seeking spontaneous sustenance to see us through until morning. How much longer can we struggle before our wings give out?

At first, I was looking for a bus to take me around blocks for a while, with warmth, but I keep finding parts of London I haven't explored before, and one thing leads to another until I'm in a street I don't know. There are signs, but to places that don't sound familiar. I've got everything I need to find my way home, but none of it makes sense. It's like a book I haven't read, which makes me nervous. The rain has eased off, deciding a better use of its time is to hammer on the ceilings of Parliament, rather than in my path. It was relieving at first, it sounded like white noise, until it drenched me and left my clothes abrasive with every step, but now that it's gone, I miss it.

It also exposes all my other senses now, I don't have an excuse to be inattentive. Because of this, I can hear water pouring into drains, I can see the darkness barely 10 metres ahead of me, and I can hear the very human sound of laboured footsteps, of someone not trying to hide. It is Isaak, he is closer behind me than anyone would dare to be as loudly. I hate him right now, I don't want him right now, but the scared little girl in the core of my chest sobs uninhibitedly and tells him that I'm glad he's here.

"Isaak..." I don't know how to follow up an argument with gratitude, they're not complementary exits and entrances to conversation, so I just try to hold him. My hands retract like a snake shedding skin when I'm met with a stranger, and even rain wouldn't disguise the alarm bells emanating from the man in front of me. I get an eviscerating pummelling of deja-vu, like I've seen him before.

"No, not quite." He answers, with a weird entanglement of snappy and optimistic, like he's finally satisfied after a long-term, sinister yearning. "But thank you, that's all I need to know." He stays a little too long, and begins to walk. I know his shadow.

"What do you want with Isaak? I thought you were after me. You never came to that concert, you promised." It is a flirtatious attempt at protecting myself from sudden aggression. I don't usually take this approach to safety, but I have to for certain men. Men who behave like they've never known a woman. Men like this.

"I thought I'd attend your last week of performances, it's a shame you're...how to put this, permanently retiring. Too soon, too soon...pity..." He murmurs to himself. It sounds like a threat but he's smiling, the narrative doesn't match the tension that's brewing. *Last week of performances.*

He rocks around brazenly with a gun, held straight in my direction, and I'll never ignore my instinct again. Don't let him shoot. He pulls the trigger gently, not enough to release the bullet, bracing himself to do it, excited. I can't run, so I beg him instead knowing that if he doesn't shoot now my racing heart will kill me first. My love has laboured too much to die early from palpitations too heavy for me. There are books I haven't read, there's sunsets I haven't seen, there's Isaak. Isaak. Isaak steps in front of me, just as the bullet clicks, and fires.

I am frozen. My anger and fear metamorphose, hotter than a summer dusk, bursting into a burning fiery hell inside my body. My world becomes darker than a soldier's nightmare and my heart, more bitterly broken than a heart has ever been broken.

CHAPTER XXIV: HELP

Sebastian.

I've given up my virginity to the purest of souls. It doesn't concern me that the shockwaves that rang out through her body left my scalp reeling from the pain of her climactic pull on my hair. I know I've given my service to her for good, and she returned it in all manners of equal. For one, my ambition had one foot out of the door until she led it back inside her body, treated it with kind hospitality and made me a better man, one with passion and pursuance. She reminded me what those traits meant to me, with love. An injured woman has healed us both, and for that, she takes my breath away. She has the blanket folded around her curves, tucked into herself using her stronger wrist, holding it close to capture the warmth we created. I reclined, naked, marvelling at her. I could have chosen submission, I chose apostasy. I could have easily nominated myself for Sierra's rescue, but I chose Betsy. It feels like, tonight, the world turns frictionlessly, happily. The moon beams, with the appraisal of a charmed decision made between two brothers, months and months ago. Everything is at ease.

Betsy looked at my body in a way I never have. I don't need self-esteem when I have a clone called Alessandro, cloaked in confidence. Even though it's a facade, it's convincing enough to keep me from ever thinking I needed to meet standards. Alessandro thinks he's enough, so I thought that way too, until I met Betsy and I *felt* it. The way she hung to me, clung to me, trusted me enough to tear her apart with kisses from the heart to the stomach. You don't do that with someone who isn't a soulmate. I threw away everything I used to cover my own wounds whilst I romanced her, they're all at the roots of the tree, all my dependencies that hid my pain. My clothes, gone. My emotional strength, abolished. The orders I've always had, disobeyed.

I saw her scars, but she saw mine. Marks I didn't know I had, sustained from fights I didn't want. She traced every one, letting her lips run wild and transparently across them all, regardless of where they were. I didn't know how much she wanted, how much of my vulnerability she could take, but she kept going, desperate to know me. Everything about me. It was more than sex. It was more than intense, because she didn't have the mobility to explore me, she couldn't find my pain herself. I had to show my pain to her, inch by inch.

When she found the scars, from carrying logs and uncovering shrapnel, on my left hand, she brushed her lips over them and then her eyes rolled back and she was searching for more. I'd never learned this signal. Was it my forearm she wanted? Exclusively with her mouth and her working hand, she touched every part of me that I thought would hurt underneath my skin forever. In return, I kissed her wrist, gentle on her fractured bone. I kissed around the wound on her neck. She found more scars on my chest, scrapes, blue bruises I didn't know I had, and kissed them back. It hurt her, but with her tongue's limited licks, she blessed my injuries with arousal and sensuality. Every part of me reached her mouth throughout the course of intimacy, and her lips movement did every word of talking. She spelled every silent letter on my tanned parchment body, whilst mute.

She's fast asleep now, but I remembered how she kissed my cheeks, making the punches and hits that I'd had laid on me, and laid on others, forgettable and forgivable. I didn't grow up wanting to hurt anyone, and yet now I've killed tens of soldiers to be by this woman's side, and to have this woman here beside me.

I feel a light dabbing on my cheek, with a corner of the duvet. Betsy's awoken and is wiping away my guilty tears, she caught the salted freight before it caved into my ear. It's strange how crying isn't just torture spilt from tear ducts, it's your body saying no more in every way it can. I don't want to miss my father but I do, I don't want to wish at night that I could meet my mother. I don't want to force myself to be okay because my brother isn't coping, I want to do what he did, change his name and run away. I want to be the lost one.

Betsy's troubled expression, watching me cry, say *no you don't, you want to be here.* I agree with the North Stars in her eyes, the wisdom they hold. I want to be here forever, but I need to leave her just for tonight. I've spent too much time languishing with my emotions, my whole body available to her touch, tolerating the cold night, when I could have made use of my life and saved another soul, saved my brother. Feeling selfish is the most damning motivator, but I need to know one way of pursuance and passion to enjoy another. My mind is beginning to wake up from its sexual slumber and ready me. Ready. Ready. Ready.

I kissed her. I wanted her to feel it, whilst she recovers from having fulfilled me, and healed me. I want this kiss to be present in all her dreams, I want her to receive it so clearly it will never forget what it feels like to be loved by me. I don't come from much and I don't boast anything but a combatant brother and a death warrant stapled to my name. I own absolutely nothing but love for her.

Love for her, and a flimsy piece of plastic to keep me connected to Alessandro who is miles away. I have to go now. "See you in the morning." I hesitate, needing more. "Darling, promise me, don't open those eyes, until I'm back to hear your dreams?" I whisper, with another kiss,

sliding my clothes back on. She groans, gesturing to further down the wooden floorboard. There's a stone there that I roll towards her. With effort, she begins scratching into the floor.
I love you.
I smile, and Betsy looks so relieved. Expectantly, and innocently, she awaits my reply. I can't do that to her. We are equals, and it is all we have been from all the time I sought her out, to the first time she called me 'Seb', to the first time I heard her, the first time we suffered together, and the first time we healed together. I ease the stone from her hand, squeezing her fingers in a demonstration of security, and tuck the duvet back around her. I make my own engraving, beside hers, into the floor of the house I built for her.
I love you. I love you.
If she has no words, neither do I. Some things don't need words. Just a sharp stone, and wood, materials as natural as love itself. And some things, like walking away from a sleeping beauty, like the end page of a fairytale, are so damn difficult. I can't wait to see her again.

The more I walk, the more the stretch of road extends ahead of me. The moon rises with London's lights in the distance, and the sky is more purple than usual. Purple is royalty, reminding me I come from nothing, a place where ascension favours only one person.

I head straight towards where I know Alessandro will be. By default, I head to where Sierra is, but it's a blind triangle. She doesn't know about me. Except that I'm the face of a perpetrator that shot a man - and the face that mirrors her lover. She can't know about me.

The building looks gothic in darkness. It's on a corner, leading into two streets, and gives the roads a red, gold and black edge. There's no purple here, because royalty garners attention and that's the opposite of Nicholas' wishes for the place. A palace is large, has more doors than can be opened, more ornaments than can be counted. This pub is a trove of books and paintings, history hidden in plain sight, more resemblant of Colmoorian aesthetic than I can account for as a coincidence.

Nicholas himself is a private character. Bartenders hear whispers, they vacuum drama from the city, they can be dangerous because sometimes power is not in strength or heroism, but in knowledge. Nobody knows more than a bartender in London. The taxi speeding towards me as I cross the road towards the pub's entrance seems intent on killing me, but it won't, not if I walk with stature.

Everyone is possessed by rage tonight. Even Betsy's frustration at her inability to speak must be gnawing at her dreams. It's as if, in a matter of hours, society has realised there's no good turns or right answers. Living in each other's space, pretending to be a community, won't prop us up indefinitely. The greedy will get angry, the weak will die, and who knows what will happen to those in the middle, non-affiliated to either trait, Alessandro and I, Sierra and Betsy, Nicholas. Colmoor's curse is affecting London, and maybe it's the fault of me, the messenger who trespasses between two starkly different worlds, not quite belonging to either. If London's people catch Colmoorian temper, it'll all go down from here until it's over.

I'm glad mother and father died so they didn't have to live minute by minute in this horrible night like I do. Living is cruel. My mortality has placed me here tonight, every street around me meticulously arranged to make it feel like every snapshot is a backdrop to kill. People will be left behind, and the good ones will scarper too far away to recover them, to remember them, to rescue them. I'll do what I can. My plan starts here, by hauling my weary feet up the concrete steps.

"We're closed." A voice mumbles from a corner.
"Your unlocked door says otherwise." I say flippantly, catching the smile from Nicholas as he emerges, fatigue in his walk, in his eyes, in his gesture. All over him. He's diseased. Alessandro did something else this time, something different.

"It's good to see you, Sebastian," Instantly, I feel at ease. This man knows me from my brother. "You're not allowed back there." He continues, as I swerve behind the bar. He knows me from my brother and disciplines me the same, it's amusing. I start making him a drink, and he gives into arguing, slumping back down in a chair. This isn't a man in need of sleep, this is a man in need of mental safety. I despise that I have the power to make him forget.

I poisoned Sierra before she arrived in London. Well, Alessandro and I poisoned Sierra, in what we thought was good faith. I'll take my involvement in that to the grave, because at the time I feared I'd almost built a robot.

We diluted the Amnesia, and because of our cowardice in doing so, Sierra has shown vague memories. The happy ones. As a woman who approaches life graciously, all of her strongest loves were preserved, immune to the poison, and she retained them. She doesn't know where Colmoor is, or that it exists, but she remembers times on its beaches with Alessandro, and she remembers her home with Bridgette. Alessandro is scrambling now to rewrite the truth, as the diluted drug ceases to work, and he's creating a narrative for her that we never intended to mechanise. It's not a concentration that's strong enough to use in Colmoor, or tie us to them, but I still don't want a hand in this development.

The poison in question was a vial of gas I stole from Colmoor. Invisible in the daylight, silver in the darkness. Its purpose is to stimulate amnesia in the victim, disabling neurons in the brain, but its effectiveness is inhibited by the selective memories it targets. It tries to attack them all, but the stronger the memory, the harder it will be to make the individual forget it. It was just a small amount of Amnesia cooled to room temperature, so it became a liquid we could work with, and slip it into her drinks. The state of the drug meant it didn't act as it should have. If she remembers even an ounce of Colmoor, it'll force its way back in. It's a town that is known, by the locals, for vengeance.

The chemical was manufactured by officials to stop the good people doing good. It removes their conscience, and without stable footing, you'll walk wherever the closest authority sends you - which is always a trap. I'll bet that from my encounters with Colmoorian forces, ninety percent of them used to be family men. Jasper sends men out to find anyone he doesn't have control over, bursting into their private spaces, and drugging them, pulling them by the ankles back to his army. The drug knocks them out for a while, then they wake up with no family, no values and no mercy. It's a tainted world.

A tainted world from which we tainted Sierra, with stolen Amnesia.

I love London for the equality, unthinkable and unheard of in Colmoor. Politicians of both genders, people in power. All genders are allowed to sing. Every person is given the right to self-expression by a bloody unitary set of ideas. Colmoor would never be so lucky, and Jasper would never be so democratic. My hometown is centuries behind modern day fairness, and I am ashamed of my birthplace. I am ashamed of my actions. I am ashamed of myself. I need to bring myself back to reality, the things I can do in the moment, like making a drink for a melting man. Snap out of it. Out of it. Out of it. Now.

I don't use Amnesia on Nicholas, having learnt my lesson. I use the alcohol he has stocked already, which may suffice. I pour, he drinks, and I have to ask him. "Why aren't you asleep?"

Any direction he looks he can't avoid an answer, because I stand in front of him, committed to not moving until I know the reason for this man's pain. There's a selfish reason for my standing too. I want to know what Alessandro has done. We know Nicholas in different ways. Alessandro sees him as a safe for deferment, a place he can deposit Sierra until a better time. I scour the city when my brother requires it, more so when he claims he doesn't, and see this bar as a rest stop for wanderers like me. A good conversation with a bartender, brief safety, a place to go.

Nicholas massages his chin with one hand, balances his drink with the other, and struggles to draw breath without it sounding like a sigh. I wince, it reminds me of Betsy's plight. The people I care for most always hurt in complex ways. "Alessandro is attacking high above his station. I'm worried he doesn't know…"

I look on with encouragement. Finish the sentence, man. Please. "Doesn't know…" I echo.

"How to handle this." He coughs, and takes another swig of the drink. He's not trying to forget anything. He's trying to rack his brains to find out how to help.

"Handle what, Nicholas?" I push.

"Sierra's missing. He's only got a lead on Warner."

Nicholas knows so much for a bartender. He's accepted everything Alessandro and I threw at him from day one, swallowing all the urgency, confusion, danger and responsibilities in his stride. He met Alessandro first, and I sought to introduce myself when I could. I struggle to lie to kind men though. I told him about my brother, underneath the man he calls Isaak, and his need for a low profile. Without revealing Colmoor, I explain we're in danger, and that's all he's ever probed for. All along, a confidante that we've needed, all without a formal agreement of secrecy. He's that type of man, caring for Sierra, fostering safety in this place straight from the first step on the doormat. It doesn't faze me that he knows about Warner, or the telescopes.

"Drink. I'll find them both. All three, if things start looking up." I assert, looking out the window into the nothingness that somewhere contains a trio of people that I want to restrain all for different reasons. Sierra for safety, Alessandro for relief, and Warner, to finish what I started. I should have killed him.

"Hell, Sebastian, be careful. It's not nice out there. Things are off. I just know."

On the way here, I'd reasoned with this night to spare me tragedy and instead the outcome was that I founded two philosophies.

Number One. Anyone could be anything they wanted to be without limiting factors. My father could be a father, a proper one. And me, I could be a man or maybe explorer, at peace without threat.

Number Two. Safety is underestimated. You can be in a safe place without safe company, and within safe company in a dangerous place. I am in a safe place with a safe person in Nicholas's pub, alongside him, but I know the instant I exit, the same can't be said. No sensible person thinks they can have both elements of safety at once.

"Do me the honour of being the second person in the entire world with my number. You should feel privileged." I say with a half-smile, scribbling down the memorised digits onto a white portion of a menu. He doesn't care that I've vandalised it, and tucks it into his pocket after taking a second to examine it.

"Oh, I do, son. You're a good one."

"Call me next time my brother pulls a stunt like this. It's not good for your health." I poke at his stupor, pallor and age. I find it more humorous than he does, but we both know of the mutual care between us. He'll never replace my father, but he is all of my closest living relative beyond Alessandro. I'd prefer him alive for as long as possible, my family doesn't have a hugely successful track record.

"Hey, I'm healthy." He retorts.

"Makes one of us, huh? Alessandro is a liability." I feign a chuckle, bringing life back into a verbal mortuary.

"Must make self-loathing easy."

I know I will be in danger. I'm throwing my life on a thin tightrope of safety. One slip and I'm dead. Nicholas also receives the anathemas of tonight, spilling from the darkness, and looks at me with pity. The pattern of his eyes bears into my mind, the pyrography of an honest, kind man into my heart spurs me on. Nicholas becomes my courage.

"Sebastian?" The bartender calls me before I'm about to face the rain, that's just about ceasing. "Thank you." It's sincere.

"All part of the Gray Brothers service." I humour him, not believing in one bit that me and my brother are a team right now. Alessandro should have called me, on something like this. Regardless, Nicholas needs confidence more than he needs to drink, and there's no room on a battleground for apologies, explanations or sensitivities. Only orders to charge. Charge. Charge. Charge.

But a headstrong charge can't wind back time. I turn a corner, hear voices, and stop, and let my eyes do the rest. Where is Alessandro? He must have been so riled up by the damage to his own pride by losing Sierra, that he's forgotten the only thing to do is to think like her. In a dark night, what would she follow? Where would her heart, if it was hurting, guide her? Somewhere equally dark to match. Somewhere alone. Somewhere closed off. There's only a limited amount of these hiding spots in such an open, tourist filled, nocturnal city. It's only a matter of which one.

The first one failed me. The second one was an equal success and failure for he's reached her, the final rotten element in a moulding street, on moulding cobbles, with a girl whose innocence doesn't belong there. I refuse to walk away. I was too late the first time, I couldn't stop Warner from hurting Betsy, in fact she did that herself, but under my watch he'll never touch another Genieva woman again.

The orders are telling me nothing. My brain doesn't know what part to command me with. My logic is scrambling, my instinct says interfere but it also says wait. All reason knows that if I wait, I'll regret it, and if I go, I'll risk Sierra seeing me, which requires more explanations that I can't give on a battleground. Where *the fuck* is Alessandro? Nowhere. The realistic answer is nowhere. He isn't going to be. It's down to me, for the sister I didn't take responsibility for. The way this world works will spite me one day.

He spins and brings up a gun to her head. If he shoots, she'll die. She'll die. I decimate the orders, and run. Run in front of her pleading cries, run in front of the gun, run in front of my brother's love, and at that, an incredible woman. Run to greet the painful sound of the air being torn in two with my last whole breath.

My chest gets warm. The elasticity of adrenaline has snapped back and it dawns on me what I've done. The severity. My morality. It's entered just above my right breastbone. I have a bullet in me, like Father, and I haven't got long. I want to let death take me, but no member of the Gray family died for nothing and I can't be the first. I stagger to my feet, Sierra screaming "Isaak! Oh, Isaak!" I look around for my brother, wanting to see his smug little face. I want to die, the same way I lived. Bordering fatality with Alessandro. Sierra isn't screaming for Isaak. She's screaming for me. I have his face, the same tattoo, the same idiotic drive to do stupid things for another's protection. What I don't have, is the explosion of love, and need, and despair he has for this girl - and she needs to know it. I need to see her know it, or my brother will be repressed forever.

On my feet, barely, I crumple up as I walk. I hate the pain. I hate that I'm trying to wire up my body through the shock. I need to remember what I know about fighting. You have to give in, sometimes. I streak a bloody hand on Warner, using the last of my strength to push him away from her and knock away the gun. Sierra has the sense to rush to it, and stop it serving anyone else's hatred. My hand plunges into Warner's pockets, drawing out the telescope. I fall to my knees and pound it, grinding the metal into the floor with a closed fist. Hitting it. Hitting out the pain. It's searing. *Fucking hell.* "There-" I suck in breath, "Go. Fuck off. You've got more time." I wince, knowing there's tears streaming from my eyes. I'm on the floor, completely, and convulsing. This is the end. The glare of the moon on my tears means I can't see Warner, but I still talk to him, "Don't think he won't find you. He'll kill you." There are a few quiet seconds. He conferred with himself if he should take the opportunity. Two kills in one night is greedy, not when there's the chance to space them out. I hear him scuttle away, through the frenzy of panic and blood in my eardrums. Then there's Sierra.

"Isaak, don't die…please. I'm sorry. I said horrible things. I-" she frets over me, trying to press the blood back in, "I'm so sorry."

I haven't got the breath to explain. There's one last thing on my mind. "IM…" My brother, by the identity he wants. "In love with you." I die to the sounds of her screams. My body dies a little before my mind, the night's exhibitions running through my mind like a film tape that runs on without an audience.

Betsy's smile and sleep. Her heart. If I think too much about the girl that I'm leaving behind, I'll die twice.

The last image of Colmoor. I left unafraid of what would happen, that place is too far gone, with or without me.

Nicholas' trust in me, that I carried until I couldn't. His eyes. His words. He warned me Alessandro had gone too far, now I know how.

Alessandro. Nicholas said Alessandro. The orders siffle in, in depleted beats. Alessandro. Alessandro. Alessandro.

Nobody outside of Colmoor calls him Alessandro. Nicholas is a Colmoorian. Nicholas has Sierra's eyes. Betsy's eyes. I looked into those beautiful eyes, full of love, only hours ago. How did I miss it? The clues I ignored all fall into place as the lack of oxygen starves me, and my mind surrenders. I didn't do enough, know enough, to tell them Nicholas is their father.

CHAPTER XXV: MISTAKE

Sierra.

Affection is a hyperbolic attachment to death. I could bring myself out of it before, on my balcony, when it was just a man. A man I didn't know, a man that wasn't Isaak. It sounds awful that I can simply depersonalise a man, to help me forget death. I can make him just a figure and a figment of my imagination. I've seen two people die in short succession, and yet one hits me harder than the other because I have affection for one. Affection exaggerates the pain of death, especially when there are so many more words left unsaid. Affection is the debt that the living owes to the dead, and that debt piles on twofold if you held affection from them whilst they were living, whilst you thought you had all the time in the world to say how you felt. To portion your heart.

Maybe it's a good thing Isaak never accepted a share of my love, because if part of my heart belonged to Isaak now, it would be somewhere halfway to heaven, irretrievable, and where would that leave me? To trudge the rest of my mortal journey with a semi-heart, loving someone in the sky.

He's mourned by me, and the lights he loved. The moon aches to wrap him up, but can only scratch the pavement lazily, both me and the wind can't move for we're stunned by the loss of this wild night roamer and romancer. All is still. I want it to be still. I don't want there to be a time where I abate all the feelings I have inside me for this dead man, just to conform to uniformity, to reality, to the pretence that time will heal pain. Time is my enemy, what will follow Isaak's death is an endless cold, and an endless darkness until my own death in years to come. How can cruel society expect me to obey with a smile, and exclamations of healing when my sanctuary in a man, my home in *un hombre*, is shattered? Time has surpassed itself. Time has won the game. I need to remind myself to breathe, because right now it is all I know. I am entirely broken.

Isaak speaks now, and I can hear him spilling numbers rather than blood. The sound is as clear as day, yet the emptiness looms dark because I know he is dead. He's in front of me, more scarlet than butterscotch, life escaped him, one thing he couldn't run from. *5, 4, 3, 2, 1.* Why is it so clear? I've read about trauma, auditory hallucinations, and whispers - the brain's way of stapling the gaps. Still, no amount of research or anecdotes could prepare me for the pain of this feeling. Hours of moments with him ripped away, because nobody remembers him in that way but me, in his beautiful rebellion and incapacity to fully let himself relax, the hurt in his eyes on the stairwell, blinded by pride so much that he couldn't see I was what he wanted. Now he'll have no chance to tell me.

A gunshot cracks in the air whilst I'm in the middle of breaking. If my heart was slowing, it isn't anymore. I check, and as expected, the gun I hold in my hand is dormant, sleeping, exhausted. So, whose gun is awake - and when do I run? I stumble closer to Isaak's body, my legs hardly pulling their weight, pretending he'll protect me, not wanting to believe I'm on my own. I raise the gun to the darkness. I'm an egregious statue, stony-faced and shaking, standing, waiting for something to pounce so I can prove myself to myself.

Nothing happens. Nothing emerges from the darkness, but there's gasping. I want to investigate but my heart won't let me leave Isaak's body. Then there's a scraping sound like shoes on a dirty pavement, and Isaak has to get up, smile, say he's only joking. I look forwards and back between whatever's approaching and my love, then when the alternating fear and longing reaches its limit and I don't want to see ahead, I stare away. My gun faces forward, my eyes do not. The noise stops and I know that there's someone in front of me.

My finger is anchored on the trigger, I don't know why I can't pull. A hand pushes down hard on the weapon, lowering my aim until if I shot now, I'd shoot the floor and either of us could die.

I might die. I didn't shoot and now I'm going to be killed. I still can't look. I don't want to know who takes my life. My life is mine and Isaak's, and if I don't look, then nobody can take that away from me. That's my last morsel of decency I award myself, whilst I still have autonomy over my heart. Then, the gun gets dislocated from my hand. Gently, for a murderer.

"I know we argued. I expected anger. I didn't expect a gun." A voice I've heard so often in my dreams meets my ears. I snap my eyes back on him. It's him. Isaak. This is real life. I'm not delusional. This is real life, I think. But a man that looks exactly like my lover still lies dead behind me, so which part of this is a dream? Isaak is painted with relief, until he sees himself on the floor. His face changes. It's ugliness. Written all over him. An indescribable expression. Searing pain. Quickly, it's back to normal and he ducks, then lifts me neatly over his shoulder, carrying me from hell.

I don't know where we end up. I can describe it little more than I can place it somewhere in London, but I can try. A room no bigger than a cloakroom, unfurnished, a musty smell, and Isaak. Alive. I can't have made it here supported by a phantom's frame, so he must be real.

"I know you have so many questions," he ruminates, "and I will make it all make sense, Sierra. I promise you." To my surprise, he sank to the floor, a deflated version of the man he was when I'd last seen him and he'd held a chase all the way out of our apartment. Still, I suppose, this is better than dead, although he ought to start talking before I change my mind. "Talk. Then I won't need to ask questions."

He coughs, rubbing at his temples, getting rid of the sweat and the hair sticking to his forehead. This isn't because he doesn't know what to say, it's because he just doesn't want to and will just wait for something else to happen that calls him away. I'm regaining all feeling in my hands and feet. My blood is warming up again and now my fear is corrosive. There's no more shielding my outrage.

"I just watched you die. You jumped in front of me. He shot you, and then you just suddenly turned up again, large as life, and slung me over your shoulder. I almost shot you for Christ's sake, I know I didn't, but I could have done. For *fuck's* sake, Isaak, that warrants an explanation at the very least! You, you saved me." I burst out.

"He really jumped in front of you..." Isaak buries his head in his hand, clutching his scalp, strengthening his grip until his knuckles whiten, "shit."

I think he feels me looking at him, and knows he dare not meet my eyes unless he wants to use his own to cry seas of apologies. "I didn't save you, Sierra. I just somewhat pathetically assisted in the prevention of your death. He saved you, and it wasn't even his path. He came here especially for you, because he knew it wouldn't be long before I lost control. He knew you needed saving and I needed someone. Now he's dead...because of me." The realisation hits as he speaks.

Careful not to ask questions, I crouch beside him, placing a hand on his arm. My anger dissipates, because some hearts are psychic, and I can tell that whoever else had his affection, admiration, for this long, is the one lying dead in the street, metres away, heart not beating. Isaak doesn't want me close to him, shaking me off his arm and walking to the door to accept that his heart no longer has a receiver on the other end. Who's the dead man, and who is the living one leaning against the doorframe? I don't feel I know him anymore, and yet I pursue him out of hopeless faith. "Isaak, name him. It'll help the pain. I'll speak my pain. My pain is Bridgette. Tell me who you lost." I try to encourage him.

"My brother. Sebastian." He breathes, his Adam's apple disappears and then resurfaces as if he's trying to cram the pain back inside by not speaking through it. He's said enough.

I don't remember deciding I was going to hold him, one moment I'm watching him swallow his pain from a distance, and now he's against me, wheezing, "Tell me what he said when he died, Sierra. Please. I need to know."

He's turning the tables, in his tried and tested, heavily predicted, technique, but I can't deny him as he grieves. It's a case of remembering, through replaying the moment, filtering out my own screams to make out what his brother said. They look so alike in my memory that it scares me. I've seen a counterfeit Isaak die before the real one, and worst of all, I believed it. I wonder how much that says of me as a lover. I need to take the time to be assured I'll never mistake him again. *I'm in love with you.*

"I'm in love with you..." I parrot, and before I realise what I've said straight to the face of someone I've been loving for years from three feet away, he interrupts me.

"The bastard." Isaak mutters, and breaks away from me. This cycle of attraction and retraction is messing with my mind, and with the last of my dignity I approach him, clasping his hands.

"I know you're grieving, and I will give you time to do that, but I, I am at a limit. I'm keeping calm, but you've fucked me up and if I don't get answers, I swear to you, you won't see me again." I release him so he knows I mean it.

"He told you I love you. IM. Me. Isaak Macaluso. That's just the way he does- did- things with his bloody initialisms. I owe it to him to follow through, but I can't love you Sierra. I just can't." Isaak sounds defeated, but he's not the one on a knife's edge. I'm devoid of empathy.

"There's more to whatever this is, Isaak. I wouldn't let my heart be as bruised as it is for just anyone, so you've got to keep talking. I wish I didn't, but I care about you. Tell me you don't love me. Let me leave."

"I can't love you. There's a vast difference." He can't look me in the face.

"There's no difference, Isaak. It's just what you want to believe. What you think. What you feel. If that's all it's going to be then tell me goodbye." I know that I'll want to scoop all my words out of the silence and apologise, but I can't keep buoyant on this ocean, on waves of emotion. I know that what's underwater could either kill me or make me breathless.

Constantly weighing up this risk has slit my wrists and kept me blood-bound to this man who sneaks around London like the plague. I can choose to scream 'man overboard', find new land, and cultivate a place around me that won't nurture lies or secrets. I can crown myself the captain. I picture Columbus and a dead rose. Singing with sirens. Loving my freedom.

"You can't love me because of this city. Polyamorous since the day we all met. London's your mistress." I can't avoid what I'm about to do. My tears are flying off my cheeks as I throw my encore in his direction. "Isaak, I always thought there was something else to you, something I could unlock. I thought I could be the key, that breaks you apart so I can love every bit of you that you hid from everyone. There wasn't ever a key, was there? You just had your lock. Sebastian. He kept you contained. Now he's gone, you're broken and you don't know what to do to stay the unafraid way you were and pretend you're a pillar. People get scared, Isaak. It's who we choose to feel safe with that protects us, and if I can't have your love and safety together, I don't want you at all."

"This is insane." He's hot on my heels to the door. Everything moves so fast.

"Is a woman with standards how you define insanity?" I bite.

"No..." he exhales, stepping towards me, edging his hands around my waist and pulling me close without time to lie to me. "It's insane you don't know I crave you. It's insane my brother has just died, and I'm about to leave lonely the only one in this damn world that cares enough to see inside me. A woman with standards isn't insane. This night is. The notion of being without you. Everything I could use this *fucking* moment for," he finishes by kissing me. I see bright colours. Romantic colours. Deep colours. A breakthrough. It's obvious now he was holding back when he kissed me a galaxy. This time he's got my veins tugging my blood along astronomically fast. I could be beyond this universe if I dared to open my eyes.

He keeps his lips firmly on mine, tugging like he wants to extract my thoughts of escaping. I need to humble him, and turn the tables. "I could escape you if I wanted. Don't get...cocky." I gasp, wrenching his neck forward to make his tongue forage past my teeth.

"Escape me then." Isaak's hands ride up my back, the skin to skin I've wanted. Although neither of us will ever understand our own ways of working, we've stumbled across this middle ground. I'm a captain, turned pirate, turned outlaw - *he collects my hands behind my back and finds a wall to hold me to* - turned prisoner.

"No." I shudder, through flustered kisses and a headache, neither of which bothers me in the slightest. I didn't take Isaak for an arsonist but my skin is on fire with his touch. Nothing comes as a surprise anymore, life, death, borderline surrender and sacrifice. Intense. Bittersweet. Necessary. It's all the same to me.

He pulls my necklace from his pocket, reclasping it around me. "You lost this."
I scowl, but let him fix it.

Isaak deals with nothing appropriately. He upholds his brother's legacy by trailing me back to our apartment, planting his lips on my neck whenever he isn't glancing back at our path, delivering on his duty and acting on his urges. I'm so enamoured by him, and he's so desperate for company that my heels drag through puddles as he pulls me with love, towards privacy. Outdoors, it feels like all eyes in London are on us, creatures preying on our primal attraction, lashing out at our happiness because we stand out as two lovers clueless to grief and the world. Our bodies are pulsing, demanding sex, accompanied by cosy candlelight in the corner of the bedroom. A flicker bright enough to illuminate our skin and make the shadows of his fingertips against my waist spread like fireworks, the silhouettes of his touch dripping onto the warm bed sheets. They weren't warm when we got here. The heat came from us. The candle wax and its burn, is just dim enough that it doesn't shed light on the gloom of Sebastian's departure from the world, so we can forget for a while. It's not ignorance. It's the thrill of being alive, of touching, of loving, of exploring. Death reminds us to live, and to Isaak, it's an automated notification, albeit one that hits a fraction too close to home, to fuck me against all four walls whilst the opportunity, and the impulsion. He has an impulse for me.

The first wall he goes slow, a perfect virgin. Sensitive, tentative. Knowing that firsts come only once in a lifetime. He kisses me in places I can't love myself, areas I've never been kissed. I can't control the tremble that follows. I'm possessed with the feelings I've suppressed for him, exotic nymphs and pixies that make me scream his name. I feel them tingling at my hair, relentlessly dancing, until they hear me beg for him. If I opened my eyes, it would be him pulling me by my hair, and not the fairies twisting at my roots, but I can't open my eyes. I don't like to see, when these feelings let me fall asleep in the back of my imagination, a lazy, comfortable journey. He drags my underwear to my ankles whilst I call for him to be closer. Yet, he keeps his distance because if he's going to love me and all my demons, and dig up all our repression, it's going to be his way or I'll be sleeping alone.

Effortlessly, I find myself responding to his energy in rotation around my room. I'm seeing an aesthetic I've spent so many nights in, become a playground, become a boudoir, become a scene that my lust will revisit again and again. The window stretches the length of the room, a thin pale curtain dividing me from London, keeping it out of our affairs, but when Isaak casts me against it I'm sure my figure can be seen hazily from the outside. I'm both breathing a mist in response to the cold glass, and breaking a sweat in retaliation to his touch. Isaak takes my shirt off, wasting no time on buttons, and knocks me around to face away from him, in one fluid movement. His hands are all over me, my exogenous beloved meets my erogenous desires, and he's not polite about it. He bites, like he can taste my aching, and it's his new favourite flavour. A prodigious cup of coffee has nothing on my pheromones.

Third wall. Between the window and this one, he's lost all but his grey boxer shorts, our tattoos spy each other like strangers with a hidden past, trying to catch a shared glimpse before Isaak pulls me to him, so I can't question our markings. I can only try to guess how long I can withstand my torso being so close to his beating heart. *He does have one.* Discovery after discovery, and it overcomes my affliction, and angst, towards mystery. Isaak has a heart. I, as it turns out, have a wild side. He's not the only one with a bite. He scrounges for a capable grip on my legs, to lift me around his waist, groaning as I leave teeth marks on his neck. He has more to give, and now I've engaged in a competition of our mouths, he's bringing the force. The last mystery underneath the waistband of his boxers is uncovered, and I feel if there were any more secrets between us, they would have all been washed away. My lover is beautiful. Golden. Alight. Mine.

I don't know how to remain standing. I want to fall to my knees for him, but Isaak works in a series of numbers and we're one line away from having drawn a full, equal, square with our passion. We've touched in all four corners but there's one more line it's imperative we cross, to box us into a lover's kingdom. To find ourselves the king and queen, and complete.

The bed is against the fourth wall, and we've forgotten what words are. My thighs are doused with a smattering of love bites, because he whispered to me three words, I thought he'd never say to me, and I put my signature on permission for his free reign. A siege of my being, bestowed upon one man. A man who changed my world by whispering *I love you.* As he said it, he stared into my eyes, loving me inside out, my body meaning just as much to him as my voice, my heart, my attitude to the world, and apparently my newfangled libido. Our new rhythm.

"Sierra, I'm afraid to hurt you."
"There's no need to be afraid." I say to a man who has more fear, and strength, than he knows what to do with. I have more trust in him now than I ever have, and it would be a wreck for us both if I misplaced or mistimed it. I feel now is right.

There's a record player standing proudly on a chest of drawers in my room, only existent, until now, for daily decoration. I have records, so we christened the mechanism, letting music play to disguise the sounds of Isaak churning his fear into passion inside me. I all but expected it to be over in moments, pinned in memory, but it lasted enough for me to remember how he slightly takes his bottom lip into his mouth when he gets overcome. I know what his hair looks like from underneath him, I know where he positions his arms to keep himself above me. I know all these things I yearned to know at least once in this lifetime. I remember it all: music, dim light, warmth in four walls whilst London was cold and whilst a dead man lay in the street where we'd left him.

There are truths we try to hide, but we are weak. Kind people, or those with good intentions, have brittle resistance to morals. This can mean we fall into the guilt that arises after sex that happened so fast with someone who we've only just learnt to love in person but have been loving in our mind for the better part of forever. This can mean knowing we can't leave a dead man out in the pouring rain, to suffer over and over until he can be dry under soil and buried with a legacy.

Isaak dresses himself, helplessly kissing me with the promise he'll be back. Satisfaction, gratification and belonging are preserved in the condensation hanging on every mirrored surface. With reality and fatigue settling into the early morning paradise, and my clock reading a blurry 3am, the rotating record provides soulful consistency.

Before he leaves, Isaak treads towards the sound, tightening his belt around his hips. He doesn't want to think too deeply about what he has to do once he leaves these walls, and I don't want to know. His eyes scan the cyclical spin of music, and he pauses, only briefly.

"Does this song have a name? I can't risk forgetting it." He asks.

He asks. I answer and I don't register the milestone through my fifth headache of the evening, or the same one recurring, until I hear the front door shut. *He actually asks.*

CHAPTER XXVI: HOLD

Isaak.

Red carpet events look like a magician's work to a naive individual. I roll my eyes when I walk past them in London and I'll tell you why. It's a parade of the walking dead. These people were put on screen, their demise written into a script, and they saunter as large as life in reality. Shockingly unrealistic deaths, some of them. They'll make any screenwriter famous as long as they can hold a pen to paper or who chirps up at a table, regurgitating an idea they saw on a lesser-known show. It's merely characters that die, and the actors live on. We see them die, we mourn them in the credits, then get hounded by the paparazzi in hours. These people play on the audience's emotions and get celebrated for it.

I've seen my own body die from a distance, and find myself still breathing, working, functioning. I watched my lookalike brother get shot, from a distance, firsthand. Which means the actors and I have something in common aside from a stage name. We both get to cheat death. It's both an honour, and dangerous. It's horrific and haunting to be the one to bury a brother, but when all is said and done, Sebastian Gray, a man who loved harder than I ever could, is with the people he yearned to love the most. Reconciliation six feet under. That's no reason to be jealous, so I wipe away those green streaks from my predilections, and instead remember the promise I made. I'll live for you, in your footsteps, and one step ahead to clear your path, my impossible girl.

When I reach him, he's reclined like he's sleeping, crumpled in the middle of the road. Dark, looking like clothes and red wine, looking like waste until you realise it's a person. My brother, for sure. He's staring at me.

Sebastian died with wide open eyes, unsettling me. I've seen his eyes before, they're my eyes for fuck's sake, but I've never seen them glassy and lifeless. The first thing I do is press them closed, because I can't stand the fact he thinks he still has to watch me move after death. You can sleep now, brother, leave things to me. Let me be the protector I should have been, whilst you frolic in the land of the dead with our parents, poking fun at me because I'm the only one who hasn't realised how easy it is to be dead. No responsibilities, but also less beauty, and less heart, less Sierra. Which is why it's not an option for me to die.

"I loved her, like you wanted." I speak at deaf ears as I try to pull him up from the ground. He weighs too much, all his limbs and organs, putrid and slackened. Heavy. "It was everything I thought it'd be. I fell for someone who's going to destroy me, I hope you knew that when you told her. Bet you thought you were real smart." I try to lift him by shoving my hands under his arms and dragging him up onto my knees. He slumps forward, neck swinging loosely. "At least *try* to cooperate or you'll be late for Mother and Father, wherever they're waiting." Eventually I manage to achieve momentum, albeit a crawl, with a corpse slung over my shoulder. It feels disrespectful, but it's the most effective display of pragmatism so far. I'll talk to him, so it makes hauling a body through an abandoned London street seem more humanitarian.

"I even asked her a question. Just came from nowhere. I didn't have to pretend." I keep talking to myself, hearing Sebastian in my head. The first stage of becoming completely delusional.

But did you tell her your real name, AG? Get out of my head, if you're going to ask those sorts of questions, the conversation's over. Terminated. You're dead, remember.

Why Isaak with a k and not a c, did you think it looked pretty? Don't be pedantic. I'm not concerned with the aesthetic of a name. Words don't constitute fashion. I just liked the punch. Sounded impactful. *Right. Impactful.* Go away.

It's silent when I banish him from my mind, and for the first time in my life, I realise I'm without family. I'm not without people though, there's two that depend on me, and several I have to avoid whilst carrying a deceptively large tarpaulin up several flights of stairs, tucking it behind the sofa. It's no more suspicious than any other trip I've taken, but I feel red hot, like I'm being watched. Dead bodies won't be on the contract of any level headed landlord. I massage the crushing pain radiating from my ribs, and I will my collarbone not to collapse with the ghostly feeling of Sebastian's weight still on my neck, wondering how on earth I'll tell Sierra we're hosting my brother's skeleton until the sun sets again tomorrow. I reached an easy conclusion, which is that I'm not going to tell her. Partially because I don't want her to relive the trauma, and also because it's an almost unapproachable conversation. I feel immature and dysregulated from the incongruous hours of death, sex, honesty and questions. The night is almost too dissonant to fulfil a promise, yet I am many things but a coward.

"Sierra, take me in." I kneel beside her bed, nursing my shoulders, and hoping it's too dark for her to see that I'm covered in my brother's blood. Hopefully, I won't have to remind her of her desires for me.

She stirs, mumbling. "I thought you'd never ask."
"Note that I didn't ask," I'm trying, shamefully, to reinforce the man I was and wanted to be, but one question was all it took to open floodgates of integrity, now that's all she'll expect from me.

"A conscious effort now?" She laughs. The mocking that follows is sweet and delirious, deliciously fictional, with the ways she tries to echo me asking questions that I'm confident I never asked. *Sierra, will you touch me? Sierra, what's the time? Sierra, can you make some space in the bed?* I frown with the audacity she takes, loving her courage. She finishes her taunting with, "Get in here, before you change your mind and run back off to fuck London."

"I can assure you that you're my capital. Move over." I grunt, effusively. Everything's all wrong. I'm in Sierra's bed. My brother's in the living room, without his life. She's mere inches away, and I don't thirst to be outside. There's more to deliberate, to make things as right as they can be. A girl called Betsy Genieva, who before this time tomorrow, will be evenly heartbroken and whole again. Without a lover, but reunited with a sister. I'll be burdened too, for having to deliver the news back to Colmoor, having to bring her to London, and having to leave my brother there to decay. Having to watch two siblings have forever whilst mourning that the past stole my brother from each one of us in a different way. Sebastian will be remembered as a multifaceted custodian; one who saved Sierra from a bullet, Betsy from her adversities, and me from myself.

Insomnia and paranoia slice me in half so much I can't sleep, and I know that it's because Sebastian is dead. As much as I can kid myself that Sierra will numb me, it doesn't detract from the fact my brother is turning cold in the room next door, all the fluid that hasn't spilt still swimming in his ashen body. It doesn't all feel real. Staring up at the ceiling, the blame jumps at Warner, because he held the gun. But we've all held guns. Then when I toss and turn, I'm furious at Jasper, then Colmoor, and then Sebastian himself for prying. Then it's on me. If

I'd have been there quicker, then nobody would have died. Sebastian would smile, tell me it was a close one, and follow his heart back to Betsy.

I stumble to the kitchen, mumbling to Sierra, scapegoating coffee again as an excuse for the space I need. My skin is itching, and my nostrils are flaring involuntarily. I feel like the smell of death is carrying into the bedroom, and I need to shut it all out. I need to get rid of my brother, because as soon as he's buried, the better. I won't be reminded of grief or guilt. The fucking grandfather clock haunts me, an omen of death, ringing and ringing like it lacks social awareness for the actual time it is. It bellows at me before the sun has even risen, reminding me of my father. It patronises me, pretending to know that my father would be ashamed if he knew I let my brother die. I can't know what he'd think, I can only hope he'd pity me - but I've got to exhaust a whole lifetime until that question can be answered, and I'm not in a rush.

My footsteps abide by their own programme, and launch me next to Sebastian. Before I know what I'm doing, I've grabbed the limp hand of a dead man and am combing through my hair with his frozen fingers - begging his death to also claim my flashbacks. I don't care that it's a bloody encasement of bones and flesh. There's been so much pain that Sebastian's been freed from, I need him to act as mediation, and ferry my pain somewhere I can't feel it.

"Order them out. Make them go fucking anywhere else. Go on. You can stop them. You can." I seethe, whilst crusted blood flakes away from Sebastian's forearm and onto the carpet. I can't keep him here. Throwing his hand back onto his chest, I lie beside him and look over again. It landed at a funny angle and my gag reflex stirs. I'm by his side until the flashbacks leave me alone, and I need to think, seriously, about how to haul him back to Colmoor tonight.

"Isaak! If you've gone out again, I can't even begin to-" Sierra gets up just past lunchtime, and calls from the bedroom, her steps are travelling down the hall to start a search for me in every room. I don't recognise how long I've slept for, and only realise once I'm met with the sunlight. I hastily shut the curtains, so the neighbours can't cry murder, and step out into the hall. "I'm here."

Her face is drowned in relief from seeing me, but then the rosiness vacates her cheeks. Without colouration, her eyes seem to sink into her face. I launch forward to cushion her just as she falls to her knees, wailing, breaking apart in front of my eyes. Her mouth is open, but when she consummated her louder scream, she kept it open, her teeth pushing into my sleeve. I know she wants her muscles to hurt. I've been acquainted with that feeling before, waking up from nightmares. She's heaving, haemorrhaging tears. Each lurch of her body expels a pain she's incurred because of me. I clutch her as she scratches at the carpet, wheezing and not in control of herself. It's making me itch to be inside her mind. "I can't go outside Isaak...I *can't*..." she evicts a muffled howl from somewhere deep in her throat into my shoulder. She's completely terrified. We wasted the energy she had to stay robust, on sex.

"No weapon, or behemoth behind it, has the power to silence Sierra Genieva. Tell me there's still a part of you that knows that." I compel her to understand, guiding her to look into my eyes.

"I'll sing...a barricade." Sierra mumbles, tasting her tears on her tongue.

"Attagirl. And I'll do the rest. They killed Sebastian, they know what I'll do if I see shadows in this city." I begin to rock her because, when she hears my brother's name, she seizes up.

"*Oh, Sebastian!* I was stubborn and it wasn't worth your brother's life, Isaak. I'm so sorry. If I'd never left the pub, if I'd listened…"

"If you listened to anything or anyone but your instincts, you'd only be half the woman you are today. Your desires lead you. It's arrestingly attractive, it's an honour to exist in your sphere. My brother made his own choices, and he made that one for the both of us. You owe him nothing but to keep on keeping on."

I make sure she knows this, but let her grieve, the spiel I was anticipating since I let her watch from the balcony.

"The shot. It's not left my mind. You were so calm. *How* could you be so calm unless you had something to do with it? I just, I want to ask you all the questions but I don't even want to hear the answers. Witnessing gunshots and just being expected to live with it, *isn't normal*, Isaak. Then being stood up, the late nights, the cocktails I've surrendered to, to try and feel okay, *crying* in a *pub bathroom*. Getting *stalked*. Getting *shot* at. In and out of love with you, even though I *fucking adore you*, and then finding out you have a twin brother after he stands in front of a bullet meant *for me*. What the fuck. The life I'm living with you, for you, this life is psychosis."

Impressively, not a single breath entered or exited her mouth throughout the whole recital. I shouldn't be surprised, but I've never seen performance endurance to express a mental state. She promptly makes up for the lost breaths, going into shock. In mourning, I reap my privileges of being unassailable, not answering a single question as her hyperventilation ensues. I need this to escalate. If it gets fast enough, once it declines, she'll be tired and will want to sleep more than answers. I can sneak out as soon as it's dark and deal with Sebastian.

Sierra hasn't mentioned the legality of leaving my brother's body in the street, but perhaps that's her quiet faith in me. Faith that I'll deal with it. I keep a thumb on her pulse, until it softens. I nurture her before I depart from her. I give her food, water, and a safe place to sleep, with the words *don't leave without me*.

The night arrives late because it knows I'm waiting for it. I'd have thought it'd rush to spectate me burying my brother. I start a rhythm against which to haul Sebastian's body, and it's an endless march all of the miles to Colmoor, with minimal slip ups. Pull, stop, breathe, again. Imagining Sebastian and I grunting these words in synch helps, when really it is just my voice alone, swept up in the lashing wind. The taste of Colmoor's nastiness reaches me earlier than usual, it's the taste of blood in your mouth, which I like, interspersed with mould, which I don't. You're already in a jail of scents, sounds and tastes before you see the sights.

At a suitable distance, I shed the tarpaulin from over my brother and let the skies salvage it. I use this as an opportunity to sit and watch the dark covering get smaller as it travels into the distance, and I would be sweating, if the air hadn't stolen the beads as well. I'm interested in what the sky collects, there's so much that falls back down to earth, that it must just be holiness and souls. Every other material thing, or intangible concept, is too heavy to be held. Envy is on earth. Fear is on earth. Violence is on earth. Killers. The sky can't even hold onto sadness, that's when it cries.

I know for certain, one voice that remains in heaven's library. Never stop, Mother. I still think I hear your voice on mortal earth on a still night, spurring me on. Not like tonight, when the wind is winding me up and I can't hear you to save my life, and neither could Sebastian when he needed you. That's not to say I don't crave particular weather. I love the rain. The skies remind me that I'm playing in the corporeal filth, and I adore the thrill of only having one shot at it. How much damage I could do, how many lives I can save, how many I can end, how much trouble I could be. Everything I could do to those who threaten me. Too many people haven't realised that at anytime, anywhere, not a single human actually has more to lose than their life. Pain could be exciting, emotional, entertaining. Pain is a plaything. That's why they encourage you to share it.

I share my pain with the dirt. The exhaustive volleying of my hands into the mud, digging my brother's grave in between our parents'. I don't leave space beside him for me. I want to be buried atop them all, with my arms outstretched. I don't know when to stop sharing the pain. It's exhilarating. It goes on forever. I can't get enough pressure underneath my fingernails, I can't spear enough insects, cracking their bodies if they happen to be in my way. I can't move enough ground. I can't demonstrate to my parent's bones enough that I'm trying. Trying to be what they wanted, feeling as though I'm failing anyway. Returning the more honourable of their sons, back to rest with them. I line the crumbling soil casket with blood-laced saliva, and keep lifting Sebastian in and out of it to experiment with the depth. I'm wasting time, but I don't care. This is the non-negotiable amount of effort going into a send-off this man deserves. I wasn't prepared for the reality of Sebastian's body finally being eclipsed by the messy grave I've pulled apart from scratch. This is it. No more digging. No more make believe that this is fun.

I deposit the soil back on top of him. Not his face first. I can't. His feet first, his legs next, to delay the inevitable. By this point, I'm kicking the mound of soil, creating avalanches so that gravity can do the job my heart can't. Eventually, it is unavoidable. I hesitate, unsure whether to do it incrementally or all in one so I don't have to think about him suffocating. Dead people don't choke as the dirt hits their windpipe, but the alive people burying them can only imagine what it's like to not be able to breathe. All in one. No, in increments. Shit. Sebastian can't make me indecisive. I'm Isaak, Alessandro, alive. Not one of my identities waits, especially not for my dead twin to make a choice. I throw the last smattering of soil across his eyes. *Goodbye, brother.*

I take a moment to disassociate. Then, continue. It's not my last duty tonight, and it wasn't the hardest. Quickly, I finish shovelling the dirt, and then I smooth the ground and leave my family to reunite, taking one last look at the unmarked grave. No Colmoorian will think any differently of the churned-up patch in the graveyard, new handmade graves are commonplace, but there may be a rumination of respect for the hand that killed a revolutionary. An anonymous grave means a Colmoorian soldier killed a Gray brother. They don't know who or which one, although it is only a matter of time.

I am satisfied that for now I know more. I know that two legacies were sealed with a bullet. I know the names.

Sebastian has told me about the treehouse. We both took our girls to higher ground, to guard from a platform, so I know I'm headed to the trees. There's so many but I'll hunt the forest. Don't shoot the messenger, but tire him so he'll beg for it. I'm apprehensive. I don't know how Betsy will take this without a voice and with a broken arm, she can't scream like Sierra, and can't curse or pound the ground with her anger. She has lost her lover, but never his love. "This is the worst thing you've ever had me do. Worse than all of it. I detest you." I grumble to the dial tone of Sebastian's phone.
You love me, that's why you're doing this. I know. Praise fraternity.

But of course, there's no reply. The phone is underground with him.

The disappearance of watchful eyes is how I know I'm close. Brown eyes from a window, at a height, and a distance. They ignited with the sight of me, and awaited my return at the top of a stepladder I've never ascended before. Those eyes belong to a face, as pretty as anything, and a body, that comes up to me close. She rests her head on my chest, feels my beating heart, for a second believing it beats for her. Those eyes belong to a body that takes a breath before realising I'm not the brother they expected. Those eyes host tears. She takes two steps back, and she knows. Her head tilts, trying to take in how I can look so much like her lover, and yet not be him. Deducing that if I'm here, he isn't, and he would never leave her unless for heaven. He loved her too much. "He loved you, more than I've ever seen him love. More than I thought he could, or would, love anyone." Slowly, she nods and I follow her sadness to a beam on the floor. *I love you. I love you.* An unfamiliar handwriting, and my brother's. Nothing needs explaining when she knows everything. I extend my arms to her, standing in my brother's shoes, offering myself up to her if she needs to know him one last time. The appreciation is in the knowing nod she gives me, and the hand she places on my chest, simple and kind rejection. She doesn't need me. She knows loss. She knows love. She is bravery, with brown eyes.

"You'll always live with memories, and that's a beautiful thing, but Sebastian wouldn't want you alone." I invite her back to London, to live with Sierra and I. I'm not here to save her from Colmoor, but from grief consuming her in an affectionless place. Thoughts about travelling away, in the worst of scenarios, have already weighed on her mind. Betsy raises her hand, asking me for a moment, and I let her take it, turning away from her to look at Colmoor from a novel altitude. It looks like the innards of an engine, dark and tangled. It's resemblant of a mechanical pig sty, a dirty system in which things run dangerously smoothly. It's a different world. The echo of a loud beating sound makes me fly around again.

This woman is ripping up the wooden beams, with her feet and her able hand. I realised she already knew she wanted to come to London. The moment she needed was to work out what to take, and she decided on Sebastian's words from the floor. None of her research, or her photographs. She wanted his words above her clothes, the only time I ever saw Sierra's sister hopeless. A staggering amount of sadness exploded from us both through the medium of strength. A booming snap of human activity and anger, instead of a mammoth animal, gave us less than a minute to leave before the authorities began a customary search. Betsy had the inscriptions she wanted in a splinter of wood under her arm, and we were going to run either way now, the decision made just by locking eyes.

Hysterical with feelings that shouldn't be human, and with no belongings, I carried Betsy down the ladder in my arms. I realise her lover's, and my brother's blood is in my hair. I hope she can't tell in the darkness. The hysteria lasts until Colmoor is just an accidental streak of black acrylic on the canvas we travel.

Then, it begins raining, and the world is ruined once more. Pain is solely painful again.

CHAPTER XXVII: REMEMBER

Sierra.

Before spending a beautiful morning with her, I shut the door in my sister's face. A decades-kept secret isn't something Isaak can present like its breakfast, so when a girl of a similar stature and face to mine is ferried into my room before sunrise, I panic. I can only just see the rainbows cast onto her smile from the window, I can't see her pain. I can only see my own, and it's suffocating.

My insecurities mismanage me. I conclude that just because she has my face, she also knows my lies and what I love, a vessel of my own vulnerabilities, as if Isaak has found my inhibitions and brought them home. Flustered and emotional, I banish them both to the hallway and collapse on the floor at the foot of my bed, talking to myself. I nearly made it to the mattress, but I fell here, so here is where I'll stay. It's not fair that there's another Sierra in the world. It's not fair that I think she's fascinating. It's not fair that Isaak brought her here as late as he did. It's not fair I love her, and that my fear turned what should have been a graceful and excitement-filled reunion into an apology. I ease open the door humbly, as though I'm existing in a dream, because my eyes are puffy from tears and confusion.

She thrusts herself towards me, wrapping one arm around me close, restraining the other, which I later came to understand was broken, tentatively. My doubts are assured, because in this embrace, I know she doesn't know me, but is willing to. Who I want to be, and who I was - for after all, our past binds us to each other. Isaak introduces her, as she cannot speak to me, "Sierra, this is Betsy," and she steps back and smiles, nullifying my initial reaction. It feels as though we were never apart, but why are we apart? Why is Isaak, like always, the first to know? Do I have other sisters hidden away? Betsy seems calm in the absent gaze of my lover, making me think she knows more than I do about what's going on. I'll play innocent until I have her alone, and then maybe I'll encourage her to divulge the truth how I've always yearned for it. In paper and pen. In black and white.

Isaak strides beside us all day, like an escort, without speaking. All day, prioritising protection and sacrificing speech. Although, it occurs to me that it may be out of respect for my sister.

Betsy made the sun shine a little brighter, which made Isaak's paranoia worse, because London was busy in every direction. The heat was unusual for spring, and my nose and cheeks burned with it, so we took detours through shady stations - packed with people roaming wherever they liked for business, for leisure. My brain fights not to make anyone who's hood covers their face, a murderer. Introverts are ripe in London, more so than murderers. As are the homeless, that approach me and beg for money, for apparent betterment. Isaak pulls me sharply away. "They know you have money, because they see your face on the side of a building in Leicester Square. Your success doesn't need to guarantee your philanthropy. Superfluous money won't make you a saviour."

"Kindness could. Just look at saints." I look at them religiously, when passing by churches and cathedrals. I've spent afternoons researching about kings and queens in the library, and putting together a tableau of London's paragons. This city decorates itself with its gratitude, you only have to look at the statues and plaques to realise. It's a treasure map from above. As always, Isaak dampens the subject.

"Kindness could also get you killed. All the saints I know are dead." Sebastian's name aches in the subtext. I stop trying to outwit him, and give him a nudge towards Betsy. I suppose wanderlust is genetic. Is this what I looked like: obsessed with the confidence of strutting pigeons stealing food, confused that London only carries the smell of either bodily fluids, pollution or food in the majority of areas? For this to be novel to Betsy means we must share a past in which a blossoming and busy society was unfamiliar to us. She knows where she's departed from to have arrived here, and she's luckless in that she can't speak it to me. She travelled with no luggage and no voice - but she must have smuggled the rainbow that flexes above the distant buildings and steeples. It's a colourful reminder that she ought to feel as beautiful as she's made today, and I have the means to make it happen for her.

Gala does a double take when all three of us enter the shop. She's used to Isaak, who stands there sheepishly now, but she can't make out the duplication of me. Betsy and I aren't exactly identical, mostly through lifestyle choices. The way we've done our hair. My makeup, her lack of. We're slightly different heights. However, despite our differences, we're obviously sisters.

"Any day seeing Sierra twice is a lucky day!" Nothing flusters this woman, and I love her for that. Betsy is offered a handshake, which she stares at blankly. I'm not used to being the one explaining, the sister on the other, reflective side of discovery.

"Betsy grew up in a world away from this one. It's her first day here, she's taking time to adjust. Particularly with her injury, she's not able to speak, but I think in time you'll find nothing quells the ambitions of a Genieva."

"I know that well. Let us look for blue."

"Blue?"

"A dress. You didn't come just to fraternise with Gala. Betsy's colour is blue."

As Gala shuffles between racks of clothes, with a sixth sense for the rustle of the right fabric, I feel the aching absence of Isaak no longer behind us. I lightly guide Betsy to follow the elderly woman into the silk hedges, with a small touch on her shoulder, before scouting out my lover. Fittingly, he's in the shadows. In a nook of the shop, where the dressing rooms are, surrounded by mirrors. Immediately, I see what he sees, but I will never be able to understand the way he sees it. Flexing his fist, the rising temperature of his blood makes veiny peaks and valleys in his hand. He's steadily testing to see if he controls his reflection, or if the image won't copy. He sees his brother in every habit of his own, but rather than upset him, it has boiled the reptilian haemoglobin in this man. It has transformed his restraint to simmering vengeance. It's Isaak versus the mirror in a face-off, his look is piercing. Eyes locked on eyes, both attestors to dilapidated faith. I watch as whatever he sees inside himself unnerves him, and his fingers clenched tightly into themselves. "Isaak, don't." The enchantment breaks, and his gaze flickers to me - or rather, the reflection of me. His shoulders decompress, avoiding shattering the mirror to incorrigible fractures by only a split second. The voice of a lover is a rope, towing us away from the riptides we walk to, tugging on our heart through a keyhole incision between our shoulder blades.

I ease him away from the refracted memories of the short-term past, the glass unknowingly frivolous in how it bounces memories across its three walled, four dimensional, boxed-in clique. Isaak is led away, and synchronously the image of Sebastian shrinks too, with his back to us, disappearing into the shop on the other side of the mirror, without so much as a wave.

"Ah!" Isaak's ears prick in response to the female scream. Apparently not to the tone. If he was an animal, his ears would be up on end. He returns to his purposeful stride, no longer stewing in complex grief, until he meets Gala's fervent gathering of the perfect blue dress. It has flared sleeves, cut-outs in the waist and is a deep blue colour. Like a pebble dropped into my brain, there's a transient moment as flashbacks ripple, like water. An ocean so beautifully blue. I glance at Isaak, to look for the familiar sheen of recollection to glaze his eyes - the pulsing of an identical pebble dropped. I wait for our tides to meet. I waited too long, before I knew the water settled still again, or that mine was the only pebble. Perhaps then, my visions of blue were simply just a dream that named itself a memory.

I'm thinking of the forgotten blue as I sing on this unusual night. Unusual, for Isaak is sitting beside Betsy in the wings to my right, each of them watching a different thing. Isaak is watching the audience, leant forward on his creaky bench seat as if in prayer - his poise similar to the night I decided I'd never again touch a white flag. I see, in his pain, how much I mean to him, and I realise, as I exercise arpeggios, that maybe our connection is in how we commit rather than how we love. Betsy, on the other hand, knows commitment but not long enough to reap the sweetness of it being lost-lasting. My lyrics grieve on her behalf, song to sister.

My microphone projects my shallow breaths into the silent room, before the accompanist raises their hands to the keys to play.

I'm not sure what I believe in. I've learnt about religion, but I can't seem to work out how to conduct myself vicariously through the mistakes and morals of the first ever person to have put a foot wrong. I want to experience shaping myself, in contrast to my being having been moulded by writings. I'm hesitant to believe in a higher power, but when the pianist's music was ripped to the ground by an impromptu gust of wind in an otherwise still venue, I believed in something. I believed in luck and I believed in the world. The first notes were never played, because the musician leant to the ground to gather the papers meant to escort my voice through the evening. For once, I heard life in the same frequency as Isaak. An inhuman click, in place of what should have been an F Minor chord. A sound that relied on the music on stage to disguise itself. The greasy squeak of catching metal that discarded a boulder, which then came crashing down into Isaak and I's memories, the waves of both our realisations meeting and accelerated in superposition. We never would have heard it, if the music had been played as it should. No warning, that the weapon that precipitated Sebastian's death, sat somewhere menacingly in my audience. A ticket booked to hear me. A trigger cocked to kill me.

I watch Isaak's open mouth, scream soundlessly at Betsy to go and then latch on to me, meeting me halfway on stage, his body shielding me from the audience, and his arms trying to protect me more. He rushes me away, so helplessly, that I cannot apologise for the bullet that ricocheted from the stage floor and toward the pianist, who had no time to cover her own face with her hands. *It was meant for me, it was never meant to end your music*, is what I would have told her had she not died there and then, crumpled up and bleeding out onto the black and white keys. The ugliest end and metaphor for the way she played for me. Her heart was always in the music, and now it spills out all over it, staining the pages she saved from drifting away. Isaak, remorseless in his focus, tells me we have to get to safety. I can hear the kicking pandemonium of people screaming and tripping over each other in the stalls, and realise that humans have an innate capacity to recognise a gunshot from a firework. Killers don't wait to celebrate in miraculous colours, they kill in monochrome with a twinge of red. Painted like a murdered pianist slumped over their instrument.

I believe in a half-hearted type of luck. Haphazard in its philanthropy. Luck volunteered an innocent individual for my bullet, but fortuitously made her the only casualty of that night. Gratitude is as complex as a sin, when luck makes survivor's guilt an ailment you have to suffer your whole life through. It makes me wonder who has the short straw: those who die first, or those who watch. Those who absorb looted accountability that they don't want, forced to be grateful for their survival, which may be putting a name on the cost of love.

It was my fault for challenging the circumstances, I'm a glowing target and yet I stood myself up for auction. My promise to Isaak courses in my head. *I'll sing a barricade.* I did, and it wasn't strong enough to protect a soul. I'm stumbling too slowly in my dress, as Isaak is stressing, "They didn't see you die, they'll be coming after you as we speak. You've got to move faster."

The chaos will obstruct them, part of my brain tries to reason, but then I'm upside down over Isaak's shoulder and he's hurrying me down the stairs. Betsy must be in front of us, for all I see is the swaying inverted view of the frenetic audience scuttling for exits like ants. A gruesome termination of what my heart accepts was my final performance. Once we're outside and the sticky humidity of a fermenting thunderstorm makes itself known in the air, Isaak ducks around a corner. Escaping people are flooding from the other fire exits and the building's entrances. Fleetingly, he crouches to set me down on the floor, and then backs my sister and I into the wall. Under his breath he murmurs, "I will try to avoid the possibility as much as possible, but I might kill a man tonight if necessary for your protection."

"That man might have a family, Isaak." The thought of Sebastian materialises as a lump in my throat, disintegration in my chest. To my surprise, Isaak attaches a kiss to my cheek, and whispers in my ear, but loud enough for the three of us to hear.

"Family is nothing without a good conscience. Anyone in ownership of a gun, is not under good conscience." To this, I have nothing to say, and Betsy lays a hand on my arm. If she could speak, I know she'd be telling me to trust him. Yet, I already knew this from the kiss, that from Isaak are as rare as shooting stars. *Shooting stars.* The heavy door of the exit we used is thrust open again with a resounding metal echo. *Hearts in the sand.* Isaak takes charge and beckons us to the busier London road, where he ushers us onto a bus just as the doors close, figuring we're safer contained than out in the open. I know where he's taking us.

The beeping of the doors, and the subsequent traffic, brings me back to the moment. Isaak's kiss still coldly creeps across my cheek like ivy entwined with forget-me-nots. My flashbacks dance around my flower collection, before I'm promptly distracted by Betsy flushing a pale green against the boldness of her dress. I lunge to bundle her hair in my fist before she is sick on my dress, excusing her vulgarity to the stress of the situation by vague flustered gesturing around her head. The contents of her stomach dripping down my dress doesn't frustrate me in the slightest, but it is my lack of awareness for her feelings thus far that I condemn myself for. The driver is not as compassionate.

I ___ YOU

A stocky man, beginning with a glare at us over his shoulder, presses down a pedal and pulls the bus to a halt. The disgust of the other passengers' writhes in the reflection of the driver's irritated stare, as he unfastens his seatbelt. Isaak keeps a sturdy hand on the driver's door, not letting him access us. He transfers money into his hand, and once the exchange is done, Isaak takes the liberty of reaching across to the button that opens the bus doors. He cocks his head slightly, freeing me to lead Betsy out into the street. Nodding to the driver, he follows us off. A couple of passengers close to us alight too. There's inevitable spite in the way the doors close again and the bus accelerates away. Fortunately, Isaak evaluates we've travelled far enough from the danger, for now. Isaak's surveillance for the remaining walk to the pub operates at all angles, whilst I check in on Betsy. It's not bothering her more than the rest of the night, but Isaak suggested to me subtly that the excess acid in her throat will be scouring her internal wounds. The thunder commences when we're a few roads away from the pub, shortly followed by the rain. It fastens my pace because I don't want to be reminded of Sebastian and the rain that fell that night.

"Nicholas, this is Betsy. She'll need water for now, she's sustained an injury to her throat so I'd be hesitant with the alcohol for the time being. Sierra will have the usual." Isaak looks at me and I nod in confirmation. "Yes. I need to leave them with you, here tonight. The situation's worsening outside." Nicholas looks slightly taken aback, on top of his normal reserved state, but he recovers and obliges.

"Pleased to meet you." Nicholas engages, quickly realising my sister's impediment. In true kind fashion for this gentleman, he suggests that he might tell Betsy a story and proceeds with an anecdotal tale about something I will never know, for Isaak touches my waist, tugging me to the pub's disabled bathroom.

"You can't relax in that. Nobody drinks comfortably when weighed down with the contents of someone's stomach." Isaak speaks softly, studying me up and down. Lingering on my chest for a little too long. I've felt vulnerable under many definitions tonight.
"I'll remind you that nobody drinks comfortably on the run from a murderer, or several, Isaak."
My lover drops to his knees and discovers the layers in my skirt, paring them one by one. Sprinkles of dried mud drift to the floor. Two layers underneath, Isaak trails his hand up the front of my thigh. There's still a couple of layers separating his touch from my skin, but I know seducing me is never high on his list of priorities. Dismally, he's aware he doesn't have to try. He applies energy to more efficient things, in this case, tearing my dress apart with a clean rip, with the strained thread creating zigzags over the pieces of the dress that remain. The vomit-blemished fabric crunches as he disposes of it in the bin. He keeps, with engrossed strength, mauling my skirt to lift the weight from me. With every damage he wrenches me a little closer. I attune to the rain, getting wilder now, and it lashes the tiny translucent window I can see over Isaak's shoulder. He uses the way the storm reverberates around the tiled walls to camouflage the sounds of the kisses he douses me with. I have to hand it to him, his pumping my lungs full of his own air, and his amendments to my dress have made me feel ounces lighter and lightheaded.
"I'll forward my apologies to Gala and pay for repairs." Isaak makes a concession so I don't begin to feel guilty about the tatters at my feet.

Although I have to be realistic. "Repairs to this degree are unlikely."

"Here then." Intrigue causes me to be limp when he tries to manipulate my hand, and rests it against his chest. My fingertips graze his skin where the top button is undone, and they twitch, remembering the bedroom before the rest of my body does. A slice of lightning hits something close outside, and as I picture red post-boxes or hanging baskets burning, my grip electrically tightens with the surprise of nature's whip. Isaak cups his hand on mine, keeping it held in a position. I'm squeezing the ruff of his shirt like I'm dependent. With a slight smile, he snatches our hands to our sides. The fabric splits as it's ferried through my palm. A number of buttons hang by threads so he picks them off like berries. I'm taken by the colour of his skin, richer than I remembered in the darkness. He mistakes my attraction for bewilderment.

"I thought you knew I believed in justice." He says, as though it justifies our shabby attire.

"On a larger scale, yes." I concede, not having to point out how ridiculous it is, that romance made us destroy ourselves.

"Incorrect." He mutters, pursued by more kisses to my shoulders. Then he meets my eyes. "Oh Sierra," the way he vocalises my name makes me tremble weakly, my legs suddenly understanding the effort of holding up my torso again. Still, he is right there, supporting my whole body with just his right arm, his left hand massaging my scalp. "I believe in justice on any magnitude that concerns you." I'm not sure if he speaks to my cheek, my neck, my ears or straight through to my heart.

Betsy's eyes travel to the alterations in our outfits the moment we step outside. There are a few glances from other patrons, but I'm still ruminating on Isaak's last words before he released me away from the chrysalis of us, and back into society. *I have to leave.* I protested, and then bargained for answers, to which I received a few excuses. Betsy needs me to be strong, and it's a chance to spend time with a newfound family. Eventually, after pushing him in every direction I know how, I'm desperate to admit that I'm afraid of everything outside of the space we exist in as two.

He'd responded, "I'd not leave you anywhere you weren't safe. I've always been there. I will always come back." As he disappears into the thunderstorm, and I should feel relieved by his words, I can't help wondering if Sebastian ever assured Betsy the same.

CHAPTER XXVIII: GRIEVE

Isaak.

Love. You can't romanticise siblinghood. At least not until your only brother is dead.

He may as well not be. I can't see him, hear him - or as was normal between us, feel him nearby. I'm kneeling on dirt, weighing down on Sebastian. I might have always been this weight on him. It's itchy. Not the thorns and weeds I lie on, but the idea that a few feet underground they may be growing through his body, winding through his stomach, growing through his skin. He's just another body woven into the ground, and I did this. I sacrificed him. I should have kept him from his grave just a little longer, to assert my claim to the one human I could ever unconditionally say was mine. Even now, I struggle to say I loved him because I know it's just a cheap forfeit for my self-pity. I wouldn't have loved him if he was alive, I just believe that it's love now that he's left me lonely. Love is nothing but an oath that we'll remember. Comfort that we'll be remembered.

Families remember families. Lovers remember lovers. Grief is an extrinsic catalyst, the fear of one day grieving what we have is what gives present love its edge. We have to promise again and again that we will vow ourselves to the memory of a person. I never promised Sebastian that. Not because I didn't mean it. Because I never thought it'd be necessary to fear losing him. I compress my ear against the top of his grave, listening for reassurance that he's still here, that I don't need to love him to remember him. Nothing. The silence doesn't give me permission to forgo the burden that is love. I can't say goodbye, because insolent love's custom still has one *fucking* foot in the door.

I ___ YOU

Love. A custom. An expectation. Etiquette. Convention, protocol, courtesy.

Sierra never knew Sebastian the way I did. Betsy and her are far from replicating the bond we had. It is courteous for Sierra to pretend she knows what it's like to lose a twin, but it is poor. There's care but no quality in her love of Sebastian. Love is a disgusting way for people to trespass between sympathy and empathy, and get away with it. I can't blame Sierra though. Sebastian was in my life longer, but played a bigger part in hers. He's the reason she still has her life, so her love is a courtesy but a justified courtesy. I contemplate who owes the greatest debt to Sebastian, and therefore who is most liable. It's incomparable. Sierra lives with the weight of my grief as well as hers. I live with the curse of seeing my brother's face every time I look at myself, and only today Sierra had to hold me back from attacking my reflection to release Sebastian's ghost from the glass. A murky dynamic between lovers, siblings and friends supersedes his death, and the irony of it all, is that he chased unity. Selflessly, he died, and two of us are reminiscing on it selfishly. I'm concerned about looking at my own face. Sierra's blaming herself, letting it infect upon the second chance at life Sebastian provided. There's only one of us left who knows authentic love. A genuine heart, broken more than ours.

Love. Unfalsifiable. Unobservable. Irreplaceable.

Terms that understand more than I do, what Betsy and my brother had. Neither of them can speak of the love they shared, and it makes it theirs. The world was kept out of it. It didn't need to know, because they did. Betsy hasn't reduced herself to the lover left behind. Each time I take note of her face when Sebastian's name is mentioned, she smiles subtly, knowing that if he will not return to her, she will one day run to him. Rushing little, she collects stories, to tell him when it's her turn. Not a soul can prove what this type of love means, or why it works. It angers me that there's no instructions. It could be so simple, that I could start with stage one and have love be the product. At any argument I could administer a factory reset. Do it again, a better way. Yet all my mistakes are adhesive, unshakeable, just suppressible until something reminds Sierra of what I've done. I'm still repressing Alessandro, but the torment of mourning is chemical, and if a battered battery in any part of my brain gets enough charge it could resuscitate my old identity. Then I'll have no idea how to be alone, and no willingness to dare loving Sierra Genieva. Isaak Macaluso has many deficits beginning to come to light, I decide, but not a short-circuited fuse. There is nothing to say about Betsy that doesn't make you question the defects inside yourself, for her grace is impenetrable. Which is why the love that she and my brother shared is inextricably bound and impossible to prove otherwise. Nobody will know what they truly shared.

Love. From myself. Love. From Sierra. Love. From Betsy. The three of us remain to carry out the duty of love. Almost as if it's an order, Sebastian's last order: that we must regard him with the rest of our love, for the rest of our lives.

I find myself on the beach where I first heard Sierra sing, scrambling through the sand with haste. My aim is to find a rock large enough to set Sebastian's last order in stone. I find a jagged dark grey one that I carry under my arm whilst I search for something better, and then I uncover one that rivals it. A light grey this time, underneath shrubbery at the back of the beach. It's a weight, but so is love. I cradle it in my attempts to haul it back up to the graveyard, keeping an ear out for life in

Colmoor amidst the slipping grains underfoot. The last thing I need is to get caught. By the time I'm at the gates to the cemetery, I'm rolling the rock at my feet. It's thudding with each rotation. I grimace, for my father's grave inspires the final momentum. Then, gravity finally is allowed to hold the stone stock-still to earth, atop Sebastian. Another smaller, more jagged, rock assists me in carving those three words in memory. Love. Love. Love.

The air picks up static, the thunderstorm from London reaching me. The wind begins to churn up the leaves around my feet, the sort of weather acclimatising that correlates with unease. Distant lightning manifests as the crackle of approaching footsteps, and I won't stand for pathetic atmospheric mind games. The first bellow of the thunder echoes for miles, sounding like a clutch of metal pans thrown to the floor in anger. It could be Sebastian, stirring up something wicked to tell me I shouldn't be here. It's not him though. He knew me too well to know I'm not deterred by the weather, but I don't know how strong a message can come from heaven. Some things I'm left to work out independently as a hermetic mortal.

It's eerily quiet in Colmoor, now I truly listen. I watch too. No heads pulsate up and down above the walls of the town, nobody on patrol. If the soldiers aren't in the streets, there's only one place they'll migrate. One motivation. A motivation not under grey clouds, but riddled between skyscrapers that tower over native Colmoorians searching for the unfinished half of the Gray pair. Any soldier that is ahead of the storm, is also ahead of me. Sebastian has merged declarations of love with a thunderstorm. One last unprecedented order that I don't know whether rings from the grave or from me. Go back. Go back. Go back.

Lackadaisical, I clean my hands on my trousers, assessing the sky. Wondering how long it'll take the electricity to chase me. There's an advantage in having little to nothing on my person, nothing weighs me down. Not a weapon. Not a gun. Not the fear of a new city, with concrete structures Colmoor couldn't fathom. Any new soldiers that Colmoor deploys are spanners in the works of their plan, which is a factor they don't seem to have realised. My poverty acts as a lubricant in the demand I'm under to work around the city spontaneously, and I take the time I need to prepare for what awaits. I'm so sedated by the comfort that I associate with coming back to London, I think I mistake the thunder for vibrations, deep in the earth. Timed. Equal measures apart as I walk. Three steps. Vibrations. Three steps. Fainter vibrations. Three steps. Mere quivers. Then nothing more. The only tremors now ache along the path between myself and Sierra's heartbeat. *I'm coming back.*

I keep my eye out for soldiers accompanying me on my route but see none. It boils down to three possibilities. One. None came, or rather, none reached this point. Most men are under the influence of Amnesia, nothing but cowards beneath the mask Jasper has wound to their faces. He has a joystick screwed inside every mind of every man he has captured, playing with these lives like dispensable pennies down a well. Each meant to satisfy his one wish, which is to end the casual walk of a man returning home in the downpour. Me. Though, cowards aren't best acquainted with thunderstorms. Maybe the misery leaks too close to home, the blasts intimidate the pitiable bullets they shoot. Maybe because thunder cannot be killed, it is feared. I'm enthused yet again at the faculty of mortality to raise the stakes.

I ___ YOU

The second possibility is that they are on a different route. Amateur hunters wouldn't know the shortcuts. It comes with time. Warner is getting quicker in his returns, but I'm confident that should we both be blindfolded, I'd find my way to Colmoor days before him. I veer slightly from my path each time, conscious of treading down a leaden trail to a town that won't welcome tourists, trespassers or traitors. It matters less when I'm on concrete. The dirt is already so thick on the city's pavements that my prints make no difference. The darkness is laid on heavy too, but I just have a sixth sense that the figures I see in the shadows on the final stretch to the pub aren't after me. If they were, they'd be four steps behind me and not raising lighters to cigarettes, or arched over, urinating on the walls.

The last possibility, which doesn't bear thinking about, is if they are there already. Highest on the hit list would be the theatre, as it was earlier, and next, the apartment. I've got a while until the pub is under scrutiny. I've got a moment to scan the perimeter, and halt as I see the sisters sitting at a table together. Sierra's gestures are animated when she speaks to Betsy, but I can see her anxiety grace her expression when they pause to sip their drinks. She's waiting for me. Losing herself to her doubts. Then, I see Nicholas, acting abnormally. Wringing his hands before edging towards their table, and then holding back. His mouth moves in silent conversation with himself, and suddenly, he looks out of the window as if he sees me, but there's no sign of recognition. I glance behind me as a precaution. I'm relieved to see there's nothing, and three faces are relieved too, when I enter the pub. Catching Sierra's eye, I just wink and resume a seat on a barstool several feet away. I don't want to promote overindulgence in our love every time I'm around, particularly as I don't want to be infatuated by her pull tonight.

I have barely sat down a minute, and now an ashen hue trickles down Nicholas' cheeks all at once, caused by pneumonia brought on by the sight of an enemy. His swollen eyes stare straight past me. With the quick realisation that he's not involved if he doesn't look, he flicks his attention back down to tending the bar. Writing out pretend orders. At the bottom, underlined - an order for me. On a ripped shred from a server book, he's scribbled *Colmoorian.* I don't have time to ponder how Nicholas knows Colmoor. Instead, I blame my brother for running his mouth, and begin to pour myself a drink.

An eight-legged whisper scurries around my collar. "You're about as inconspicuous as that ridiculous fluorescent wheel near the river. Flashy. Bold. *Ruining* my shadows with your pompous feats for *her* popularity. It's a ridicule of what Jasper stands for."

The way Warner snarls 'her' could be his most grating throwaway so far, though his disdain for the London Eye is the most accurate summary of his banal personality. "It might have occurred to you, that *I don't give a fuck* what Jasper stands for. Or that you're here. Or what you want. None of it. And it may be in your best interest, to get the hell out of this pub." The maybes and the might's are indefeasible. He is leaving, whether or not I have to manhandle him.

Warner spies the bartender, washing glasses and close enough to eavesdrop, naively thinking he's anonymous. "Hello, *Nicholas*." Warner froths, through a strained smirk. I look between the men trying to work out what this interaction means. I gain confidence due to the way Nicholas is also engaging blankly.

"Nicholas, if you know this man you need to tell me." I assert.

He hesitates briefly, and only shakes his head. Warner doesn't seem to care.

"You've far overstayed the welcome nobody gave you. You'll leave now, peace kept. No bloodshed. Know that if you stay, it'll come to that." I snap, rehearsing my attack in advance of what I know his answer will be.

"Why don't you try me?" He hisses the question of questions, finally bringing to life the warrior inside me, not adverse to learning how to turn men to slain snakes. My glass shatters all over the counter, and I rise to face the weedy soldier that thinks I'll be as easy to kill as my brother. All heads, including Sierra's, are drawn to where I stand. It would take simply a needle to deflate him, but I've just got a pint's worth of shattered glass, glistening with the drink I poured. Flecks of foam on my shoes, and flickers of red, of Karian's bursting neck, in my mind - but I won't let Sierra see blood.

The caveat was that she drew blood. She made the world turn faster when before I registered, she was out of her seat and slicing chunks out of Warner's arm with the first shard she snatched from the bar. He's letting out animal noises as everyone grows feral. People in the pub wailing though they're just witnesses. Sierra has the eyes of a wolf, uncaring, furious. I'm scrabbling for the wolf's hand to stop her making a carcass of Warner, whilst he thumps me and her frantically. My elbow closes around Warner's neck, restraining the enemy down at my hip, gasping. His cheek, still bruised and purple, presses up against my shirt. My blood retreats with his hot, desperate breath - leaving my skin numb and freezing where I have him mashed against me. All I can think is that he deserves to die. Sierra's rage decelerates disjointedly, her limbs swing with less energy but she's determined to keep fighting for all she's worth. She recognises him. Loathes him. I realise now, that this was the answer. Hatred not love, is a stronger descendant of Sebastian's memory. The fight that accrues from antipathy.

I say this because his lover, Betsy, is the only tame one here. Death isn't a variable in her justice conclusion, she just watches the world play out. It may be because she doesn't know that the man being ambushed on the other side of the room, is the one that shot the man who taught her love.

Sierra's derailing. Hyperventilating. Scrambling for her wrist was a risk. I bleed out from where she strikes me, accidentally, in her temper - but I have her stabilised now as red dribbles down my raised arm.

"Drop the glass, love." She does as I say, shocked with herself. Considerably comatose the more she watches my blood dripping to the floor. She rushes under my free arm, whilst Warner grumbles something pathetic. I massage her hair, urgently whispering, "I want to know why you did that. My conflicts aren't your responsibility."

"He, he has a..." She's trying to breathe again, and speak at the same. "A gun. Back pocket. You couldn't see. Had to..." I kiss her and release her, entrusting her to Nicholas who enfolds her in his arms as she's mumbling still, "...do something. Because Sebastian. Not again. Couldn't let it." At the mention of Sebastian, Nicholas looks up at me concerned, but I have to turn my focus on my captive weasel. I whip the gun from his pocket, smeared with sweat and fingerprints. Momentarily I inspect it, then anger encapsulates me and I hold Warner at arm's length just by his hair. He writhes, trying to break the follicles to set himself free, but there's not a fucking chance. I thump the magazine against his head as I shout, "Tell me - that this is - the *fucking gun* you used - to kill - *my* - *brother!*" I halt the abuse to give him a chance to confirm my suspicions, but he smiles sadistically.

"Maybe." He considers, emptily. "Also, maybe not. What's it to you?"
"Answer me!" I swipe his head with the gun again, leaving instant marks. It swells with my anger. Half the patrons have left at this point, the others are too frozen to move. The city vigilantes with their stupid sirens will arrive soon, but they've never dealt with Colmoorians. We are the same capable, violent, breed, in a civil war. The MET, in all their force, can't disrupt a war on family. A tussle on integrity.

Although, Warner will stop if they turn up. We'll be normal men, and return to fighting when they're gone, but looking at his shallow eyes, I can't let him escape this time. I'm holding a gun to his head. I won't stop now. MET or not.

"One more time. This is the gun that killed my brother." I say it louder this time, and in the corner of my eye I see Betsy stand up. Nicholas tries to stop her walking towards us. Someone else rises from their seat and treads cautiously towards her to hold her back, but she shoots them a look that says all of *don't you dare*, and keeps going. Her ease doesn't complement the intensity all around us, and she calmly creates a triangle of Warner, herself, and I. Raising her eyebrows at me, I read what she needs. Confirmation. Validation. "This man killed Sebastian." Her eyebrows adjust immediately, a different slope.

Tiresomely, Warner interjects. Laughing it off, he raises his hand, pointing his finger at Sierra. "Technically, it was meant for her, and…" he continues deliriously, "the gun didn't do it, completely. A hand was what did it, this one, mine." He's shaking his left hand proudly, like a wave. Betsy closes her fingers gently around the gun I still have pointed at Warner's head. There's no time to protest between her decision and when he notices she's not as patient as I am. A shot echoes around the pub, not dissimilar to a cork from champagne but with far darker consequence. Sierra looks away. I keep my eyes locked on the action. Blood flies across my cheek.

Warner screams. I can see through his hand. "Fucking bitch. First my face…and now my fucking hand. Crazy bitch!" Betsy's satisfied. I'm in disbelief. I drop Warner to the floor and I can feel the heat returning in my waist, but too much. Rising too high. I turn to see the counter alight with flames, and behind it, Nicholas with a match. He shakes the wooden splinter first, tossing it to the fire, and whispers through the crackle, "Enough's enough."

CHAPTER XXIX: NEED

Sierra.

Alcohol burns magnificently. It casts an auburn filter on everything surrounding it. *Fire. Water. Darkness. Kisses. Gorgeous.*

"Sierra, come." Nicholas nudges me further down the pub, towards the fire exit I've staged escapes from. He's bustling me so far away from Isaak. Betsy reaches for my hand but my fingers are moving of their own accord, trembling involuntarily with the quickening pace of the night. My arms are covered in the man's blood, and Isaak's. I cut my lover. *Why did I hurt him?*

"The books!" I cry, my thoughts thick like syrup and the fantasy worlds I've read about are merging with the one I'm living in. All I can think of is saving characters from burning. I don't want the pages they call home becoming charred and ending their stories. There are at least a hundred books. I can't save them all. Even if I could grasp a few, do I prioritise the ones I've read or the ones I'm yet to read? The ones that welcome me, for a familiar second time, or the ones that invite me for the first? The pub is small and heats fast. The fire licks the older wooden furniture, hopscotching across the room to anything flammable. By this point, the bar is abandoned by all but us three, plus the silhouettes of Isaak holding his victim down to the floor as he tries to escape the smoke. There's only so many incombustible items in the room that they can wrestle around, and lash each other with, before they both contribute to the ashes. Instinct tells me to retrieve Isaak, but he always survives. Anything. He comes home. Always. The smoke is stinging my eyes so I can't even take a last look or understand his movements, it's up to him.

An alternative version of myself races towards him with scrunched up eyes, trying to replace one sense with another. Feeling him, if I'm unable to see him. In the darkness of closed eyes, I see a bird's eye view of the city I thought was between us. Now, the city is unaware we're burning, that Isaak is fighting and handcuffed to the allure of dying. It's just concrete cartography, and a blazing pub is all but a scratch on the surface. These buildings aren't uprooting to find us, throwing bricks to quell the flames. It's other people who find us and bring us out of our own individual hells. It's the reason there's a name for hell. It's a summoning of fate for the unambitious. For the guilty. For those who don't look out of windows. Those who don't use doors. Human chassis ignorant to the speed of the world.

Hell is an acknowledgment for the place we all share, yet nobody seems to marvel that not one of us recall the same exact ugliness as another. Hell is magical in a wicked way. The darkness can access our insides. We see nothing in darkness, and just assume the darkness doesn't look back, and doesn't see anything in us. I testify to falsify.

The heat from the fire is exploding the fragile glass casing on some of the decorative lanterns, plunging us into a depressing type of brightness. One in which we rely on what hurts us to help us see. An aphorism suitable for Isaak and the fire. The man who found me and brought me from my hell, into the heaven of a public house in flames. A place I have a choice, and determination. A room where the temperature and pressure are stifling, but one where I have Isaak, and so much love for him.

Sierra in another world, with sealed eyes, embraces her lover in the darkness - the two becoming the candles by their bedside the night they made love. Dripping, melting, malformed as a result of choice and evolution, not acquiesance to what the outside world wanted.

But now, as Isaak disappears in a flame and a gasp, the real Sierra is looking at life like a film. Hot and stunned into one last daydream. I don't know whether or not he's still alive. Hoping on all hope that he's breathing, even if they're breaths or charcoal expulsions. I don't hear coughing, only the drum rolls getting lounder in my head, in this culminating reverie. I fill the silence with hope. Hope in the vehement, naked powers of the human race. I fill it with the faith in all the kindness, charity and the liberties we chase to encompass what it is to believe. I'm hoping for everything I now realise Isaak was to me, more than a lover or fighter. Someone who believed in me. A man who risked everything for my voice.

I consume the idea of Isaak burning, a death worse than death, without digesting it first. It churns, upsetting my guts. The world needs kindnesses, charities, liberties, mercy. None of these exist without nights with my skin on his chest. None of that will live on without how wildly he urged that I should exist. *Mercy.*

"Have mercy!" Nicholas howls as a reaction to losing sight of Isaak, and launches himself over Betsy and I as the ceiling begins to crumble.

We narrowly avoid being crushed, but bottles are leaking out over the floor and cupboards, and every abandoned glass on the tables is a catalyst petitioning to ignite. Pools of alcohol that mean any second left waiting for Isaak, is a countdown to death for the three of us. Nicholas's breathing is becoming shallower, and he's sinking to the floor - still holding both of our arms - searching for cleaner air. Betsy's breathing into the fabric of her dress, like a filter, she can't risk the smoke on her wounds for too long. I'm pitting love against love. It comes down to numbers. *I'm not the third one I'm saving,*

Isaak, I would have run to you. I would have let us burn together.

I don't consider my evacuation saving myself. I'd rather be liquefied beside him, but Betsy's drowning in fatigue by the minute and Nicholas is scanning the room, calibrating right and left. They're ready and they don't want to burn, and it cannot be that for the love of me, they stay. Nicholas uses his shoulder to navigate the edges of the walls, and his memory to locate exits. It takes a long moment of uncomfortable shuffling, and forced deceleration of panic even though our hearts throb fiercely with fear. For Nicholas and Betsy, the fear of when they can next inhale pure air. For me, the fear that I'm the only surviving memorabilia of *Isaak and Sierra*.

"Hinges. Door's here." Nicholas chokes, followed by an acute silence. I imagine he's feeling for the handle. I don't imagine for a second the real quandary, which is that the key to the locked door is trapped in ponds of molten heat behind us in the bar. Nicholas' reassurance is lost on me, because I'm detecting the loud thrumming of Betsy's anxiety. It is possibly a twin feature. Telepathic sympathetic nervous systems. The next step is just to succumb to human instinct and find the light. The indoor clouds of grey are thinner to our right so we crawl towards them, all the while I know Nicholas is fighting with the idea that he might be responsible. There is no such concept as good and bad people, only actions and intentions, and I see the best in this man.

It becomes apparent that the bathroom doors had acted as fire doors, meaning the vintage-aesthetic walls and the medium-sized window they contain are hot but visible. Nicholas lends little thought to his own escape as he begins to prepare an exit that's only large enough for Betsy and I. He smashes straight through the window and uses his fist to smooth the edges so we can easily glide through without pain, meanwhile carving up his own skin. Betsy and I exchange concern, and before I overthink it, I'm pleading with Nicholas to stop, not expecting him to condescend.

"Sierra, leave it out!" He resets his demeanour fluidly, voice softening, "Can you see another, easier, way out of here?"

"What about you?"

Nicholas smiles as he breaks the last chip away from the window. He's achieved our safety, and ignores my question. "Have you heard of the world *cingulomania*, sweetheart?"

Through tears I shake my head, "No, but some things…some moments, evade definitions Nicholas, please understand me. You have to come with us…there's always another way."

He caresses me, bringing Betsy in close too. "Cingulomania is defined as the strong desire to hold someone in your arms. Myself having taught you that word, is a memory that'll last longer than this embrace, but you'll always think of me and know that it is a desire I died with. Your protection. Both of your protections. When you think of me, think of how much I longed to keep holding on to you, and think of how beautiful it was that we all had the strength to let go."

Betsy kisses his cheek tenderly.

"No!" I sob into his smoky shoulder. This could have been a summer's evening bonfire, we could have laughed together, by the beach, and burned things that didn't mind burning.

What am I talking about, dabbling with 'could have beens'? I have fire for blood. I'm impossible, I deceive the plans people make for me and I'll outwit this course of action whether it takes all my breath or all my strength.

Suddenly, it occurs to me. I have my voice and all I need is time. Betsy can see the groundwork spreading across my concentration. I instruct her to leave by the window, and she is surprisingly adept at using the objects and furniture around to propel herself and descend safely. Outside, she steps backwards, so I can see her from my angle, and gives me a soft nod. She's telling me she trusts me.

I pull Nicholas back out into the hallway. It's smokier than seconds ago, and I know I'm working on an uncompromising scale. Dragging him around a corner, I leave him against a wall with the promise to return in seconds.

"Part of a process." I only have time to explain it in a simplified way, struggling back to the window to point to Betsy.

"That wall. Hammer on it. Watch your arm."

My sister acknowledges my instruction and runs to the indicated plaster panelling just above the layer of brick and pummels it with her healthy hand. I run back to Nicholas, and in alignment to where we crouch at the floor, I can hear Betsy's battering clearly. Perfectly. It's my turn to kiss Nicholas on the cheek. Hope visualised. "To hell with your cingulomania. There's so much more to come. Follow the noise."

There's no time to embrace but he chances it. "You're exactly like your mother was."

I blink. "You knew my mother? Do you mean Bridgette, or my actual-?"

"Savannah Genieva. A story of, and for, another time. Go, please." He ushers me away under the pretence he's said too much. I'm desperate to be taught about all he knows, with things slotting into place now like a combination lock. My long-term brain is reprogramming itself in the background of the glowing red all around me, breaking the circuit to my short-term thoughts. I adjust myself back on route. I need to get out of the window.

It takes me a dangerous number of attempts. I slip the first time, lose strength the second, and it's only when I think of the flames creeping towards Nicholas, and the thought of knowing my mother, my muscles ignite and get me over the ledge. Forwards. Inelegantly, I clamber around so that my feet touch the floor first. Scurrying along the pavement, I find a door to the rear of the pub that's open. To the kitchen. I open my lungs and sing a song that my first note inspires.

The last song of my last show. I scream the lyrics so hard I lose the pitch and my voice breaks but I sing every word to get him out. To show him there's life outside the thick, hazy room he's trapped in. Betsy still thumps the wall whilst I sing, directing Nicholas where to go. Waiting for a reply, as he edges the way we lead him he pounds back. I skip to a passion filled chorus, or nothing will release him.

The first lyric is well wishes, but to the thousands. I hope you're okay. I hope you're safe. I'm singing it to a wall, and two of the men beyond it. I'm roaring it out like a command. Be okay, because I don't know how I'd feel if you both were to go. My wisdom and my spark. If I let them die, a part of me dies too. Betsy has loss already stacked on a plate she'll waitress her whole life. I can't stop singing because my sister beside me is the epitome of bravery, and the two men I sing for are mine.

The second lyric is missing a place you once cherished, a place that made you - and as I expel sound, the empty space left inside me floods with unsourced memories of where we were before this. A town, like London's estranged stepsibling, where there should be ties but they've never been formed. A town so dark. A town that kept persisting in secrecy.

I ___ YOU

I can't tell if this is a memory or a dream I've had once, all my life the lines seem to have been blurred. I can't understand the purpose in recalling memories now, if that is what they are. I've been poisoned by flashbacks recently, buds on deadly flowers I should remember. Millions of petals I remember, and I collect. Flowers I've collected habitually to make sense of life I keep forgetting.

Nicholas is halfway to the exit I uncovered, but his knocking is getting weaker. Either a thicker wall, or a breach of his thick skin.

I wish I'd fraternised with time in the park instead of making it my enemy. I'd let time believe it could run from me, and made it familiar with lying ahead. By neglecting it, I've made it adversarial when I need it to be on my side. The third lyric teaches that time is something to be treasured. Somehow, when I sing it, time hears me. The following lyric spills easier, soothing Nicholas from the outside. We're still here, together, focused on his escape. Trying again and again. I keep singing as Nicholas' hand emerges from the exit, Betsy grabs him and pulls him away from the smoke. I can't stop singing.

A lyric about an apology. I force it through the smoke to reach Isaak's heart.

A lyric about letting go and forgiveness, and a thought for Sebastian. Can he curse or care for my living choices, in death?

Then nothing but loud silence, as the lyrics can't synopsise the reality of being in so much company, but so etiolated and alone.

The fear must have overwhelmed Betsy for she dips into the second alley to relieve herself, leaving me to balance Nicholas' breathing back to a steady pace. I sink down to the floor where he sits, and rest my head on his arm. "Cingulomania, see. A desire that is so strong to hold someone in your arms, you don't let them get engulfed in flames."

"Oh, Sierra."

With a question about my mother on the tip of my tongue, how they encountered each other, the passages and paths since, I'm interrupted by a fractured call. Nicholas and I both pause to gauge what we're hearing. A strained yelling, which would be an attack to be wary of, if it wasn't as quiet. I realise as he does. It's the call of a girl who we haven't heard speak since she arrived, which is why her voice sounds so unfamiliar. I, and Nicholas with immediate strength, scramble to her side. She's almost out of the alley but she's fallen, on her bad hand nonetheless, but she holds her abdomen, just below her navel. It doesn't take long for the pain to ease, she breathes deeply, recovering, gesturing for us to back down. As her sister, I simply can't let it go.

"Nicholas, what was that? What's there? Could the smoke be inside her?" I puzzle, with some degree of urgency.

Rocking his head back slightly to think, he talks steadily and with knowledge. "It's rather unlikely. She was out of the building before either of us, as well as having the sense to cover her mouth. There is something I'd be hesitant to...I think it's worth discussing what it isn't too, if anything. Eliminating some variables."

Bending down to Betsy, he helps her stand. I catch half of what he mumbles to her. By his tone of voice, I know I'm not supposed to hear. "Possibility...intim...astian..."

She slowly nods. A conclusion is reached by the three of us, all with different methods, in the same synchronous second. "I think there's a chance you're carrying Sebastian's baby, sweetheart." Betsy's eyes grow, and she mouths his name, pressing her hand to her belly. Nicholas embraces her like a child, whispering comforts, about how Sebastian spoke about her so much when he visited. I'm a mix of all nervousness. Happiness. Delight. There's a subdued celebration of a silver lining in the midst of a toxic evening, and yet I can't stop looking behind me, listening. Often, when my body knows adrenaline and dopamine together, Isaak has his hand in mine. I am missing him profoundly, and distressed beyond comprehension - but I know I cannot take importance away from Betsy. Nicholas holds her so gently, and my thoughts are running away with me.

"Nicholas, do you have children?" I pose.
He doesn't react instantly, but answers truthfully. "I do. I love them incredibly so. More than life itself."

It all makes sense. Nicholas isn't a young man, and has been away from his children a while now. Perhaps they moved away. He is a paternalistic man, with so much love to give. He knows my mother. It just so happens that Betsy and I came along as he was lonely, and reminded him of an old friend. I can tell that wherever his children are now, he loves them so dearly. I am lucky to know him, and feel the surplus love he has to give. I watch him now, as he holds my sister. If I will never meet my own father, I will still be filled with so much gratitude for having crossed paths with Nicholas.

Over Betsy's shoulder, Nicholas spies her bag, with an embellished edge protruding from the fabric. "Betsy, what's that?"

Breaking from the embrace, she follows his line of sight and reaches down to scoop the book and her bag off the floor. Extracting a book, she hands it to him and glances at me. I take it from his hands and turn it over. *Secrets of London's Unspoken Outskirts.* "This was the next book I was to read, and Betsy put it in her bag for me to read later. I hoped you wouldn't mind. Thank goodness one book survived the fire."

I'm staggered when I realise Nicholas doesn't look relieved. Dispirited, he claims it back and forces apologetic eye contact. I sprint towards him in my ruined dress when I realise what he's doing, but I don't manage to save the pages from their fate as he tosses them into the flames, through the open window. We were only inside that room moments ago and now it's set alight. I can't speak out of anger but I'm pausing my fusillade, hoping he'll extinguish my fury with reasons.

"Where do you think all books come from, Sierra? The mind. All of them. If not, perhaps reports on human creation, or inhuman, that particular book. The only thing with more fantasy, more plot twists, more adventure and excitement than a book is the mind of the creator. Everyone's an author. Every one of us is a character. Whether we write or not. However, we choose to exist." I see there's a point the man is struggling to reach, and my adoration and respect sympathise with him.

"Tell me what you need from me." I cringe when I realise my words could be Isaak's.
"Sweetheart, listen. Real life is the largest book you'll ever read. It's the one that is ignored too often. Look around. There are a thousand stories in that street, a million in London. I am a story. You're a story. Sierra, you've got to live whilst it's the best adventure you'll ever have. What is a book when you have the world?"

"You need me to live?"
He solemnly lowers his head. "Take my advice and write with it. Run with it. Find yourself home."

Extraordinarily, I don't feel I have anything more to say. Nicholas' earnest expression is a recognised farewell, and I don't want to tarnish his persuasion with any more inexperience from a girl who hasn't discovered the whole world, or her whole self. Nicholas is in every way, correct. A book can only take me so far, I can take myself further. I can talk to people with stories in their minds. I can take myself and Betsy home. I can be strong without Isaak.

  I can write my strength into existence.
For the first time, maybe Sierra Genieva is possible.

CHAPTER XXX: SACRIFICE

Isaak.

I don't think dying will ever be this convenient again. That doesn't mean I'll do it. It'd be so easy to die here. Too easy to collapse as the carbon dioxide takes me hostage. The air doesn't understand, Isaak Macaluso is hostage to nobody. Except like a sailor to a siren that goes by the name Sierra. I don't know how exactly compassion fed into Nicholas burning his own pub to the ground, but I can assume with certainty, it would have had something to do with love. A disgusting bargaining tool and motivator that keeps on cropping up. If any part of it was a strategy to shake Warner, it was unsuccessful because he still dangles under my arm, limp like a puppet. Just a shadow in the flames. Jeering at me. I don't know who's against who. He's apparently made an ally of the fire, blood gushing from his palm mere metres from the blaze. Absolutely unconcerned by the blitzed nerves in his hand, oblivious to our impending cremation. Pareidolia makes the room a vault of corrupt smiles, as it hits me. Warner is prepared to die, as long as I die with him, because he knows I abandon fights as rarely as I ask questions. For Warner, there is no better opportunity for me to kill myself. Even if we are both deceased, we are deceased in an altercation: and Sierra will be hunted by the rest of them straight afterward, struck down as easily as a hapless rabbit. My pride is the difference in this fight.

Warner is glibly confident he's duped me, until I unclench my fist and let him scramble to his hands and knees. As the smoke rises, staining the ceiling brown and black, the truth descends. The cold-blooded Colmoorian in this blistering room, will die here without the satisfaction of one additional kill. I register my lip twitching into a smile, despite the unbreathable air I'm offering my organs. The grin works itself into a frown as my body begs for oxygen, and my mind begs for time. Warner begs for nothing, not even his life. Though he's robbed my smile.

"At least- I won't have- you to deal with on the other-*fucking*- side." He simpers through wheezing. His glee is just the result of the burglary of so many lives. So much stolen happiness that he can use to fund his last moments with disproportionate humour. It's only fair that I play his game, and beat him at it.

"Fortunately, Sebastian's going to want his turn ripping you apart. He'll have so much fun with you. Though I doubt you're heading where he is, you're headed much further down." I begin to fumble through the smoke, following Sierra's path, but Warner seizes my ankle.

"Ask me a question, Alessandro. Just one measly question, damn it. You're so fucking stubborn, it'll be the death of you-one of these days...!"

I roll my eyes, edging left to the table the girls shared before the night was overturned and snatching the salt shaker. "How about, does this hurt in the slightest?"

Warner's fingers curl with sensational pain as salt swims into his open wounds, and I amuse myself with the second time I've ever broken my rhetoric rule. The glass bottle smashes when I cast it away behind me. He lets go and I'm free to walk, but I'm now invested in his suffering. "You didn't specify the question. Take that as my initiative, your loss, Warner. If you ever make it out of this pub, I will kill you myself. I will do it twice, ten times or however many deaths it takes."

I crouch to where he thrashes around on the floor, frantically trying to erase his whole hand. "I believe I'll borrow your phrase..." I whisper as I descend to his level, muttering in his ear up close, "try me."

His howls get distant whilst I use the mental blueprints from searching for Sierra in these corridors and rooms, to search for survival. I might be poisoned by the compounds in the air, or an overdose of adrenaline, but I'm beginning to hear noises like my father sighing. Logic says it's the floorboards upstairs weakening with the heat, but in my head the sighs are someone watching knows there's nothing left for me. Alessandro hesitates, contesting his worth, but Isaak commits carnage of his doubts in pursuit of an exit. Desperation seeks one. Ardour uncovers one. Bad luck fastens one tightly shut. Good luck is that it's wooden. It takes barrelling with my shoulder repeatedly, sustaining valuable bruises, to buckle. Once I've made an incision in the blockade that separates me from outside, I press my mouth up to the hole to draw in cold, cool air. Refreshment - though it tastes smoky because of the congestion in my nose.

The flames start to tap me on the back with searing heat. Shit. There's one more chance, and only seconds for execution. I give it everything, with the force of two men, both my arguing identities.

"Alessandro, give me a run down. Medical assistance. Whatever you need." Nicholas' voice means I've either been successful in my escape, or we're both dead. A burn creeps up my back and I push my spine up against the wall to extinguish my shirt, groaning in torment. I don't correct the man on my name. Isaak's strength is depleted, and Alessandro, meek and aching, outgrows his masquerade. All I can think about is locating Sierra. "I wasn't expecting you to still be alive. Good on you, son."

"I'm alive as much as can be expected." I raise my eyebrows unintentionally, my shirt smouldering, the fire's fault. Torn and broken, romance's fault.

He pauses. "The Colmoorian…he's…"

"Dying a juvenile excuse for a man." I gloss over the part with the salt, and the threats. I leave it all out, compromising by taking in air and finishing sentences instead of answering questions. Nicholas watches silently as I release the last of my shirt buttons to let the breeze kiss the smarting skin. He knows enough to let nothing be said until I say it, but there's anonymous thoughts bathing distractedly in his pupils.

I sigh, massaging my shoulders. I'm kneading the bruises in preparation for the next exertion, so they ache less. "Talk," I instruct, glancing at Nicholas.

"It's midnight." Nicholas asserts, hearing Westminster complaining in the wind.

"Correct." I reply brazenly, still obsessing over my recovery and recharging, wanting information on the girls but requesting it doesn't come naturally. I'm usually the one to know.

The man breaks into a knowing snicker, "Sebastian did tell me it wasn't the bells."

"Sebastian- *shit!*" I narrowly avoid a rainstorm of embers fluttering in gravity's funnel. "We need to move. I'm sorry about your pub, Nicholas. Tonight could have happened differently."

"And I'm sorry about your brother." Nicholas takes me by surprise, not lamenting his house and his livelihood, but Sebastian. "I knew if he was alive, he would have picked up the phone. All that you said to the Colmoorian confirmed my suspicions."

I cough, in a failed attempt to talk. My words don't work. My arms, cramping up, crave one thing only. "Sierra."

"She's en-route to the apartment with Betsy." I'm told the information matter-of-factly, and it comes to my attention that he's completely unaware of the gargantuan threats attached to Sierra's homecoming. A flashback of Warner scanning the wall of the tower block, surreptitiously counting windows. Failing, like an infant, to disguise his longing. Though he burns, our address will be on several more soldier's consciences by now. It'd headline a newspaper, if Colmoor cared for news. Except it favours rumours and homicidal secrets.

"Nicholas, they know where we live." I iterate, slowly. "Sierra's not to blame for that. It was one person only, who made her believe she was safe there. You." His panic and his frustration merge to sound aggressive. Aggression falls flatly in the artillery of someone as overwhelmed as he is.

As if it could stop murders that may be infesting the apartment as we waste time, I say "I've put my life on the line for her, I give you my word I'll put it further."

"When it comes to my daughters' lives, I'm not interested in a pledge. I'm sold on your resistance. " An overwhelmed man also fails to sustain enigmas, revealing his heartache.

"Of course…" I murmur, half in cognizance and the excess in relish. Larger than the revelation of Nicholas being their father, is the satisfaction of my accurate analysis. Compassion did come into it, in maximum capacity. The love between a father and daughters was the compulsion for a man to set his life on fire. My mind can't see Nicholas as anything other than a bartender. Even as he looks at me with the helplessness of a guardian giving his utmost - running himself into a debt of sweat and doubt, for he will never be reimbursed with peace - to Sierra and Betsy. If paternity is factored into the equation, the present becomes my past. I'll return to Alessandro's diet, of trying to stomach the trauma without rejecting the good memories of Father.

The streets have always unnecessarily slowed me down. Nightlife is a crowd that flocks in crucial moments. Everyone's pace declines as mine hastens, and I'm weaving in and out of typical people. Typical - those without their lives under threat on the regular. I'll take the skies to buy time. My path is a litter of ladders, tiles and chimneys. Handholds and footholds. At this altitude I have freedom of movement, taking advantage of a rooftop velodrome. Other nights I'd pause for the prepossessing views, though in this hour, I ignore them. I can't fail to be the first to reach Sierra, on the grounds of camera-less photography.

Burnt skin isn't meant to stretch to keep up with a sprint. Especially not freshly burnt skin that blisters. I tackle the side of the building, balcony by balcony, suspended by just my arms. My descent is easier by employing the refusal to look down, because then I can count as I move. Our apartment is five below the top.

We've never known our neighbours. The less people I need to be concerned about trusting, the better. I drop down outside our window, grateful nobody else spends solemn midnights on balconies. There's no noise, or any audible indication of confrontation, but without visual confirmation I don't know if I'm too early, or too late. I crane my head around at a slight angle to the door to be able to look backwards into the lounge. All the lights are off, except a soft glow from the kitchen. The aura breaks for a half a second with an obstruction, a silhouette. With the city being as dark as indoors, I won't be seen unless I want to be, and it'd have to be intentional gestures for that. The shadow looks my way, but I'm just another curtain to anyone unsuspecting. I've never been a curtain for the purpose of camouflage before. Living is many things but vanilla.

I passed my induction in blending into the embroidery, because the shadow crouches to the floor. I never cleaned the floor of the flowers that broke out when I opened Sierra's book, but unless the shadow is well versed in geography and horticulture, they'll just be meaningless petals. The worst they can do is wonder.

I stand corrected. The worst they can do is wander. In an automatic response to the darkness getting closer, I usually hold my breath, but my body rejects this, still trying to eject the smoke from my lungs. Coughing with a closed mouth is uncomfortable. I may as well start the next chapter without suffering for it, then at least I can use my muscles again rather than turning to stone. I clear my throat as the door is unlocked and slid open, rasping but poised in defence.

"You're alive...I should have known, if you were alive this is the place you'd run to." Sierra throws me off guard. The shadow hadn't been walking like her, and she's not speaking like herself either. It's slow, a little breathless, exhausted. Relief exists there somewhere, but beneath so much hurt emotion.

I take her by the waist and pull her to me, wrapping her arms around me one by one. Breathing deeply into her neck, I'm kneeling to become hers, whispering, "Almost, but I ran to the arms I needed."

She softens, cradling my head back, on the same balcony I assured her I had no time for love. I'm against her but on edge, and those positions aren't congruous. There are predators that could be anywhere around us, stopping the reunion being wholesome, and something unnerves me about the stillness. "Inside. I don't want the night near you." I mumble.

Sierra agrees through numbness. She's a passenger on my intuition, though had she seen my fear, I'm not sure she'd still be on board with me.

I shut the door firmly, lock it, and draw the curtains, turning my gaze back to the room to adjust to the lack of light pollution. Like the bedroom, there are candles in here. I've had my fair share of fire, but taking up this lighter is different. It's in my hand. It's under my control. It glimmers brightly enough to satisfy lovers, and dimly enough not to attract thieves.

"I thought you might not want to encounter a flame ever again, Isaak. Given what you've been through tonight."

"Fire doesn't bother me. I just often prefer to escape without the burns. I'm actually quite partial to fire when it burns what deserves to burn." *Warner,* and this key, that I settle next to the flicker, so the outside has no hope of a welcome. I could watch it melt, but I'd rather watch Sierra navigate the room, in the quizzical way she does. I'm so accustomed to just Sierra's company that I haven't given Betsy a second thought until now. Asleep, I expect. Sierra and I have always been more awake at night. It became our pulse whilst in Colmoor and the ticking never ceased.

"That was you." She suggests, downcast, stepping over the flowers on the floor. I could have received aggression more tolerably than sadness, and it causes me to ache. I can deal with being the reason for her fury, but not her grief.

"It wasn't out of spite, if you believe me. I was looking for answers." My primal instinct still looks for soldiers in a motionless living room.

"I've done the same on occasion, except I have never searched so hard as to drop them." It's not passive aggressive. Sad and confused in the forefront of background processing, her forced smile indicates her trying to excavate the humour. She rests the water lily in her palm. Part of her knows she'll not touch that freedom again. I've sealed us inside the flat with the key to the window melting in quicksand-like wax.

Her eyes suddenly flare at me with separate concern. "You implied you had burns."

I carelessly show her the streaks across my skin. There's limited pride in the anguish, and as I tell her, even less in reliance on ointments and creams to treat the marks. It's no good patching up my experiences. Shaking her head, she takes my hand, "Two choices. You can be stubborn, or let me stop them from hurting you." I cringe because it was always supposed to be the reverse. I was supposed to do both. Through being stubborn and not falling in love, I'd stop anything from hurting her. Now I'm in love, and letting her assess me like a wounded animal. Yet, relinquishing pride once tonight saved me. The probability it saves me again is plausible. In the bathroom, she strips me down.

"There are so many…" she curses, not at me but at the fire that smoulders in the distance. "These should be seen by a doctor, Isaak."

"Any good doctor would ask for paperwork. I don't have any, and I intend to keep it as such. I'd rather let you do your worst." I was never fully honest with Sierra about how we landed the apartment without money or documentation, and I never truly thanked Nicholas for his home.

"I'm not sure I can do much worse." Sierra teases, patting a cold compress onto my back. My fingers twitch against the sink, without the knowledge that burns could feel searing and like frostbite at once. I clench my teeth. She kisses me between the inflamed insignias of skin. "Hey, you're okay."

Vulnerability with her is becoming unexpectedly comfortable, but I despise being exposed whilst apprehension still courses through my body. There are even distress signals throbbing deep in my injuries. You've never experienced your body's worst pain, as long as you've resisted death - and the pain in store for me is a prophecy. Sierra understands I need swaying from my sensitivity. "Tell me the real reason you got the tattoo."

Her thumb flutters across the warped letters, *RWYA*, narrowly missing blistering flesh. I flinch. It doesn't stop her touch, though, forcing me to eventually slacken and surrender to intimacy. It's not as saccharin as I feared. I don't like what's happening to me. Too late for the standards I uphold of my awareness, I remembered her instruction.

"The real reason is lost on me. I've had it as long as I've been conscious of myself. I preferred it when you settled for my reason."

"I rejected your love, and branded you a liar." She says plainly, with slight hesitancy.

"The arousal was unfathomable."

She ignores me. "I left you alone."

"Yet you also came back. Albeit it, the long route. Killed my brother on the way. Left me in a burning building to die. You're a whole new category of dangerous to love." I humour her.

"And that's why you love me. The fact that nothing is easy in love." Her face is the picture of cogs working themselves into perfect places.

"Unfathomable arousal." I taunt. Satire reveals itself to be an effective antidote. I feel stronger already.

In the midst of everything I forgot about her sister once more. "And Betsy." I prompt.

I was expecting any answer except something as naive as, "I don't know, she realised something and left. Perhaps went looking for you, she didn't say. She's not thinking straight, Isaak. Hormonal, having a baby. She's pregnant."

I whip around so fast that Sierra's flannel scours my back. "She's outside…" I seethe, beginning to bleed whilst getting dressed. "…and Sebastian was going to be a father, *fuck*. Tell me anything she said before she left, Si-" Holding her by the shoulders, I can't remember her name. In my anger, in my disbelief that she's let her sister wander back out into a world that was trying to destroy them. I hiss with a vague memory of the letter 's' on my tongue.

"Isaak, sit back down. You're not healed. You're not ready to chase anyone. I've got a splitting headache…please…just sit."

"No…" I can't respond to her. It's not me. She's not talking to me. It's just a reality where I'm someone else. Another nightmare because Alessandro can't understand reality. That's it. I'm in my own head and it's maladjusted, neurotic. Though in my nightmares the air doesn't taste chemical. *Sierra. She does have a name.* It's a sweet chemical. If battery acid was a sherbet. *The scent is strongest in large doses, non-existent in small ones. If you know the smell of Amnesia, it's too late for you. Too late to remember it. Too late to remember who you are.* A voice. Not my voice. Another voice. I look over and see myself leaning against the shower wall. It's not me. He's marked on his right shoulder. Sebastian. But Sebastian's dead. I look at the girl again, and he's gone like her name from my memory. *Amnesia. We're being drugged.* I scramble to the living room, pulling the anonymous brunette with me and praying that I know I know her.

I fumble with a pen and paper. "Tell me your name. I need to write it down. I won't forget it." She's closing her eyes, drowsy and unthinking. Not knowing how to fight it. *There isn't a way to fight it, AG. You need clean air.*

At my dead brother's orders, I drop the materials I held. "No, there's no time. We need to get out. Follow me."

Nightmares aren't tangible but in this one I locked the door and burnt the key. Shit. The front door. I'm beginning to fall asleep in a dream, someone once told me that means death in real life. I twist the key in the lock and fall against the door with fatigue, slapping it closed against my will. The girl is a dead weight, eyes closed but breathing. I step back and unlatch the door a second time, shoving her through first, and she slumps over the top step in the stairwell. I give in to the headache telling me to sink. Collapsing, I try to hold some part of her so she can't be ripped away from me. There's nothing on her, so I grasp her hand but my fingers won't contract. My body is returning to a state untampered by muscular action. Hands that won't close. Eyes staying open, but pupils not working. I'm getting unsteady as the world turns three dimensional, inverted in the back of my eye sockets, like someone holding a laser to my face in complete darkness. I hear chimes. I want to recoil but my body won't react to me, it's already disqualified itself from fighting. It's the fear. *'Sebastian did say it wasn't the bells.'*

It's the keys, AG. Someone has removed the keys from our door and throws them back and forth between their thieving hands. The tiny metal templates clatter like the necklaces swinging in the window the night I saw my father. The noise brings back his death, his jigsawed face. It tells me it'll happen to me. The voice in my head warns against my fear. *Who has your keys, AG?*

Our neighbours emerge with the commotion of me kneading my limbs on the landing, clinging to the girl and the bannisters. I must have missed an occasion, or vandalised my vision completely because they are all wearing black. Normal black clothes, not out of place. It takes them all marching closer with confidence, to know the normal black clothes aren't out of place, but are not from this place. An older Colmoorian stoops down to brandish the keys in front of my eyes. I notice his jacket doesn't bear a name badge like the others. He's not a man I recognise, but nobody is anybody I know under Amnesia. I try to swipe at him but I'm paralysed.

I failed to force a successful dream. I failed and it's time to wake up. I let myself go blind completely, knowing in a matter of seconds Sebastian will shake me awake and swear at me for shouting loudly in my sleep. Then, he'll make me a shit drink of what's left in the kitchen.

I can hear the men come from upstairs and downstairs. They've been here the whole time. On stakeouts in the flats above and below. Soldiers deployed so near me as the nightmare raged on, and I never achieved the protection of a girl without a name. Wait until…Sebastian. Wait until he knows my nightmares made him a father. I picture his smirking, as I spit at the soldiers in vicinity, *"Fff…fuckers…"*

CHAPTER XXXI: AWAKEN

Sierra.

"Doesn't need this fucking thing." Phantom laughter creeps into my eardrums, pursued by an intense friction against my neck, as though my throat is being tugged away. I'm swaying by the hands and feet, like a rotisserie between two sets of uncaring arms. Metal jingles and a heavy shoe comes down hard on to earth, as motion sickness overcomes me.

"These rags neither." Another poltergeist attends the cause, tugging at my clothes.
I let out a scrambled moan as my body wakes from an unhealthy type of sleep, and I'm promptly dropped.

"Amnesia." It's an order not a diagnosis, to someone in the air.
"Here, Sir." The poltergeist complies, and fabric meets my lips. I'm too exhausted to bite back. It's like I'm breathing an electric current. Flowing to my heart, stopping my heart, putting an end to me.

"Sleep, girlie." The phantom sings, tunelessly.

Dreams have never left me as dizzy as this. It must have been beautiful, or horrible. I do what I always long for after a journey in and out of my imagination, and pick up a book to start travelling again. My collection is split between the bookshelf and my bedroom as a result of my addiction to other worlds. I must have more stashed in my bedroom, for there's a lot less spines here than I remember. I'm inspired by the glow of the sun through the window, and select a book to dissolve the nightmare. It's feeling like the morning and I both woke up together.

I ___ YOU

After strained concentration, I am sure that I can't succumb to another's words. Oddly, because my dream is still the narrative behind my eyes.

I was singing somewhere urban, like I'd never seen before, wearing nice clothes. Now, I'm back in my brown and white chequered dress, which looks faded in comparison to the colours of my dream. It's a little dusty. A good dream can bring to light the faults in an imperfect reality- my chore today will be to give it a good wash. I don't even feel like myself, mature with experience, as if I've lived a life overnight. I stand shakily, trying to step out of this cloud that follows my heart across the room. The coffee granules spice the rotting smell in the hall, and make the dingy outskirts of the town more bearable. The smell of coffee reminds me that there was a man. A man I loved. Oh, to walk beside a dream would be a dream in itself, a film of the heart's passions. *Film. What's a film?* Did I learn that from a book? I must have, before I fell asleep. Kildrift doesn't have films. *Are my dreams lecturers of a foreign social climate?*

I call out, up the flight of stairs, to Bridgette. "Gettie, I had the most familiar dream. Eccentricity if I've ever known it. I'll make you coffee, and we'll talk?" No reply isn't unusual if she's napping. The weather may be toying with our need to create *films* in our sleep. Rattles of the doorknob could be her returning from the market, perhaps with books, but there is a rhythm to how people open doors. The sound I hear isn't hers.

A cautious step takes me behind the kitchen wall that backs on to the door. I fish for anything sharp around me at the sound of hinges, but the intruder talks to me in a whisper.

"Don't lash out. I'm the first one. Stay still." I watch the reflection distort in the metal decanters on the counter. I follow as the face that made Bridgette's skin bristle, invites himself into my house and hall. I brought a chair down on his skull before I listened, my lack of trust speaking for my instincts. If he claimed to be the first, how many others followed? *Gettie.* I take the stairs two at a time, and hurtle to her bedroom. A white sheet has been placed over her body. What have they done to her? If I wasn't scared of what I'd find, I'd uncover her. She looks peaceful. Laid that way, or dead that way, I don't know. The word *mercy* courses in my conscience, but it falls upon a lost moment. She is dead, hung in a stifling, decomposing, scent in the bedroom.

I'm no medic, so it is hard to test my theory without courage, or without pulling back the sheet. I think she's been dead for a while. I don't believe I was dreaming. Voices call me back to the timeline I'm in now, which is all I can manipulate right now. The tremble of faraway conversation is far from imaginary. *There's more, and they're outside.*

Shielding my face from the air that vilely fragrances upstairs, I step inside my bedroom. At the front of the house, I can see figures outside, silhouettes diced by the lace in the curtain. The tremble of their hoarse exchange, begins a tremble in my hands. Their entitlement to turn up at my house unannounced, and Bridgette's death, are strings threading together. What becomes of the weaving is a fuse, attached to bombs cached in my brain. All explosive without answers, counting down. These bombs have voices too. Decisive. Steady. The voice of a man that lives somewhere in my heart, but not my memory. *Five, four, three, two…*

I push the door aside, denting the wall behind it, as my adrenaline floods in the direction of answers. Uniforms are only material on people with brains that contain information. Information I want. A uniform can be used to bargain for respect, but I'm past the point of respect for these animals. My house has been contaminated by the same soldier, twice. Once when I was too young for my voice, and again when Bridgette so happens to be lying lifeless. These things aren't coincidental. Therefore, a uniform won't hold me at an arm's length distance from knowledge. I'm seeing all things translucently. This reality echoes the dream I had, and I can see right through those badges and credentials, straight to secrets.

"What did you do to her?" I scream to the nearest soldier, advancing with my arms outstretched as if to shake him for the truth. Two other men aim to placate me by stepping forward and restraining me. I step backwards, away from the flesh and muscle cage of their hold on me. The middle soldier I directed my question to, saunters forward.

"Steady, missy. We're here to check everything is in order. Taking care of business." He says breezily, without any acknowledgment for the resting state of the only mother I've ever known. *There was another. A seamstress.* "Is there more to the interrogation or might we continue with our work?" He evaluates.

"What role does my house have in any of your business?" I struggle to avoid the officers stalking me, as I pace the path, trying to collect my anger and my loose memories.

"Your house? It's of minimal importance to us. We came to ensure that you're awake, and it seems you are, and defiantly so."

I'm stunned by the impassiveness. "Using my better judgement, I'd be inclined to agree with you, that I am, in fact, awake." At least, if I'm held back from physical retaliation, I can still expel caustic darts. It's what eventually eroded Isaak. *Isaak. Do dreams usually bestow names upon their actors? Every other dream I've had has woken up with its people a blur. Not this one.*

"It's protocol, and that's as much as can be said on the matter. Though, it's a shame you couldn't have employed better judgement sooner." He says shallowly. I follow their glances to their colleague splayed just past the open door. They aren't in the least bit concerned about the folded heap of man on the floor, and I doubt anything could persuade them to care because it's all about protocol. Morals, compassion, or dignity aren't protected under that umbrella - and the pouring rain falls, causing hypothermic love. Love that can't function as love, drenched in so much hatred and order.

It's a stalemate between my resistance and their impertinence, until the soldier gives way and shrugs. There are no instructions following protocol, so apparently, they are all at loose ends. I concede, the energy in me draining, and the desire to be alone resurfacing. "Take him away with you." I order, and with nothing else on the agenda, the soldiers oblige.

"Better do it quickly or we'll get given concussion, and all." One man risks joking, only to be met with a pale sigh from me, and muffled laughs from the others - but there's no life in the laughter. Whilst the trio heave their wounded counterpart down my path, I close my eyes and try to shut off all other emotions, to concentrate on my memory. *A balcony overlooking an ocean of shimmers, and I naturally, was feeling the five senses intensely. I naturally wasn't cosseting the sixth sense - love - but it was there. It was there as certainly as the shining lights.*

I hastily crack open my eyelids to see nobody around. Daydreams have different time zones to soldiers, and they're fleeing fast as I'm conceiving flashbacks slowly. I rush back into the house and rifle through Bridgette's stationary, her death giving me the liberty of inheritance. My hands take a while to awaken, but I scribble anyway in cryptographic handwriting - creating what will be a

catalogue of all I remember. I write until the table is
buried in paper, and I've turned into an adroit detective,
to solve the mystery of myself and very real dreams.

CHAPTER XXXII: INFLUENCE

Alessandro.

The night sky coats where there should be ceiling. The walls are just foundations, in a been-and-gone way. Not the start of anything promising. My hands are bound by the wrists. Therefore, I find myself trapped in the most open of places. A mattress in a derelict room, that invites the wind straight in as a bed mate. It's a pen of brick, mere inches from the ground. A simple step to hurdle if I was able to move. My surroundings introduce me to my role. I'm the tranquilised creature waking up from a hallucinogenic nightmare, but I'm lost on the type of poison and reason.

I'm lost on why I call for people that won't come. I'm lost until I crane my neck around enough to catch sight of my company a few metres away, encased in another chamber of the concrete confinement. Sitting melted in a shadow. Suddenly, I know my bearings with acute conviction. Details I first glossed over upon waking, become stark. Scattered pottery, cutlery and ornaments all present themselves familiar. A break in the brick, that had once been a wall, shows the placement of the door in relation to the bed. I remember my father arranging the furniture this way to prepare us for attacks. I lived in this prison. I used to call this home. I'm in my own bed, though there are no walls or doors to speak of. Overnight detonation has blown up every childhood ingredient.

And in my father's chair, is not my father. Hands tied, I rock with anger, not acting the pliant prisoner. "Get the fuck off that chair!" I bellow, only to find I'm gagged. The shadow extends a finger, pointing to their own chest. They're querying my remark with pretend naivety, as I continue to babble insults underneath the fabric. Fear kicks in when they stand and begin to work their way through the rubble to me. They aren't trying to avoid the bricks, rather the concrete crumbles underfoot, so I infer they may not tread lightly around the insults. I'm instantaneously grateful for the gag, and stay silent, though my fury is unshakeable in its gushing from my glare.

The shadow stops close to me now, conducting itself in a way that indicates that it's my age if not a little older. It cocks its head, and then, following a moment of hesitation, appears to make a decision. I can't twist my neck enough to grasp his features, before he reaches into a pocket. He retrieves a capsule that I don't investigate because as his elbows bend to release the screw cap, they shower dust from my father's chair into my eyes. Blind, I feel a nozzle fed into my mouth and nose. They might be connected, because as I squirm and begin to hit lethargy, they remain fixed in place.

Under a brighter light, and the midday sun, my father's chair is now situated by my bedside, occupied by a scrappy, unhygienic man in a smart uniform. I'm burning up from the light on my face, as well as my body's thermal systems overpowering to keep me warm in a drugged state. Emphatically, he glances at his watch.

"2 hours I've waited here, because you couldn't keep your mouth shut." I didn't tell him to drug me, or to sit here in anticipation of my recovery, so I don't owe him anything but ignorance. Instead, I survey the room again, trying to stockpile clues in case of another few hours of biological blackout. The books are tossed around as evidence of attempted, and failed, arson. Fury sways inside me again. I want to burst out of my own skin and throttle him. How dare they defame my father's belongings. He's going to be furious when he finds out.

"You don't know what's coming to you." I gurgle from beneath tubes. "Where's my brother?"

His chuckle is eerily offensive. "I wouldn't hold your breath. I don't think Sebastian Gray will be arriving any time soon. If at all." The tone smacks a hidden replay switch in my mind. Snippets of a nightmare. More questions surfacing. A dream tells me I shouldn't ask questions, that there's nothing to fight for, and it's like I know a depressive feeling, but I don't know its face. I'm dismally acquainted with reality, inch by inch. I don't want to believe any of the deaths circulating in my peripheral memories. The way he's speaking makes reality seem unhelpfully closer. I almost believe Sebastian's not coming, given the state of me and the house, but I know he'd never abandon me to be tortured this way. Unless obstructed.

I overcome my subconscious, creeping distaste for questions, in favour of information. "What have you done to him?" When there's no answer but another laugh, I attempt a lunge to scratch this man's face, to land a punch. Anything damaging. I lurch further than I expected the restraints would allow. He's forced to take a step back, his outrage obvious. Humour manages to alleviate his want to kill me, once again. His penchant for verbal torture saves me, and he exercises it as he retakes his seat.

"That stuff works a little too well." He says, before he uses it again. He pumps my body of this colourless disease, and I do nothing.

I wake up with a blank slate brain.

There's a man sitting in the chair to the left of me. My context and my purpose leaks from him. "You're Alessandro Gray." I nod, blankly, as the man makes my supposed identity an instruction. I can't read facial cues enough to know the truth. My mind is completely infantile, free to condition.

He continues, "Your father was Jack Gray. Meaning your grandfather was that hunchbacked miscreant that worked on the pavements, and your grandmother...ah. I believe you'll find this part very amusing. Let's wait for Jasper to tell the story, after all, he's a primary narrative." Sucking in his teeth with immature impatience, he watches me work out the atmosphere, and anticipate the arrival of this *Jasper*. I barely waited. It was a few seconds at most before we heard the crunching hobble of another's shoes.

"Speak of the devil," the man mutters, briskly standing up and smoothing his uniform.

I don't like the way this new man receives me, or the atmosphere he brings. He's a courier of hierarchy, so perhaps speaking of the devil wasn't entirely idiomatic. Where he stands, the scene and its characters become incremental based on importance. I already know the pecking order, even through being stunned in my emptiness. The man to my left has become subservient. This wrinkled, magisterial relic, *Jasper*, is unquestionably above us all. I am clearly lower than the dust on the floor.

"Hm." Jasper grunts, walking the perimeter of the bed. He approves of the display, but with condescension for the mannequin. "I'd tell you..." he wets his lips with his tongue, and swipes a hand across his mouth to catch the drips, "...all the things I did to your grandmother, except, I like how your father put it. Jack's diary, Earnest."

The man scrambles to locate a worn-down book from the bag beside him. Evidently, they carry this literature everywhere for light reading, unless it was planned that I'd be the listener. I don't like the fluency of everything around me, whilst my whole body stutters at even trying to twitch a finger.

Jasper's hands carry the diary with grim familiarity, well acquainted with the words within. When he begins ventriloquism, becoming the puppet echoing supposedly my father's words, I realise he's sickly fascinated with reading about himself, and the filthy ways he's perceived.

'As I can't puncture this pen through the following pages of this book, in fear of spoiling future, better stories, I'm forced to write today's events. I'd much rather stop here and cast this book away. The ocean can have it. There's no other way to describe it, but that Jasper is possessed. Possessed with evil that makes him believe my mother is a plaything at his bidding. I was walking through headquarters to call him out, not to find my mother that way. A cursed image, which I know will keep me from ever surrendering to these forces.'

'I opened the door to them, both naked. Jasper faltered at the interruption, loosening his grip on my mother. Gasping for breath she dragged her head away from the claustrophobia of the unwashed sheets, and laid eyes on me. I almost didn't recognise her through the puffy eyes and captive tears. I couldn't look for long because of the stench of bodily fluids in the room. Jasper glared at me then pulled out of her, and she cried out in pain. He struck her, straight down her naked back, and she fell quiet immediately, used to the paralinguistic threats. She lay on the floor, blinking at me, sorrily and silently. It used to be lovingly, but that definition was clawed away from her long ago by Jasper's hands. She's a shell for his sex. Her emotional absence paired with my father's means I'm an orphan in an unconventional way. I have no love now but for Lucia, which is why when Jasper calls for his men, I don't surrender. I escaped the planned

way. His men are all under Amnesia, meaning their memory for small tunnels and passages is limited. I use this to my advantage, and fall to Lucia's waiting arms on the outside. We don't embrace long, because I break free and march towards the front of the building. I scrawl my name on the list in front of Jasper's men sent to condemn me. I let them bustle me into the Death Room, as is known by the very few locals that remain uninfluenced by the drugs. I take a deep breath as they arrange the tubes, and protest little, saving energy. I keep Lucia as a beautiful bright picture in my mind, and hold my breath as the gas pumps hot in my mouth. As late as possible, I close my eyes, and slump backwards.'

"Always was an evasive scoundrel." Jasper breaks the narrative, but soon returns to reading before I can interrupt.

'My lungs seize as the masked men tread back in, and as they have a momentary debate about the speed of the Amnesia, I have a brief belief that I won't survive this. They drag me out, and tear the tubes from my mouth, just as my pulmonary muscles give way and start to vacuum up the closest air. The exhaustion means I don't need to make my fatigue pretend. Having no immediate order for me, they threw me back out onto the street. Either to die, or to stumble home and await being summoned to do Jasper's work. I stay where I've collapsed. Footsteps tentatively creep to my side. I know their pattern. Lucia is taking a risk. If my plan didn't work, then I've been programmed to kill women. It's in her best interest that a soldier doesn't know her face. I reach for her hand so she knows of her safety.'

'As is routine, following Amnesia, all men will go back to life. A monitored life. They will find a compliant woman, to breed more young boys with, who will

eventually be conscripted as soldiers. The cycle continues.'

'But I will never kill a woman the way they do. They kill any woman whose talent takes away from their imagined popularity. They exploit any woman whose talent provides for them. They sincerely believe they can outwit genetics. Jasper expects that he can use my mother for pleasure again and again, and I won't have a single word to say about it. She couldn't breathe, bruises on her neck from the position she's been forced into countless times. She knelt at the foot of the bed, whilst his hand tightened around her neck, no doubt liking how weak she was when he abused her. The bruises say it's been happening for months. I don't know how she's not dead at his hands. I don't understand how she's kept herself from suicide, surviving abuse to her body that has no end. She's serving a sentence she doesn't deserve. Jasper thinks she should be grateful that he didn't do to her what he did to the rest of the women. That he didn't kill her on the spot. Today came with its message. You have to give in to get away.'

"Give in, Alessandro. Your father's words. Except you won't be liberated. He didn't really get away. I took great amusement in planting that bullet in him whilst you and your brother were asleep." He chuckles, without any depth in his revelations.

"You fucking-" Foam swarms furiously inside my cheeks.

"Dose him again. Double it this time. I ought to depart, Alicia Gray is waiting for something good from me." Jasper excuses himself, leaving me at the mercy of his men.

I heave all of the memories I have left in his direction. "My father told me my grandmother was dead!"

I ___ YOU

"Oh, my dear boy. She is." The twinkling in the elderly weasel's eyes as he staggers away, are the last thing I see.

An explosive roar erupts from inside me, but it turns into the buzzing in my ears from the medical machinery. More Amnesia is pummelled into me than my body can handle.

I'm eager for darkness when I wake. It's early evening, dim light. Dark enough.

"Alessandro Gray, to attention." An officer barks.

I stand up straight, ignoring the dizziness and paying no attention to the instruments and tubes around me. My focus is directly on my superior. A series of photos are laid out on a chair. They are all monochrome images of women, of varying ages. My superior gestures to me to take note. I step closer and examine each face, archiving all the features in the forefront of my head, whilst listening for my next order.

"You killed all these women. They are all victims of your hand. Do you understand?" The officer talks at me, accompanied by an expectant glance.

Doubt, emanating from the man, trespasses our communication, making me wary. As I confirm my comprehension, it disappears. I shake it off. Death is always accompanied by doubt, but worry isn't something I carry. That's why I was enlisted, trusted, to kill these women. The evidence checks out, even if I don't remember. I look at these portraits with much ease and no guilt. I must have excelled at murder. The proof checks out.

The reason I'm brought back to work follows. "We have one more."

"Direct me, Sir. I'm at your disposal." I submit. I'm met with approval from the officer.

"Kildrift. Target is a brunette. Medium height. Singer. Goes by Sierra. Sierra Geneiva. You'll return to this address with her body." He commands, offering me a notecard. I receive it promptly, tucking it into my trouser pocket. I leave over the broken wall, in the direction of Colmoor's outskirts.

Acute geospatial awareness has replaced my emotional recall, in trade. I know exactly where I'm headed, and have no inhibitions. I turn back momentarily, newly a reputable soldier. I'm a force out for the next woman who disrespects culture. "Sierra Genieva." I verify, readily. "Understood, Officer. Consider her dead."

CHAPTER XXXIII: BETRAY

Sierra.

No space remains on the paper and parchment I've decorated with ink. The more I wrote, the more the string revealed itself. Through the morning, I kept pulling out my memories until my dream became a tapestry. Love and death, embroidered beside ambition and navigation in a new world. Now it is evening, and I have convinced myself that I've come back from somewhere different. A place where I tasted fruit on my tongue. A place with soul, and diversity, that didn't hide away from me. Rather, I was attracting them. I found animation for myself. I collaborated with the dream, and it became magical.

Theories are only foundations though. I'm sure everyone has believed that the idea of a dream is good enough, rather than achieving it, so what makes me different? Clues. Signs. I walk my stationary around the house, stopping to write when I remember things.

The disappearance of my books crucially gouges my conscience. I would have never misplaced them in my waking hours.

At my bedroom window, another memory aches. They pierce me like arrows, I only wish I apprehended the archer. The throbbing only subsides when there's a bedraggled sketch mid-page, overlapping other writings. I make no sense of it. A human shaped figure beside a rectangle. Exasperated, my eyes sting with impending dampness, until I revise my emotions. My voice is my regulation, not my tears. I can't lose myself to silly fantasies about dreams coming true. It may be nothing at all, but an overactive imagination because my whole life has been spent in custody in this abandoned part of town.

I ___ YOU

When there are no more words, there remain pitches. I sing a frustrated lyric-less song, staring out of the window.

It is not only me that the song frustrates. An aproned woman shuffles past outside, with bundles of vegetables in a basket. First, she looks tired. Then, she locates the source of the tune and looks at me. Bewildered, she frantically looks around, then back at me, incredulous. I almost cease my song, dampened by her fear. At the sound of marching, she lets out a shrill screech, and scuttles into the murkiness. Someone else emerges, their footsteps exhibiting no respect, as their thundering overpowers my soft breaths in the twilight. I'm not awarded any respite here anymore. How did the world invert overnight?

A man steps into focus, the silhouettes paralleling the illustration on my lap. A flurry of pen to page, copied from the present, and I finally have understanding. These unrelenting footsteps aren't obtrusive, they're evidence when I asked reality for it. It is not a figure and a rectangle. It is Isaak beside my gate.

"Your face was nowhere this morning when I needed it." I call down to him from my perch, his presence couples with my dream. It alleviates my downward philosophical spiral. Desperate for belonging, and my place in his arms, I almost performed the descent via the wall instead of the staircase. When I reach him, I stop a few steps short of him. I know we're not what we were.

"I assure you, I've not seen you before. Are you Sierra Genieva?" His inquiry comes harshly. There were two of him, I remember. Twins. If this Isaak doesn't know me, I have to act casually. Let nothing on, let no information out, until I know his intentions.

"What's it to you?" I confront him, although he pulses his head in a nod, wringing his hands, like I've given him exactly what he wants. He doesn't answer my question, which is on par with my memories of him. If he wants to practise naivety, I can too. Either way, it is clear that the more time we spend in each other's company, the more I will know, and the more my pages of writing will decipher themselves. I need answers more than I crave his comfort. I need this. I need to know if this is momentary anonymity, or if he genuinely doesn't remember how he romanced me.

"I suggest we take a walk." If he's using my affixation to entice me to a trap, I'm prepared to be trapped, so long as I'm jailed with him. I keep my gaze locked on his, as I pull the front door closed. He's gruffly taken aback when I touch him, ushering him to walk ahead of me. It's a threat that if he has betrayed me, there'll be hell to pay that he can't afford. He'll be indebted to me always, whether he recognises me or not. I'm not letting a dream man run away back to a place he won't remember what he was to me.

I don't close the gate, wanting him to understand I'm not afraid of people overstepping their boundaries. I like watching the damned ones flounder outside of their comfort zone, I adore witnessing the worthy ones explore.

If I am prey, I'll act persistently with spirit and spark. The Isaak I remember, doesn't like fire when it burns him. I follow in his footsteps as he leads me away from home. The trees are whispering warnings, but they don't know that inside me, is fire that'll break him.

CHAPTER XXXVI: HUNT

Alessandro.

She is incessant. Irritating to the extent, that if questions were physical barricades, my bullets would have no chance of striking her. She feigns control, but I am the lucky one because weapons supersede words. I always marvel when pacifists try to outspeak violence, as if they have true faith in vocal pain. It's a foolish belief. Anyone with integrity knows that pain is not real unless fatal.

"We're going to the beach. Why?" Her voice, again, crops up behind me. Sensibly, she's no longer singing.

I reward the effort with bluntness. "Less people around."

"You never answered questions in my dream." She pauses. "What's your name?"

"Alessandro Gray."

Though she doesn't argue, I can sense she's unsettled. It may be easier than I thought to get rid of her because her mind isn't in a common place. To kill someone off guard will be fluent when they have no guard at all, and Sierra Genieva appears overly trusting. To keep believing in a dream, is someone who believes in happy endings - which is why I'm anticipating unwinding that dull delusion.

We surface at the verge at the back of the beach and I let her fall ahead. Sierra Genieva begins running towards the water. I almost lost her silhouette to the night with no moonlight. Clouds cover the lunar brightness, like a manual eclipse. Perhaps it is fitting that the moon doesn't see me destroy her, as it may not be kind enough on other nights to shine down as congratulations. I have killed so many women, so it is curious I hesitate with this one, stalking her movements whilst she plays and invites salt into her hair. If the salt ran into her eyes, it would be a novice kill. Many people don't realise salt is as powerful a weapon, as it is a taste enhancer. Murder is fundamentally about utilising your surroundings, and turning expected purposes on their heads. The knife in my pocket, for example's sake, is intended to cut food. I'll repurpose it for flesh.

Sierra Genieva leans down to extract something from the sand, from a distance it looks like a flower of sorts.

"Isaak, come here!" She beckons, smiling with her eyes. Completely deranged.
I advance, close enough that the waves yearn for my boots, but tire before they touch them. She is barefoot, and surrendering to the water. The difference in both our approaches serves as a reminder of my duty. I am ordered to kill those who are different.

When she sees the knife in my hand, and tracks murder in my eyes, she rightfully backs up. Extending a hand in defence, it is clear she imagines that her skin and bone will break sharp metal. I twirl it between my hands, accepting a relaxed role. The point of the blade spins on the calloused pad of my index finger. I can't escape that this kill is different. I don't remember ever obtaining this much wealth from victims, or this much interaction in a hunt. Unprofessionally, I tease her beliefs. If she wants to believe we're in love, I'll take her there. I'll take her into my arms. Despite the knife, and the gun she hasn't yet seen in my pocket, she curls into my chest. I'm surprised how natural and complementary the collision is. "Am I Isaak?" I whisper, facilitating her dreams.

She fidgets defeatedly, agreeing. I savour it.
"Right." Behind her back, I draw the knife. "Did I love you, Sierra?"

Prematurely, I touch the edge of the knife to her shoulder blade. The iciness shocks her into forgetting my question, and asking another.

"Why do you have that?" She mumbles shakily.

"The knife? For protocol. The wolves." I need to buy time, to torture her heart.

She eases out of my grip. The blade only nicks her neck slightly. "I've never seen a wolf in Kildrift. Are there wolves where you come from?" Her inquisitiveness stops her from feeling the bead of blood trickle down her back.

We've been conversing far too long, and my mouth cramps with the want to reveal the reason I stole her away to the beach. "There are hundreds of wolves across Colmoor. The type that walks on two legs, looking for girls like you." I outline. At this point, she breaks apart our chests and stares at me.

"You're going to kill me, Isaak." She predicts, and I feel as though we both finally view this encounter for what it is.

Tightening my hold on her in case she runs, I introduce myself formally. "It's Alessandro Gray, and I'm going to do my job."

Sierra Genieva barely flinches, making my confidence uncomfortable. Perhaps it is the acceptance of fate, or impassioned cynicism in my plans, that causes her to challenge me.

"Is ruining good, innocent lives your forte?" She refers to her existence here, in Kildrift. The monotony of waking up, in a desolate home. Filing through forsaken literature to nourish the mind, as there's no pertinent adventure for miles west of Colmoor, and miles east is merely ocean. There is, in essence, no life capable of ruin. Just a lonely life, hunting love, with a stark invitation to cease. I am the one to perform the termination, for she has wronged society with her tongue, wrestled control from

Jasper with the exhibition of her voice, and still expects fascination from any man in the direction of whom she bestows her ignorance.

"I trade lives for the preservation of Colmoor." Rationalisation that empowers me to kill. For as long as I serve, I am worthy.

Telepathic or psychoanalytic, she shovels into my guise. "You crave proof. I have proof that you aren't just a dream to me."

Intrigued, I prescribe her the freedom to walk within the vicinity. There's no question I'd overtake her if she ran, so she doesn't. She only retracts into herself - closing off her chest with her arms, her head with her hands - as she frantically assembles her truth, or an artificial version.

"There's things that I remember..." she calculates, and I raise my eyebrows in suspicion, "..a brother."

It would be arduous, not impossible, to learn about Sebastian, and trace me to him. She could have done it, particularly with a predilection for learning, and interfering. My brother is my only family, and I am grateful to the force for enriching my knowledge. If not for the additional illicit inscription on the back of the notecard, I would have never learnt of my brother's existence, working as a travelling espionage for Jasper - and it is immensely admirable to be linked to a man of his military position. I also read of my parent's traitorous conduct, and I am thankful for their death so I no longer have to be associated. I owe the force. My parent's murders are only a symbol of judicial importance and the necessity of having soldiers who enact the consequences of defying Jasper's rule. I have pride in working to secure Colmoor's prosperity.

"The fact you know that, means nothing." My airy response seems to stun her.

"They killed him after you took me away."

Everyone dies. For such a solid concept, death is such a malleable tool in conversation. Sierra fears death, so she adopts two emotions and forces them together, with the intention of making me afraid. It's all a presumption, and void. It will not work to dissuade me.

"And where would I take you?" I enthuse, mocking the conviction on her face.
"Somewhere better than this, that you fell in love with. Somewhere where I was someone you loved." Sierra pleads loudly, scratching her forehead to catch her lies under her fingernails. Apprehensive that her beggarly behaviour will draw more eyes to the beach, I clasp a hand over her mouth.

"That's just not possible. I'm not interested in love. I never have been." I remark, as her teeth grapple at my palm, trying to sink in and make me release her. Incisors detecting nowhere to break skin, she becomes heavy in vanquish. Clearly, I state the circumstance needed to detangle us - that she concludes the calling out. Sierra thrashes from side to side, but my arm is locked, and I remind her of my upper hand by neatly slotting her into a chokehold with my free arm. In doing so, the knife drops to the sand.

I let it fall. I have the gun, its advanced counterpart. By stabbing the grains at the end of the descent, the handle of the blade is concealed, and its blade, partially concealed but upright. It would only be a shame if Sierra's bare soles stepped back onto something buried. I was sharpening with fervour the whole time I walked to Kildrift.

"Quiet." I hiss, and she looks up, unblinking. Tossing her on the floor, her face, eyes open, drops mere inches from the hidden blade. Gun drawn, I withdraw a stride or two, but I pause. I want to fire as soon as she knows she's going to die. The thought of a victim's last moments being somewhat unsuspecting riles me up, they ought to know. It revolves around honour.

Sierra scampers to her feet. I'm holding my breath for the metal skewer to meet her foot, yet it never does. Breathing in precursory shock, she frowns with vulnerability. "I'll show you."

Her exhibition consists of hoisting her dress, higher and higher. I shoot at the sand beside her, hot debris flying around her ankles. A flash explodes in the darkness, and raucous staccato builds as the bullet scuffs the shore - not echoing, just skimming out to sea until inaudible.

"It is an offence to expose yourself to a Colmoorian soldier!" I bark in her direction, over the sound of the gunshot.

Voice breaking, Sierra shudders to the floor, legs and arms repressing convulsions. "Is that you, a soldier? Are you a soldier?" She dares me. "Or are you just a follower? Scared? There's no fucking agency behind that gun. Nothing that makes you any different to the others with carnivorous hearts. You're a human that chose to be animal. What's love to a predator who hunts pleasure in murder like the world is expendable? When you turn around, who's going to be left?" She surges. Boiling lips don't accuse in halves. "Who's going to be waiting for you, Isaak?"

Sucking my teeth, I apply pressure on the trigger. She's trembling. I should love this, but it's the misery of mysteries that creates an impregnable sludge between my finger and the trigger. Sierra Genieva knows the way second guessing looks on my face, after only minutes spent together. She now preys with a prayer. "If you're intent on killing me regardless, could you bring yourself to look at my *fucking* waist?"

I avert my eyes to think, and she extracts permission from my actions. There is no harm her naked body can do to my armoured hand, so I compel myself to examine her. Potential proof of our existence beyond this beach, narrows down to four faint, distorted letters: RWYA.

This murder will be as straightforward and unapologetic as the breeze. A dead woman, with no truth. She won't even call me by my name. There's no evidence, and with that, the sludge of hesitancy drains from my gun.

CHAPTER XXXV: FEAR

Sierra.

His gun is of the opinion that I'm lying. When he leant across me, touching the barrel to my skin as a gesturing instrument, he sneered, "What does it mean then?"

It is a simple irony that my life is condemned by the one question I've been searching for, since I knew there was a vacancy for its answer. Inventively, I could fascinate him with my own interpretation, though he appears to have lost every connection to me aside from the ability to know when I lie. I have read enough books to list things alphabetically linked to four letters. With the exception that, I am sure pirates never thought coherently at the brink of a plank, or people with poison infecting their veins remained calm. I am utterly terrified, having given no thought to the absence of stories in death. There is no stimulation where I'll land, in the earth somewhere, with a blown apart mind. Everything I own with true value, is materialistic in the form of neurons, brain fluid, and electrical currents. All of these materials are the ones that paint my pictures. If a bullet destroys them, then it destroys me.

I elect for fact. Shunning fiction, entirely unlike Sierra Genieva.

"I don't know the content, but the context." I articulate, slowly. I'm on a minefield. Isaak, or his body double, is still, so I proceed cautiously. Reprehensibly, I maintain my want to touch him after he's cut me and shot at me, to reveal his tattoo. It'll bind us, but I know he has to be the one to do it.

"You have an identical marking, in the same place. Look. Please." I plead, and he only stares irreverently. Bracing myself for the bullet, I become a statue as I start to think he believes me. Desire to see the skin I remember still agitates me, but he turns away. Though it's more important to me now, that in any manner, he lifts his shirt.

He does. He believes me. Untucks his shirt, and folds up the corner, to see the skin I indicated. Strewn in puddles across his back are burn marks, scarring and recent. Recollections of smoke inflate in front of my eyes, a vivid flashback of fire. Amidst the flames, I didn't realise I missed a crucial sign, pointing towards my annihilation. The flinch of recognition never happened, when he saw my body. If a matching tattoo had belonged to him, there would have already been a motion, one that said he knew.

Isaak scoffs, and the smoke clears. He rotates with satisfaction and I feel death snatch me. I beg for my life, as I see the torso of the man I loved without the imprint we shared. A new burn covers the exact placement where I could have sworn those four letters were inscribed. I bartered for it, with my life, that they'd be there, and in their extinction, I will die. Certainly, someone has embossed a new burn, so close in the aftermath that it looks as though the indentations happened at the same time.

I implore Isaak not to get closer, and he only grants me that one request. He ignores the following requests and the way I beseech him, that his own wounds were appendaged, yet it falls upon deaf ears that only understand the language of murder as he raises his gun. I can't have been dreaming because the only difference is the way his flesh is scoured there, every other part of him is indistinguishable. Flailing, I feel his stare inhabit me, and he becomes the homeowner of my thrumming ribs, admiring my anxiety from the inside. Dread is my skin's internal wallpaper, and he lavishes in the decor, balancing on every rocking surface. Every organ exaggerates its own, lone earthquake. This man's dark eyes climb my ribs, fearless of the pit that expands destructively below the ladder's bone rungs. Adhesive fear, used to affix the wallpaper, is quickly turning tumorous and clogs up my lungs, seals my arteries and closes my eyes.

The idea of him leaps out of my mouth, spurred by ferrous foreign blood in my saliva, at the same time as real blood bursts from my chest, splitting my breastbone. I hear my own skeleton crack whilst I fumble. Fingers understudying as plugs, my arachnid hands scuttle impulsively across the front of my dress and plunge themselves into the muscle and tissue. My heart, struggling to beat, approaches my fingertips for reinforcement. I try to put a liminal cork in the cavity, but I'm not made to supplement cardiovascular functions with feeble manual strength. *Fuck*, it's wrecking me. I grapple at Isaak when he comes closer, but he only advances *to check it's working*.

The volcanic unsteadiness in my core convinces me to squeeze. Mashing my own insides results in projectile eruptions of blood. The scarlet streams coagulate on the sand like textured lava, and that's where I notice the ersatz artefact, not of the natural world, but of Isaak's world. A sunken knife. It's armament, but it's *a fucking blessing*. I coalesce my corpse with the rise and falls of the sand banks, towards the blade in stages, giving all my body can manage, as Isaak's shadow feasts on my decease, just for a meteoric, undignified death.

The cutter, an extra felon, will end me quicker.

CHAPTER XXXVI: WATCHED

Betsy.

It is necessary to point out, at this moment in time, that my sister's death was a slow one, in two parts. From the forest on the other side of the verge, I watched him kill her. Then, I watched her kill herself. I watched the cremation of that beautiful word 'protection'. They both thought they were fire, and they were. Dangerous to each other. Stifled lovers. It is after Alessandro Gray is unburdened by the thought of Sierra walking free, that he recalibrates to find my waiting eyes pinned to the nape of his neck.

A second glance means one thing for a lover, another for an enemy - and a separate something entirely for a woman in his memory. He doesn't know what to make of me, because he's just killed me. I'm in knots at his feet on the floor, and simultaneously chronicling the scene from under the boughs of trees. I think he is afraid, underneath lashings of Amnesia. A dosage so historically high, it has never before been heard of in Colmoor's dark communities.

I did my research.
Amnesia was, of course, manufactured in Colmoor. The quandary affected Colmoorian people for years, because pressure was drilled into making a discovery to make soldiers more obedient. Unsurprisingly, as Jasper's ideology was in multiple ways immoral. Men were expected to put the law above their women, and kill their wives, daughters and sisters for governmental credit. Jasper, almost immediately, realised threats weren't going to bring to life his intentions in the same way that numb humanity would. Consequently, people with scientific backgrounds, regardless of whether they claimed to be

medically competent, were shuttled into isolated bases situated behind Jasper's own buildings. It was the hypothesis of a resident with psychological understanding that finally coddled Jasper's pining. The hypothesis was that swelling the brain to impact memory recall would inhibit the human prerequisite for affection. In turn, this was expected to lead to fluid recruitment and increased recidivism, and thus, decrease accountability and defiance.

The conclusion that this was indeed possible, and Amnesia emerged from the trials. Earlier trials occurred, and were tested on other men. Those men swiftly disappeared. The disappearances were talked about in Colmoor's streets, until the day the scientists found what Jasper wanted, and Colmoorians got scared because they knew that the paper threats had come alive and could be enacted.

The threat was now a colourless gas, meaning several men forgot their aim before they could figure out how to contain it. It was in the air in the bases, until they knew to produce it in metal canisters. Men were going to work and coming back not recognising their families, becoming hostile and aggressive.

These bases still stand now, to produce and bottle Amnesia - and to construct the machines that administer the gas to patients - in large quantities. The machines are cardinal to Jasper's control, but underdeveloped as far as machinery goes, particularly compared to London's technical advancements. At basic cognizance, they employ a pneumatic system to funnel the gas out of a one-way metal cavern, through valves, and into the breath of innocent men.

This was known by nearly everyone as the Era of the Conventional, categorised by Jasper recrafting his town for his own convenience, and began deploying Amnesia into the towns. Kidnapping men who hadn't yet been cursed by the medicine, and returning them to broken homes. A collection of broken homes, became a broken town. It was never thought to repair what had gone wrong, because that meant overcoming Jasper, a task no army could achieve. Sebastian once told me of his ambition to lead that army, or become it all by himself.

It was after Seb's words, and seeing Alessandro march around London with more furious determination in him than I'd ever seen in his brother, that I decided to investigate if reversal was possible. I couldn't do it around my sister, she was rightfully torn with her own struggles of love and ambition. My lover doesn't burden me now, and never did whilst he was alive, and my ambition came after the fire, when I understood there was a possibility of a better world existing in time for our baby. I undertook the research everyone else neglected for the fear of Jasper's condemnation. I figured out how to counteract it.

Not sure what to make of me, Alessandro abandons Sierra for dead and charges across the beach in my direction, poised for another murder. Psychotically, he lunges at me when he's close enough, brandishing the gun. I flex my fingers subtly, telling Nicholas to stand down. There's a rustle in the bushes where he's sought asylum as a lookout, but he doesn't emerge. He's acknowledged that I want patience to deal with a broken heart shivering inside a gutless carapace that boasts a proud exterior.

Nicholas broke as soon as I sought his help, I left the apartment with the hope of finding him where we'd left him. Instinctually I knew that he'd still be there, and he was. Knelt on the ground wheezing, wringing his charred hands. A spectator as his own pub burned. I sat beside him, my silence unloading my doubts about how easy it was to return home with no further altercations. Through touching his hand, I'm expressing how much, without calling it vengeance, I wanted what happened to Sebastian to never happen again, to anyone. How there was so much death developing in the name of pride, and how I loathed it. He had asked if I regretted the bullet I put in Warner, if wisdom taught me inflicting pain was wrong.

No, *I had indicated with a shake of my head, whilst what my inner monologue retched was:* I relished every bit of it, because that part, that selfish fraction of a second, was enough revenge.

After knowing I wasn't going to back away from safeguarding legacy, and deciding that was enough to determine true trust, Nicholas had removed his metaphorical cloak to reveal honesty. Shredded to rags with the input of time, I hadn't, until now, believed there were more curtains to draw back. I thought I had figured it all out, with the exception of the last thing on my agenda, a cure for Amnesia. Nicholas asked if he could chance a phrase that could change everything, for better or worse. I like the addition of righteous people's words in the world, now I can no longer eject any.

When he tells me he's my father, an oracle of my existence becomes of him. Tousled with exhaustion, this man has within him pristine details of my mother. The reason I kept believing in reasons, whilst Arlen whipped and beat me. All the tears I cried facing walls, welts on my neck and skin, and how I endured them, finally will mean something. There's no space for anger, because it has already been evidenced that Nicholas is a kind man. He cannot be blamed for what I went through, there's no cause for that. He's here now.

In my polished ecstasy, I replace every thought I've had about him, that contains his name, with the word, 'father', and they become sweeter in my mind. My father was ready to burn alive, to hold me one last time. Perfect does not mean flawless, but I'll take this version of perfect any day, now or ever. I tow his hirsute forearm into my lap, firmly tracing Sierra. *Intently, his focus remains on me.*

My father understands. She still doesn't know, *he confessed.*
I wonder if he holds guilt, for that she now never will.

Alessandro contrasts my calmness with the impatience of a fake soldier, struggling to work me out. It buys me time. Particularly, to try not to accept that he looks like Seb. I retrieve the voice recorder from my front pocket, and Alessandro raises his aim in defence.

"Drop it!" He bellows.
Not letting it go, I press the button on the edge so that brittle music starts playing. The strength of the sound is whipped up by the coastal wind, but I have faith that the Amnesia will dissolve before Alessandro decides to shoot. Faith is all it is entirely. Logic could have him shoot me immediately. I'm entertaining hope.

I mask the baby with my hand regardless, I'll break all the bones in my body with bullets just to keep it alive. The dissolution of Isaak's neuroticism is a trial of a process I devised only recently.

Nicholas and I agreed to initiate Sierra, leaving the smouldering building in our wake, intent on the comfort of the apartment. Neither of us were ready to see Colmoorian soldiers hauling two poorly-obscured body bags. More horrible than the action itself, was the disciples attire. Londoners wouldn't know what they were looking at. Murderers dressed like normal people, infesting healthy society. Inside all of them, is a flood of Amnesia and trained antagonism. It churns inside Alessandro now like a virus.

Following the theft of weighted, dark cargo, I assumed the worst. My father assumed worse, his whisper cracking. Colmoorian soldiers don't murder, they massacre.

This meant his daughter, and Alessandro, weren't dead. It meant they were worse off. I could never have known it would mean they'd be bred to the point of not knowing each other. That Alessandro would be enlisted for her murder. A man who only ever swore to protect a voice, would end up silencing it.

With the forewarning of Amnesia in the building, owing to the men with masks, we postponed our entry to the apartment. I trembled with the effort of theories, because I couldn't give in to grief. I remember this feeling well, from when Sebastian's homecoming was substituted by Alessandro.

Alessandro whose gun is now wavering side to side, unsure. It's a trait of Colmoor to evict you from your own mind with anaesthetic torture - and I think he's beginning to reclaim his tenancy.

I spent the night conceiving what could make things right, though formulating mostly what could go wrong. An interval in my thoughts was Nicholas determining that it was safe to head inside, and then I restarted. Tired, but sleep would only make up for hours, not the days I'd spend alone without my sister if I didn't persist.

As damaging as it is for the people who suffer, Amnesia is worse to comprehend, and after hours of sitting with myself and no clues, a spokesperson in my brain thought I'd prefer being on the other side. Drugged with them. Morals would then become something I'd never have to think about again, but instead it's all I chased as if the fact that one girl with good character will ever overturn a regime.

Everything about Colmoor and London is mutually exclusive, from the way that people are allowed to live, to the aesthetic. Colmoor has winding streets that lead to unsafe places, London has boulevards that connect attractions. Colmoorian thirst for death, and this city's breadth of life, are completely antonymic. At the crux, Amnesia is a sedative. It acts to make people unnervingly calm in their villainy. It occurs to me that an antonymic resolve has been black and white this whole time, plainly on display as I've stressed. Sedatives need to be excited by stimulants.

Love alone is not an adequate stimulant.
Love anyway, in the common sense, is experienced at face value. Attraction to stereotypes and impermanence, like beauty and bold gestures.

Stronger love, in the more uncommon sense, has depth. It's why love cancels out distance, illness and death. Love is a multidimensional substance. When a sedative as powerful as Amnesia makes the whole world shallower, love is forced out to make room for the worldly colonisers such as greed and hatred. It didn't occur to Jasper that Amnesia didn't mean love was gone, just forgotten. The hope in me jumped at the thought that love was not extinguished, but waiting to be liberated.

I reached Alessandro's house in the morning when he first woke up. They had him chained, and from afar I heard his shouting and the repeated instructions to dose him. I realised then how much love Alessandro had in him. That man resisted three bouts of Amnesia, an amount that would and has killed others, and still had love to defend his father. Unfortunately, he didn't have enough love to resist a fourth overdose. Nobody, until him, has ever surpassed two doses in the same day, and now he's overcome four.

However, now I deal with a Colmoorian soldier, doubled. He has ingested more than Warner, except I think if Warner's Amnesia was to dissolve, he would still be a loveless man. I can be certain there is a confused call of love, bullied into exile by the drugs, that is worth rescuing inside Alessandro.

Once Amnesia has taken hold, it does not need to be re-administered. They do that for pleasure, and occasionally for reassurance that the new soldier is truly enrolled. If supplies ran low, one dose would condemn a man for life, but Amnesia production is obscenely rife. Perhaps promisingly, there is no such thing as exportation. Jasper knows that if the rest of the world knew what he was doing to create armies and his paradise, Colmoor would cease to exist. Some Colmoorians know about what lies beyond Colmoor, others don't. It comes down to tales within families, and who is losing memories.

I searched the apartment for any materials that could function as emotional transport, something that could unite common and uncommon love. Alessandro recognises Sierra Genieva for her face, but he does not remember their brawl of love. He has been lied to, steered away from making those neural connections, by the officials. Casualties of Amnesia have clay brains, mouldable. Superiors can choose what emotions to bury, they can ascertain the density of memories, they can choose how to engrave a mind. Depending on the person, they might do this differently. Some victims will be kept airily oblivious, the clay scrounged and metaphorically removed, so the killings are just jaunts. That's what happened to Warner, likely because he was captured possessing no love in the first place.

Alessandro is a separate case, and one that exhilarates the force. He has so much previous love, angst, determination and activity, that there is so much for the sculptors of his mind to work with. They've decanted the passion from his love, and drowned his conscience in it. As for his love, it's discarded in the centre of a blockade of harm.

I'm pulling apart the apartment for something that might destroy a blockade.

If materials of love were anywhere in the apartment, they'd be in private places. Though, Sierra's bed and wardrobe hold nothing of Alessandro's. The couch holds nothing resemblant of her. Physical proof of love that they shared is scarce. I could trust them both to be as contrary.

I am slightly incorrect, for there are frail petals on the carpet turning grey, but I know that if flowers were to reverse Amnesia, Alessandro would not have crept in that body-bag without a fight. It needs to be something more, and there is nothing here. Nicholas comes to sit beside me, reassuring me. In the absence of ideas, and justice, we still have each other. It starts me thinking about ideas and justice. Abstract concepts. Then, in a matter of seconds, I see the whole room in a different way. The scents and the sounds. I enter every room again with new eyes. Sierra's bedroom has a record player in the corner, with sweat-stained fingerprints on the start/stop dial. If this was the last song they heard together, I'll make it one they hear again.

I snapped up a sheet of paper and scrawled to Nicholas to leave immediately and purchase a voice recorder. He soon returned with my request.

It is the same voice recorder that is my shield from Alessandro. I should have made these conclusions sooner. At the sound of a female singing, Amnesia enrages whoever it occupies and prepares them to kill. An occupant programmed that way. If Amnesia can have a powerful adverse reaction to music, there is a chance there is an unexplored positive. If Amnesia is programmed to throw the world's most tremendous emotions at music, nobody has a say in what the limit of these emotions are. Colmoor just channelled them negatively.

I press play on the voice recorder. A song starts, second-hand and croaky, but slow and sensual. Recognition seeps back into his eyes, it is dawning on him who he is. I'm at ease now, grateful that he is too lost in remembrance, to remember pointing his gun to me. Amnesia, wearing away, he is still disorientated.

"Sierra..." he beholds, relieved, discarding his gun and dropping to his knees, blissfully thinking I'm the one he wants. I have, and hate, to be the one to tell him. I point over his shoulder, where Sierra is lacerating her own body with the knife he delivered. Blood spraying, she's wheezing as she punctures her own lungs and stomach, significantly less energy each time she stabs and stabs. Screaming as much as she can through the neck she's cut and slashed, but only as a release for how much it hurts. Hoping for a larger release in seconds, and savaging herself more when she doesn't receive it. She is barely recognisable as a woman, in the dark oasis of blood.

A guttural, acidic, vomit-inducing, gasp rumbles from Alessandro. "Oh, *fuck*." He scrambles up onto his feet, and charges to her, "Sierra, shit, stop now! We can get help-*fuck*..."

I would have been at her side, if I believed she could be saved, but she was gone after the gunshot. There are too many unanswered questions that she would have died with, our twin status potentially reversing the Amnesia with our intrinsic connection.

She never stopped, not as her lover was on his knees imploring her to drop the blade. She had already cut herself too many times. It took her to be lying still, twitching in the posthumous belief she was still stabbing effectively, for Alessandro to regurgitate his own stomach inches from her death sprawl. Once he's finished heaving, he reaches for the knife in her hand, but it slips around in his palm with the blood and flesh slices, so then he pats the ground around him for the gun. That's when he looks back, bleary-eyed at me.

He staggers over, slower and at an end. Scooping up his gun carelessly, he swings backward, holding it by the muzzle so that the handle points towards me. "Kill me. Do it."

My father emerges from hiding at this point, easing the gun from my hands, and becoming my voice to reason with the broken. Alessandro doesn't bat an eyelid at another presence for his one and only person is dead, killed by him. Artlessly diplomatic, Nicholas gives him a choice.

"Son, the Amnesia you were under killed her."
"It was my hands-" Alessandro's plea is eerily similar to Warner's delusion.

"It was the drugs. Look at me. She was my daughter. If I blamed you, I'd already be retaliating." Nicholas reminisces, though only minutes have passed. He was battling with the probability of her death on our journey to Colmoor. To him, she was already lost. He just wasn't expecting to have to watch. Even now, he studies me a little more intently to reassure himself not at risk. "Betsy is having your brother's baby. You could come back to London with us, and be family. You'd be welcome."

Alessandro shakes his head and sobs, reaching out his hands to my stomach. I almost think he'll make contact, until he sees Sierra's blood trickling down his fingers. "There's nothing in London for me...there's no her. I don't deserve to be around her family, when I've taken her from you." He relents, powering himself to look back at her, dead on the sand. Averting the course of his outstretched arms, he clasps Nicholas' hands and connects his own head to the gun. "I will never forgive myself for what I did to your daughter. Pull the trigger."

"I feel it's unnecessary, son, I-" Nicholas struggles to encourage Alessandro's rational judgement. My father doesn't want to kill, but he won't sustain suffering. It becomes clear we're at a stalemate.

"Kill me, please!" Alessandro exhorts, preparing himself with short, sharp breaths. I myself breathe in, and close my eyes. Indescribably, I feel Sebastian's presence, bowing his head in acceptance. Alessandro needs this to be at peace. Nicholas is looking at me when I tempt another glance, and I understand he's requesting it to be a mutual decision. Alessandro has already advocated for his death, and he will act on his wishes, if I agree. It's abhorrent to feel, and have the responsibility to terminate, Alessandro's pain. He needs to die or else he'll always hurt, as the man who murdered his only lover in a sleepwalk.

CHAPTER XXXVII: OUTLIVED

Betsy.

An unborn child shouldn't have to listen to human sacrifice.
I am getting wary. Alessandro is still begging.
"Nicholas, you're a good man. Do good. This is what I want. I adored your daughter and I still can't fathom that I lost her. Say it for what it is, fuck it, I killed her. You have every right to-" Nicholas' finger spontaneously tightens. I see red. The bullet grazed the grass and then came to rest on the verge, after ripping in and out of Alessandro's skull. I protected my belly from the splatters.

Nicholas looks away until he hears the body slouch. Alessandro's legs twist awkwardly, with the weight of his torso pressing them perpendicular to the natural angle. Blood leaks out of his mouth from his brain.
"I didn't want him to anticipate it." Nicholas admits, insecurely. "Do you think-"
I place a hand on his arm.
"I took a life," he continues.

You released a tortured soul, I want to justify. I shake my head at him with a comforting smile and hope he knows how much of a beloved father he is.

Nicholas guardedly kneels to Alessandro's side, and takes a pulse. Expectedly, the wrist is devoid. My father is an able man, but I never considered the extent of his strength until I saw him pick up Alessandro as if it were nothing. Like a decanter, more blood pours as Nicholas tilts the corpse in his efforts to move him. I stay back, but he gets a lashing of brown and red saliva down his back. It runs quickly, like water, with the occasional island of tissue.

I ___ YOU

Sierra's hand is open when we reach her, in the cast of the knife handle, before Alessandro took it away from her to turn it on himself and failed. Humans have an abundance of limbs which makes a dead person hard to manoeuvre. Nicholas performs admirably, without tiring, to work Alessandro's body next to Sierra's. Hand in bloodied hand. Torso beside mauled torso, two adaptations of perforated skin that'll soon turn to ice by ice. Nicholas packs sand into the wounds so they won't be torn apart by gulls, and then around their sides so they won't get tossed from each other in high tide. I curl their fingers to lock, so in death they may forget their betrayal of love. This way they'll be everlasting.

I was unaware that there's sometimes so much love in slaughter.

People dying and killing out of moral need. Nicholas' instinctual duty to protect Alessandro, from the lasting effects of guilt and grief, that made him pull the trigger. Alessandro's love for Sierra healed his Amnesia. Sebastian's love for people, for his brother and for my sister, made him decide to take that bullet, and in the end, my love for living found the answer.

There is sometimes so much to love, in ambition and entanglement, that it overcomes what we risk and lose.

There's so much love in loneliness and a cold night. Nicholas walks ahead, but love lingers. Sebastian is all around me, always.

The thought of him interlocks with my fingers as we look upon his brother, the expression on Alessandro's face, no longer tormented, and my sister, chopped up but at peace in the arms of a man who cursed the word 'protection' but introduced her to idiosyncratic romance.

A ghost and I promenade, to an unpredictable new style of belonging and beginning, leaving the dead where they lay.

I ___ YOU

THE END

EPILOGUE

Nicholas.

Savannah kissed my hair, light and smelling of vanilla. I've kept vanilla at bay since because it reopens an irremediable hollowness, as it did when she said those words I've never forgotten.

"You can't stay here." She murmurs, kicked halfway through her words by a foetal heel.

"Oh, I don't believe for a second you'll have me far from this baby" I chuckled.

Savannah sighed and received my hands on her waist. "I mean it, Nicholas Genieva. I wouldn't say it if I didn't believe that you were better for them back in London."

I often tried to ignore my love's sixth sense. It was, aside from her voice, powerful and accurate. Meeting her eyes was the only way to tell, and I disliked everything I saw. Not for how beautiful she was, but that in that moment, I knew I was leaving for London. I didn't know I was never to see her again, except to have her likeness in my, not one but, two beautiful daughters.

"Savannah. Are you certain it's a daughter? There's every chance it could be a son." I heartened, only to narrowed eyebrows.

"What's the difference in having a son? Do I have to remind you what they'll do to him here?" This talk is upsetting her. She doesn't want a soldier son, or a dead daughter, and I think she resents me for our story. I knew so desperately that she wanted to be a mother, but it is too late now to sneak her away to London, and Colmoor is no place for a baby who doesn't want to grow up a machine or a monster.

"I'll be gone by morning." I say, trying to massage the pain away, transgressing down her spine. Screams resound outside, from a few blocks away, and she tucks her head into the bedsheets. When I met her, she was timid, but the more she knew love and consequence, she grew afraid. Regardless, she leaves to sing with Lucia Gray every day. I've told her it's a risk, but she won't listen, naively confident they won't catch her, but they catch up to everyone eventually. I feel she doesn't understand risk unless it is physical and imminent.

She is expecting, and I'll be miles away for the birth. It is right to ensure survival of at least one parent, but it'll destroy me as a father.

I can't speak of destroying fathers. Mine was infuriated that upon becoming an adult I wouldn't engage in the family law firm that made us as wealthy as we were. I refused to adopt a lifestyle where I could sleep and indulge in luxury, because my parents profited from defending the vulnerable and guilty. Sleeping was burdensome knowing someone could spend that night without a home or their families, because of my parents' advocating for their abuser in court. You can't argue with lawyers, or your parents, and I brought myself to the task of doing both the night before I left. Voices were raised and chairs scraped and thrown, neighbours complained, yet my parents knew that the police wouldn't challenge the Genieva household. I was living in a reprobate cage, and now I've encountered another.

I ran away from my parents' house at midnight, with some clothes, and walked for miles. In my bank account, there remained enough to build pyramids, but I didn't run from the lavish life to enter it again. I was chasing inexpensive escapades. At London's borders, I walked as far as I could, until I came across a girl my age sunbathing under the moon. Freckles were the sequins that decorated her fear. I sat and told her not to fear me, all the while thinking how the elegance of my mother's jewelled dresses were mirrored in the natural beauty of this girl. Money meant nothing, and that same night I made a ceremonial show of letting my paper notes fly like eagles; a tumbling, flipping avalanche off the side of the hill.

"Are you a soldier?" I can't criticise her for her assumption, in low light with my baggage, I could have escaped war. I did, in a sense.

"I am not. Are you?"

She laughs, and introduces herself as Savannah. I know now we are friends, not only for our light-hearted moonlit-licked conversations, but for the mannerisms of another escapee that she unknowingly exudes.

I later learnt of the town that made escapism her vitamin, I stayed for too long. Friends turned into frantic nights of overflowing escapism. Escapism came full circle and now we both have responsibilities.

Early in the morning I left, before the sun rose, I woke her to kiss her goodbye. The previous night she had said she couldn't face a farewell, but selfishly, I couldn't face leaving without. I'm glad I broke her rules, because I remember how her lips quivered in sadness and surety as I rejected Colmoor. There was unfinished scrutiny though, even after the last kiss, so I waited as much time as I could allow. Creeping to her dresser, she brought out ink and a needle and told me to breathe like I was a copycat of the receding waves. Pinpricks, I learnt, are nothing comparable to the pain of leaving behind good love in a bad place.

She spoke as she wrote, lastingly.

"Remember...who...you...are."

Savannah's phobia of me being caught and enlisted is excessively wrought in advance of my departure, though

I ___ YOU

she seems to settle when I promise her that I didn't enter Colmoor as a soldier, and won't leave one.

"I'll remember who I am, and I will remember who we are." I vowed, the letters RWYA etched on my skin forever. Crossed paths created a beautiful chemical flare, and having dabbled in convergence, we now must, like many a light source in a dark world, refract. Divergence is obligatory, when there's more than an entwined partnership at stake. There is their baby.

Forsaken by paternity, I couldn't bring myself to abandon my first proper life immediately. Months went by, and I slept under trees, on the beach, or under the sky. Anywhere safe that there was solace. In every location, I was free from parental juries, injustice and materialism. I counted the days with a rock and scratches on a tree trunk, that I returned to mark each evening without fault. All was planned, up until the morning I staged an entrance back into Colmoor and I discovered Jack Gray hovering anxiously in an alcove, two babies in his arms. The extent of my vision wasn't enough to see their faces. Could it be possible I fathered twins? At his feet, resources Savannah had for the baby, but in two piles. A blanket couldn't be divided, but the clothes could. Every indication suggests Genieva twins.

Privately, the babies were given to two women. I overhead the second address, so I was forced to stalk the first, and do my last duty as a father to ensure that one day my child might find me.

I followed the first woman as she hobbled home, to a house with a furnished but dusty exterior. Someone had tried to maintain the house's presentability, for it was the most decorated in the street, but had lost track of organising the upkeep. That afternoon, I rapped loudly on the door and puffed out my chest, strapping a vacant expression on my face.

I ___ YOU

A frail woman, cloaked in a woven quilt, takes a while to open the door. She relies very heavily on the strength of the hinges to support her remaining upright, and introduces herself as Cecile. Hearing my daughter coo and squeal inside the home, I have to fight not to drop my masquerade and force my way to her side. Past Cecile, further in the hall, is a gruffly perched man. People don't take kindly to soldiers.

"Taking information for the census." I bluff, in as droll a tone as I can manage.

The man in the hallway examines me from a distance.

"We gave our information to authorities just last week." She informs me, apprehensively fussing with the edge of her makeshift shawl.

"I've been informed of a change, since." I further my pretence.

"Gosh, the force is fast. Um, yes, this morning." Cecile explains nervously. The man, I assume to be her husband, clomps forward with his walking stick, in the same trembling hand, shaking papers.

"Cecile went and adopted a child. All completely legal. Documents here." Impatient and combative, the man's body language is keen to shut the door on me.

"That won't be necessary. I just require a name."

"Oh, well we've only had her since this morning, we haven't-" His wife contemplates under pressure, but her husband is having none of it.

"Betsy Genieva. That's her name as we got her. No point confusing affairs. Good day, sir." The aggressive man closes the door, just as I break into a smile.

I can hear them arguing in the hall. "It's a good thing I like the name Betsy, Arlen. Honestly, you can't afford to be so crass with the force, count yourself lucky you were too old to be drugged."

I ___ YOU

Betsy was one of the names we considered, nights after nights, spent making lists after lists. I forge a letter from Cecile, confirming the adoption and name to the authorities, and store it in my pocket, heading for the other address. It's been circulating in my memory so as not to forget it. Nobody answers the door when I arrive and there's no lights flickering in the cottage. It's thrown me off course.

"May I help you?" A voice is croaking over the squeak of the garden gate opening.

I struggle, I haven't had time to acquire the soldier facade. A man of my age in Colmoor, stuttering slightly with anxiety, reveals I haven't been caught and forced to ingest Amnesia.

"I trust your intentions," the lady decides after a brief appraisal, "but you ought not to come in, you never know who's watching. Stand there."

I thought I was careful to be aware of my surroundings, but her words make me paranoid. We stay on either side of the doorstep. Next to the porch lantern, she looks elderly, perhaps older than Cecile, but less ill. Colmoor, with its darkness, makes it hard to find elderly people who are still exhibiting signs of emotional intellect and life. Cecile's husband's aggression serves to prove my point.

"I'm Bridgette," she smiles and uncovers the bundle of cloth in her arms, "and this is Sierra. We've just come back from the drapers to find some fabric for some new clothes."

I lean forward, unthinking, and stroke Sierra's cheek, accidentally awaking her. Peeling her tiny eyes open, she blinks in the light, and smiles like Savannah. Bridgette doesn't withdraw the baby, but evaluates my actions. You tend to find that women older than Jasper are wiser, they are the ones that have significantly witnessed the shift between the Era of the Conventional, and life beforehand. She knows I bear relation to Sierra, and she is already imagining the complexities behind if I were to keep her.

"The less I know the better, for all our sakes." Bridgette assessed, and I consent.

"Ma'am, I have only one question," I hesitate, and she bows her head to invite me to continue, "will she stay Sierra Genieva?"

"I hadn't given it thought until meeting you. It is a gamble on high stakes. You'll be linked." She purses her lips in contemplation, but doesn't deny me.

"It's the only hope I have of reuniting with her."

"Then it is what must be done. Leave now, you've stayed a while longer than they'll appreciate. It was a pleasure to meet you…"

"Nicholas Genieva." I hold my daughter's small hand, the last time it'll ever be that size, and then step back. Bridgette, as understandingly as I could have asked for, protects Sierra from being associated with me, a Colmoorian runaway.

I posted the fake letter from Cecile to the authorities, and then purchased the apartment and the pub on the same day, as soon as I returned to London. If you're looking for runaways, the first place you'll look is the streets, so my bank account and credentials now have purpose, but I still wanted what I always had. The ability to know everyone. I aspired to know different lives and hear the stories of people, not just those who walked a fake life, using the hearts of others as steps. 18 years passed, and although I stopped imagining - what my girls would sound like, look like, or what I'd say if I ever saw them again - I never forgot them.

The dark-haired boy that told me to talk to him got my attention. Customers don't ever ask for things other than drinks, let alone instruct me.

"Tell me where I can find a place to house a girl." He had said.

"This isn't that sort of place, son."

"Then I need you to tell me where one is." It becomes clear to this adamant teenager that without more information, I'll dismiss him. "I have just lost my father. I am alone, and so is she. We've both come from a dark place, and she could make something of herself here, but there are people that will eventually follow us from that dark place, and if I don't find somewhere-" he recollects himself. "The streets aren't good enough for runaways." Heavily cryptic, I hear more in what he doesn't say. It's a description of Colmoor, if I have ever heard one. This boy is me, when I returned to London eighteen years ago.

"I have an apartment. You can call it home, just give me until morning." Obviously, the boy examines me for signs of fraud. Bartenders don't give away apartments. I've been too generous with my discernment of Colmoor, so I dial back. "I do this sort of thing, for people I trust."

The boy nods slowly, appreciatively, and extends his arm over the counter for a handshake. "Isaak."

"Nicholas."

A brunette step out from behind Isaak. I hadn't seen her lurking. "Sierra."

Bridgette was right. Too many runaways in one place were a gamble on high stakes, and one that took Sierra from me, but it was also a recipe, like every act taken in life. The result it yielded was Betsy, next to me in the graveyard now, searching for stones to bury her sister. The largest rocks are those that make up the wall, a pen of skeletons, which is crumbling. I call Betsy over to help me ease the rocks from the top, that are loosening with wind and rain erosion. Extracting two, we haul them back to Sebastian's resting place before we carve them. Betsy writes for her sister. I write for Alessandro, who suffered like his brother, like his father, his mother, his lover. One of life's recipes that went tragically wrong.

We are scratching into rocks, on limited time and with torn hearts.

Minutes in, Betsy raises her hand, concerned enough by a sound to stop me. There is nothing, then a vibration travels through us both, and I point to the stormy sky almost above us. My daughter shakes her head, cueing another vibration. This time a tremor buzzes under my hand, from underground. I drop my ear to the earth, and almost miss another vibration. Viable, and timed. Betsy makes a calling motion.

"Impossible. The only people with Sebastian's number are me and Alessandro. Alessandro is dead and my phone," I empty my pockets, "is right here. Neither of us are calling."

In a split second, Betsy is scooping out the shallow grave with her hands. The soil is barely solid, having absorbed water, and more so as the thunder above us breaks into rain. It makes a puddle of the grave, as Betsy keeps pitching handfuls of mud aside. She'll reach his corpse in a quick moment. I assist her from the opposite, one of us will excavate the right pocket. There's been another two vibrations since we started our panic. Then, Betsy and I spot different things at the same time. She sees Sebastian's curdled face, tunnelled into by woodlice and maggots.

Barely illuminated, I see the phone and lunge for it, snapping it up just as the vibrations cease and the battery dies in the rain. I slap it against my thigh, trying to trick it into restarting, but it is clear it is finished. The only hope is to take it back to the apartment to recharge, and on the way, ponder the only initial I saw on the caller ID. An initial that means this number was known to Sebastian. Someone is trying to reach him, someone unaware he's dead and less than two feet under, as his lover weeps over his ruined body in the rain. I give her the moment she needs to grieve, never once forgetting the letter I saw.

G.

I took the phone back home and worked on it into the night as Betsy slept. At exactly 3:08am, the digits flashed across the screen. The device and I both woke up. Wiping the excess dirt off the icons, I found the call history and without thinking, pressed the number titled G. I should have been more careful, dialling to reach a person that could inspire heaven or hell. *The number you have called is currently unavailable.* I curse at it, and try every day for twelve weeks.

However, it was eight months and a half that had passed when they called back.

Betsy gave birth to a gorgeous baby girl. Sebastian's spirit, I know, right beside her. Gala fusses and potters around her bed with towels, enjoying a purpose, and the excitement of another tiny body to create dresses for.

I rushed into the room as the new mother beamed. "Her name is Alessi Bastienne." She breathed, in homage to love from every soul that had more to give.

Before I register my new status as grandfather, the vibrations happen again. I'm taken back to that night with little Alessi's father unearthed under dirt, vilely rotting. I remove the phone from the pocket I've not unlatched since I stopped calling those months ago. The letter *G* broadcasts into the bedroom, though Betsy's urgency is lost under love for her daughter. I step away.

Betsy does not know of the research I have done; she is not the only with a keen eye for resolution and adjudication. She doesn't know of the nights I've stayed up and the denouements I've guessed at.

I ___ YOU

I clamp the phone to my ear, listening, then interrupting with the knowledge I was right and the whole word changes because of it.
"I had a feeling it'd be you."

I ___ YOU

ABOUT THE AUTHOR

Mollie Mardel, was the student in class who always considered light reading to be scouring the dictionary for more ways to enhance her writing. During her writing career, she is most proud of the fact that she has been commended for her work on a community scale. She has written for the council on political and social themes, and has significantly ventured into psychological and interpersonal literature to begin her writing career. Her writing style is varied and she enjoys trying to mash modern day prose with Shakespeare's tongue. There is nothing she loves more than literature that demands dissection.

She writes with an ounce of her dreams, a helping of experience and a dash of what her friends would call 'an old soul in a young heart'. She believes touching hearts and teaching lessons, through words, will help connect with those that need it most. The command of words, crafted regardless of quality and entirely with feeling, is an individual's most valuable ability.

Printed in Great Britain
by Amazon